I0779206

<u>**Hatshepsut**</u> (hat•SHEP•soot)—
First woman to be king (or pharaoh) of
Egypt.
She ruled from about 1472 to 1458 b.c

Q

H

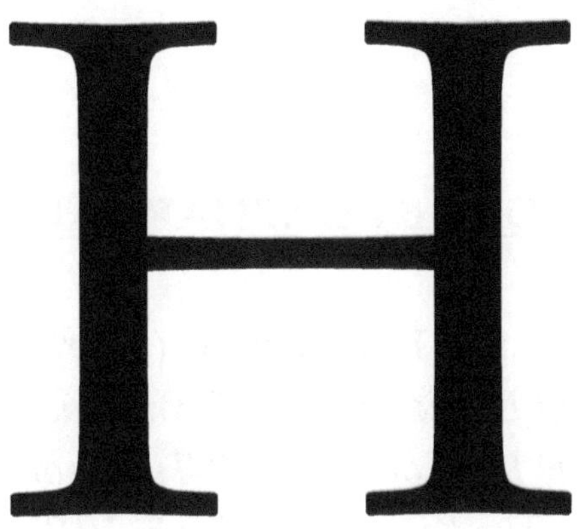

CALL HER *Queen* HATSHEPSUT

BY

Dapharoah69

BOOKS BY DAPHAROAH69

The King of Erotica 1 The Throne (Short Stories Only)
The King of Erotica 1: The Throne special edition
The King of Erotica 2 The Crown
The King of Erotica 3: VIP
The Official King of Erotica 4: The DeTHRONEment
Some Men Wear Panties
The Diary and the Strap E-Book

Coming Christmas 2009
The King of Erotica 5: WAR:Dr.O.Be.

ANTHOLOGIES

Voices From Within
WSN Network Anthology
Mocha Chocolate

Dedicated to

Angellique Phillip
And the Memory
Of your beautiful mother,

Joy Peters

1970-1990
God called you home for something greater.
But your daughter, who I used
For the Hatshepsut book cover
Lives on.
And she's a dear friend. And my biggest fan.
I may never meet you, but I know you
Through Angellique's compassion.

Dapharoah69

✠.Ḳ.Φ.Є. Publications

ISBN 978-0-557-20086-3

9 780557 200863

LIBRARY OF CONGRESS CATALOGING-IN-PUBLICATION DATA HAS
BEEN APPLIED FOR.

PUBLISHER'S NOTE:
ALIYAIH AND SUNJARAIH are my nieces.
They will own everything with my name on it when I perish.

Edited by Kevin McNeir: GBMNews.com
Cover photo by **Angellique Phillip**, New York
Back Cover photo by
The Wonderful **Steve Shires**, Ft. Lauderdale, Florida.
Cover wording text, cover touch-ups
and the king of erotica logo by
Maddaphobia
Meak Productions Agency represents
Dapharoah69, The King of Erotica ™

Fran Briggs, Publicist

Matthew 10: 21-22

Brother will betray brother to death,
Fathers will betray their own children
And children will rise against their parents and
Cause them to be killed!
And everyone will hate you because of
Your allegiance to me.
But those who endure to the end will be saved

Jesus spoke.

The King of Erotica 1
The Throne

Some enticement for all sexual appetites. DaPharoah69 serves up a sinful dish of erotica that feeds your own desires and introduces you to some new ones that will have you thinking... That's the sign of a great writer: being about to take you up and out of your comfort zone and put you in bed with something new and exciting.

C. A. Webb "Conversations Book Club"

Words can't express this book changing my life
by *Str8guy*

I'm a straight man, and never in my life dreamed of reading an erotic book written by another male, let alone a bisexual male. I bought all four books, his tetrology or erotica, after an interview I read about him on www.unheard-voices.com. He is a soldier, a warrior and has survived some very heartbreaking things in his life. I applaud him for publishing his own books and watching them slowly take over the world. The book opened me up a great deal and allowed me to see behind some of the reasons people are gay. He has allowed me to befriend a gay guy at work now and treat him with equality and respect. Thanks Dapharoah69, The King of Erotica.

The King of Erotica 2
The Crown

I am woman. And I love to read. He can't be touched. Frankly I love the man better than Zane. Better than Eric Jerome. Why? He not only writes well crafted, gritty, in your FACE literature but he borders perfection in the process. His poem 'Barbra Streisand' touches on racism that he experienced in his classroom. "What is Africa" is another magnum opus college professors seriously need to PRINT out and give out with lesson plans. Every black man should read this poem. The boy not only writes good fiction but he is a very well-versed POET.

FATE WILLIAMS. Was so shocking I was left in tears reading about the abuse she endured at the hands of her own mother. BOOTY-DO. The title was comical but the story of a reformed prostitute who bangs her best friend's husband was such treat I read it twice. FREAKY DEAKY. Melissa is back, from Part 1 of his book. This time she gets freaky with candle wax, and her own selfish pleasures that left me panting and desiring her myself. Dapharoah has been touched by God with the gift of GAB. Dapharoah will always get my last twenty bucks. He is worth it. SHAME on publishing houses sleeping on this magnificent writer.

From Lover_of_Black_books:

I've been reading that he's Zane's competition. Why do we as blacks pit each other against each other? Pharoah clearly says in his book that he loves ANY BLACK AUTHOR who opened the doors for him. He says he's HIMSELF! He says "I'm not trying to be Zane or Eric Jerome. Why would I want to be a woman? Why would I want to be Eric? My Mom gave birth to Larry C. Wilson, Jr. Compare me to myself." Quite honestly, Pharoah shatters Eric with character descriptions. He blows Zane out the box because all she writes is butt booty naked Sex. Pharoah explains WHY they have butt booty naked sex. Which draws you in emotionally? Everything is perfect! From the way he grabs you with his eyes on his book cover, it lets you know that "HEY I WROTE THIS AND I STAND BEHIND IT LIKE A FIERCE WARRIOR!" From the very beginning you can feel his energy; you can feel everything he writes. He writes with a style unlike any other. His descriptions are on point. And the sex is off the chain. Pharoah69, I'm glad I discovered your world. Looking forward to Book 3.

The King of Erotica 3
VIP

The King of Erotica 3 concretes his legacy. By the time I got to book 3 I was left breathless and mystified from book 1 and 2. Just when you think he can't top himself he effortlessly does it again! This time he changed up his prose and it reads like poetry mixed with blood raw sex, trauma, beauty and skill. He has become my favorite author and I can see WHY E Lynn Harris selected him for the literary cafe. Dapharoah69 can't be touched with a ten foot pole. To me he writes better than Eric Jerome Dickey and Zane. He doesn't have million dollar editors editing his stuff, he does it himself.

By: Love_Stoned

A pleasant surprise of both passion and prose: Dapharoah gives the world not just a book of steamy sex, but story lines that explore sexuality in ways few authors of "erotica" are able to achieve. Though definitely not for the faint of heart, this is another triumph for the author and literary pleasure for the reader.

C.A. WEBB CONVERSATIONS BOOK CLUB

The King of Erotica 4
The DeTHRONEment

If he doesn't write The King of Erotica 5 I will be hurt. What a way to write a book! I read all four of his books in less than six days, and man what a ride! He has outdone himself with this latest installment. Dapharoah69 is a lyrical genius! The King of Erotica 4 has made his competition look like complete fools. Every story, magnificent. He has a Nutrition Facts Label for the book, never done before. Original! EACH SHORT STORY HAS IT OWN NUTRITION FACTS LABEL! And The Freak of the Oath is genius. The man out his heart and soul in the book, and the story Jadish Houston 3 changed my life forever. *A Barnes and Noble.com review*

I am awe struck. And I will use my review to write a personal letter to Mr. Larry Wilson, Jr. Dapharoah69. I have TWO WORDS for you: THANK YOU! I love the book. I love the author on the front cover. He reaches out to his fans on sites like Facebook, Myspace and Tagged. You write him a message and he will answer back. His politeness, his humbleness and his willingness to help a stranger with a simple problem is why I bought all four books and waited for them to get to Trinidad. With that being said, The King of Erotica 4 has saddened me. Why? This might be the last book in the series. I really hope he reconsiders. Because he has created a juggernaut of success with taboo subjects other authors will never touch. Because they are chicken. And any other trying to follow his formula or success will FAIL because he started his own legacy and did it his own way. Overall the book is awesome, awesome, and awesome. If you want deceit, lies, trauma, sex, passion, love/hate, ups and downs, then THIS IS THE BOOK FOR YOU. BUY THE ENTIRE SERIES. THE MAN IS A MYTH AND A LEGEND AND AN HIV SPOKESPERSON. HIS BOOKS SAVED MY DAMN LIFE. THANK YOU THANK YOU THANK YOU DAPHAROAH69, MR. LARRY WILSON, JR FOR SHARING YOUR TRAUMATIC CHILDHOOD, YOUR LIFE, YOUR FAILURES, YOUR SUCCESS AND FOR REMINDING A STRAIGHT MAN LIKE MYSELF THAT WE ALL HAVE A STORY TO TELL, AND WE ALL CAN SURVIVE THE STORMS WITH PREPARATION.

I LOVE YOU MAN.

TRINI_BOY YOUR FAN FOR LIFE!

The Coronation:
FOREWORD
Written by: D. Kevin McNeir

In the lead to a story I once wrote about my friend and the incredibly talented writer, Larry C. Wilson, affectionately known by his fans as DaPharoah69, I mentioned that with his cover-boy looks, chiseled abs and wickedly inviting smile, that he should be on the front of magazines instead of toiling for hours at end to perfect his craft. But DaPharoah69 is not motivated by the exterior but rather that which lies, sometimes hidden, inside. Instead he is a driven author whose poignant tales reflect the pain, passion and vicissitudes of life that have shaped him.

Poverty, sexual abuse, abandonment and even succumbing to the HIV virus due to the extraneous skirmishes of a dishonest lover, have been his challenges but not the marks of his defeat. He has risen above his circumstances and is in a word, a survivor.

This book, *Call Her Queen Hatshepsut,* is his first venture into the world of historical fiction and moves him outside of his more comfortable and established genre of erotica. And it's one of his best works to date. It's a haunting story of a young boy who is forced to live his life as a girl due to the irascible motivation and musings of his mother — a woman bent on revenge

Thus our protagonist, Hatshepsut, becomes a pawn as the author illustrates, in a deadly game of chess. The story deals with the age-old question of whether sexual orientation is something with which we are born or some argue, a choice. But in the final analysis it is an extraordinary, coming-of-age tale of a young boy who hungers for the same thing that all children, no matter what their race or economic circumstances, long for — love.

In Egyptian history, it is clear that Queen Hatshepsut was one of only a handful of women who ruled Egypt as pharaoh and during her over twenty years on the throne she had great success – both in warfare and in improving the economic welfare of her country. But she was met with great resentment, particularly by her stepson and nephew, Thutmose III, who was too young to ascend the throne at the death of his father, and who would succeed her in power.

Some of the few remaining statues of her show Hatshepsut with her arms crossed, reportedly to take attention away from her breasts. In addition, many speculate that she dressed as a man, presumably so that she would be given the respect that was normally reserved for the male pharaoh. However, whether she really lived her life as a man is something that cannot be confirmed.

Wilson plays on the history of this so-called cross-dressing queen in the development of his story about his main character, the confused young boy/girl Hatshepsut. But the book further addresses one of the more controversial aspects of the gay community – transvestites. And he pushes us to consider if this minority within a minority is viewed as anomalies, even freaks by those who face prejudice themselves from the larger heterosexual community. And it asks if they should be treated with dignity, despite their unique differences or if they are more suitable as a means of our own entertainment at the local drag show?

Free will is one of the major human characteristics on which the book is based and whether we really have the choice to be who we are destined to be. Wilson pushes his query as he contemplates whether free will is really an option when our environment places us on a divergent path? In addition, he skillfully addresses the impact that religion, faith and tradition have on our lives.

Meet Avarice, Rosa and Kayak – the tantalizing trio that prove to be young Hatshepsut's nemesis and ironically, his salvation.

This novel marks the seventh book penned by the prolific Wilson, but if this is your first time savoring his creative skills, prepare yourself for a full course meal of twists, turns, unexpected surprises and bizarre revelations. His time has come and you are witness to his coming. Prior to his death, the bestselling author E. Lynn Harris wholeheartedly took on the role as a mentor to Wilson – even reading this novel and

Call Her Queen Hatshepsut　　　　　　8

affirming it as a book that takes chances, confronts conformity and forces the reader to reevaluate how we view the world, our fellow brothers and sisters and ourselves.

Enjoy!

D. Kevin McNeir
Senior Editor, *Centre Stage Magazine*
Senior Editor, *FootNotes Magazine*
Senior News Correspondent, *www.gbmnews.com*
dkmcneir@hotmail.com
Atlanta, Georgia, 2009

THE VALLEY OF THE KINGS

The Tombs:

Call Her Queen Hatshepsut:
Acknowledgements

I titled this book *Call Her Queen Hatshepsut* for a reason. I've given it many titles. Each one wasn't befitting. It normally takes me a millisecond to title a book. It usually comes to me very easily. But I was so flabbergasted after writing this account, so in touch with myself emotionally and so disturbed that I searched for the best name to symbolize my raw feelings. They say the title of a book can make or break it but that wasn't my concern; I could care less if it makes or breaks me. I write to express myself. I don't care who likes it or not. As long as you get something from it to apply to your own life then my mission is complete. I don't do this for money. I do this for awareness.

You can't make everyone happy so I don't try. The book is not about Queen Hatshepsut. It is a fictional account of a mother's scorn over a man who married her identical sister and shared with her a son. In this case, I first titled the book "Dear Grandma: Mama's Gone." But it didn't grip me. It did nothing for me. If it does nothing for the author then it won't do anything for you, the Reader.

For many years I always wondered why I was entranced by the story of Queen Hatshepsut and why I felt compelled to read about her. I didn't just study her…I dissected her. My own father abandoned me as a child and my inner feelings have always spilled over into my writing. In this case, writing allowed me to feel, to self-examine and to accept. Of course I'm not an Egyptologist or even an expert on Egypt. But one thing I have that keeps me in the league with certified whatever you wanna call them is my ability to comprehend. I have a heart, a brain and I can read quite well.

Queen Hatshepsut came across my eyes at a time when I was learning in school that blacks had only been slaves. I read whatever I could find on her. I read about her reign potentially being erased from history by Thutmose III and wondered what motivated him to do so. Thutmose III uttered things about Queen Hatshepsut he wouldn't say to her face if she'd been alive. Why did he wait until she perished to destroy her statues, memorabilia and paintings?

Queen Hatshepsut was his stepmother and aunt. In those days, it was a common practice to marry your sister, half-sister or even your mother who would serve as your primary wife and then to have secondary wives. Queen Hatshepsut failed at one thing in life, despite appointing herself King of Egypt the way Napoleon crowned himself king. She never had a son.

Queen Hatshepsut's memorial temple is considered an incredible architectural achievement of the ancient world. She used to wear gold sandals and highlight her very existence with gold in a way today's rappers and Hollywood starlets could never touch. She used to drink from one-handled enamel jugs and rule her kingdom baring gold collars with falcon head terminals.

She was born during an important time in Egyptian history. During the birth of the New Kingdom Era, it's speculated that she drew her first breath during the coronation of her father King Thutmose I, c. 1504 B.C. It is further believed that she may have been just a toddler when her father set sail to Thebes with the naked body of a chieftain swinging from the bow of his ship. It was a warning to those who would seek to cause havoc on his empire.

It's also legend that she reburied her father in a tomb she was having built for herself. She said that her father once named her successor to his throne if he was to perish. From what I've read, many scholars felt this wasn't the case. Thutmose fathered two sons with Queen Ahmes. They predeceased him. The son of a secondary wife, named Mutnofret, was crowned Thutmose II. To redefine the bloodline, Thutmose II married his half sister, Hatshepsut. She was Queen of Egypt at the tender age of 12.

Thutmose II was a very ineffective ruler. Hatshepsut used that to her advantage, playing on his weaknesses to get what she wanted. She birthed him a daughter, Neferure. Thutmose died in his 20s, and Hatshepsut had not given him a male heir, so his throne went to the son of yet another secondary wife, named Thutmose III. At the time of Thutmose II's death, Thutmose III was an infant.

It was common practice in Egypt for widowed queens to become regents, handling the business of government until their sons came of age. In this case Queen Hatshepsut was looking after her stepson/nephew's throne until he was to become a man. During her seventh year of rule, however, Queen Hatshepsut did something that would mystify scholars for centuries to come:

She reinvented herself. Gone was the polished, beautiful, graceful Queen *Egypt* had come to know. Appearing before them was a King with broad shoulders, a fake beard and a bare chest.

She dressed as a man to concretize her reign as ruler of Egypt. Some say she acted unscrupulously. Others say there were threats made against the kingdom and she had to declare herself king to protect Thutmose III's kingship.

I always enjoy reading about her and I thought about her when I wrote this book. I used certain elements of history to carefully shape this harrowing story of love, lust, lies and deception. I have never attempted to write anything of this sort because I was so used to writing erotica. I don't want to be remembered only as the King of Erotica. I wanted a change. I wanted to write something daring and different…something that would raise eyebrows and play on their emotions…But now that the book is completed, I present this with an open heart and a satisfied smile.

Queen Hatshepsut died in c. 1458 B.C. Her stepson, who loathed his stepmother, ordered the destruction of whatever she had touched. He tried to erase her from history.

In this book, someone was being erased from history.

But who…?

November 2009

Minister Kayak Burke, a very eager, arrogant, sexy man, moved throughout his establishment almost like a zombie. He was totally unaware of the 890 members watching his every move. Several women in the assembly crossed their legs and couldn't take their eyes off him. A few other men secretly lusted after this powerful motivational speaker, philanthropist and self-published author.

In his hand was the Holy Bible and on his mind was his son, life, God and a host of other unspeakable things. His son threatened everything he was as a man, everything that he has become would shatter if the congregation found out he had a homosexual son. He prided himself on setting the standard, being that he was in a position of authority. He cared about people and cared about what they had to say.

Images of yesterday exploded in his mind. Back when he got married to his late wife, rest her soul, life was good. He loved his late wife with every particle of his being.

He closed his eyes as the pictures danced in the darkness. In the past, when he married his first wife, his son was his best man. And what a mockery that turned out to be when everyone realized his son was gay.

Opening his eyes, he approached the podium, overlooking a huge group of well-dressed members. There were a few new faces in the crowd, and he set the Bible on the podium and chugged on the bottle of Zephyrhills water. "Welcome, everyone. I'm glad you all could make it. A rather lovely bunch today. We all look good in the eyes of the Lord."

Amen.

Hallelujah, Pastor Burke.

A sea of applause swarmed him with love and understanding.   He rose up his hands. "Let's take a moment and give thanks to God. For our lives."

People jumped up to their feet. A few women had their open palms in the air and their heads hung low.

"Praise him. Reach down in the pit of your stomach and scream your praises."

Out of the blue a dope dealer with dread locks took off running around the church, shouting he loved Jesus.

Pastor Burke was pleased.

He raised his hands in the air and everyone became quiet. "Let's get into the Word. I will be reading from the book of Job today."

Everyone sat down, gathering their thoughts and getting themselves together.

"Before I do," he went on, a strikingly handsome man in a purple and gold robe, "I want to say a few things. There is something that troubles me about this church, our church. Some of you I am told are showing up late for Bible study and a couple of you pulled out of last week's sermon for a *Beyonce* concert. When we start putting musicians before our God they become false idols."

The church was quiet.

Power oozed from his intimidating eyes. "Let's get it together, people. We have 6 days to go to work, go out and do whatever, but let's keep God in mind when we do these things. We are about to collect tithes, and remember, give with a cheering heart. Don't give out of obligation. God so loved us he gave his only begotten son. Let's keep that as the mental framework of giving back to the Lord. Those seeds aren't ours. They come from God."

A series of ushers started walking around collecting

white envelopes, cash and change. Two very beautiful black women, in their early twenties, stood before the church, behind a table. As the tithes buckets came they started counting all of the money and opening the white envelopes, neatly putting ones, five, tens, twenties, fifties and hundred dollar bills in piles.

Pastor Burke didn't believe in robbing his organization, so all money, every Sunday, was counted before the members of the body.

While the two women counted money, and the ushers collected tithes, Pastor Burke talked about hypocrisy.

"I am not a hypocrite. I do the right thing according to God. I walk a fine line," he said, grabbing the microphone from the miniature stand on the podium and making his way down the carpeted stairs, into the main assembly.

"I have hardly done anything wrong in my life."

His Caucasian wife, Olive Hills, a very beautiful blonde, quietly crossed her legs, closing her Bible and focusing on her husband. Her left heel dangled from her left toe. "I hardly made mistakes," he went on, his voice rising with confidence and power. Everyone hung onto every word with respect. "God has always been number one in my life."

Olive Hills closed her eyes, folding her hands in her lap. She was humming.

Pastor Burke closed his eyes, and thought, *Lord, please erase my past.*

So I don't have to keep up the charade.

When the two church accountants were done tallying up the funds, they collected a grand total of $14,589.89 in cash and another $3,589 from personal checks.

They were ushered into the back high tech offices by the ushers.

"God is pleased with your tithes." One thing Pastor Burke would never do was steal from the church.

He never thought of it.

Dapharoah69

C

***

A few hours later, after church services ended, Pastor Burke entered his lavish office and closed the door, drained from all the hand shaking and pampering of the congregation members.

His wife, holding the arms of the suede chair, stood up and said, "You lied, darling." She wasn't pleased.

He looked at her a moment. He was madly in love with his wife. He must admit, before he married her he had bad credit, lost his car and was dealing with his wife's death. Since marrying Olive, his credit rating skyrocketed because she paid off all his outstanding debt.

When his late wife was killed by her sister, he didn't want to live anymore, and he promised to kill himself.

Now he loved himself, his life and his wife.

He strolled past her and she said, "So you're ignoring me."

"I'm not ignoring you," he said quickly, sitting down in his high back chair. He poured a cup of coffee and looked up at her. "So you want some coffee, sweetheart?"

She avoided his eyes. "Sure."

He poured her a cup. Just the way she liked. Black.

Handing it to her, she stood before his desk, leaning into his face. "Why did you lie to the congregation?"

He loved her beautiful blue eyes. "About?"

She set the coffee mug down. "Everything you said about hypocrites. You're the biggest one, and you run a church."

"I lead a body of members who want to better themselves through my example."

He shook his head. "Yes. I give them false examples and look what I get in return. God's blessing for keeping his children in the Word."

She glared at him. "I can't believe I'm hearing this. When I married you you were a very honest man."

His feathers were ruffled. "When I married you I wasn't over my dead wife. You came along and gave me Miss Prissy pussy, had me all in my feelings and I married you because I thought I was in love. I mean, now I'm in love with you, because I *grew* to love you."

She stood up straight, glaring down at him. Crossing her arms across her bosom, she said, "That is not fair and you know it. I mean, when we met (at a local bar) I overheard you telling yourself that you wanted to kill yourself. I sympathized, because when my late husband was killed in Iraq, I felt like I couldn't go on, so I knew the feeling of loss. I came into your life to help save you from yourself."

He smiled. "And I thank you for that sweetheart."

She frowned. "But you still lied."

He stopped smiling. "Know your place," he said dangerously.

"And what is my place, Pastor Burke?"

His forehead low, he looked up with his beautiful eyes and said, "You're my wife. Trust your husband. Press the submit button and sit your tail down on this subject."

"No," she said, walking around the desk so fast her hair whipped behind her head. "You lied to this church. I'm your wife. I'm a member of this church so that means you lied to me. Your life wasn't perfect!"

He turned away from her and she walked around the chair, and back into his face.

"*Leave*, sweetheart." His voice dropped. His temples twitched with anger.

"No. Let's put it out there. Tell the church you have a homosexual son. You deny your own blood child. Gay or not, what kind of real man who loves the Lord, who puts God first would deny his child?"

"Fuck that faggot ass bitch!" he exploded, jumping up to his feet and pointing at his wife. "I had it with your accusations of me lying. Shut up and leave this office."

She slapped his hand out of her face. "Listen,

sweetheart. I'm not your little wind up dolls."

"I will never accept him. He sucks dick, doesn't he? He wants to be a fucking girl. He's walking around with tits doing shows and dressing in drag. I don't want a transvestite as a fucking son!"

Olive smacked him across the lips. "Not in the house of the Lord! Watch your mouth! You defile God's house."

He slapped her so hard she stumbled back into the wall. She held her face, evil eyed.

"I will not respect my gay ass son. I don't respect a man fucking another man in his ass."

"He's your son! If I were you I would extend an olive branch to my child. Especially after what he's been through in his life. How could you be so *heartless*, Kayak?"

In his eyes was concern for his son. Even love. But his own selfishness and what the community would think clouded his judgment. He was never there for his son.

"My son is a he/she with a dick and tits." He walked up to her. "Look, I'm sorry for slapping you. But you struck the first blow. You can't go around slapping me for having feelings and my own personal thoughts and morals."

She walked past him. "I don't know who I married. I think I married a monster." She picked up the coffee and he sat back at his desk.

"I will never accept him."

She turned and dumped the coffee on his crotch. It scolded him so badly he jumped up screaming.

"Don't wait up for me tonight," she went on, walking towards the door.

"I won't!" he said angrily. "Stupid bitch! Go take my gay ass son out for poker or something. I'm going out with the boys. Have some drinks."

She turned to face him. "If you do, pack your shit and get out my house."

Check mate. He fell into a deep silence.

Part 1

The Valley of the Kings
Prelude

Back in the early 1980's

A staccato of bone-chilling thunder boomed from an embossment of dark clouds agglomerating above the thriving, enigmatic county of Miami-Dade. In Liberty City, Florida, there were reports of gusty winds so strong it blew people to the ground without apology. In Carol City, a small, local concert was in progress. Nice and sunny skies. Energetic and upbeat people of all ages and creeds were dancing to the hubbub of pulsating guitars and well-delivered percussion.

A handsome, sleek, local singer danced across the stage like James Brown but came off looking like a young Michael Jackson ala the "Dancing Machine" Era. He was well on his way to superstardom. And then out of nowhere, thick black clouds slowly and gradually erased any sign of light from the sky.

The sun ceased to exist as the scorching rays inevitably vanished. There was a fusillade of noise, cackling lightning violently striking trees and acres of bushy terrains.

Outrageously deafening thunder sent frightened people running in all directions. Heavy rains spewed from the sky, soaking any and everything it touched.

A group of young thugs with the all-seeing eye, from the back of a dollar bill, tattooed on their backs accidentally stomped over an elderly woman who was desperately calling for help.

She died ten minutes later from internal injuries. A very powerful spurt of wind shattered certain store windows and sent people flying into trees and the pavement.

Hospitals were put on alert. A hospital in Kendall was receiving calls from people being struck by lightning. Another hospital on NW 95th street couldn't handle the number of people being brought in, soon to be diagnosed with concussions, internal bleeding and broken arms and legs. Patients were arguing with registration personnel and security guards had to apprehend a few belligerently intoxicated men because they didn't have medical insurance.

Around the entire city of Miami-Dade County, freakish storms were being recorded. News stations, ranging from Channel 6, 4 and 10, quickly sent incessantly confused news reporters out into the violent weather to alert the public to stay inside, to turn off electronics and to lay low until the thunderstorms ran their course.

But there was one woman who didn't care about the cackling lightning and deafening thunder.

It didn't match the hurricane in her heart *or* the tropical depressions in her sad brown eyes. An empiric woman, she cautiously tried to stop the extrusion of hate spewing from her spirit as she haphazardly drove her Lincoln S.U.V. along U.S.1, pulling on a joint.

She normally didn't fancy drugs or alcohol but tonight was different.

Something died inside her heart. Something wicked has curtailed her very soul. She felt it every time she attempted to do something for herself. A very selfless woman in public, behind closed doors she was a very disturbed black woman.

The glowing red tip of the cheap joint, laced with cocaine, sizzled in her ears when she hungrily pulled on the joint once more.

Her eyes were blood shot red, hidden behind thick Hollywood-type Bandi shades. The speed limit along the road was legally posted at 45 M.P.H., but she didn't really care.

She was driving at 80 M.P.H, her foot firmly pressed on the accelerator; ducking and dodging slow cars, which she could barely see because of the heavy rains. She totally ignored the fact that she could end her life if her weak, wearing-thin tires decided to slide over slick, rain-swept roads.

She didn't have a clue that her Firestone tires were of low pressure, and the nail in the back passenger tire gave way to air slowly seeping out into the atmosphere. She didn't know if she was coming or going, but she knew she wanted to get far, far away from this town.

Miami-Dade County.

But how can I leave when I have unfinished business? I can't just up and go! That would be admitting defeat and I'll be damned if I let the enemy win! The enemy can never win. Oh no, no, no-no-no-no-NO!

On the radio were startling news reports:

A Homestead, Florida resident nearly escaped death as lightning shattered his windshield, sending his Ford Mustang careening off the Florida Turnpike…

A Cutler Ridge resident was blown into a tree, his cane sent up the block and his dentures winding up in the neighbors pool.…

I hope he drowns, she thought to herself, her heart black with hate.

Violent lightning strikes the daughter of activist Fred Dryer, the best friend of Bishop Gregory…

Ask me do I really care…I have my own problems. They say there is always someone going through something worse. Who cares what they say! I am not all together in the brain right now. I want to kill something. I want to break things. I want the world to match my heart. My body is Storm Central.

Violent lightning knocks out half of Miami-Dade's power!

Living life in the darkness is a good thing. It's a very noble thing these days. To do what you do to the people you love and deny it when the sun comes up. Someone did that to me once. Convinced me he set the sun. He convinced me he was God. I built a home while he worked. I had complete faith in him! I carried his child to term! It all blew up in my face!

He knowingly lied to me! His promises were hogwash! HOGWASH!

Over 30,000 people are in the dark…FP&L are working around the clock…

ξ

Devastated, she quietly sat in her vehicle, hot tears falling down her lightly made-up face. With the exception of the light pink rogue, her choice of green lipstick did nothing for her mood. Sibilating noise rampaging through her warped mind, she was slowly losing her grip on reality. Why *shouldn't* she lose her mind? She lost some of the most valuable, priceless things in her life. She could never get them back. She wanted one of those things back, mind you. She needed it. She convinced herself she couldn't live without it.

Now I am forced to live without it. But I have a plan and I hope it works because it's premeditated and I actually took down

Call Her Queen Hatshepsut   22

notes in little composition notebooks. And I drew it out and I made little dialogue boxes. I mapped everything out like a script. I will follow it to the tooth and nail. I will never deviate from my purpose.

The death of her husband has gotten the best of her. She didn't want to go on.

He was a man she loved; a man she looked up to and valued. He was a sweet, caring man who taught her things she would carry in her heart for the rest of her life. He taught her how to love and how to honor; he taught her how to truly respect herself and those around her.

He once told her that she couldn't wrap her entire life around one person. She had to do her own thing, sometimes go out with her own friends and have her own life.

Build a career, read a book and help someone in need. But she didn't listen. Oh, no she didn't. The dick was too good and he was hitting spots she could only imagine.

The more he told her to find her purpose and to execute her plan the more she cut her own existence and made her husband the axis that spun her earth. Now she had the darkness to keep her company.

When she put her husband before her child, *God* decided to call her home. Her daughter was the sole reason she kept moving and striving for her husband.

She learned, while in the delivery room, that she had to live for her child first and herself second. She would never forget the delivery room…the room she experienced the brut of her pain…a delivery room in the Pennsylvania Hospital back in the late 70's…

Oh, God! Now my daughter is gone! Mama misses you. Mama misses you so much!

Mourning the death of her daughter, she was filled with rage and misunderstanding. She felt like God played a trick on her. Lord, why would you give her a child just to snap Holy fingers and take her away? Were you that jealous, Lord? Was ailing her daughter's heart and transfixing you own spiritual time stamp your way of

Dapharoah69

showing her who's boss? Didn't she eat healthy foods and be there for her child's father the way she should? She was barefooted and pregnant and still kept a clean house.

The questions spewed forward in her head like a bad song she didn't know the lyrics to. She seemed a bit out of it as the traffic came and went outside of the crowded parking lot of the shopping mall in Kendall, Florida.

Lighting her tenth cigarette, she hungrily pulled on it for dear life, her hands shaking.

I need nicotine! I need these cancer sticks! The marijuana is doing nothing for my mind. I still feel the same way I felt when my child died. Drugs were supposed to make you feel like Superman and take you up, up and away from your misery. I'm looking around, God. I'm still sitting in this vehicle. No, Lord.

I NEED TO KNOW WHY YOU TOOK MY DAUGHTER!

"You have to pay," she mumbled, looking over photographs of her daughter's funeral. She closed her eyes so tightly she felt her pulse. "And you will pay! The very people responsible for my child's demise…"

She pressed "play" on the corroding tape deck. The sudden sounds filled her ears like a wishing well. *A penny for your thoughts, Lord!*

Johann Chrysostom Wolfgang Amadeus Mozart was the composer flowing through her ears. Laughing sinisterly, she tapped the dashboard like it was a drum set…nodding her head like birds swooping through the air during the spring…

She inhaled deeply, the cool air filling her lungs with hate. "…Ah, Mozart. Born on the 27th of January, 1756 and died on the 5th of December 1791. Was this a form of Alpha and Omega? Was this the beginning and the end of life? January and December symbolized that. Even teachings of the Bible graced the front pages of Earthly publications, yet I don't remember when my daughter was born because I was so wrapped up in my child's father. I lost sleep wondering why he was late coming home…I

Call Her Queen Hatshepsut

always wondered why he never called when he stayed away for days on end. What kind of mother knows more about a Classical era composer than she knows about her own child? What kind of man left his woman home pregnant, making her fend for herself? Could this be why you took her, Lord?"

Tears fell from her itchy eyes and dropped like rain on the pictures…her sweaty, shaking thumbs were smearing the color, staining her fingertips like a brandished sunset over Paris…the pinks danced on the silkiness of huge puffy clouds as if Van Gogh and Di Vinci battled canvas to canvas…brush stroke to brush stroke and Van Gogh unceremoniously pulled Di Vinci's ear and tried to vindicate thee and his hand slipped and he lost footing and cut his right ear and the pinks and the beiges and the purples and the blood spilt all over the earth…yes, that's how the photographs were colored to the Perahia piano concertos of Mozart!

"I should have never trusted you, Kayak Burke!"

The words were filled with deadly venom as she eyed the shiny pistol on her lap. She should end it all! She should pick up the weapon and end her misery. Her daughter meant everything to her. *I don't deserve to live, to honor or to have a meal. I don't deserve to enjoy the pleasures of life. I couldn't even protect my own son, I meant daughter!*

Her child couldn't have come at a better time. Back then she had no sense of direction, no dictation. Her life was an endless journey underlining the U-turns and one way streets that always brought her full circle back to the start. It was like continuously running in a circle, a dog aggressively chasing his tail.

She cracked open, taking a small hand towel from the passenger seat and wiping the make-up from her face. She felt as if she failed as a parent. She couldn't protect her child from death. The photos fell to the floor. There was no need for them. To look at them and to hope and to dream of your child and to be one with your heart and finding beats unparalleled with reality was a beast without the beauty of love.

Every last one of the photographs was cleverly sheered blank pieces of construction paper.

Without images, pictures or memories.

ξ

The years she lived before the birth of her daughter were sad ones. At least she convinced herself of that. After Kayak Burke left her she slept with men to find her place in the world, she selfishly gave away the nectar of her honey to use them…defile them…to drain them dry of their resources to help her on her journey. The act of love making has died in her soul.

The thought of making men fall in love with the biorhythms of her vagina was climatic, potent and cunningly real.

She loved taking what wasn't hers. She refused to realize her psychosexual state of mind was set on propelling her growth as she continued to grow up and mature, yet she indirectly and unknowingly rushed it, acting out what she saw in her environment when she was growing up. In the beginnings of her life Haiti wasn't what she wished it to be.

Her little friends lived in poverty and she always had a hot meal in her tummy just before her parents hastily tucked her in at night. She slept on silk and cotton, deported from Puerto Rico. Her friends had to cover up with worn, dirty jackets and pray to a God that seemed to ignore their pleas for food, help and nurturing.

Seeing all the drugs and illiteracy in Haiti had changed her. She made a vow to say NO to drugs and she had, up until her life started spinning out of control and drug use seemed to be a sweet escape. Her Chronological Age was set at 18 but her Mental Age was 5, which was understandable because after the traumatic event she faced as a kid, she stopped mentally growing around that age…back when she was brutally attacked by vicious pit-bulls.

The dogs belonged to her step father, Miles, who bred dogs just to make money entering them into dog fights all over the muggy, muddy ghettos of Haiti. The act itself was unlawful, but he bought a house, three cars and a shitload of clothes off the winnings and provided his family a better life than those who lived in Port Au Prince. There was a pricey Olympic-sized pool in the back of mangroves, oaks and tall evergreens.

Miles loved his step children. He had a name for her. It was "Flower." Flower never wanted for anything. She had a room filled with pricey drapes, curtains, bed linens, furniture and walls of dolls! Yes! All four walls were loaded with hanging dolls. As for her sister Rosa, a startling beauty, she didn't have the best of everything. In comparison, Rosa's room had black drapes, black curtains and black walls. There wasn't a doll in sight. The floors were mildewed and her room was located behind the house, next to a small cemetery and she had to go to bed hearing the voices of the ghost and ghouls and goblins that hid under her bed.

When Flower tried to talk and play with Rosa, nicknamed "Dark Rose," she would say mean, malicious things to her and Rosa meant everything she said. You have the best of everything…why were you bothering her, she figured. She never understood why Rosa got the evil end of things, but it was quickly forgotten. The more she played with her dolls the happier she was. She became one with them, confiding in them…building a bond with them she should have built with her sister Rosa. Inevitably, this would bring about their ruin…the sisterly love would be crushed like a bug under a sharecroppers boot and dried like a raisin in the sun.

Life in Haiti wasn't a walk in the park. In fact her

grandmother periodically lived with them because her mother, Pauline, was always running the streets, doing the devil's work, despite playing the Mother of Mary role in the eyes of society.

Mozart bringing her back down from Jupiter, she smiled now, thinking about that time period as the rain built back into the torrent affair it has been all day. It rained so hard she couldn't see the parked cars or the looming mall ahead.

She remembered sneaking out into her backyard when Rosa was sleeping. She just wanted to play with the dogs. They were so adorable! She had tons of baby dolls and pretty toys but she wanted the dogs. *Can I become one with them?* In her hand she had bloody steaks. She remembered Miles telling her mother "I don't feed the dogs, and when I do I feed them raw meat. So by the time fighting competition comes up they are so fixed on appeasing their appetites all they see is blood."

She remembered waiting until her parents were sleeping before she went outside. Her parents forbade her from going into the back by herself around the swimming pool and the dogs in the man-made cages that was filled and smelled of feces.

The illegally-bred dogs, three of them, had eleven pound steel ball chains tightly hugging their bulging necks. Rummaging through their thick veins were steroids.

Salivating at the mouths, they eyed her as she naively smiled and talked to them.

Her heart pumped wildly. She was so excited! She just loved dogs!

"Here doggy doggy! I brought you something to eat! I can't wait to play with the doggy! I just love dogs!"

Inside, unknowing to Flower, Miles, who was mixed with Japanese and Haitian, and her mother Pauline, a Haitian nurse, were making love.

He was gripping her amazing breasts, tongue kissing her, flowing into her emotionally and physically as she wrapped her legs around his sweaty waist, digging her nails into his back every time he pumped his eleven inches into a hole too tight and small to handle what he had.

But she loved it. Releasing her inhibitions, she came over and over again, vowing to get pregnant and to birth his child! After all, any man with stroking ability of its own design deserved a living and breathing child in the process. The hell if she would go through endless hospital visits and unbearable hours of labor for a man who couldn't stroke vaginal walls like a dentist tool between teeth or rock the boat through ravenous seas to the shores of America.

Outside, the Little Dog Lover set the pan of meat on the ground, overrunning with blood. Some of it got on her white furry slippers, but she didn't mind. She would have her mother wash them. But what if her parents asked where did the blood come from? What would she say? They would whip her if they found out she fed the dogs! What did she do? Think, Flower! *Easy! I will bury them under the roses in the garden. They will never find them!*

The dogs were growling at the meat, licking their chops and ready to pounce. Rosa watched from the bedroom window, wondering what Flower was doing outside, alone, with those snarling creatures. On second thought…Rosa smiled to herself, closing her eyes and putting her hand over her heart, the evil washing over her face.

Kill her, Lord! Then I could have the dolls! I could have her room and get rid of the room next to the cemetery!

The moment Flower opened the gate…the dogs lashed out at her, biting into her arms and legs, her face and feet. Not once did they touch the meat…

The instant Miles came inside his wife, they heard the piercing scream. The lights came on at the neighbor's house.

Pauline, pushing Miles on the floor and grabbing her pump shot gun, fled from the room and down the stairs, her eyes and heart about to explode.

Dapharoah69

"MY DAUGHTER! BABBBYYYY!"

Miles, already knowing his dog fighting days were over, was right behind her, clumsily trying to put on his pants.

Pauline shot out the back glass door instead of opening it, and she took aim and shot all three dogs BOOM, BOOM, BOOM without skipping a beat.

Her daughter was twitching on the ground.

Her life was slipping away.

Pauline's world was swept from beneath her feet. "MY BABY!" she screamed in sheer horror, feeling helpless.

There was a popping sound in her ears, making her deaf as Miles quickly ran towards the dead dogs, digging holes by the rose garden and trying to bury them. The neighbors couldn't see over the huge wooden gate and the surrounding bushes.

Good, thought Miles. *This could buy me some time.*

Pauline was outraged. "Your daughter is bleeding to death and all you think about is saving yourself, you fucking prick!"

She turned the pump shot gun on him.

Death in his eyes, he jumped up and ran towards the phone, calling the authorities.

The little girl remembered everything was black at that point.

Miles calls me Flower! I am a flower…a rose unlike my sister…who hates me. Why does she hate me? Why don't we talk? We have the same eyes and the same chin and nose…

She didn't know at the time she would be in a coma for five months. She didn't know how Pauline lashed out at Miles, her burst of anger decapitating their marriage. She didn't know they lied to the police and said a pit bull dug a hole under the gate and attacked their daughter. She didn't know they would convince the police and never tell them Miles took down all the dog cages and got rid of all the evidence before the ambulance arrived.

When she came out of her coma she didn't know who

her parents were, or who she was. Her face suffered severe bite marks. A plastic surgeon was called in and after a week of therapy he agreed to recreate her face to the way it was. The procedure was very risky, and very daring but he pulled it off and made all the national newspapers for being a saint.

Over the next few years Miles's and Pauline's relationship deteriorated. She never forgave him for being careless with those dogs.

He finally divorced her after six months of heated arguments and misunderstandings. The sex dwindled to hell, unpaid bills and mounting torment. Rosa and Flower grew up and grew apart. Their hearts were cemented in evil and selfishness and neither or did a thing for each other. Rosa vowed to take any and everything Flower touched…she believed that with everything in her.

When the divorce was final, Pauline, who was a very head strong woman, slipped into oblivion. She started doing drugs and taking her failed marriage out on her daughters. She would shoot up heroine and smoke crack until she passed out in front of them. Her once thriving, beautiful face was now sunken and scary. It scared Flower and Rosa to see their mother that way, but ever since the divorce Miles met another woman and he forgot all about her.

When Pauline overdosed on drugs Rosa and Flower was fifteen years old, able-bodied and sexually aware. They thought life was over and they acted out in revenge. They didn't want to live. Flower briefly saw her step father, but he was so into his new wife and new family it was almost as if she didn't exist.

Then Flower met him, the man of her dreams. He was a man that single-handedly brought her back to life and back to sanity.

Shaking away the memories, she nervously lit a cigarette and began chain smoking until the pack was empty.

Kayak Burke. When I met him I still shouldn't have trusted him! But my flesh was so weak how could I not? A woman never thinks straight when a man is moving inside of her, bringing her orgasm after orgasm. Tired of Mozart, she wanted to hear some good, uplifting music. But as she turned the dial, searching for a good station, the only songs she heard were sad, sappy songs of loss, love gone wrong and autonomy.

That's just great, she thought miserably. *They're playing all this sad music. Making me feel worse.* The songs powered her up like an electrical generator. She was laughing hysterically, her huge blonde wig filled with gorgeously silky curls. In fact she laughed so loud she started to sneeze, the force of the laugh tickling her throat.

"Oh, yeah, you will die! If not, you will most certainly rot in jail. Or maybe prison."

Her daughter was all she had in this world as far as family was concerned. Her late husband, Rodney Lamley, was a very smart, intelligent man. But he died. Oh, yes he died. She wrapped her life around him just to…crush him. The life he shared with her turned into shambles and debris when he died. She was lost without him. He left her behind to raise her daughter. She was only eight years old.

Now her daughter has been dead for four years, and it has been four years of hell. Something inside of her snapped. She wasn't the same and she never would be. She couldn't eat or sleep. When she did try to cook the smell of food caused her to vomit. She quit her job and closed off herself to emotions.

When friends called her she didn't answer. When they came to her house to check on her she answered the door with a loaded pistol and they ran away fearing their lives. They never called her again and she didn't lose sleep.

Clad in a come-stained nightgown and huge rollers in her hair, she would laugh psychotically into the air, twirling the gun on her finger, her hand on her hip. She remembered purposely getting pregnant with her daughter because her mother had overdosed on drugs and she thought by having a baby she could replace that motherly love. And it failed miserably, because she found out the love of a mother could never be replaced. This killed her even deeper inside.

Nothing seemed to be the same. A circle seemed to be a triangle. Friends seemed bitter enemies. Love seemed to be hate's long lost betrayal.

NOTHING MADE SENSE!

"Enough," she uttered, cutting off the engine, the keys dangling. Sighing, she hastily grabbed her purse, angrily pulled the wig on her head tighter and quickly re-applied some make-up on her sweaty face.

She said, "It's time. To set up the game pieces"

ξ

When she entered the business she was surprised to see it nearly empty. Small, wooden chairs were neatly circling a polished oak-wood table. On the table were fake orchids and some old magazines. One of the magazines had Michael Jackson and his Thriller album on the cover. HE SAVED POPULAR MUSIC! The headline screamed and she rolled her eyes.

I wish he could have saved my child instead of worrying about Bubbles the Chimp. But that's life. The rich got all the breaks, the money and the fame. Normal, hard-working people such as me got the low end of the totem pole.

"Good, I'm glad it's empty in here," she mumbled, marveling at the brilliance of the room. The Art Deco bull crap was to die for. The old-school-looking windows added an old Renaissance Era feel to the room. The light brown wainscoting and brilliant green sea weed rugs were oh so ala gorgeous! It smelled like an ocean in there, complete with real hanging plants and hanging pictures of ships and people smiling as if there wasn't a care in the world.

I wish I could smile and be like the people in the pictures. But pictures are just that: images. Phony. Surreal. Gimmicks! Photographs are tools designed to trick the public into having false securities. They challenge your love. You find out that if you don't have what the people have in the images then you are no good. You have failed. And if you failed then give it up. Drop dead. Crawl in a hole and die.

I want to crawl in a hole and die!

She approached a very pleasant-looking woman clad in a Barbie nursing uniform. She frowned at the sight of Barbie imprinted all over the shirt. She was hugging Ken, driving a Porsche. On the name tag was "Jeannine Reynolds."

Jeannine was upbeat. She loved her job and she loved people and it showed when she made the woman jump by saying, "Hello, ma'am! How are you?" so loud Flower dropped her purse.

Startled, she said, "You scared me." Flustered, she picked up her purse, flinging the strap across her shoulder.

"Oh, I'm sorry! I am celebrating my eighth anniversary today!"

Flower gave a fake smile. "Well congratulations. Marriage is a sacred thing."

"Oh, yes it is. But I got a confession to make, darling. I'm not married. I have been in a serious relationship for eight years. His name is Fontal Clements, from London, Chile. And we are going to get married in a couple weeks."

Ask me do I care? Women and their hopeless bullshit I never fancied. I just want to wipe that smirk off your face! "Well again, congratulations."

She was shifting through some photos. "I'm sorry. Where are my manners? Business first. How can I help you?"

"I'm here for a free consultation."

"What, specifically are you seeking? And your name is…"

What name could I use? "Miss Up. Flower Up."

"Miss Up. Nice name, up, up and away," Jeannine joked, trying to make Flower smile and failing embarrassingly.

Bitch, you're not funny. "Cute. I am interested in liposuction."

Jeannine blankly looked at her. "Right! You have wash board abs, what more could you possibly want?"

"A husband," Flower said blandly, lying.

They were laughing.

"OK, one of the doctors is here. And as you can see we're dead today, because of the freakish weather. So go on in the back. His name is Dr. Samuels. He's the oldest, shortest, whitest doctor back there. You can't miss him."

"Thanks for your time."

Feeling uneasy, she shook Jeannine's hand. "It's my pleasure."

"Do you happen to have a sheet of scrap paper?" Flower asked, her eyes darting all over the place.

Jeannine blinked twice. "This is an office. We always have scrap paper. Frankly I need to get rid of some of the papers on my desk. It's too cluttered."

She was shuffling through papers. Memos. Documents. There were pictures of people who had successful operations. Very breathtaking work. Miss Up was impressed. *But why isn't those pictures carefully documented and filed away for safe keeping? What kind of doctor's office was this? What happened to confidentiality laws?*

"Well, I don't have scrap paper at my desk." She stood up, looking around. "Wait here."

"OK."

She didn't wait. When Jeannine vanished into the adjoining room, Miss Flower Up raced into the ante chamber, towards the back offices. Miss Flower Up was walking down the huge high-ceilinged hallway, inside the pricey and expensively built office. The walls were of cream and showed no signs of life. *Like my heart. There is no sign of life.*

There wasn't a hanging photo or a hanging poster. She felt dreaded and depressed.

The photographs I saw in the main waiting room should have been signs. And now the hallway leading to my destiny is blank. Is that another sign,

God? God? God, are you there?

They say when you pray you come right on time. Well, looking at my diamond-encrusted watch it's a little past 8 p.m. and you're still not here.

There is no God! There can't be a God!

She held her purse close to her body like she used to hold her daughter, so lovingly close she could feel her heart beat against hers. She smiled then, trying not to cry.

Today, the tears stop. And the ball gets rolling. Yes. Yes, Lord. The ball drops. It's only a matter of time.

She paused before an office door. It was made of oak wood (the same wood as the table in the waiting room) and polished to a shine. Wow. Even the door came with a hefty price tag. Told her he had regular clients. And why shouldn't he? His office was located in the expensive part of Kendall. All sorts off white girls walked around here like episodes 1, 2, 3 and 4 of *The Facts of Life.*

She politely knocked on the door. She waited a moment.

Then the door opened.

Dr. Samuels smiled at the beautiful woman standing before him.

It's time to set up the 16 pieces on the Chess board. Checkers is too typical, too fast paced. Chess?

Ah, yes. I loved the eight-by-eight grid and the 64 black and white squares.

I am supposed to have two bishops, two knights, two rooks; eight pawns a King and a Queen. The game I'm playing requires patience and understanding. It requires skill and dominance.

One wrong move and you are done.

"You made it," Dr. Samuels enthused with a smile, embracing her. She barely hugged him back. *Why is he*

hugging me? We are not friends. We aren't even acquaintances.
Holding her breath, she entered the expensively-designed office, smiling. Once the door closed she opened her purse, digging around. Where was it? Oh, there it was. She pulled out an inconspicuously unmarked, white envelope. In it was $8,500 in cash.

I just moved my first pawn. It's your move, doctor.

Falling in love with the sparkles in her eyes, he gracefully and appreciatively took the envelope, putting it in the inner pocket of his lab coat.

He fought himself not to get an erection.

Good move, Doctor. You moved the pawn off to the far left of the board. Great diversion, Doctor. Now it's my move.

She handed him a picture, saying, "Can you make my face and body look like this?"

I moved the pawn to the right of the board two places into the black square, Doctor.

His eyes glittered. "Consider it done. And I get the rest of the $20,000 when?"

Goddamn it! It's your move, Doctor!

Chess is a game of patience, not talking.

When the current form of the game emerged in Southern Europe during the second half of the 15th century I don't think they were doing much negotiating.

"I'll tell you when you get the rest of the money. When you make me look like the picture you will be paid and not a moment sooner, sugar britches. Now clear out this office. Oh, and send the clueless Barbie-looking bitch home and let's get on with the procedure, Doctor." Her eyes glittered dangerously. She didn't have time to play around. No, Sir.

"Money talks," the Doctor said, having second thoughts about doing the procedure. She seemed psychotic and a little intimidating. "But since I want this over with I'll get right to it."

Doctor. Move your game piece, please. Before I move it for you and if I do that it won't be pleasant.

Dapharoah69

"And once you're done, the bitch walks," she said, taking off her blouse, her breasts making his mouth water.

Meanwhile, out in the lobby, Jeannine smiled, thinking about Miss Flower Up. She was such a pretty, homely woman. She was pouring a cup of coffee because she was exhausted and she couldn't afford to fall asleep on the job. Pulling 12 hour days five days a week was taking a toll on her.

When she saw the note taped to the conference phone she grew pensive.

Don't marry your fiancé.
Trust me.
If you don't trust me call this number:
305-320-4433.

Her hands trembling, she guardedly picked up the phone, her heart about to explode. She clumsily dialed the numbers, but her finger kept pressing all the wrong numbers.

This has to be some prank. Ha, ha, Doctor. April Fools. But wait. It's not the month of April!

She sucked in air, dialing the number again. She knew the number by heart. Oh she knew the number well. Her stomach was in knots, bile rising in her throat. When her fiancé answered her best friend Rainey's phone she died inside. She had to hold her forehead, her breath failing her. She was suffocating.

"*Who* is this?" he asked groggily. "What do you want? We're trying to sleep."

She forced herself to say, "May I speak to Rainey!" using her best Texan accent to deter him.

He had an unbelievable attitude. She never knew he was an attitudinal person. He was always so accommodating and sweet with her. "She's asleep."

"And with whom I'm speaking with?"

I just have to hear him say his name. To confirm it. To confirm

Call Her Queen Hatshepsut   38

the deception.

Say your name, baby.

"Fontal. Listen, are you a bill collector?"

GOD! FONTAL! HOW COULD YOU? "No, I'm not a bill collector."

"Then who the fuck is this? You're waking me and my girlfriend up out of a deep sleep."

Hot tears redirected her vision. Nothing made sense anymore. Love was dead.

Life was dead.

Her world was a vindictive, lonely place. "It's funny, Sir."

"What's funny?" he asked, releasing a large gush of air.

"I have a bill from Hack's Jewelers for $59.99 with your name on it."

"What are you talking about?" Alert, he sounded very awake and she smiled bitterly.

"Aren't you set to marry Jeannine? And you said that you're at your girlfriend's house, who happens to be her best friend Rainey?"

"God! It's not what you think, lady. Whatever you do—damn I messed up! Don't tell my fiancée, Jeannine. I don't want to hurt her and I never will hurt her. Why am I telling a bill collector this?"

She was quiet, biting her lip. Her world exploding all around her, she said, "Hello, baby. It's me, Jeannine. It looks like the wedding is off."

She heard his huffing and puffing. He was silently waking up Rainey with a whispery "She knows, Rainey. Oh God she knows…Oh my God baby, how….its not what you think."

"GO TO HELL! And take that little tart, too! IT'S OVER!"

Slamming the phone down, she fell to her knees, sobbing into her sweet-smelling hands. She couldn't do this. She had to be strong.

Life didn't stop or start with a man.

Dapharoah69

Struggling to stand up, she pressed her hands flat on the desk, the ring glittering in her face.

Tears fell all over the photographs. She looked them over.

Where had they come from?

There was Rainey and her fiancé.

Together.

Skinny dipping.

On a nude beach.

They were having sex.

She was throwing objects all over the office, ripping up the photos, photos that appeared out of nowhere.

How did they get in her office?

She was grabbing her hair, wide eyed as outside the rain continued to pour.

The lightning and thunder continued playing a symphony too melodic for Miami-Dade County and Dr. Samuels led Miss Flower Up to the back operating room, and closed and locked the door.

Miss Up smiled evilly.

The doctor just moved the pawn in the middle of the board…
Good move, Doctor.

Tomb 1
Kayak Burke

Closing her eyes, Miss Flower Up (Avarice James) was slowly losing consciousness, being snatched back to a world that was very different from her present reality. She wasn't known as "Flower" anymore. Flower died when her mother perished from drugs. Or did she truly perish from the use of pharmaceuticals? She was remembering the fast-paced, forgettable days of high school. Those empty, depressing days she never wanted to relive again. The operating room was now high school. She could hear the leaves rustling in the trees as she, clad in a plaid skirt and blouse, walked inside the noisy Main Lobby.

"And what's your name?" a tall, handsome young man asked Avarice on a warm, sunny spring day. He was sipping a soda, his back pack too small for his sexy body.

Avarice grimaced, hugging her books up to her amazing breasts. "Don't play with me. Why are you trying to talk to me? Don't you have all the girls?"

He licked his lips, a knock out in a nice pair of blue slacks and white shirt. "Yes." His white sneakers were dirty and he did an annoying thing with his eyes.

She tucked her chin back, rolling her eyes. "Then you need to leave me alone."

He shifted on his feet. "I can't."

She averted her face. "And why can't you?"

"Because I want you to be mine," he admitted, giggling with a few of his friends that passed by them, trying to eavesdrop. Avarice noticed.

"Be yours?" she asked, leaning against the lockers.

"Yes," he answered, leaning up to her. Their lips were inches apart.

"You are a liar." She wasn't falling for his spell. In fact she wanted to kick him in the testicles.

"Come on! Why are you treating me like this?"

"I hear what they say about you. The ladies do whisper, you know. They say that you screw 'em and leave 'em before the door closes, and that you ruin their reputations before the roster crows."

"That's blasphemy against my good name."

"You're not God to call it blasphemy. So is it true?"

He tried his best to look innocent. "What?"

"I heard you went down on Cindy for so long she had four pissed rivers sliding down the back of your tongue. Samantha said you slid it in and caressed her velvet room so good she snored before you were through."

He pats himself on the back. "Yes, it's true."

Egotistical prick. "You sound proud. And that's turning me off. I'm wasting my time because you will never have me."

He challenged her. "I get what I want."

Men and their pride. "I don't want what you got."

"Oh. I like this conversation."

I am about to puke! "I'm late for class."

"I'll walk with you," he suggested.

Call Her Queen Hatshepsut

"Don't stalk me. What's with you selfish boys?"

"I'm not like the rest of them."

"Oh, yea? All you guys do is run around, talking about women behind their backs. Then you want to have sex. Life is more than sex. I'm a virgin and proud of it."

His eyes sparkled. "You're saving it for me."

"I'm about to go." She walked past him, gripping the strap of her book bag.

"Wait, Baby."

"I'm not your baby and you're not my Daddy. I never met him and I don't want to meet him now."

"I'm sorry. Did he abandon you?"

"Sorry? How can you feel sorry for someone you don't even know? What do you possibly know about empathy?"

This one was a tough cookie, he thought gravely, slowly losing interest in her. She was too aggressive and lippy. "Easy. You are supposed to love your fellow man."

"I have breasts. I don't have testicles. I'm not a fellow man."

"You're playing hard to get. I'm not used to that."

"I know. You're used to women throwing their panties at you. Well, I don't know you and I don't like you."

A few women were giving her the evil eye, whispering vulgarities. They didn't like seeing Avarice walking with the sexiest, most handsome boy in the school.

"And what are you tramps looking at?" she asked with acid on her tongue. A few women absent-mindedly pat their wigs and a couple other women stood up, laughing at her insecurity. "I don't want his used behind. And I will run up on you bitches if you don't cut your eyes off this 'cause you'll never get like this."

"Fire. I like that." He wrapped his arm around her and said, "This one here is mine. Step off, men. She's taken."

She slapped him so hard he fell to his knees. Instant shock waves gravitated through the school.

"A). Keep your hands off me and b) we are not together. I don't want you and I don't care about you. I

want to be a doctor when I finish school, a plastic surgeon
at that. I don't need a guy who can't keep his zipper up
claiming something he will never have. I want things in life;
I want something *out* of life. My Mama wasn't about shit
and you obviously aren't about it either. You are a whore
and whores have no say in anything I do. So get it through
your head."

A crowd formed around them.

"Tell him, Girl."

"Stand up for the ladies."

"If you don't want him I'll take him."

"Girl he boned you eight different ways already."

Deeply depressed, Avarice shook her head.

*I never had sex with him. Why do people make up such horrible
things about me? Is this what life is about? Find a handsome man
and you let him disrespect your body?*

He never took his eyes off her.

"Be with me…"

Avarice was unsurprisingly appalled. "I think not! You
think I wanna kiss you and taste these whores off your
lips? Please. I don't want to taste Samantha or Cindy. I'll
pass. Next."

He looked up at her with a smile, holding his cheek.
He knew then he loved her and he knew he would have
her. No other woman had ever been this feisty with him.

He never heard the word "No" and she told him and
it felt good to not always get what he wanted. It felt good
that she wasn't going to spoil him.

Finally. He needed that in his life. She was a real
woman. He said, "Will you marry me?" He held up his
hand, remaining on both of his knees.

He had the most gorgeous smile and she melted in it
without showing it on her hardened face.

"You can't have me. Sorry." She walked past him, her
big derrière jiggling in her loose fitting jeans.

Avarice James built her entire life around the man of her

dreams. There was nothing she wouldn't do for him: Kayak Burke. He was the most beautiful man in the world.

Who would have thought she'd wind up with the catch of the century?

Who would have thought that the man she slapped in school would capture her heart in ways cameras never could?

God knows she made the wrong decisions before he came along. She had eight boyfriends. She kissed three of them, one of them slapped her when she didn't do his homework, another one played her by trying to talk to her friends and the other one had seriously mind-boggling mental problems. James (was that his name?) was too possessive and Hank had problems with his hands because he couldn't keep them off her buttocks and she wasn't with the program.

At a time in her life she should have been happy, she used to be sad in school. She would trek the hallways with her head down and black, unruly hair dangling in her face like vines.

People rarely talked to her and the few friends she did have talked about her like she was a three-legged dog.

Home life wasn't what it was supposed to be. Her grandmother, an alcoholic seamstress, required her to cook the food, wash the clothing and mow the lawn.

Her sister Rosa didn't have to lift a finger. She could come and go as she chose. Avarice hadn't ever met her father.

In fact her mother never told her who he was and when she inquired about it her mother slapped her so hard in the face she accidently bit down on her teeth. She could remember how her eyes welled up with tears.

She didn't understand the reaction. Why had her mother struck her? Her lips didn't have the desire to utter the question so she never bothered to ask again.

She felt like fifty percent of her existence was out there somewhere, probably worried about her. Was he roaming the streets a zombie?

Was he tall and handsome, like the men in the romance novels?

Did he whisk her mother off her feet with roses and cotton candy, uttering promises of the moon in her ears?

Was he heart sick with guilt? How could he feel guilty?

He was probably the typical man; get 'em pregnant and move on to the next boulder. Was it his fault Mama left him? Was Mama ever with him? Did they have a relationship? Did they go through the typical ups and downs of a burgeoning relationship?

Avarice thought she was to blame. And this played on her self-esteem. She really thought she and boys weren't a mix, and all her girlfriends tried to tell her to be patient.

Don't rush to get a man, but she was young and dumb. Caught up in romance novels, hoping some Prince come to her house and sweep her off her feet.

Then Kayak Burke came along and changed her life. In high school all the girls wanted him, and most of them momentarily succeeded.

Getting him in the sack and tasting the seeds of his flesh as a means to trap him. But he never stuck around long enough to write love letters.

Didn't those harlots understand you couldn't plant seeds in a river and grow a vegetable garden? Kayak was always interested in her.

Undeniably, he was a very intimidating man. Rough around the edges with deeply rooted southern views.

He loved wearing flip flops and long tube socks and gym shorts one size too big.

He had a nice butt and the shorts sort of clung on to his butt cheeks in a very seductive way. He loved sports and hanging out with those he loved. He rarely took anyone around his family, so she was honored when he took her to meet his mother, who had osteoporosis.

Avarice James loved falling asleep, looking into his heavenly eyes. She loved being wrapped in his semi-

muscular arms while he talked about the world, his
ambitions, which seemed over the top, and his goals. She
wanted to give him the world. She wanted to believe in
him and fight his battles and quite possibly have his
children, when the time was right. The way he kissed her
was magical. She could have sworn Tinkerbelle flapped her
silky wings from her heart and left stardust all over her lips,
eyes and hair. She breathed his air and couldn't breathe
when he was gone. Even though they didn't live together,
she always held out on dating other guys because Kayak
told her he was going to marry her. And she believed this
with everything in her. Wasn't that what love was about?
Logic, understanding and faith? The shape of his lips
always did a number on her. The sight of him made her
soft inside. She was glad when he made her a woman by
taking her virginity in his own sweet, patient way. Even
though she was in the 12th grade, she knew she'd love him
forever. He was slow, masterful and tender. When they
rose on tidal waves of bliss he was accommodating,
beautiful and fulfilled. She then got it.

It all came together in her heart and soul with a
resounding click. He practiced with those other girls, going
through some sort of manhood training, to prepare himself
for her.

The way he kissed her breasts made her feel gorgeous.
He moved slowly and deeply within her, her rosy lips
agape with fear, longing and passion, the blood of her
virginity shining along the incredible inches of his shaft.

Her nails in his back ignited Rome into Eiffel towers
growing along the Goosebumps on her arms and the
Spanish Steps on her shivering, sweaty thighs. When she
saw the mountain she never knew the peak would be
elevated so high in the sky…she caught the wind and
spiraled towards the cliffs…he moved deeper within her,
his thrusts more powerful than the next.

She wrapped her legs around his waist and refused to
let him move so they rocked back and forth…the breeze

pushed her over.

Oh, God! She was flinging her arms, trying to scrape the edge and got nothing but clouds.

"I love you," he promised, kissing her lips, reaching a climax of his own.

She stuttered. "I love…love you…"

She arched her back and it happened. An explosion so intense she screamed out in pleasure as he lay spent like last year's ten dollar bill on top of her body, her chest heaving.

Wow! She used to write poems for him and wait up late into the night, hoping the powerful beams from his vehicle would light up the block before his car turned on it. Her heart would pitter-patter when he parked in her front yard.

She would secretly smile when the car door slammed. She would hold her breath waiting to see his beautiful body. Ever since high school, in Philadelphia, the man has been chasing her. Initially, she found it to be annoying. She went to school to better herself. She wanted to be better than her mother had ever been.

She tried not to think of her mother because when she did she started having nightmares. And to make matters worse she was apart of a Haitian Gang. She had made a hobby of robbing people.

She loved being Haitian and ever since her Grandma fled Haiti and set up camp in Philly she and her sister used to get spat on. They were ridiculed and talked about. She grew tired of the insults and the boys throwing dirt in their hair, calling them sick little bitches so she and her sister retaliated. They found a few other Haitian girls who'd gone through the abuse and they started causing havoc.

Gone from her heart was the soft spoken, kind hearted little girl she'd grown accustomed to.

The little shy thing her Grandma fancied. She didn't take any mess and she did it with a smile and an attitude. But meeting Kayak proved to be heaven.

High school seemed like another world. During those

times she thought she had life figured out and she found out she didn't know the half.

Her sister Rosa hardly ever spoke to her in school, since they were in the same grade.

And people were always marveling over their breathtaking good looks and banging bodies.

This drove Kayak Burke crazy. Ever since he laid eyes on Avarice he knew he wanted her. Having bedded most of the females in school, Avarice was different.

He'd sit under the huge tree in the front and watch her when she was bused to school. Avarice always rode alone, her sister riding to school in the Porsche of a Caucasian jock. The way she carried her backpack, the way she wore her long dresses planted a huge Cheshire cat smile on Kayak's face.

Her hair was always pulled into a tight ponytail and she seemed too shy to speak. He was never aware of her drop-dead gorgeous sister. It took him a few days to realize he wanted Avarice to be his wife.

Avarice slowly opened her eyes. Discombobulated, it took her a while to realize that she was in the operating room. Her body was sore, the last of the drugs starting to wear off. She opened and closed her hands. They ached with a pain she never felt in her life. Had everything gone perfectly? In her heart she knew that she had to complete the game. She had to merge as the victor. She couldn't afford to kill time or play around. Every second counted. Every minute added up.

The pain shooting all over her body was excruciating. Were the drugs wearing off?

Moaning piteously, she looked around and found the doctor smiling down at her, standing by a row of tables. The lights were dimmed and soft chamber music played. In his hand was a manila folder. He set it down and there were two black and white photographs. Her Before and After photos were startling.

Dapharoah69

Dr. Samuels grinned. "How are you?" he asked, pleased with his work.

"Fine, I guess," she said, her voice cracking.

"The surgery is complete."

She smiled, closing her eyes, a feeling of euphoria engulfing her and making her sinister against herself.

At last. It starts.

"Is it really accomplished?"

"Yes. It is. Now the only thing left to do is…"

"Is what, doctor? I don't want no record of this surgery."

"But I have to document this procedure."

"Truly, do you want to destroy yourself in that fashion?" she asked sheepishly.

He stared at her. "What do you mean?"

"With all the illegal things you do in this clinic, surely you don't want it to get out, do you?"

He stuttered. "Well, no."

"The overcharging of your patients, Doctor, is just one flaw you will be found guilty of. Hell, you overcharged me. I'm sure the IRS will have a field day combing through your mighty fine establishment, doctor. Your record books and account sheets would be public record and a jury of about, what, twelve people will have your ass in prison so fast your unruly panties will ride your ass faster than sunlight can touch your paling skin. Want to test that theory, Doctor? I can be the singing canary if I'm…tempted."

"I see you don't play by the rules, Lady," he snapped.

"Well, don't document this procedure. I want no record of it. Make like it never happened, Doctor."

He shook his head, his temples twitching with anger. He turned to walk away. "As you wish."

I'll get some rest. After all I just moved the Queen. I'm coming after you, King…

Tomb 2

Queen Hatshepsut

April 2008

With everything in me, everything that comprised my body into the molecules and cells it has become…I loathed this place, a place that was unlike any other place I have ever seen in my young life. I would like to think I was a multifarious person but I knew that deep down I was just like any other human being. Mother named me Hatshepsut many years ago and I wound up studying Hatshepsut's life and legacy in Egypt from dusty text books hidden deep in the back of the public library. The dust itself told its own story of racism. I knew then that the country known as North America was a racial mess. Any country that would condone slavery, any country that had people bashing Negros, beating them, spraying them with hoses and making them work for little to nothing, any country that looked at blacks as property to be sold to the highest bidder and not even offer them three acres and a mule when slavery was allegedly *abolished* should be ashamed. The Emancipation Proclamation really didn't free the slaves. If you read the documents blacks weren't to be equal economically or socially to whites. So Mr. Abraham Lincoln, tell me how did that make us free? I heard his John Hancock wasn't even on the document. So it's not endorsed.

I bitterly watched *Roots* and had more questions than answers. Kunta Kinte has become my hero on many levels. They way he endured hate, the way he handled slavery, the way he said his name was Kunta Kinte when he was being beaten gave me hope that I could make it through anything. Bow down to no one.

Why would Caucasian book keepers hide Egyptian rulers and pharaohs in the back of the library, out of public view?

That's why I loved children, educating them. They loved, were influential and non-judgmental. The eyes of a youngster, I was told, were pure and unbiased.

I closed my eyes now, searching for my childhood. I looked for the trivial things…

I searched for the simple things, back when life was a crystal stair. Back when my mother paid the bills and cooked the food and all that was required of me was to come to her when she called my name and play with my dolls like she had when she was a little girl and go to school and make the grade.

In my mind I saw a robed figure dancing behind my closed lids…beating a gavel on my skull…there was a jury made up of the most bitter, illicit people in the world. I couldn't make out what they were saying. I didn't even know if I was on trial or not. But I did know that I hated this place. And I wanted to leave.

I couldn't think right now. To think would be a

monstrosity of the facts. What *were* the facts? I would tell you.

The facts were simple. In my young life adults have destroyed the very fabric of my being without sincerity or apology. I didn't know what to do or say. I was confused.

When I came here…I didn't know…I felt…alone, deserted and abandoned. It was a dark place filled with bad memories…memories I didn't care to remember.

Who was in charge of issuing a memory? Was it supposed to be good or bad? I didn't know, but I did know this: I was on my knees with rain soaking in my hair…my silk dress stuck to my skin and my ample-sized breasts…my make-up ran down my face with my tears…

I taste the tears and the mascara and the rain…black rings were around my eyes.

Devastated, I placed my well-manicured hands on my lap, leaning forward until my forehead touched the cold tombstone like I was offering my body to the Gods. There were two concrete slabs before me.

Each with a name.

AVARICE
ROSA

There wasn't a last name or a date they were born or a date they demised.

One was my mother and the other was my aunt.

Their last names were "James." Deciphering the names into mother and aunt didn't serve a purpose.

Mama was dead.

My Aunt was deceased as well.

When they were alive they were bitter enemies, trapped in a war they both lost. Satan claimed their lives and he set them in his lake as the horrid trophies they were.

Beauty was a splendid thing…but even beautiful things tarnish and the dust rids the fine writing of its luster.

My heart cracked at the thought of my aunt and mother fighting, bringing each other misery. There wasn't a victor. Crimes of passion never made way for utter sunlight to sheepishly erase the darkness.

Yet it was dark right now…the glow of a crescent moon trying its best to penetrate the rain…the towering trees with twisting branches were all around me.

There were too many dark purplish clouds and too many ghosts. They were saddened and blurry and I kissed Avarice's name, then Rosa's…

Life was a mystery of sorts…you had to sort through what was left of a bitter war fought between the two women I loved most in the world.

I didn't want to think about it. Mama had taken something from my whorishly jealous, trouble-making aunt and my aunt had unapologetically taken something from my sick, twisted mother. And they lived a lifetime retaliating, seeking vengeance, vowing death on one another, and the worst crime of all filtered through my brain as I gathered the strength to stand up in these high heeled stilettos, covering my face in shame.

As sisters, they tried to eradicate each other like blood thirsty vampires.

I was the reason they tried to destroy each other. The memories I would always remember.

I was the memories.

Good or bad.

God, *you* tell me.

For the next few hours I lay, soak and wet, on satin sheets. My mattress wasn't strong enough to hold me and I weighed a measly 134 pounds. I needed to purchase a new mattress but buying one would be outside of my budget and I didn't feel like restructuring my finances.

Entangled in the past, I cried and I cried. The fire in the pit of my stomach was real, redundant and unflinchingly wicked. I tried to eat, but I chewed the food for the taste and made myself throw it up.

I battled myself profusely; I tried to erase the fact that I didn't have high self-esteem. My own father didn't love or want me in his life and he spelled out a few terms and told me if I couldn't live up to them then me and his relationship was utter hogwash.

I was fine with that. Because If I was going to change it would have to come from within, a decision I would make the day I learned to love myself unconditionally.

But it wouldn't be so easy.

When you spent a lifetime being something you were not, tell me, how could it be easy to make the transition? A lot of people loved me for something I wasn't because I was too afraid to lose them for something I was.

Was that a mockery?

Was that right?

Every day on television you heard lying politicians boasting about change and vowing to do it differently than those who did the job before them. I felt that the President was actually chosen before the election. Illuminati rumors are running rampant all over You Tube and the Internet, and I studied every single thing I could find on it.

Everyone lied to get what they needed. Politicians thought they knew God and the world's secrets and those very same politicians were busted trying to have sex with homosexual men…tell me, from whom the world should seek advice? Ignorant parents, I say, would always raise ignorant children. Ignorant children grow into ignorant adults. And when they have children the cycle continues.

If you couldn't get people to agree on one God, Buddha, Jehovah or Allah, tell me, how could you get them all to agree on abortion, gay rights and marriage? Gays hated each other, bashed each other in online communities if you didn't praise Beyonce and disrespected black women like it was the *in* thing to do yet they wanted equality. It's impossible. I didn't praise any female singer who thought she was Jesus or God.

Dapharoah69

In one way or the other our upbringing and the environments in which we were raised has affected us beyond repair. I know it did for me. I could only speak for myself. If you couldn't recognize the bad seed growing amongst the plentiful how could we change the core of ourselves to reinvent what our parents destroyed in us? What did they destroy, exactly?

They destroyed our ability to make choices.

I said this because if a child made up his or her mind to wear a suit when the parent distinctly told him or her to wear a pair of jeans and a T-shirt the parent goes off the deep end and would tear you down, talk trash in your face, write a voided check on your confidence and tell the world about you wearing a suit and tarnish your image in the process until your decision ails and you do what they said.

Parents wanted puppets for children as a means to correct all the wrong decisions they made in life. Live through the child. Once you surrender then the tongue-lashing and the bitterness and the argument diminishes. You aren't their child at that point, you were now a puppet.

Wear this, do that and come back saying this. As long as you do those things…a parent would give you the world…But the universe would remain out of reach.

Those who were lacking love sought acceptance. Those who needed to feel special would spare no expense to purchase it. Didn't they know true values and morals couldn't be bought, that it had to be taught, practiced and executed?

I was still learning this. Even in my own lie.

When was I going to accept, acknowledge, and execute self-love? I knew deep down I had to love myself first. And I hated myself with a passion unknown to Christ.

A few weeks horridly passed, and I just got through attending a comedy show in Coconut Grove (Miami, Florida). Traffic was ridiculous and I saw a few men that I knew. Honking my horn, I waved and pressed my foot down on the accelerator. They waved back, not sure who I was. When I got home I realized I hadn't had dinner. Over the past month I gained ten pounds so skipping a meal was like skipping Christmas.

You save money, you remained steadfast and the more procrastinate you become the more you endure.

Despite my unease about the past and battling self-loathing, I felt at peace roaming around my cul-de-sac, stoned from too much marijuana and alcohol.

My place, my safe haven, was beautifully furnished to my liking of course, but there were some things that had to be worked on before I could be completely satisfied.

A woman was never satisfied; at least that's what Mama once told me. Thinking of my late mother really disheartened me because she was a sick bitch hell-bent on destroying her sister Rosa. I was still shaking with anger.

There were still things I held on to. Grudges that made me very uncomfortable within my own skin. I never knew I had an aunt named Rosa until Mama Avarice took me to my father's wedding and I saw her. She was looking as beautifully elegant as she could be. I would never forget that day. So long ago.

The day Daddy Kayak Burke tried to cut off my beautiful hair. The day he called me vicious names. He said things a father should NEVER say to his child.

I was surrounded by elegant things so I could forget the unworthy artifacts in my soul. Red drapes of silk that danced on a morning's breeze when I opened the windows. Potpourri stuffed inside huge life-sized ceramic bowls and strategically placed throughout the fancy living room. Two identical China cabinets filled with gorgeous artifacts from Japan, Beijing and Tokyo were along the far wall leading to the kitchen.

I'd gone to Tokyo earlier this year to do a show and I didn't want to leave. I stayed at the Century Southern Tower Hotel and lost my breath at the beauty of Shinjuku.

I fell in love with hotels at that moment. When I was

done doing dance shows (and feeling homesick and experiencing culture shock) I checked into the Keio Plaza Hotel, which has been a centerpiece hotel since the 1970's, and had a few one-nights stands with narrow-eyed, little cocked Asian men who couldn't stroke it to save their lives. The Keio Plaza Hotel was also one of the tallest hotels in Tokyo.

I didn't even want to leave. The food was incredible, the sights around the hotel were mesmerizing and the people were accommodating. I smiled thinking about it.

I even bought a little translation manual and taught myself their language. Well, I learned a few words.

Pushing Asia to the back of my mind, I could see the den from here, furnished with all black leather couches and sofas, a plasma TV was mounted into the wall and surround sound speakers were carefully hidden so you know it's there by the point of hearing yet invisible to the naked eye.

A picture of Rosa hung on the wall. In it she wore a red dress and her smile radiated with her breathtakingly gorgeous almond-colored eyes. Since Mama was a lover of books I had every book she ever read on the polished shelves at the start of the rotunda. After all, this used to be her home. I inherited it when she passed away. There was a lot more to that story. I was sad now…some things about my life I didn't care to remember. Mama died a bitter, sick, twisted woman who had too much surgery done to her face and body.

I was proud of this home. After it burned to the ground I had it rebuilt a year later to remind myself of what I lost?

Daddy used to have a rotunda at his home in Philadelphia. I absolutely loved when I first saw it many rains ago.

A huge painting of Queen Hatshepsut, my favorite of the Egyptian Queen, regally hung above the mantel by the front door.

I just love how I felt when I ran my fingers across the hardened paint. But that was short-lived…because my father never accepted me.

Mama kept me hidden from him for years. Initially, it bothered me *but* when reality sunk in and the events that transpired over the years changed my logic and reason about my parents, tell me…how did I get beyond being abused on so many levels?

I inherited my Italian chairs from my Aunt Rosa. There was a story behind that as well.

The taste in paintings came from my father's grandmother, even though I never met her.

My mother's mother Pauline, a very serene Haitian woman, an upstanding citizen who did everything by the book—even fucked her husband by the book before he was killed in Haiti, then she married Miles—was a woman I was glad I didn't meet. I should be truthful.

I never met Miles.

Mama Avarice told me the story. She said she was once bitten by vicious dogs.

She told me she was in a coma for five months.

After years of believing it I stumbled across her diary and everything made sense.

Everything morphed into the Lie of the Century!

Passing off a whore as a woman of taste put a bad taste in my mouth. I really didn't care because people came into your life for a reason or a season. Great Grandma Sasha François was a season in my mother's life and now its spring again in my own life.

I mournfully looked at my Great-Grandma's photo. It was a breath-taking 5x7 sitting in a gold frame in the middle of my low-table.

It's the only thing on it.

Her gorgeous eyes and her flair radiate. This photo used to be in Mama's room on the nightstand. Now it sits here, where it would be until I died. The photo somehow survived the fire…

I had to have it restored. Unwanted feelings of abandonment redirects my heart beat. I wished my Great-Grandma and I were close…but we weren't because I never met her.

I didn't have house guests. I didn't invite anyone over. I liked being alone.

I was a Shrek of sorts. Leave me to the swamps of my mind and I'll be just fine with a donkey.

My eyes dance across a book on the end-table. Authors Lynn Margulis and Dorion Sagan, in my opinion, didn't know what life was, as their book "What Is Life" entitled.

I read this book from cover to cover a few times and each time I do I spark a joint and I pour a tonic and I walk around my house topless, contemplating the different themes written within.

Again, I looked at the book. Even the "Foreword" by Niles Eldredge didn't do a damn thing for me. Where do these people get this shit?

Distraught, I turned on some Nina Simone and let go, sipping the drink, feeling it burn my slender throat. Burning in my mind the way the spark burned the tip of my cig was page 119 of the book.

TWISTS IN THE TREE OF LIFE. I marveled at how they talked about nucleated cells and the whole nine. Tell me, if they were so goddamn smart…let's talk about the developmental biology of my parents. Who made them?

Clearly God was love and he wouldn't make two destructive people just to fuck and bring me here.

Or what about the information on page 209? Charles Darwin (whoever the hell that was) called the origin of the flower an "abominable mystery." Was Mama an "abominable mystery" since Miles nicknamed her Flower? Charles also said that fossilized flowers revealed that flowering plants appeared in the middle latitudes of the Northern Hemisphere approximately 124 million years before I sipped this tonic in the mid-Cretaceous.

Call Her Queen Hatshepsut

If that was so, explain my upbringing. Did mothers brainwash their children 124 million years ago? Did your fossilized plants reveal that, Mr. Charles Darwin? Did your Great-Grandma Sasha call your mother a whore?

Did your mother have surgery in the 80's, and died one delusional bitch who was convinced she had a daughter who died when she was eight?

Yes, Mama had a daughter but she was still born. She was born the same time I was.

Again, this was what Mama told me but her Diary revealed something different.

She never carried a daughter in her womb.

Yet God let me survive to deal with the nuclear fallout. The lies that unraveled have changed my life. My life was not what Mama said it was.

Mama's life was contrived lies.

Women came from Venus and Men from Mars, so the good book says, yet where did *I* come from? I was a demon of Mama's design. I didn't feel like a whole woman.

Maybe I came from Jupiter because Saturn had too many rings and I couldn't afford jewelry right now. Couldn't find a man who wanted to turn my finger into Saturn and marry me.

Who would marry me when I was in this state?

Disillusioned, I spent the next hour on my sofa, contemplating going out tonight.

I was a loner but I didn't run the streets. There was nothing out there but a man waiting to give you an STD. And it was best to treat all men like they had the clap.

I looked in the mirror, fingering ashes from my cigarette into the ash tray, looking at a woman who needed to work on herself.

I was drowning in my own waters of hell and there were no dolphins to push me to shore. Where were the life jackets? I hated my face.

I used Botox injections to smooth the aging lines. Not enough to freeze my face but to keep everything smooth, despite being in my late twenties. With that in mind I didn't feel like being the found tomb of Nefertiti so I got up, showered and found a dress from my closet I made and I put it on.

I took my time applying sweet-smelling lotion to my legs and put on some panties.

Checking myself in the mirror, I took a sporty light red wig from a clamp in my closet and I put it on.

I completed the package.

Grabbing my keys, cell phone and purse, I locked the door behind me and walked to my light blue Nissan Maxima.

The one I haven't made a payment on in eight months.

ξ

Trapped in my own world, which evolved around the past and finding ways to overcome it, I left Club Mansion a few minutes ago, thankful I didn't sweat out my wig.

I was happy to see my car still in one peace. I looked at all tow truck as the potential repossessed freaks they have become since I stopped paying my car notes. Quite honestly I got in the club for free, since I once gave it up to the bouncer ions ago. The sex wasn't memorable, and I had plaguing vertigo a few days later trying to shower and erase his scent from my body. Seeing him again wasn't the homecoming he was expecting.

He gave me a hug and I cringed. He said a slight, "Hello," and I walked right past him. Once I leave your bedroom you become another face and another lay. Somewhere down the line your face gets lost in the crowd.

Hmm, I initially met him at another club in Fort Lauderdale. I wondered did he remember.

I remembered it well. Why I thought of it beats me. After my second free drink I was in your car and bumping against your groin seconds later. I gave you the anus because I wasn't ready to give you the front. You didn't have a condom yet I happened to have a Magnum in my bra and you were a little too small for that but you seemingly made it work. You were happy with that, telling me you never banged a girl in the ass before.

Glad to meet your acquaintance, Mr. Inexperienced. I hated his choice of words. I mean, you didn't tell a classy woman "I want to fuck you in the ass." For some women that was a complete turn off. We like to have poetry read to our anatomy parts and rose petals trailing along our limbs. The key wasn't even in the ignition for ten minutes and your tongue slithered all over my breasts…you fumbled between my legs and I abruptly pushed your hand away.

Get back, you didn't know me like that. Trust me; you didn't want to know me like that just *yet*.

Some kind of way you managed to drive me to your house ten miles away. I was so horny I forgot I drove to the club. My car was still parked in the parking lot. I didn't stay in your wife's bed for twenty minutes. And don't you think for one moment I had any…remorse about getting some of you in your wife's bed while she worked.

To be real with myself, a) I didn't know you were married and b) I really didn't care when I found out. Giving you some more ass (as much as you begged to be in the vagina), I rode that little needle in the haystack, rolling my eyes and taking your cash from your wallet, stuffing it in my bra.

I could tell your body still had a foreign attitude to your wife's touch because your eyes were slammed shut the entire time. Her photos were up all over the room and I got off on her pretty eyes bearing down on me. With all the trappings of your bedroom it was safe to say that she only married you because you had four bank accounts. So if she truly didn't love you then why should I feel guilty for taking her only prize?

When you finally did tell me you were married, when we were finished, I didn't care. I figured that out already.

Why did men cheat without a conscious? My own mother once told me I would understand this one day. And she was right.

So you tore your room up looking for your wallet and I sat like a prima donna on the settee by the closet. I picked dirt from my acrylics. I told you I had to go get my car. You listened and decided to drive me back without your license. When we got to the club the cops stopped you just as I opened the door.

I kept walking. That wasn't my scene and I hated dealing with cops. You were yelling "I don't know where my wallet is. I don't have my license!" and that didn't sit well with the big boys in blue. I happily walked to my Nissan Maxima with the $7,000 rims, unlocked the door and got inside, closing the door. I crank it up and was out, speeding past you, giving two honks.

Good. Night.

Dealing with you pissed me off and reinforced the walls I built around my heart because I refused to let anyone hurt me in this lifetime. Seeing you tonight at Club Mansion brought all that up. I had gone through enough hurt in my life growing up and I really didn't feel like going through it as an adult.

They say there was always someone in a worse position than you but I wasn't trying to hear all that mumbo-jumbo. All I thought about was myself. No one saved me as a kid from destruction. No one threw a lifejacket into my rapturous seas when I was in my teens.

Just like they didn't think of me why should I be the bigger person and think of them?

I remembered I used to always say that I couldn't *wait* to grow up. When I became an adult I was going to do this and get that and this person would get cursed out and my house would be built from the floor up but none of those things happened.

You're trained by your friends in school in ways your parents never thought about or maybe they forgot about.

"Girl, when you become a grown woman its smooth sailing. You come and go as you please," said my friend Veronica when I was in the eleventh grade. "…You do what you want. You get a job and make your money. You get a car and ride to the clubs. If you're smart enough you go to college and get a degree."

And when high school came I fell on my face. Things intensified and got harder. I wished I was a kid again. I had to fill out résumés for a job. Interviews and rejection after rejection became my life at that moment. Did you speak Spanish? Miami was diversified and we want someone who was bilingual, they said. Yet the Spanish people who worked there couldn't speak a lick of English.

When I did find a job, as a waitress at the local restaurant, I thought getting a car would be easy. Wrong.

I didn't have credit which was just like having bad credit. Where do you work? Do you have a co-signer? If you work you need to fill this out so we can contact your employer to verify your annual gross pay. What about insurance? Do you have any? You have to have it in order to drive the car off the lot.

And even when I got my first car, a raggedy Mazda, '87, it gave me all sorts of problems. Oil changes and breakdowns on the turnpike were the end result. I didn't have anybody to call and when you did get a hold of someone they claimed they were at work when it was actually their day off.

I thought you just bought a car, hopped in and drove until the gas light lit up. Wrong. Check the radiator fluid. Put water in the goddamn battery. Check the carburetor. A pain in the ass was more like it. When I got tired of that, not getting anywhere with my job, I applied for college. Smiling while standing in the admission office, I thought it would finally be "smooth sailing," like Veronica had said.

WRONG!

Papers and fees. Are you under the financial support of your parents? Student loans. Wanna know where you work. Select your classes…go to this building and that building and that building. How many classes you wanna take a semester. Three or four? And still had to work around your employer and they didn't even want you going to school. They wanted you to choose – school or work.

Horny boys who run around with overzealous hormones, trying to poke every female with a bubble ass and a Big Red Bubble gum smile got on my nerves. They flashed their expensive car keys to lure you to bed. Glad I was never a victim to that. Those very same men said I was stuck up in college. I smiled and said, "I'd rather be stuck up then your penis stuck up in me."

That shut them up quick.

Being an adult comes with its own problems, problems your parents never prepared you for and I was raised in a broken home.

My mother was never married to my father. She hated the man and the very ground he walked on. She had problems of her own, but as a kid you're ignorant to all that.

You just think life was all about Christmas and Valentine's Day and Thanksgiving. You only dressed up and went to church on Easter.

After that you ignored God until the next go round. I knew very little about Mom's past.

I knew her name was Avarice James and when she was little she was nearly mauled by dogs her step-father owned. She met my dad, Kayak Burke, in high school. She once showed me pictures but I was perturbed because the pictures had his face cut out.

I was caught up in their emotionally entangled mess by the time I was twelve-years-old. Some of those things I still haven't recovered from. I couldn't even look in the mirror without hating what I saw.

Hell, I didn't even love myself. My daddy didn't love me. I thought he'd bend over backward for me when I went to his wedding but that proved to be very disappointing on so many levels I lost count after three. Men loved my body, men loved the way I did things yet I was not that experienced in the Game of Sex. I still haven't given them my vagina. I only gave up the booty. Anal sex was risky but they either take it or leave it.

My vagina I always said would be for someone special and black men weren't that freaking thrilling these days. Many people called themselves freaks, got their sexual advice from Zane books and spent their life savings at the nearest pornography store; they frequented prostitutes, went to bed with members of their churches while trying to keep it "sanctified and Holy," and had problems releasing inhibitions in the sack.

I wasn't into those types of things. Despite not getting to know my father, I never really learned how to bond with another man. Or another woman for that matter.

I briefly met some people from my dad's side of the family at his wedding. But after that day I would never see them again.

According to Mama, Dad's family was very evil and simple-minded. Mama shielded me from that. She kept it away from me and tried to make me happy and I was happy at certain points of my life until it all came crashing down in my face, changing me forever.

I didn't have brothers and sisters. Honestly, I never thought to have one, either. I always made myself happy.

I always found solace in my room, playing with my dolls and make up and dressing as Marilyn Monroe and all the Hollywood starlets in the black and white movies, trying to reenact their lines and prancing in front of my mirror like I was Ginger Rodgers.

I loved being the only child because that allowed me to get all Mama's attention. But that wasn't to be. Mama always had to work, pay the bills and keep the house running smoothly. She was also in medical school and her life was all about studying. She only spent some time with me when it was convenient for her.

I had been caring for myself ever since I was about eight-years-old. Mama taught me how to cook and clean. She bought me books on recipes and baking.

She used to give me little quizzes. How many cups of flour go in a cake? How much sugar? When do you add the frosting? What's the difference between a bell pepper, an onion and an apple? What are the major food groups? What are the benefits of calcium? What was malnutrition? Does milk do the body better than candy? Does fruit provide natural sugar or sugar from the jars?

I loved those moments because you always walked away knowing something you didn't previously know when talking to Mama.

She taught me to dance and sew clothes. In fact, she bought me a sewing machine for my tenth birthday, as a way for me to kill time while she attended classes or had to work and she taught me how to make my own dresses, how to pick the threads and the fabrics.

I found this all fun because I loved to create things. I always had a very vivid, colorful imagination. That's the one thing I used to love about myself and I knew I got that talent from Mama.

She read every book she got her hands on. But Mama's creativity poured into her work in a very horrid way. And it hurt a few people, including me.

I still suffered tremendously from it. I still sometimes face the trauma of my teenage years, going through puberty and finding out it was all a lie. I lost most of my life and childhood and didn't know it because an adult made the decisions for me and society taught me to do as my mother said.

You didn't back talk or you got a spanking. Even though Mama never hit me, she abused me in another way that wasn't sexual but it was traumatic enough to leave a permanent mark on my psyche.

Going through the ups and downs of high school just to have it all snatched away because your mother had lied to you about certain things was embarrassing. I wore my feelings on my sleeve.

If things were too complex I would curse you out. Being a Sagittarius didn't help matters either.

I wasn't much for zodiac signs and astrology's being in the Third House of the Sun, yet the way the waves crashed across the seven seas tugged at me at any given moment of the day.

I was a growing rose in fertile soil and when I reached my full potential I found out I was a generic rose, grown in a lab, observed and charted, metered and categorized and I was still recovering from the shame, the embarrassment and the experiment.

Yet I still loved Mama. She taught me to take care of my body and how to douche my anus. She taught me very keen things that followed me into adult hood. She also taught me how to hold onto bitterness and how to carry grudges.

She taught me to lash out at folks who did me wrong. She taught me about Karma. She taught me about the birds and the bees.

One thing I could say about Mama, she never brought men around me.

I never heard her being screwed through the paper thin walls by men. She never had a boyfriend after Daddy left her.

And when her husband died she stayed alone. She refused to marry. If she did have male lovers she kept it well hidden. She didn't trust anyone around me. It's like she died inside when Kayak left. She thought it was best if I didn't know the man and I never pressed her to explain.

He was her entire world at the time; she modeled herself after the man.

He was very charming and loving, from what I could remember. He loved life and was very loyal. Extenuating circumstances caused his untimely decline in society.

You know me.

I always loved "discounts" or the "free of charge" things. Half of my friends worked at Macy's/Burdines, Bloomingdales, Sears and Roebuck, or the electronic stores and you best believe half my house was furnished with things I got on "discount" or "clearance" or using their "twenty and thirty percent off" cards. It paid to have friends in high places.

Yet I learned the hard way that just because it was free didn't mean it was good.

Committing suicide was free. You just picked up a gun and boom—you ended it. Did that make it right? I was still learning. Jumping off a building was free. Did that make it right? No.

Maybe I should have stayed home and read "What Is Life" again because the club was so boom: dead tonight. I took advantage of the free drinks, since I handled my liquor better than I seemed to handle money these days, which wasn't saying much.

After the eighth guy tried to get my phone number without asking my name, H.I.V. status and favorite color, I decided I'd had enough.

Men were just as small-minded as their dicks.

I was persona non grata. The men were typical, the drinks were kind of flat, the bartender put in too much ice and there was a fat guy, loaded with cash, who thought that buying the bar appeased me and trust me it didn't because I had enough money to buy every closed bottle behind the very same bar.

I wasn't trying to kill off my liver with hepatitis drinks anytime soon.

I didn't believe in washing my wig on the delicate cycle like my girlfriends.

I believed in replacing the product when it was worn out. I was all about image, and growing up image was all my mother was about.

After all she taught me how to talk and think like a lady—how to be a lady.

There were so many well-dressed people surrounding me, vehicles slowly parading up Washington Avenue.

Car horns wailing, loud music booming, Spanish people uttering romantic sounding phrases and dancing across the street.

I was flying solo tonight without a guy on my radar.

I yawned, standing outside the club.

A few women walked up to me, each extending their hands. My guard went up but the more they smiled the more I relaxed.

"You look nice, Sistah," the taller one said, a knock out herself in an off-white suit with huge oval buttons keeping the tits in place.

"Thank you," I told her, shaking the short, fat one's hand. She looked gorgeous in an ankle-length red dress with matching hair.

The skinny one, with a huge overbite, looked flawless in patent leather, which was refreshing, because if it rained again tonight she didn't need an umbrella or raincoat.

"And what can I do for you ladies?" I asked.

"We love your dress. I'm Keisha," said the taller one.

"Thank you," I told her.

"That is Queen Hatshepsut on the back of your dress, right? In the sequins? Oh, my manners, girl. I'm Lolita."

I looked her over with a smile. "Hi, Lolita, and your name, miss?"

Miss Overbite said, "Sasha…"

"I'm Rosa," I lied. "My great-grandmother's name was Sasha." I looked at Keisha. "Yes, that's Queen Hatshepsut."

"That's a unique dress. And the way it flows into the slanted ruffles just above the booty. Girl, knock out." She was walking around me, checking it out. I liked the praise. They were very forthcoming and cordial.

"Hello," said Lolita, snapping. "I agree."

"Yes, ma'am," said Sasha. "I give two thumbs way up." I think they were part of a sorority because they snapped together.

"Thank you," I said. "I hate to be rude but I need to catch a cab," I lied again. My car was parked on 8th Street.

"No problem, sister. Where did you get that dress?" Keisha asked.

I looked her deeply in the eyes. "I made it."

They stared at me.

Lolita, skeptical said, "You made that?"

I smiled, really needing to be getting home. I didn't like staying out late.

"Yes. I'm in college for fashion design and I created this."

Sasha walked up to me, shaking my hand again. "A Sistah doing big things. You should have seen how the bitches gawked at your dress. Half of them don't even know who Queen Hatshepsut is."

Keisha said, "I know, right. They don't know she dressed as a man but was really a woman."

"Right," said Lolita. "They don't know she ruled for over twenty years and her life is somewhat of a mystery in Egypt."

Sasha snapped again. "Snaps, Girls."

They snapped again. I liked the snapping thing. Hmm, I started snapping.

"Can you teach me that?" I asked and they showed me.

I was a snapping bitch by the time I collected their phone numbers and stored them in my phone.

Each wanted me to make them the dress and would pay the $500 I asked.

One thing stuck with me when they walked off, chasing the cute guys.

It was what Keisha said about Hatshepsut.

They don't know she dressed as a man but was really a woman.

I was looking in my purse, searching for my wallet when a guy took me by the hand.

"Say, Ma'am. How are you?"

I smiled, summing him up in three seconds.

He wore a pair of nice Dockers' pants, a crisp white T-shirt, a pair of Jordan shoes and he had a Kangol hat slanted above doe-shaped eyes.

He smelled really good. His top tooth was slightly crooked but that made him more appealing.

He was a gorgeous man. But was he full of himself or full of crap?

"Hey, dude. How are you?" I kept looking in my purse.

He was persistent. "I'm Dexter. And I like what I see."

"I'm Rosa…I liked the reality show I watched last night on VH1 but a funny thing happened…"

He looked around, winking at a few ladies. "Yes, Ma?" He kissed my hand. He had thick, soft lips.

Mr. Playa-Playa. I knew his profile already. "I changed the channel when it was over. It was time to move on, you know. No matter how much I stared at the screen the show would not come back on, no matter how much I wanted it to."

He looked me over, my sarcasm flying over his head. Which told me a) he wasn't that bright so b) I had to do or say something to get him out of my face because if a man didn't listen to you right off the bat then he wouldn't listen to you after you started having sex?

"Are you alone tonight?"

I reclaimed my hand and closed my purse, looking him over. I kissed his cheek and said, "I've been alone for ten months, Sir."

"We should change that," he went on, taking my hand again. He pulled me to him. "We should get to know each other."

"And how do you suppose we do that?" I asked, realizing my feet were killing me. I should have never worn these one size-too-small stilettos. But no, I just had to be cute.

"Let's grab a bite to eat."

"I don't do food after wolfing down free drinks. I'd puke that up, brothah and I'm not in the mood to upset my stomach the way you're upsetting me holding my hand like I'm an old lady about to cross the damn street."

He released me with a faint, "I'm sorry. No disrespect."

I checked my watch. "Look, where are you from? Do you have a number?"

His eyes lit up. "I'm from Seattle. I'm here for two days. So if you still want my number…"

So he wants to screw all the loose booty he can. These men kill me. They want a decent woman yet can't stay in town a week to appreciate her.

I kissed his lips, reaching behind him and held his butt. Nice and plump.

I felt for the wallet. There it was. Hmm. I ran my fingers over it, his nature poking against me.

His breathing increased. "Like what you're holding, Rosa?"

His wallet wasn't thick enough. Sorry. My insides went dry instantly. I took a few steps back, my scalp itching like crazy. I patted at it ferociously, wanting to smoke a joint. I inhaled the wet, muggy South Beach air and popped a few Tic Tacs in my mouth.

"I'm about to go. I have to work tomorrow," I lied, turning on my heel, letting him get a look of my huge booty.

"Wait, Ma."

I looked over my shoulder. "I'm not your Ma."

And I was gone, my heels clicking against the wet pavement, sucking on my Tic Tacs.

Thinking about my mother.

Part 4
Labyrinth

*For all have sinned; all fall short of God's glorious
standard*

Romans 3:23

*No one is good—
Not even one*

Romans 3:10

Tomb 3
Diva

The life of a Diva could be a very happy one, if you played your cards right. I was the type of woman who always played her cards right, but they were in the wrong game. Having a killer hand in spades didn't work in poker. I threw out the Ace of Spade to trump the heart in poker and was sadly disheartened because the Game of Life had no rules and knew no boundaries.

I considered myself a Diva. My pain and inner turmoil was my driving force. I learned more when I was angry and upset. I was a very hands-on type of girl.

I didn't have many lovers; in fact I could count them on one hand. Like Leonard. He was tall as the trees and smoother than silk. All we did was screw across the sheets.

I didn't mind, though, because I was too afraid of commitment. Why commit to a man you knew was a dog.

That's why he never had the luxury of my vagina.

But my fear of commitment goes deeper than that. Leonard was everything a girl could want: passionate, romantic and caring.

We waited a good month before we did anything and he never understood why I wanted the lights off.

I was very vulnerable. I hated a guy staring me in the face while we played Let's Drill for Oil with my anus being the well. After trying several times to screw with the lights on he gave up on me. I figured if he left because of a light switch then maybe he had some bigger issues to work on.

Ralph was a street thug and came off looking like a huge softie. He couldn't watch a drama without crying. He was a big water bucket. He was more of a brother to me, and I seriously didn't need that in my life. I felt incestuous just thinking about it.

Ted reminded me of a little kid who never grew up. In a lot of ways I related to that because I was crushed as a child. Thank God I was never molested or raped by my mother, but the abuse I suffered at the hands of a very dear loved one left permanent scars on my body and soul and would be my Egyptian hieroglyphic forever.

But if I really wanted to remember a guy it would be Javier. I met him in high school. He was a bad ass Hispanic, with a heart of gold.

When I needed him the most he was there. He was my first everything. We did the wild thing. It was a very brief, uncomfortable encounter. We were in my mother's bathroom at the time. Sitting at my dining table enjoying a cigarette and some fresh Hennessy, tears flowed down my face, messing up my make-up as I thought back to that time. Mother's bathroom.

I'd hurt Javier, but it wasn't intentional. I never intentionally hurt anyone in my life.

Mama always raised me to treat people the way I wanted to be treated.

But she didn't follow her own advice.

On the kitchen counter were twelve mannequin heads holding my wigs. I had the Nina Simone Wig, the Janet wig, the Beyonce wig, the Ciara wig. I also had the Barbra Streisand wig and a few others.

Which would I wear tonight?

It wasn't that my hair was short (because it was very long, down my back), but I didn't feel like being bothered with bumper curls and curling irons and moisturizers and creams.

I'd gone to the store early this morning because I needed a few items. I hated going to this one particular store because I would see him. Javier. After we graduated from high school he'd never been the same—I had basically hung him out to dry. Just because he was my first didn't mean I had to commit to him. I was young, and on top of that I was confused. I was still healing from the life of misery that was my childhood.

But of course at the time I didn't know it was so miserable.

Javier used to be a thriving, sexy Spanish/black man in high school. All the ladies wanted him yet he only had eyes for me.

At the time I loved his attention, even though I hardly got it because I always hung with the girls. Boys were just sexy diversions from a day of grueling school work.

He used to rush up to me and hold conversations. One particular time, when I flipped out in the middle of the football field (over something very painful) he was right by my side, making sure I was all right.

Now he doesn't talk to me or look my way. I speak to him but he turns his back and stamps off.

I really hurt him. I did that by not being with him. He wanted to marry me and make some babies.

I didn't want that. I couldn't want that if I tried.

Because one thing would keep us apart.

One thing about me was certain—I would never materialize into a barefoot and pregnant woman.

I had what he had.

We played for the same team. I had a penis between my legs. I used to be a man.

I lived with that every day, knowing I was something the public had yet to embrace. I was a very sexual man/girl, and I thought as a woman. I really wanted to be a woman so I spared no expense to achieve everything my Daddy detested. Was it that he looked at me and saw failure? In myself, my choices and his parenting? He has never done a goddamn thing for me. He didn't raise me, so I knew the flaws in my life wasn't because of his parenting. He has never supported me, because my mother did an amazing job of hiding me from him. And I guessed he truly didn't love me because he never bought me a Christmas gift or wished me a Happy Birthday. We never played sports together, never threw me a football and taught me how to play catch.

He never cooked me a meal and he never disciplined me. Never. Nothing. And now he hated me. And I hated him and I hated mother. I didn't know *anything* credible about her and everything I *thought* I knew; even certain things she wrote in her diary were lies. Lies, lies and more lies. All she did was lie. She made up so many things about her life that she seemed surreal.

How many people told themselves they knew their parents but their parents were hiding deep dark secrets, mistakes they made in their own lives?

They live everyday bashing their children for wanting to be themselves because the parents hide in the dark and couldn't *be* themselves yet they run to church and verbally pray to God for all to hear, pretending to speak in tongues, jump, shout and yell real loud…yet no one knew *what* they *really* ask God for mentally.

There were many discrepancies in my mother's life, things that didn't make sense and was confusing. Things, now that she's dead, I would never know the truth about.

And her diary she left behind didn't help matters.

TOMB 4

Discipline

"Rosa! Rosa! Rosa, Darling! Glad you could make it tonight to the Bumperton Lounge!"

Ecstatically, Rosa boomed, "Great to be here."

They kissed each other's cheeks. Smooch. Smooch. Rosa beamed, her eyes sparkling with her diamond earrings. It was a little chilly and she'd forgotten to bring a coat. Plus she was a little soaked because it started to rain just as she was walking in the door so she had to redo her makeup. Thank God she found a small bathroom by the exit door and quickly re-applied herself.

Thank God I lost that Queen Hatshepsut crap from my name. Mama was a total whack job. Seriously. She mentally and physically fucked me up. Will I ever recover? I thought my father was the problem. He was a victim as well. Played out on his emotions not knowing he was trapped inside Mama's jigsaw puzzle. I used to love doing jigsaw puzzles with her.

The Queen Diva of the Bumper Room walked over, her long white dress flowing with sequins and a long five foot train. Her huge blonde wig was reminiscent of the late Marilyn Monroe. Rosa thought he/she overdid it with the makeup. If she caked on any more she was going to call her Pillsbury Dough Girl and not the Diva she was known to be throughout the Drag Queen circuit.

"Are you excited about performing?" asked the Queen Diva, her voice shrieking to the point Rosa had to twitch her nose.

Rosa winked at a couple guys that walked by, looking straighter than an arrow. "I'm very excited!"

Why am I here? I should have stayed home.

The Queen Diva wrapped her arm around Rosa and posed for a few pictures. The photographer was a short, stocky man with an old suit, old values and was a bit of a prude.

"Stand by the tall fake plants," he ordered and the Queen Diva took Rosa's hand and snatched her over by them, wrapping her arm around Rosa's lower body.

This little gay photographer is pushing my buttons! Look at him in that old suit! Get with the times. This isn't Fred Astaire's birthday bash.

The Queen Diva was snapping her fingers when Beyonce's *Get Me Bodied* sounded into everybody's ears.

I'm so sick of this song. I've been patting my weave all night. If I pat it anymore I will get a headache.

"Pose for the camera, sweetie. I love to flick, flick, flick, don't you?"

The bitch didn't even ask me did I wanna take pictures. I control my images! I guess I'm being nice tonight. Rosa smiled, playing the role.

"Sure, I do."

"Pucker those lips," said the Grand Diva, taking Rosa's lips and horribly squeezing them.

Rosa glared at her and said, "My make-up! Don't ruin

it! I still got to go out on that stage."

The Queen Diva tucked her fat chin back. "Calm down. *You* are a Diva!"

Rosa needed a cigarette. Badly. "I know that."

Tension started to build. Before she said something that would have them cat fighting (and Rosa used her fists like a boxer), Rosa walked past the Queen Diva and took in the scene around her. The air was charged, the people were pumped. An editor for the *Express Gay News* danced through the crowd several feet away from her. She got an e-mail from them stating they wanted to interview her. She declined. She did those shows for one thing: to fit in. And she needed the money. The past two years alone she had banked over $45,000. She spent her money smartly, saved for rainy days and hot nights, and lived in her mother's house. Well, her house now.

The Queen Diva kissed on any and everything on two legs, laughing incessantly and lying just because. Deep down Rosa detested phony people. She preferred individuals that were real about themselves. She'd had enough dealings with the hypocrites. Her life had been one big hypocritical mess.

"Oh, that grassy dress is gorgeous!" Smooch, smooch. "And the pumps have hints of soil! How clever! You've been touched by the Queen Diva!" the Queen Diva told a skinny white woman with pink hair and blue eyes, touching her on the head with her fake magic wand. She then dug into her bra and pulled out glitter, blowing it over the woman, who spun in circles like there was no place like home. Rosa wanted to puke.

Such bullshit! Rosa thought both the dress and dirty pumps were horrid.

Why did she lie to that girl?

This was why Rosa didn't really enjoy doing Drag Shows. When you were losing them everybody wanted to be your friend. Offer you advice. Tell you what they thought you did wrong when they couldn't even excite a

Dapharoah69

can of paint. But the instant you were the Star! The Main Attraction! The Diva! Winning the past few Houses and winning the Best Everything in the process you suddenly had haters, little punks who wanted to ruin you, gay men who would slam your name in online forums and give you a bad reputation and half the stuff they wrote about was a) fabricated b) lies and c) embellished.

And let's not talk about the Drag Shows with stingy people who'd rather buy the bar than shell out money for the performers. One place she'd never do again is *Goodfellahs* in Perrine, Florida. Shabby. She performed Natalie Cole's "Unforgettable," dressed as a Drag Queen on one side and as a man on the other side, turning here and there to present a different side. The crowd of gays and lesbians threw out ones and maybe a couple of fives. She won a total of fifteen dollars by the end of the performance. It was like eating out and not leaving a tip for the waitress. She packed her shit and was out the door.

The Queen Diva was getting on Rosa's nerve. She just wanted to come, perform, get her $1,500 and be done with it. But this Messy Queen wasn't letting Rosa out of her sight.

The Queen Diva smacked some Bubble Yum. "We sold advance tickets for this show."

"Ok, you did?" Rosa was shaking her head, her stockings killing her legs.

"Yes, ma'am. When we have high profile entertainers such as yourself we always sell advance tickets just to get a sense of how many people will be coming…"

"That's new to me. I am just the performer, Chile."

"And a performer you are! No, no," The Queen Diva went on, adjusting his blonde wig. "You are a Headliner."

Rosa shook her head again, clutching her purse.

Before the Queen could say anything further a small white guy with glow-in-the-dark thongs and piercings paused before them.

"Queen, what about the back tables? They are out of
Grey Goose and Alize and they are crying for more
Hennessy!" he was shaking all over, clearly afraid of the
Queen. "What do I do?"

The Queen said, with an attitude, "You go out, buy
more bottles with your money, give the secretary your
receipt and we will reimburse you before you leave
tonight." And with that the Queen put a diamond-
encrusted stiletto on the guy's vanishing booty and booted
him away.

Hugging her purse close to her, Rosa thought that was
rather rude.

The guy stumbled and rubbed his butt, looking back at
the Queen with a sneer.

*Poor thing! I'm about to liven it up a bit. I'm getting bored and
I'm supposed to be performing.*

"You're doing a wonderful job!" Rosa boasted,
sashaying up to him, and giving him a hug. He was about
to hyperventilate.

"Oh my God! Rosa hugged me! I am so honored,
Rosa," he went on, crying so hard he couldn't breathe. "I
look up to you, I thrive for you!"

He had haters. They were jealous Rosa gave him
attention and not them.

Deeply upset, The Queen paused behind Rosa. "We
don't honor the hired help here," she said and Rosa
pivoted, snapping for the photographer. "They are here to
work, get paid and go home. Forgotten. Out of sight, out
of mind. Be-gone."

Rosa planted a huge lipstick kiss on his cheek. He died.
He couldn't control his jitters.

"Well, if you want me to perform here you treat
everyone in this building with respect or you refund these
people their money."

The photographer said, "Yes, Miss Rosa..."

Rosa had another idea as well. "Take a few shots of us.
And give him the photographs." She snapped at the

reporter from the Gay Express. She looked over, smiled and waltzed over to her with a drink in her left hand and a small recorder in the right, clad boyishly in a suit.

"Are you still interested in doing an interview with me?"

"Why yes, Miss Rosa."

Rosa looked at him. "What's your name?"

"I'm Jake. Nice to meet you. I know I look weird. I'm making you look bad, I'm sorry. I should go…"

Rosa hugged him, planting her tits on his chest, puckering her lips.

"You aren't weird. Any child of God is a child of mine."

The Queen Diva wasn't pleased.

The photographer snapped four good shots.

Rosa looked at the reporter. "We can talk. And make sure you mention Jake is the life of Bumperton!"

Jake couldn't believe this. "Thank you, Rosa! Oh, thank you!"

"And feature one of the pictures I took with him. I want everyone in the state of Florida seeing what an incredible man he is."

"Will do, Rosa. So when do you wanna sit down and chat?"

"We can do it now – get it out of the way. I perform in about 20 minutes."

"I bet you are going to put on a helluva show. What song are you doing?"

"Janet's *Discipline* with a touch of *Nasty*!"

"That's gonna rock!" said the reporter, buttering Rosa up.

"Thanks…excuse me…"

She opened her purse and gave Jake three hundred dollars. He was hesitant to take the money, wondering what it was for.

Rosa kissed his lips. "That's to buy the liquor. Make sure they reimburse you."

Call Her Queen Hatshepsut

Jake couldn't believe it. "You are a Godsend! You made my life bearable, Queen Rosa."

The Queen Diva was so pissed she stood there with her hands on her hips and didn't utter a word.

When Jake went back to work, with an autograph and a new attitude, the Queen Diva said, "I didn't appreciate that."

Rosa snapped. "Get off your high horse, please!" The Queen grabbed her pearls, toying with them, clearly embarrassed. People were looking.

The reporter was laughing, sipping her drink, the tape recorder swirling. "I'm a grown woman. Keep your negative shit away from me. The last thing you want to do is piss me off. I have enough anger on the inside of me…"

Rosa held her forehead. She was getting a migraine. Squeezing her eyes shut the images burst from her brain and danced behind her eyes.

Mama, what are those?

Breasts…You have them, too.

And what is that?

A penis.

A penis, Mama?

She smiled. "Yes."

The Queen stood corrected. She didn't want to upset Rosa. If Rosa left Bumperton would get bad press. And she couldn't afford that because her superiors would have her ass handed to her with her job. She changed the pace of the conversation.

"…Rosa, we heard about you shutting down the Miami, Florida House last year. We also heard you shut it down for Best Face and Best Dress in Atlanta a few months ago, Girl. These kids are here to see you. We sold out of tickets. All 6,000 of them! This is the biggest Show ever!"

Rosa smiled then, not believing her fortune. Just a couple years ago, before she graduated high school, her life had turned into the biggest lie known to man. She didn't want to live anymore.

She was in love with an amazing man and had to leave him because her life was a lie.

She had to stand up to her darling mother because of The Lie. She had to face her Aunt and her father, who were getting a divorce.

She had to battle her inner inhibitions and her demons. Her entire life had been conceived and used as a chess board.

Her mother controlled every piece and had added some new pieces for good measure.

Shaking huge curls out of her face she decided not to think of it. She didn't ask for this life but it had been handed to her. At what point does it become a choice? At what point are you supposed to move on?

After so much damage has been done can you possibly move on?

No amount of therapy can replace years of hardship and lies. No amount of drugs could redirect the past into another type of future.

All around her, backstage, was chaos. Gay clothing designers were running around like chickens with their heads cut off making sure all the models were wearing their respective clothing properly.

A tall blonde had her wig on backward. A short black girl was crying because the makeup wasn't right. A Thug type cursed because he wanted a blunt.

"You should have smoked it before you came to the Bumperton Fashion Show!" wailed a tall, gay designer with a Jamaican accent that looked more Irish than Black. "You cannot smoke around the clothing. That hat and jacket cost more than your Mama's life savings!"

The Thug type steamed, keeping his thoughts to himself.

The Gay Jamaican slapped the Thug's plump ass and said, demandingly, "Let's go, line up. You go out behind the next number…"

He mumbled something, stormed past Rosa, looking her over with a sly smile, and lined up behind eight other well-dressed specimens.

"Hello, Rosa!" said the Grand Ball. She was the owner of the club. The Queen Diva slumped to the background without uttering a word. Smooch, smooch. "You look dashing, Girlfriend!"

Rosa ran a slick tongue over her lipstick. "Thank you. I am so happy to meet you."

"Everyone knows about me, The Grand Ball of the Bumper!"

"And Grand Ball you are!"

"I love this dress, Rosa!"

She heard the roar of an eager crowd, ready for the next number. Patting her huge blue hairdo, she turned to face the mirror, loving what she saw and hating how she felt.

Her breasts were as large as ever, just the way her plastic surgeon had done them. When she first got them she was on top of the world.

Opening her huge purse with her life inside, she brushed past a diary and a folded letter.

She pulled out her compact mirror and decided to use that to check her face.

Huge mirrors sometimes made you look terrible.

She rubbed her nose with fresh tears falling down her face. She was next.

Closing the mirror, she started to perspire under her arms. She knew she was supposed to shave but she decided not to.

All through her teens she'd been shaving and it turned out to be a lie.

"Ladies and Gentleman!" shouted the announcer, clad in a peacock outfit. He snapped up to the microphone stand on the octagon-shaped, marble stage.

"Are you guys ready?"

The crowd roared.

"We have here, performing two songs back to back, Miss Rosa! The Diva!"

A deafening roar filled Rosa's ears. Brought tears to her eyes.

She was clad in a tight black cat suit and a kitty cat mask, displaying her green eyes and shapely lips.

She crawled out onto the stage to Janet giving her favorite definitions to the word "Discipline."

Rosa then stood up, and mouthed, "Like a whip…"

She raised her hands, snapped her hips better than the Columbian singer Shakira. The fans were ready, they were amped.

Rosa slowly gyrated out to the microphone and put her hands on her hips, surveying the crowd, making Beyonce look like shit. The photographers snapped away, thinking, *She looks like Halle Berry in "Cat Woman".*

The Queen Diva smiled, standing on the side of the stage. Happy that Rosa had generated the most money the club ever had.

What an accomplishment.

She watched as Rosa growled, commanding the stage and working the crowd like she was another person.

The Grand Ball was in tears, sitting at the V.I.P. table, sipping a tonic.

"Rosa is marvelous! She is a star! She is a Star, Honey!"

Rosa told the crowd she misbehaved, as the Janet Jackson song states. Touching herself when her man told her not to. That she needed some Discipline because she had been very bad.

Rosa had been very bad. For years she let men screw her.

But never the vagina! I always wanted the lights off. Didn't want them the see the weed amongst the roses…

She pulled a whip from her back pocket, slowly

pranced down the marble stairs and over to the Thug from back stage.

She wrapped the whip around his neck, twirled her hips to the floor and Rosa's huge ass made a couple guys fan themselves because they couldn't control the activity in their briefs...

She was notorious for making men cum on themselves.

With just a look.

And the flick of the tongue.

Photographers snapping picture after picture, Rosa gyrated all over him, closing her eyes, remembering her childhood.

She tried her best to push it out of her mind but her heart wouldn't let her forget. She just had to remember, remember everything that transpired in her life.

How her mother betrayed her. How her Auntie hurt her. How they justified it. Rosa had to remember that she paid for her parents' mistakes.

How her own father called her vicious names and abused her, telling her she could never be in his life if she didn't...become a man.

Dancing and entertaining for her audience, she tried to pretend those events never took place. This took a toll on her but she raised her head high, gave face and flashed a killer smile, working her hips and kicking up those long, beautiful legs, showing off her high heels with the spikes.

God why can't I let go of the past? I walk around pretending that I have all the answers, that I can just shove my feelings like clothes to the back of the closet and pull my hanging attire right above it to hide them.

But they are still there. Taking up space. How much longer can I deal with this? How much longer am I going to go on pretending that I don't have deep psychological problems?

I miss two parents I didn't really get to know. I miss a man who said he hates me, and even though he is my father, my biological father, that didn't stop him from throwing a glass of liquor into my

Dapharoah69

face.

> GOD! GOD MAKE ME FORGET! *I don't want to remember right now! I'm giving it to these bitches in this club! I am the Grand Diva! I am internationally known! I have won award after award! I am in all the gay newspapers! Everybody knows my name in the gay circuit!*

But do they know my life and my past?

She was remembering the lies!

Remembering the pain.

Remembering the deceit.

Remembering the bitterness.

Remembering what events shaped her into the transvestite she was today, part of her still wanted to die.

God, help!

Help me before I self-destruct.

TOMB 5:
Do I Look like Daddy, Mama?

I was raised differently. Before I became a transvestite I was a very handsome young man with promise dancing in his eyes and the Bible always on his dresser. When Mama married Robert Lamley she seemed to be on top of the world. I could tell it was all an act.

Bills were too much and she only wanted a man to soften them so she could keep a little something in her purse and pay off her college loans.

She was studying to be a plastic surgeon. I knew that deep down she never got over my father Kayak leaving her.

She enrolled in school and started studying medicine just to keep her mind off her depression.

Nonetheless, I had a man in my life, a father figure who took me fishing, helped me draw things and had high hopes for me. I grew really attached to him.

The only thing I hated was his alcohol intake.

Then something drastic happened.

When I turned five-years-old, a little after I blew out the candle on my cake, Robert kissed my cheek and told me my gift was out in his beige and black Ford truck.

He forgot to bring it inside. Sam Cooke played on the stereo at a moderate volume. Framed pictures of Martin Luther King were on the cream-colored walls. I was so excited.

Mama was outside. She had just gotten back from the local market. She bought some more ice cream because Robert had eaten it all up.

When she came into the house she seemed pleased, her eyes sparkling. Setting the ice cream on the table, she sighed and sat down, picking up one of her medical books. Robert leaned over and kissed her. Her lips didn't move.

I happily looked at Mama but she was studying her medical books. I never understood why she was so focused on a book with a bunch of words. She used to always tell me that she loved me more than anything in the world yet when I wanted to talk to her she was too busy reading and researching. This alienated me so badly I simply kept quiet and never said a word until Mama spoke to me first.

She was dedicated to her studies. On the cover was a picture of the human heart. Her long hair pinned up in a bun, she looked highly intelligent wearing her thin-rimmed reading glasses and a red ankle length dress with black flat penny loafers.

Robert, clad in polyester pants and a plaid shirt and boots, stood up, the wooden chair noisily sliding back on the floor.

Call Her Queen Hatshepsut   92

Mama looked at him. "I love you, Honey."

He beamed. "And I love you."

"You know we're going to have a little celebration when our child goes to sleep."

He kissed her. Again her lips didn't move. "Oh, yeah?"

"Yeah. While you're in the truck I want you to close your eyes and meditate…think of ways you're going to…pleasure me."

"Will do, baby."

"And something is wrong with the engine. There was a knocking noise when I was driving home. I left it running so never mind it."

"I'll check…"

"No!" her outburst startled us. She calmed down with a warm smile. "Just let it run. I have to learn how to work your truck; just in case the day comes when you can't show me the way. Then I'll know how to fix it."

"My wife is so self-reliable. I love that about you."

On cloud nine, Robert went outside to retrieve the gift.

I was fingering icing into my mouth. Yummy. I looked at Mama.

Her eyes stopped sparkling.

With loving thoughts of his wife, Robert opened the driver side door and sat in the truck, closing the door. Why was the truck still running? Oh, yeah. His wife said she left it running. He shook his head, closing his eyes.

And began meditating.

"Do you want some cake?"

She ignored me, humming the Sam Cooke tune.

"Mama?"

Her eyes peered over the glasses. "What?"

"Do you want some cake?"

Her face was expressionless. "Do you know that the esophagus is a part of the throat?" she asked and I squirmed in my seat.

My stomach turned. "No, Mama. Do you want some cake?"

She drifted back into her studies, and I felt alienated.

What was taking Robert so long?

I stood up from the table and said, "Mama, I'll be back. I'm going to check on Robert."

She glanced up at me with a weird smile.

"OK. And tell him that his vagina isn't what it used to be."

What did that mean?

I walked up to his truck and fear bit at my throat. I found him dead, his truck running and the gear in "Park." All the windows were rolled up. Snatching the door open, I tried to scream but couldn't because I was so hurt. On his lap was my birthday gift. My world was destroyed. I screamed for Mama and when she rushed outside and saw him, she didn't show an ounce of grief. She swept a palm over his open eyes and said a silent prayer. She reached in the truck and turned off the ignition.

I grew quiet, tears falling down my face, my heart broken in pieces. My eyes scanned the truck.

I saw a green hose dangling from the back passenger side window.

Why was a hose in the car, running from the exhaust pipe? I didn't understand this. My heart was torn in two.

Without any emotions, Mama looked at me and said, "Now the games begin."

I closed my eyes and prayed to a God who ignored me.

And would ignore me throughout my childhood.

From an early age Mama taught me every Bible story known to man.

And even though Robert's death deeply pained me I quickly got over it when Mama told me to hold onto God.

"Without God nothing's possible," she said.

She forced religion on me and since she was the parent I had to be obedient.

She told me to pray over my food three times a day and to pray for the little things so when I got the big things I would appreciate it more. She didn't tell me, of course, that that pertained to the male genitalia as well. Because, as it stands right now, I will love men until the day I die. Many have said I was born gay. Others said it was my choice. What if I told you it wasn't either. I wasn't born gay and I didn't make a *choice*. Rather, I was…molded into this life, to accept this as my reality. Mama made that choice for me. She birthed a son and brainwashed me into the female mind by the time I was six-years-old. I would find out a few weeks later that she actually killed Robert because she had "bigger plans for me," — at least that's what I overheard her telling herself in the shower. Carbon monoxide had killed my stepdad.

When I was 16-years-old, Mama died and I had to fend for myself in a very confusing world. I found out more about her when she died than I actually knew while she was alive.

Mama was a beautiful woman born in Port-au-Prince, Haiti in 1959.

She and her mother Pauline moved to Jacksonville, Florida in the late 1960s after her father was brutally killed by the government (he had been charged with treason). Mama always had it hard, despite being the gorgeous vamp she'd soon become.

Her skin was flawless. Looking at her light skin one would never guess she was a Haitian and she wore her flag and her colors with a sense of pride I uphold 'til this very day.

After a couple of years she moved back to Haiti. She missed it and the home sickness was unbearable.

She always had dreams of finding a prince charming who would sweep her off her feet like horny men seemed to be doing to all her girlfriends before they turned 18.

Plenty of guys hit on her, but she fought them off. As a fifteen-year-old young woman she got with four other Haitian girls and my Aunt Rosa and formed a gang called the Mess You Up Good Bitches, because she was tired of being badgered and picked on by women of other nationalities.

They called her skin a disease.

Others used to spit at her and say they hated Haitians. Her own black people shunned her. She got tired of lying up all night and crying to a God who seemed to ignore her. When she formed the gang, Mama and her goons were in and out of jail, robbing white women at night and taking their money or beating up girls in school when they spewed forth insults. Mama had the best clothes and shoes, money in her pocket and a reputation as a bitch that'd cut you quickly if you were on her crap list.

Mixed with the Gemini in her she was a force that no one could control. That was until she met my father Kayak Burke.

She never told me much about the man, but she did say she once loved him and was set to be his wife when she wound up pregnant with me when she was 16.

I did remember being brought up in a single parent household when Robert was murdered, and that proved to be life changing.

From the beginning, she raised me to do girlish things. Brush my hair, manicure my nails and paint them with clear polish.

Treat women and men with respect because it's earned not given. She always taught me about women in history who paved the way for others.

She rarely brought a guy around so I never had a role model, someone I could look up to.

The realization made me miss Robert even more. Now that I think about it, when the police closed the case she didn't even give him a funeral.

Call Her Queen Hatshepsut96

She said it cost too much and he didn't have life insurance.

All the money she had she put into paying bills and paying for school. I think he was cremated.

Yeah.

He was. I remembered Mama dumping his ashes in a lake where Robert and I used to go fishing.

I remember I was curious about wearing Mama's panties so I took off my underwear and put on her panties.

They were softer in content and style than my underwear and I found it fascinating.

I smiled, looking in the mirror. Mama had walked in and smiled when she saw me.

She, kissing my cheek, said, "Try putting on some lipstick."

"Are you sure, Mama? Are men supposed to wear that stuff?"

She looked me deeply in the eyes and said, "Sure, baby. Never let society dictate your life. If you feel like doing it and it makes you feel good you do it."

She was always an understanding woman. She got on her knees, while I was holding her panties up (because they were too big) and she applied my lipstick. To calm herself, she hummed a Sam Cooke song.

She then took mascara and spread out my lashes. I felt incredible, not knowing that Mama shouldn't have been doing that.

"Mama, where's Daddy?" I asked. I missed Robert so much and for some reason I had the urge to find my real father.

She kissed my cheek.

"He is engaged to another woman," she said bitterly. I shook in her panties.

"Why doesn't he live with us, Mama?" I asked, shuddering when her tears spilled over her eyes lids.

"Good things come to those who wait, Sweetie. At least that's what the fat lady said when she couldn't get that slice of cheesecake."

We giggled like witches.

"You're a comedian, Mama. You're so funny!"

"I know, baby. I used to hear that all the time when I was a child."

"Do I look like him, Mama? My Daddy? Do you have a picture?"

TOMB 6

Erase any lineage

"Yes, baby. You look like your father. You are the spitting image of him. Kayak Burke used to love life and people. He was a ladies' man. Then, one day soon after I had given birth to you and still weak from childbirth, he screwed my sister in my bed. I happened to walk in on them. I moved out. I haven't spoken to my sister in years and I don't ever plan on speaking to her. Your Aunt and I were never close. We hardly ever spoke to each other."

I was confused. "Mama, what's cheating?"

She took one of her long, flowing red wigs and put it on my head. Hair framed my angelic face and dropped just above my ass. I didn't know she lied about walking in on my aunt and father having sex. According to her diary, I would find years later, she didn't know Kayak was screwing Rosa at all…until they gave birth to sons at the hospital at the same time.

"You'll find out what cheating means one day, baby." She seemed to morph into another person. She barely looked at me as she opened the dresser and pulled out the photo album. She cracked it open, sitting on the edge of the bed, her face long as the legacy of slavery.

"Mama, why are you so sad?" I traced her lips with trembling fingers. Her lips were soft and tempting. I wanted my lips to look like hers.

She said, "Nothing for you to be concerned with, Son." She waved for me to sit down. "Here's your father." She pulled out a picture and her hand tightened on it briefly, hate dancing in her eyes. "Did I tell you that you have a sister on the way?"

"Really, Mama." I cautiously took the picture. He was so handsome. He had arrestingly gorgeous brown eyes that trapped the sunlight. He was wearing a black suit, kissing my cheek as a newborn.

She took the picture back. "I look just like Daddy."

She lowered her head. "Go look in the mirror, Son."

"OK, Mama. If I do, will you smile?"

"I'm smiling already."

I was walking towards the ceiling-to-floor mirror. "Why, Mama?"

"Because you're *gorgeous*. You're so pretty, son."

"Thanks, Ma." I paused before my image, holding the panties up, my little nipples erect, and my genitals showing. The long wig was flawless and brought out my cheekbones. And the mascara and lipstick was simply irreplaceable. "Do I look like Daddy *now*, Mama?"

She laughed, standing up and pausing behind me, running her hands through the hair of the wig.

"No, baby. And that's just the way I prefer it. Erase any lineage of that cheating creep from your life, face and existence."

I closed my eyes. *I don't look like Daddy.*

TOMB 7:

That Bitch

Mama was a plastic surgeon, having finished medical school when she was 29-years-old. She always loved helping people alter their bodies to their liking—anything to uplift the soul.

I remember I used to have blackouts as a child. And when I'd awaken sometimes it seemed like days had gone by.

Mama used to take me to the clinic to find out why I used to black out. After a while I accepted it as a part of my life and stopped thinking about it.

Whenever the subject of Daddy came up she turned into the most horrible person.

She never hit or cursed me, she loved me more than life itself, but she hated that man with a passion.

And she always bought me clothes that bordered on

the feminine side.

I loved them, the pretty pink shoes and shirts, the red pants and ruffled shirts. She grew my hair out to the middle of my back and she kept a perm in it.

The females hated me in school because my hair didn't have weave and it was a hundred percent real — no horses were slaughtered in the making of my hairstyles.

Over the years I began to look less and less like my father and more and more like my deceased grandmother Pauline.

Mama loved the fact that I favored her late mother. She used to tell me all the time.

One day when I was ten-years-old Daddy came over.

I had a heart attack when I saw him walking up to the door of our home and, excitedly, I ran into Mama's room.

I am finally gonna get to meet him! He looks better than the photographs!

I was about to hyperventilate. It took a while to get it together. "Daddy is here, Ma." I tried to sound calm.

I could have told her an elephant was eating peanuts. She didn't care.

Opened all around her were medical journals and books. Three pencils pushed into her hair, her tits about to pop out from her too-small black bra.

"OK, sweetie. Stay in here," she said like the girl next door. She didn't look happy at all. I think I learned at that point to always expect people to call before they came over. "I'll deal with him."

Yes! And then she is going to bring Daddy in the room to meet his son! I can't wait! I had never been this excited to meet anyone in my life! This man helped give me life!

"Can I see him, Mama?"

Her eyes flashed dangerously, "*No.* But you will see him when the time is right." She got out of bed and kissed my lips. "I promise.

I was so disappointed.

My heart slowed down and I barely looked at her.

"Are you just saying that, Mama?"

"I mean it, my boy."

"OK."

She kissed my lips, making me feel better. "Now get up in bed and sit down. And be very quiet. I don't want him knowing you're here."

"Yes, Mama." My eyes drifted off.

She touched the picture of her mother on the nightstand, mumbling something.

Then she went to greet my daddy.

I sat on her bed, flipping through her journals.

I was feeling a lot of things I couldn't explain. Life seemed so simple yet so confusing. There was a lot to living I just didn't understand.

For example. Mama told me to always love God, and to keep him first. I told her how I could love something I never saw or laid eyes on. And she whipped me so bad with an extension cord I didn't question her again, but I questioned myself. I had a hard time loving a being I never saw. I used to look at my Bible, a gift from Mama, and shake my head at it.

I noticed when Mama had a bad day she read the Bible, yet she never applied any of the scriptures to her life.

How did you do that? And in the same breath Mama said she didn't even believe in God, yet she was whipping me for denouncing him.

I just didn't understand. After awhile I just put it out of my mind, especially when she put me in church, which was a world within a world, and left me there. I was scared, watching people speak in tongues, and catch the Holy Ghost and jump and shout all over the place.

Were these people possessed? I couldn't wait till church was over. Sometimes Mama would show up late, and when she did she would have a medical book in her hand, a tape recorder in the other and she was on auto pilot. Hi, baby. How was church. Is that right? And I hadn't even responded. She was talking to herself, stuck in her studies.

Mama had this life thing down pat. She seemed to know what to do in every situation.

I don't know what happened, but a few minutes later Mama came back in the room with a smile. She had a sweet look on her face, like she had won a battle I didn't know she was fighting.

I've never seen Mama smile like that!

I was putting on red nail polish. She'd taught me how to do it when I was nine.

I wasn't allowed to wear it to school, of course, because Mama said she didn't feel like explaining herself.

Of course I didn't know what that meant.

"Your father is getting married in two days. We have a wedding to attend."

"OK, Mama. I already know what suit I'm going to wear."

Her eyes glittered deceptively. "Son…"

"Yes, Mama?"

"He wants you to be in the wedding. And I have the perfect outfit for you to wear when he marries that bitch."

"Mama, what's a 'bitch'?"

She kissed my cheek, her hair pinned atop her peanut-shaped head.

She closed her eyes, her hands balled into tight fists.

"My sister. And your father just moved the bishop on the chess board. It was only a matter of time. "

For some reason I shuddered when she said that.

Tomb 8:

Lollipop

Two days later Mama kept me home from school. She had never done this before so of course I wondered why.

I actually liked school and I was disheartened because I couldn't see my friends.

She was mopping the raggedy kitchen floor, an open medical manual in her hand. Humming, she seemed to be in her own world, not missing a spot. At odd moments she would mumble the different joints in the human body with aplomb, not missing a beat.

"Mama. Why did you keep me—?"

"—When you talk to me," she said, shutting me up. "It's like you're talking to God." She mopped behind the dining room chair without looking up from the book. "You don't question him and his work and you don't question me."

Bitch! I spun on my heel, rolling my eyes and went back to my room.

She was adamant about me not going to school so this really bothered me. I liked school.

Despite the boys picking at me calling me girly and the girls somewhat taking me in because they seemed to have more empathy, I really liked doing my school work and making good grades.

Mama expected that from me, I give that to her. Plus, I loved to read and watching Mama always keeping her nose in a book influenced me to do the same thing.

So why is she keeping me home?

A few months ago I threw up. I was eating some cornbread and greens she cooked and something in the food didn't sit well with my stomach.

In fact I puked through the night and found out I had food poisoning.

She didn't take me to the doctor. She looked after me herself, saying she had it under control.

She called a friend she knew from the hospital and told him what happened.

About thirty minutes later a strange guy in a doctor's coat dropped off a small brown paper bag with pills. I was sitting on the sofa, wrapped in a blanket, feeling woozy.

"Don't tell anyone I brought this to you. I could lose my medical career," I heard him whisper as the night's breeze blew across my frowning face.

"Don't worry. I won't. I have my demons, you know."

"We all have demons."

Avarice licked her lips, her nipples swelling. "I know that better than anyone."

"Do you really?" the doctor asked.

She kissed his cheek. "Yes…"

"You're a gorgeous woman."

"And I'm tired so you need to be going…And guess

what?"

She shook his hand, slipping him some money. "What?"

She grinned wickedly. "The knight has just taken a pawn."

A few seconds later I heard tires biting into the pavement and he was gone.

Mama had a small light in my eyes and my pupils followed it. Very attentively, she told me to stick out my tongue and then to say, "Ah."

She smiled, kissing my cheek. I beamed. She then gave me the pills and a small glass of orange juice. She concluded that the greens hadn't been thoroughly washed when she chopped them up and cooked them.

"How do you know, Mama?" I asked her, wanting to know.

"Because they tore up my stomach as well."

But she didn't vomit.

And she didn't take any of the pills.

The next day she stuffed two Tylenol pills down my parched throat and kicked me out the door.

"Don't miss the bus, sweetie." And she handed me my lunch neatly packed in a pink bag and some money. "Just in case they have some ice cream or something in school. When you go to P.E. don't be running around all day. You're classy. Dirty boys run and get soaked. You sit and be prim and proper. Ladies have to be classy."

I hugged her. "Yes, Mama." And I was off, my long, silky curls blowing in the breeze.

Now she is sending me to school. What is going on, Mama?

A few days later, after we got home from Bible study, I

was hungry. Mama said she would make us a salad and I was happy with that. She sent me to my room and told me to read a Mark Twain book. I hated Mark Twain but I did what she asked. I sat in my bed and cracked open the old-looking, dusty book. I sneezed a few times. I wanted to see my father and I missed Robert Lamley so much.

Why didn't Mama discuss the two men? It was almost like they never existed.

I got tired of sitting in my room so I set the book on my unmade bed and went back into the kitchen to get some water. Why was I so thirsty?

I was extremely hungry. I looked around for Mama. She wasn't in the kitchen.

Where was she?

Mama didn't allow me to go in the fridge without her permission but I didn't care. She wasn't in there and I was thirsty and hungry, and as a matter of fact she was late cooking dinner.

My heart pounding, I opened the fridge and pulled out a small container of juice, cracked the top and took a swig. Snatching a napkin from the roll, I wiped my mouth.

I looked at Mama's medical book on the dining room table, next to her Bible, purse and car keys.

I read the cover.

The Effects of Plastic Surgery

Mama drove me around in her Mazda, enjoying the sights of the city of Miami. In the tape deck her medical tape swirled.

She had the volume turned up loud. It annoyed me. I didn't want to hear about the different joints in the human hand and all that jazz.

But I actually learned a lot of stuff, so I guess listening to the tapes wasn't a total waste.

She decided to go to the hair store. I was still trying to figure out why she didn't let me go to school just to turn around, after giving me pills, and sending me to school.

I missed Billy. He always read me stories during our nap time. The teacher liked the way he read so she never said anything to him.

Once we got in the crowded hair store, she knew exactly what she was looking for. Mama hated to shop; she always hated to shop. Even in the grocery store she frequented the aisles closest to the exit door.

She bought a few accessories and bangles. She also bought a large piece of human hair ponytail and then decided she wanted a refund.

"I was going to use this, but I got wigs. That'll do."

I smiled.

Mama, you're cheap as hell.

A few people told me I was cute and I said "thank you." My confidence level boosted up twelve notches. When a handsome, tall guy pinched my cheek Mama snatched me close to her and pointed at him.

"Grown men don't pinch little kids' cheeks, pervert."

He was very offended. A few people were laughing, agreeing with her just to instigate something that was completely harmless.

He said, "I don't know what planet you fell from, bitch, but don't take your mess out on me. I didn't mean any harm. I have four sons of my own. See them over there with their mother on Aisle 4?"

"I don't care if they were standing in line for Walt Disney cups, you don't put your goddamn hand on my fucking child."

"You're going to lower your tone, bitch. If you were mine I'd beat your ass for not staying in your place."

Mama got in his face, and she meant business. "And I would cut your balls from your worthless dick, stuff it down your throat and write a check your motherfucking ass can't cash."

"Anyways, I'm outta here. I have my own damn children. Don't nobody wanna talk to your ugly ass child anyway, bitch."

Ugly? I thought, rolling my eyes and sucking my teeth.

Despite her uncontrollable anger, Mama reluctantly looked at his family and saw that he was telling the truth.

She relaxed, but not much. She walked over to them and he immediately started cursing, his children laughing and Mama held up her hand and said, "I'm sorry for my outburst earlier, man. But I'm in deep with my kid. I die for that right there, you feel me, Man? Keep your hands off my child. She has a daddy and even he's been flaky. I got to raise my child alone, you got help so have some empathy is all I'm saying."

He shook her hand. "I appreciate the honesty. I got you. Have a nice day."

She smiled.

When he walked off he mumbled, "Psychotic bitch…"

I stifled a laugh.

She glared at me.

"Find that funny?"

I said, "No."

Why did Mama call me a "She?"

The cashier was a gross-looking woman with black moles all over her face and she was snapping to an up-tempo song booming from the small stereo by a half-filled cup of soda, and a sub sandwich.

She had the gall to say, "Chile, I'm cute. All the men want me. Yes, ma'am Sarah Lee. I tell you no lie."

The other cashier, "Bell" (according to her name tag) said, "Girl, on what planet? You can't even stop eating fried chicken long enough to take a test on men let alone write his first name on a pregnancy test."

Mama chuckled at that one and the cashiers laughed back.

"Cute little girl," Bell said to me, leaning across the counter and handing me a lollipop. I started to smile. I loved lollipops!

Mama said, "Thank you. She looks just like my mother…" She was eying me.

The big cashier, clad in all black, told Mama, "If you need her hair braided bring her by my house. Shit, I charge about forty dollars. I stay right up the road on Sugar Hill."

She was licking her lips in a strange way at Mama. Mama looked at me and shook her head. I stopped trying to bite the wrapper off the candy.

Mama took down her name and number and when we got back in the car and she started down the road.

She rolled down the window and threw the number out.

"I don't trust strangers around my child. And secondly she's a lesbian."

I was dumb-founded. "What's a lesbian, Mama?"

She shook her head. "When a woman likes a woman the way a boy likes a girl."

"Oh," I said, confused as hell. There are too many rules to life. How many more rules were there?

She took my lollipop and threw that out the window, too.

I was infuriated. Hate burned across my face and this time I didn't hide it. That was my damn lollipop, Mama. If you wanted one you should have asked the lady for one.

I puffed up my chest. "Hey, Mama. Bell gave me…"

She spat, "Fuck Bell!" Her voice boomed over the medical tape playing. "And never accept candy from strangers. If Bell was a real woman she would have asked me was it all right to give my young child candy."

She snatched me by the hair, managing the road. It hurt. I was deeply hurt by the onslaught. She had never done this to me before.

"People wanting to pinch your cheek and do your hair and give you candy! You listen you little bitch! You refuse any help from a stranger."

She pushed me back in the seat.

Her eyes were hot coals.

"GOT THAT?"

With tears falling down my eyes I said, "Yes, ma'am."

"Good. Your Daddy isn't pinching your cheek, braiding your hair or giving you lollipops. So don't expect it from anyone else."

And that was the end of it.

All the air deflated from my chest, and I sunk in the seat.

Brooding with rage.

TOMB 9

Mama, what are those?

We stopped by J.C. Penny and she bought herself a silk black dress with matching sling backs. I wanted a book from Dr. Seuss and I was shocked when she bought it.I was happy again. She got on one knee at the register, looked me deeply in the eyes and said, "I'm sorry about earlier. I just don't like people I don't know around my child. When you meet people they almost always have ulterior motives."

"OK, Mama."

She then took me to Miss Francine, a friend of her late mother's (another lie), and she put a perm in my hair. I hated sitting there with the burning white, gooey stuff in my hair. Twenty minutes seemed like twenty hours. But I had to do it. When she rinsed it out she used shampoo and cleaned the rest of my hair. My scalp tingled. I felt refreshed. She added depth and character to my hair with conditioner that smelled like pineapples. I loved pineapples. That was my favorite fruit. The conditioner smelled so good that when she turned to get a cigarette I took the bottle, squirted some conditioner in my hand and ate it.

I had heart failure. I was rubbing at my mouth ferociously, startling her. Mama looked up sharply from her book and shook her head in silence.

"Yuk! This doesn't taste like pineapples!"

"I know she's gonna be an alcoholic bitch," Mama said, disgusted with a smirk on her face. "The bitch trying to drink conditioner. Dumb ass child!"

I was spitting on the floor and Miss Francine popped me with the comb.

"Don't spit on my floor!"

Mama was laughing. "That's what your hardheaded ass gets. Learn how to ask questions." She was sitting on the couch, reading another medical manual.

"And Miss Francine?" Mama called out politely.

Silently, Miss Francine was brushing lint from her pants. "Yes, young lady."

Mama stopped smiling. "If you ever hit my child again bitch, I'll kill you." Miss Francine instantly became silent.

By the time she was done an hour later my hair flowed to the small of my back. She pinned it up in the front.

"He looks just his grandmother," Miss Francine said, her house smelling like mothballs and the ten cats she had roaming around. What was worse than dog shit? Cat shit. And that shitty, fishy smell was throughout the house. I could hardly breathe. Buy some air fresheners, bitch.

Mama smiled, slipping her fifty dollars. I certainly hoped she bought a steam cleaner and cleaned the shit off these old ass rugs! Why invite people to your house when shit was on the floor and your central air blew shit all in your face.

"How do you know what my grandmother looks like?"

Mama asked her with an attitude.

"You showed me the picture."

Avarice thought about it. "Oh, yeah. I forgot."

"Wow. He looks the spitting image of your grandmother, Avarice. It's striking."

"And that's the way it should be." Mama reached out for me. "Come on; time to get out of here."

Miss Francine stuffed the money in her bra.

"Who gonna clean up his stuff?"

Mama said, "It's your floor, Girlfriend. Not ours. What the fuck we look like? Maids? I paid my money; *you* clean your damn house."

And the door closed behind us.

For the first time in my life, Mama and I showered together. I had never viewed her naked body before and, quite honestly, I didn't know how I felt. She had so much definition to her body, her skin tone glowing under bathroom lights. She had a soft glow in her eyes.

I was curious about our bodies so I asked her, "Mama, what are those?"

She pointed at her tits. "Breasts," she said. "You have them too."

I was looking at my chest all crazy. "Why don't they stick out?" I asked, careful not to get the plastic cap covering my perm wet.

"Because you're a child. You have to go through puberty."

"And what is that?" I asked, pointing to the bushy area of her hips.

"A penis."

"A penis, Mama?"

She smiled. "Yes."

"And what do I have?"

Indifferent, she pinched the little thing hanging from my groin.

"A vagina…"

TOMB 10: <u>Guess What Karma Does?</u>

After we dried off and got dressed, Mama smiled at me. "Go look at yourself in the mirror," said Mama nervously, sitting on the edge of the bed, pulling hungrily on a cigarette. Her eyes darted all over the room. Rather bouncy today.

Playing into our ears were medical tapes. Maybe she was thinking about the information pouring into her ears. She constantly played them like she did her music. I never paid it attention. But being that you heard things automatically, I was learning shit I didn't want to know about the human body. It got to the point that I didn't even wanna look at my "vagina" in the tub because it would remind me of these damn medical tapes!

I was giddy. "Ok, Mama."

I looked myself over in the mirror. I smiled.

"This is perfect, Mama."

She picked up her purse and grabbed a lace-front black wig and put it over her nappy hair with the haggard split ends. She said she didn't feel like dealing with styling her natural hair or paying to get it styled. Mortgage was coming up and the light bill, also.

"Let's go."

ξ

Mama pulled up in someone's back yard and cautiously parked by a huge, dirty white tour bus. I saw balloons, crepe paper and a lot of well-dressed folks all over the place. Talking amongst themselves. Sipping bubbly under the gorgeous sunshine. It looked nice.

The ladies all had on lavender dresses and the men had on off-white suits.

I slowly took in the magnificent house. The huge pool was awesome. We didn't have a pool and Mama never taught me how to swim which worried me because even when my teacher sent permission forms home so they could teach me and the other students how to swim Mama set it on fire and let it burn in the sink.

I asked her, "Mama, why did you burn it?"

She smiled sweetly at me. "Because God promised us one thing—He isn't gonna destroy the world by water. He's gonna destroy it by fire. So why learn to swim?"

I shuddered when she said it.

I looked behind me, slightly lifting my butt up in the seat and noticed many parked vehicles. I'd never seen so many nice cars parked in one spot in my life.

"We're here," said Mama, picking up her huge designer purse. She took a deep breath and exhaled silently.

Call Her Queen Hatshepsut　　　118

I was shaking my head, hot as hell. I inherited the word "hell" from Mama and it sounded good when I put it to use. She turned off the car and undid her seat belt.

"Where are we, Mama?"

She kissed my lips. "Your Daddy's funeral, I meant wedding."

I had never been so happy in my life.

I get to see my father! Yeah!

We were ushered into the back door like we were bums begging for change by a tall gentleman with the softest eyes and the yellowiest teeth. He did a double take when he saw the doll Mama was.

He kissed Mama's cheek and said, "How have you been?"

She grabbed my hand and told him, "I've been studying, going to school. Working and dedicatedly caring for my child."

I was nervous being around all these strange people.

Can I go to school, Mama?

"Well, it's good to see you. The family didn't think you were coming…"

"Well, I'm still surprised I came. That's probably why everyone is staring at me."

"True. But you're gorgeous and fine, of course."

"Men always revert to the One Eyed Snake Syndrome. You can't talk to a woman without throwing that in there, 'huh?" she joked and he kissed her cheek again. This threw me for a loop.

Why didn't she snap on him?

"Well, take your seat, Avarice."

"I will. Soon."

He leaned over and kissed my cheek.

"And how are you? You look very nice."

I blushed. "Thank you."

Then I snapped viciously.

"…But please keep your filthy lips off me, jerk! Don't touch me, pervert! Grown men shouldn't be touching little girls and if you so much as offer me a lollipop I will make my Mama kick your butt!"

Mama was proud. "Like Mama like daughter…"

Embarrassed, he ducked his chin. I remembered how she snapped on ole boy from the hair store. "I don't let strange people kiss me, isn't that right, Mama?"

She was about to burst with joy. "That's right! That's my baby!"

I kicked him in the shin and he began hopping up and down. Mama and I left him where he leapt.

One thing arrested my attention—

—My vagina hardened and pressed against my clothing when he kissed me.

What does that mean?

Mama sat in the second row, behind a fat lady wearing a balloon-of-a-dress and a huge lavender hat with red roses pinned in the front.

People were everywhere.

I saw my Dad. He was standing at the altar. We were in his huge living room. Mama told me he was an architect. "He designs the female womb and makes them cry."

In her hand was a program. She shared it with me.

I just wanted the picture of Daddy.

She said, "Are you hungry?"

I told her, "Yes. I didn't eat anything today, Mama. I've been running around with you."

"I wanted to save your appetite for the main course."

"So we're eating here, Mama?"

"Yes."

Someone tapped Mama from behind. She turned and smiled.

"Hey, Vanessa! How are you?"

"I've been fine!" Mama hugged her. "So you came to

my cousin's wedding!"

"Yes. I wouldn't miss it for the world," Mama said through clenched teeth. "He is marrying my blood sister…"

Vanessa looked around, looking flawless in an ankle-length lavender dress with ruffled sleeves. Her hair had hints of lavender on the tips and the diamond earrings glittered just as ferociously as her eyes. On her right hand was a small tattoo of a heart.

"So what have you been doing for yourself? Long time no see?"

"I finished medical school. I'm a plastic surgeon."

Vanessa smiled. "Oh, Word? How much for a consultation?"

Mama opened her purse and pulled out her business card. On it was a close-up picture of Mom, smiling and her credentials.

"My business is picking up. I'm swamped with schedules and new clients. I'll give you a family discount." Mama handed her the card. Vanessa stuffed it in her bra.

"Thank you. I need to get some liposuction as well."

"I got you," Mama went on, not meaning what she said.

"Can I have your number?" she asked, sitting on the opposite side of Mama. I just looked at her little protruding belly.

"It's on the business card," said Mama. She pulled out a scrap piece of paper from the pocket on the side of the purse. "What's your number?"

Vanessa took the pen and paper and scribbled it. Mama stuck it in her bra.

"I'll be in touch."

"I hope so, because when you and my cousin broke up you vanished off the face of the earth."

"Chile, life goes on. I was in college."

"Tell me about it, Girl. I tried going to Grambling State and got kicked out and lost my scholarships."

Dapharoah69

"Are you kidding, Girl? How did you manage to do
that?"

"I couldn't leave the boys alone. Couldn't stop beating
the women down over them. Sex, sex, sex was on my
mind, Chile."

"I don't get into all that. I set an agenda. I make a plan,
a list of goals and affirmations and I meet them."

"You have always been a strong woman. You seem to
handle chaos very well."

Mama smiled, putting her arm around me. "Yeah, I
do. But I'm not a saint. I have my flaws. I do my share of
quirky things."

"Where do you live?" Vanessa asked, patting her hair.

"Here, there and everywhere."

"Mysterious…"

Mama thought to herself, looking at me. "Yeah. For
now, it has to be that way." Mama squeezed Vanessa's
hand. "I'll let you know one day, right now I just need my
privacy."

Vanessa looked around, snapping her gum. "I can
respect that."

"So, where are you gonna sit?" Mama asked. "You
know, for the ceremony? Are you in the wedding?"

Vanessa snorted like a pig, making me laugh. Mama
laughed, too. "Girl, I'm sitting here. My cousin didn't let
me be in his wedding. He let your sister pick her family
members to stand behind her."

"Well, she asked me but I declined. And we don't have
much family at all. I mean, we have people we call our
cousins but my Grandma isn't alive and the rest of our
family is dead."

Vanessa took Mama's hand in empathy. "I don't blame
you for declining. You know I've always liked you.
Personally I can't believe you came. I really can't believe
you didn't blow this house up. Your sister took your life.
He was the man you were supposed to be marrying."

Tears spilt over Mama's gorgeous light brown eyes. I

stroked her left thigh, crying with her. I hated to see her so emotional.

"I know, right," Mama said. "Sisters are supposed to be loyal. A man shouldn't come between you and your loving sister, you feel me? But my sister's heartbeat is in her pussy and that has always been her problem."

"Mama what a 'pussy' is?"

Mama snapped on me and Veronica giggled.

"Watch your goddamn mouth." She glared at Veronica. "And you can wipe the smile off your face before I snatch it off.

I covered my mouth.

Veronica ignored mother. She said, "I don't wanna blow smoke but she was wrong for lying to your late grandmother, making everybody in town think you cheated on him. Hell, she even paid men to go around saying they had sex with you."

This was news to me. I sat there, soaking it in like a sponge. I only heard snippets of Mama's life during times like this and I was always fascinated because she never opened up to me.

Mama smiled bitterly. "I can see you're a Post Production bitch."

"What?"

"Bitches always claim they knew something about my man yet when I came to you, you told me you knew nothing about it. Now you talking? Too late now!"

Vanessa lowered her head. "I just didn't wanna be in the middle of it. You know how people put you in shit you don't have nothing to do with."

"So you would lie to me? We were friends."

"Girl, it was hard to keep it a secret, trust me. But I had to. Kayak is my cousin. Blood is thicker than cum."

Mama looked sad and then she smiled. "Girl, whatever. Those people standing behind my sister ain't our family. Those are the bitches she chose over me. But it's cool. Grandma is dead. I had to deal with it, you know. Life goes on. A man doesn't dictate who I am or what I do. He fell victim to circumstance. What man you know stays rational when a woman puts her body in his face to do with it as he pleases? There's no room for talk, body language comes into play."

"Girl, Amen." She slapped palms with Mama.

"And a hallelujah, God," Mama said joyously. But the pain was all over her face. She was reliving it. It danced in her eyes. I felt it.

"So now you gotta watch them marry and keep your cool…"

Mama held my hand tightly. "Tell me about it. Guess what Karma does?" Mama looked into my eyes and kissed my lips with so much love. "It always comes back to do one thing."

Vanessa looked over at me with a smile and a wave.

"What's that?" asked Vanessa.

"You really wanna know?"

"Yes!"

"It comes back to fuck you."

Vanessa shook my hand. "You look very nice."

I said, "Thank you."

She kissed my cheek.

I looked her dead in the eyes.

"Don't put your filthy lips on me, please!" Embarrassed, Vanessa tucked her chin back, holding her diamond chocker. A few people were laughing but I didn't find it funny.

"My Mama don't like when strangers touch on me. Thank you."

And I turned to face the people in front of me like I hadn't said a word.

Mama said, "That's my baby…"

Unfortunately, my vagina didn't get hard.

I was as confused as ever.

Call Her Queen Hatshepsut

Part 3
Your Majesty

TOMB 11:

This is my Daddy's Wedding!

Mama looked over at me and said, "Do me a favor."

I gave her my undivided attention. "Yes, Mama."

I couldn't take my eyes off Daddy. He was such a beautiful man. His eyes captured every light known to man and redirected the glow of my universe across his pearly-white teeth. He had perfect teeth and looking at him made my heart scream with joy, even though I never spent an hour with him…even though he wasn't married to mother…even though he never tucked me in at night or critiqued one of my stick figure drawings with the whop-sided clouds and the skinny, anorexic-looking birds. My stomach growled. Vanessa was talking to some lady in front of her.

Mama turned to face the back of the room. Her eyes danced gracefully over every flower, person and thing. When she found what she was looking for she pointed behind her, towards the start of the rotunda.

"See those handsome men over there in the all-white suits?"

I had problems looking. It was too far back, and my vision was blurry. I think I saw what she was talking about.

"Yes, Mama. I see it." I really didn't.

She nodded. "Go stand in front of the very first one."

"Why, Mama?"

She smiled, squeezing my hand.

"Because your father said he wanted you to be his best man. Go give them a hell of a show."

"Wow. Daddy really wants me to be his best man?" I asked, exasperated, not really knowing what that meant.

Her eyes glowed. "Yes."

I was scared. "But I don't trust these strange people."

She pats my head. "This is your family, baby."

"But I snapped on the man and Vanessa for putting their filthy lips on me, Mama."

"That was different. Just because they are family doesn't mean they have the right to touch and kiss you without your permission."

I was shaking my head. "OK, Mama…"

"I love you." She helped me stand up. She patted my rump as I started to walk off.

"I love you, too, Mama."

Vanessa closed her eyes when I walked by, shaking her head.

Yeah, bitch! Stay mad.

My vagina still didn't get hard from her kiss.

I walked in front of a short-looking guy with a too-thick beard. You could barely see his lips. I thought about Bright Light Gizmo from the *Gremlins* movie Mama always showed me.

"Hey, what are you doing up here little one?"

I looked at him. "This is my Daddy's wedding."

He held up his hands. "Any child of your father's is alright with me. I didn't know he had a kid."

I turned my back with my hands on my hips.

"Now you do."

The other five fellahs looked at me with a smile, shaking my hand and kissing my cheek.

"Hey, little cousin…"

"Nice to meet you."

"Glad to finally see my brother's kid…I'm your Uncle Jack…"

My vagina was harder than ever.

I saw Mama glaring at me.

I snapped. "Don't put your hands on me!"

Game over.

The music was cued up and I got excited, my heart pounding. I noticed everyone looked towards us, in this rotunda, as Mama called it. I enjoyed the attention because I was amazingly beautiful and nothing could tap into the fuel tanks of my spirit. Saddam Hussein couldn't have the oil of my fire.

I looked behind me and I immediately saw a picture of Daddy and Mama's sister Rosa hanging by the huge oak wooden door.

One of the women in lavender took my hand, smiling down at me. I cringed inside. My blood boiling, I had to slam my eyes shut to keep from killing her because her bloody hands were on me!

"How cute. Who are you?" she asked, her breath the exact reciprocal of Mama's stench when she was on the toilet, reading *Ebony* magazine.

Sucking my teeth and sassily rolling my neck, I said, *"I'm* my father's *son.* And I'm not telling you my name because you're a complete stranger and Mama said never talk to strangers."

Her eyes bulging out of her head, she frowned, releasing my hand as if I was a demon...as if I was fire and she was a barrel of gasoline. Her reaction lowered my self-esteem...compromising my self-confidence.

The six men frowned as well, in complete silence.

ξ

We were walking down the aisle. A little girl, about four years old, clad in a lavender dress and huge ponytails, was throwing red rose petals before our feet. She had too much makeup on her face and her lips coated with too much red cosmetics. I guess parents were teaching her how to be a phony bitch relying on make-up for a mask a little too early.

My shoes were killing me. I felt unbalanced.

The woman holding my hand kept glaring at me like she had a problem. I didn't sweat it. I knew she was jealous of my divine beauty and she was an aging drama queen who probably hadn't been touched by a man in years.

I saw Mama, standing up, snapping photos. Vanessa was standing up too, infuriated. She kept glaring at Mama, shaking her head in disgust.

All around me people were smiling at me. Some snapped photos and were wondering who I was, judging by the confused but happy looks on their pleasantly made-up faces.

Daddy looked at me with a smile. He was shaking his head, his hands folded before him. He was the King of my throne and he didn't know it. I would do anything for him if he asked. I was so excited about him finally being in my life. We would play with dolls and I would try to cook for him and I would help iron his clothes and he would tuck me in at night. Oh, yes, God! *You're finally looking out for me! Thanks for giving me my father! I couldn't have asked for a better*

Call Her Queen Hatshepsut   128

gift.

When I got up to Daddy I stood behind him and the woman holding my hand looked at Daddy for a minute and he nodded. She was silently moving her lips and he was reading them like they were an open James Baldwin novel. I was at a loss for words because I didn't know what was said nor did I know what Daddy comprehended.

The woman stood on the opposite side of me.

Mama was still snapping pictures. I looked at her with a smile.

Snap.

My Daddy got on his knees and kissed my forehead.

"You look very nice," he said, kissing my cheek. *Oh my GOD! DADDY KISSED ME! Daddy loved me! See, I KNEW everything would be all right!*

"Thank you…"

He stood up and faced the crowd of family.

When the bride appeared, in a huge pearl-white dress that took up the entire aisle, people stood up clapping. A veil covered her face. Her diamonds glittered through it.

She was holding a huge bouquet of flowers.

Slowly, she made her way up the aisle, looking here and there. People really loved her stunning look.

I didn't care.

I was having mixed feelings. Daddy had barely said three words to me. He didn't look at me or hold my hand.

With that said I let it go. I was just happy to be here.

My auntie looked at Mama. Mama smiled at her, snapping a couple of pictures.

My aunt stopped and lifted the veil. She had a blank look on her face, not believing that Mama was there. I really didn't know what that was about, but I started putting two and two together. Mama and Daddy were together. They had me. Sister took her man from her.

Emotional, Mama walked up to her and they embraced.

Dapharoah69

129

"Thanks for coming, big sister," said my aunt Rosa to Mama, with huge tears in her eyes. Despite her tears, her words seemed forced and rushed.

Reluctantly, Mama hugged her again, looking me deeply in the eyes.

"I wouldn't miss it, little sister," she lied beautifully.

People were clapping and whistling.

"I wish Grandma was here," said my aunt.

Mama released her and put the veil back over my aunt's face.

"She's here."

"In spirit." She squeezed Mama's hand. "Wow, Avarice…you look like grandma…"

I paid my plastic surgeon years ago to make me look like this. I remember the day well.

I remember asking the receptionist to give me a scrap piece of paper and I put pictures of her man cheating on the desk. I then handed my doctor my grandmother's photo and had him nip/tuck my face away so I wouldn't look like my identical twin sister anymore.

I got tired of looking in the mirror and seeing your face knowing you took my man.

The bride gripped the bouquet and made her way up to Daddy.

It was clear he thought she was the most stunning creature in the world.

But for some reason, looking at Daddy, one thing occurred to me:

I looked *nothing* like him. Why did Mama lie, and tell me I looked just like him? Why would she do that to me?

And why did he keep giving Mama the evil glare.

TOMB 12:

Isn't he gorgeous?

The pastor delivered a very powerful sermon before he got into the vows. I was actually moved by his stunning words. He spoke of empowerment and not depending on mortal man for jubilancy. That true happiness comes from within and if you looked for it to come from outside sources you will be damned into a life of dependency and misery.

I was still figuring this all out; after all I was still a young child. I was shrouded in confusion. I knew one thing…my shoes were killing my feet.

I was thinking, "Why did my vagina get hard for the men and not for the ladies?"

I didn't quite know. I didn't think I wanted to know.

Daddy held up his hand when the pastor started to talk about him and my aunt.

"Kayak, is something *wrong?*" asked the gregarious

Pastor, his neatly-cut white hair bringing out his gorgeous eyes.

My Daddy looked at Mama. "*Where* is my son?" He asked it politely, with a smile. "You know I wanted him to be my best man?"

Vanessa pointed the camcorder at me, frowning.

The people wondered themselves, looking right past me.

"Your son is here," said Mama, pointing at me. She walked out into the front row and up to Daddy.

My aunt dropped the bouquet and snatched the veil from her face, glaring at me.

"That's not my son! This is a little beautiful princess-of-a-girl clad in a light lavender dress, low-heels and curly hair pinned atop her head."

Mama went in for the kill. "That is not a girl. That is your son. Isn't he gorgeous?"

Demons could have been the attendees as pandemonium took over the room. My aunt grabbed her chest as if she was having a heart attack. Wide-eyed, she couldn't breathe. Devastated, Daddy sank to his knees, taking me into his trembling arms, in a state of shock. I held him, not quite knowing what was going on. I was so afraid. At that point I just wanted to leave.

Mama please! Get us out of here! Oh my God! Why is everyone looking at me?

Mama looked at my aunt Rosa. "Doesn't he look like Grandma?"

Aunt Rosa was a beast, lurking…preying. "You sick bitch!"

Mama savored the moment, looking slightly to the right. "As a matter of fact I look like grandma too, huh sister?" She used the back of her palm and pulled her hair back from her face to show the devastation in her pupils. "There is a reason Mama pushed me outta her womb ten minutes before *your* earthly debut! I don't know why they call us identical twins. I look *nothing* like you. Thanks to my plastic surgeon, bitch, any resemblance of your whorish life is nipped from me and my son's face!"

Savagely, as if being attacked, Aunt Rosa ran past me, pushing a few brides' maids out of the way. They plummeted painfully into the pews and against the wall.

When my aunt got up to Mama she snatched her by the hair and Mama brutally slapped her across the face with the camcorder.

"You stole my man, bitch!"Mama said sadly, becoming an irresponsible monster. "What, you think I wasn't going to say anything? You pit Grandma against me! She died thinking I actually cheated on my boyfriend before *you* took him. I had to marry Robert when my heart wasn't set on him. You took my life because you were jealous! Her last words to me were, '*May your life be filled with whoredom!*'"

Mama was snatching my aunt's wedding dress off. Rosa's full breasts (with stretch marks) tumbled free, like escaped convicts.

Mama went on. "You stole my life! You lied to my child's father and told him I cheated on him when I hadn't. Just to get him, bitch because you were jealous! Take off this goddamn dress! I WAS SUPPOSED TO BE IN THIS DRESS! THIS WAS SUPPOSED TO BE MY DAY!"

Then Mama took a basket of flowers and dumped them on my aunt, kicking at her frail body.

One of Daddy's family members ran up to Mama and she grabbed a poker from a breath-taking display of flowers and swung it at him.

"Get back, bitches!" Mama had had enough. "The game ends! Right now!"

It was Mama against the world with me in the middle clad in a dress and women shoes and women's curls in my hair. The room was in an uproar. Some people fled the house, not wanting to be a part of Mama's obsession.

I felt like a complete fool.

Dapharoah69

Mama spat on my aunt.

"Karma screwed you like you screwed my man!"

She walked past her sister and the other bridesmaids, and stopped behind my confused daddy.

Mama glared deep into his eyes. "Tell your son good bye. He looks nothing like you, does he? He's gorgeous! He loves wearing dresses and his hair in curls. He is a beautiful little girl. He is a she, what am I talking about. Isn't she lovely, Stevie Wonder?"

I felt good the way Mama praised me. I started to smile.

Mama said I'm a girl. I'm a she. Fitting. Yes, Mama knows best, right I'm a girl I'm a girl I'M A GIRL! Yeah!

"Daddy," I said, reaching out for his trembling hand. "Don't I look pretty? Aren't I everything you wanted me to be? Aren't you proud of me?"

Daddy snatched his hand back from mine as if I was on fire. I was so devastated I sank to my knees with my face in my perspiring hands. Daddy rejected me. I wasn't good enough for him. The hell with him. All I needed was God and my Mama.

I knew this was too good to be true! I knew he wouldn't love me. Mama was right! Men weren't worth the piss from their vaginas!

Daddy looked back at her and said, "You're sick! I understand why you are so angry. It wasn't fair what your sister did. Initially, when I found out she was not you I was angry and I felt betrayed. I never knew you had a twin sister. She used to wear your clothing and fragrances. I was fooled. But fools fall in love, Avarice. It wasn't my fault. Her lips I couldn't live without. Her smell, her flair turned me on. I had to leave you because my heart set sail. My heart was turned asunder. When I slept with her I thought she was you. Both of you are identical twins for God's sake. I was in love with you but not anymore. Attacking me and ruining my wedding is plausible…but to hurt a child? To dress my son as a woman to get back at me is sinister and unforgettable?"

"She's a pretty little *girl!*" Mama boasted with pride, tears falling down her face. "Don't call her a woman. Let her enjoy being a little girl. She loves her dolls and her doll house! Let her stay in a child's place!"

"A what?" He was in shock, his lips trembling.

"She's a little girl! He is a girl! A he/she! For years I raised him as a girl! I taught him that he has a vagina, that one day he will meet a man and they will marry and have children. I once believed that, when I used to sit at home and wait for you…I used to cook your food. I wrapped my life around you and you were banging my sister and making plans with her! I told my daughter…she will get a period when she's about 13-years-old. I taught her about pads, because I don't want her sticking tampons in her pussy until she's 18!"

My Uncle threw up all over himself. A few family members in the crowd were yelling nasty things at my mother.

Daddy engulfed me in his arms. "I love you, Son. I will take you to live with me…I will take off all these female clothing. Your mother isn't fit to raise you."

People started yelling at Mama and she was holding the poker, about to protect herself and suddenly I wanted to defend my mother.

I, in Daddy's arms, screamed, "DON'T YELL AT MY MAMA, YOU BITCHES!"

It felt nice using the word Mama taught me. The word used to describe my aunt.

My aunt, the messed-up bride, was still rolling on the floor, moaning in agony.

No one helped her up.

Mama laughed so loud it shut everyone up. It's like I didn't know who she was anymore. Her ambitious, unscrupulous antics brought misery to so many lives, but of course she was Mama – they never did anything wrong. *Honor thy mother and thy father. Or my days will be numbered.* So

I'd remain loyal to her until I figured all this out. I was just a child. Why did adults thrust their children into adult situations?

I saw a couple dabbing their eyes, staring at me like I was a disgusting creature. I wanted to crawl into myself and die so they would stop looking at me so questionably. I can't begin to tell you what this did to me. I felt weird, like I didn't belong. Was this all my fault? What did I do wrong, Lord? I have every miracle you performed stored in my memory. Mama used to give me little quizzes. So why aren't you performing a miracle for me today, Lord?

Why isn't Jesus feeding thousands of starving people fish?

Why isn't Jesus walking on water?

Where is Moses with those Ten Commandments?

Why isn't he freeing me and Mama from bondage, Lord?

Split the Red Sea so I can travel through unlevel shores, trying to battle my own River Jordan!

Mama said, rubbing her throat, "My child will be a pretty ballerina!" There were gasps filling the living room. Daddy's eyes bulged out of his head. "She starts classes next week. So much for football, huh? I know how much you love it, but my son um my daughter *won't* be into things like that. You and my sister can have each other! Fuck your wedding; I turned it into a funeral!"

Something taking over him, Daddy took my hair from the pins. "Son, listen to me…" I was petrified, clearly frightened of this man who was suddenly a stranger to me. "You have a dick." *What's a dick, Daddy?* "Not a vagina. You are supposed to like girls, not men. Your Mama's a psycho!"

"I do like girls," I told him. "I like boys, too. I have a lot of friends in school, Daddy. So I can't like them?"

He had concern and fear on his face. "Oh, my boy! I don't expect you to understand. You even talk like a girl. You don't have any bass in your voice. Your mother has ruined you."

I started to cry. "I'm ruined, Daddy?"

Mama defended me. "She has a lovely voice. I put estrogen in his bottles when he was a baby…he turned out exactly the way I wanted him, I meant her to be!"

He was hugging me tightly and Mama stood there with her hand on her hip, looking like the ruler of Hell.

"All the tightness in the world won't squeeze out your bullshit, my handsome Baby Daddy. My child isn't ruined! She's beautiful! Just like my dead Grandma."

He stood up, reached behind the podium and grabbed scissors.

Like a monster he started chopping off my hair. "You are supposed to enjoy sports, play ball if you choose to. Date women, have a family with a girl. Men don't have periods and they don't bare children."

I was in an outrage. "…You cut my hair, creep!"

I started picking up my hair, the men in all-white suits quiet and petrified because of what was playing before their eyes. One of them took out a silver flask, cracked the top and took a swig.

I had to get back at Daddy. No one messed with my mother!

With all my strength, I swung at him, my fist connecting with his balls.

Wide-eyed, he cupped them, falling to his knees.

I was just as demonic as Mama. "I BELIEVE WHAT MAMA SAYS!" I screamed at him, running up to her. She held me protectively.

"I don't want a faggot for a son!" My daddy shouted as the room fell into a deep silence. Mama was laughing so hard, stroking my face. I cried in silence, my heart burning and my stomach churning. My pulse I could feel in my feet.

Daddy slowly approached us. He has lost all sense of reasoning. Now he wanted to get back at Mama.

"…If that's the life he chooses or you *make* him

choose," said Daddy, "then I want no part of it. NO PART OF IT! What kind of woman destroys her son and raises him as a…"

"As a what?" Mama interrupted. "You are entering dangerous waters you sack of shit. I will kill you over my seed. You made it and you abandoned it."

"I won't say it. My kid is innocent in the scheme of things. He didn't do anything wrong and he didn't ask to be here. I wasn't the *only* one who abandoned him, girl. There are so many factors you choose to ignore."

Mama said, "Ignore? You don't want the world to know the truth or have you forgotten? Shall I tell them you…?"

He held up his hands, shaking his head. He was backing away from us and I hated how he was looking. He looked just like how I felt – confused and drained. His voice cracked.

My Aunt was leaning against the wall, watching it all in silence. She looked a mess in her dress. A dressy mess she would always be. I didn't understand why she didn't come to his side and help him fight Mama. Maybe she was in shock. Maybe she was just embarrassed. For some reason I felt her pain, I felt what she felt. We locked eyes and she was shaking her head at me. I felt a connection to her that I couldn't explain. Daddy detested me, looking at me with the love he once had when I first walked behind him to be his best man.

I turned out to be Daddy's Little Girl.

He called me a *faggot! I still didn't know what that meant.*

"I will disown him," Daddy said. "I *hate* faggots! This family don't support gay bullshit, you dumb woman! How could you corrupt his mind?"

Mama remained unfazed. "Karma always comes back to fuck you!" She looked at Vanessa. "Isn't that right, Vanessa? You still want a consultation!"

Vanessa lowered the camera.

When my Aunt slid to the floor, sobbing, Mama said, "Look at my child! I've been performing plastic surgery on him, secretly, for months! And I'm not worried about any of you calling the authorities. I covered my trail and it's your word against mine. You can't prove a damn thing!"

She took my hand and stood over her sister. "I told you Grandma was here."

My Aunt looked up at Mama with a bloody lip and a swollen eye. She refused to stand up; my aunt was clearly embarrassed in front of family and invited guests.

My Aunt said, "You're crazy. Why...?"

Mama said, "Don't worry yourself. You have a wedding to attend, even though it resembles ancient ruins. He looks like Grandma, doesn't he?" You could see the hurt on Mama's face, fueled by the betrayal of my aunt and father.

Mama sat next to my aunt and leaned towards her. Her lips were a few inches from my aunt's right ear.

"I used Grandma's photo on my nightstand when I performed the procedures from my bedroom," she whispered. "...My son actually thought he had blackouts. No..."

She was laughing again, people looking at her like she was Satan and I didn't appreciate that because anything my mother did for me was out of love and I understood that. "I always gave him sleeping pills when I fed him. Then I used gas to put him to sleep. I have an EKG machine in my closet I used to monitor his heart. He doesn't remember a thing. I have the manuals all around my bed and floor. After all, I did my internship in there..."

"But why?" asked my Aunt, her shoulders shaking. "You hate me that much?"

Cupping her face, Mama kissed her lips. My Aunt cringed. "Yes. I hate you. Have you forgotten we were pregnant at the same time? We even went into labor together. You had me thinking your boyfriend at the time was the baby's father. I never knew that the man over there saying he hate faggots was your child's father."

"I'm sorry. I wanted him and I didn't know how to go about…"

Mama whispered harshly. "So you go about that by deception? Whores always use their bodies to lure the serpent. Isn't that what Eve did when she offered Adam the Forbidden Fruit of her vagina? It wasn't an apple, honey britches! There was a time I didn't curse. I didn't talk back. I was kind-hearted and full of patience. I wanted to be a doctor. I wanted to marry that man over there," Mama went on, pointing at Daddy. "My entire world was built around that. Grandma told me I was being unrealistic. Then my world blows up. Your kid was born and so was mine. Your child died at birth and mine lived. It was a glorious day because when my kid was born I still harbored the pain of losing the first child I had ever given birth to."

"You never had a first child, Avarice. You were so demented that when Kayak left you started hallucinating and talking to yourself."

"SHUT UP!"

"It's true! You never gave birth to a stillborn child."

"You don't know anything outside of Kayak's penis, do you?"

"Your son right there doesn't deserve this, Avarice. That's who you gave birth to! You didn't give birth to a daughter. Are you insane? You *have* a piece of your child's father…I don't!"

"And that erases the hurt and the betrayal of my sister paying people to say they slept with me? Our family disowned me. People called me a slut. A whore! I wasn't either of those things. My son's father was the only lover I'd ever been with. And you fed on it, talked about me with your friends. I was your sister. I did any and everything for you."

"BUT I WAS JEALOUS!" my Aunt exclaimed and Mama blinked twice. I was taking this all in -- dissecting it.

Even my father listened intently. "Grandma loved you from the beginning. You were her favorite girl. I always paled in comparison. You always did everything right, Avarice."

She was getting to Mama emotionally. Mama was like a little girl.

Mama said, "You always supported me, sis."

"Yes, but you got all the attention and all the pretty gifts. I didn't. If you cooked for Grandma she loved it. When I cooked she trashed it. I couldn't deal with it. There were nights I asked God to kill you in your sleep. I wanted you dead."

"So that's why you destroyed me, over jealousy? Because of things I couldn't control?"

Wickedness danced in my aunt's eyes. "*Yes.*"

I was looking at Mama and my Aunt when something dawned on me. My mouth hanging open I looked from one to the other, trapped in a trance. This could not be! Why I hadn't noticed this before.

I had my aunt's eyes.

Mama looked at Daddy, who was on his knees, rubbing the Bible. It hurt her to look at him. Then everything she'd gone through with him burst from her heart and she was on her feet and swinging the poker.

He ducked, the iron rod swinging over his head. He picked up the huge Bible from the floor and the poker connected with it. He didn't want to get struck by the poker.

"I hate you! I hate my whorish sister! You will *never* see my child again!"

Dropping the poker, Mama snatched my arm and tugged me past family and friends, people I never knew existed. This was like a nightmare and nothing made sense. Why did Mama destroy the wedding? Why did my Aunt try to marry Daddy when Mama was her sister? Why hadn't I been told about this Aunt? Mama *never* told me I had an Aunt and Uncles. I barely knew my Dad and quite frankly I

didn't want to know a man who called me a name whose
meaning I didn't understand.

Faggot!

Mama sprung the existence of my Aunt on me when she
called her a bitch a few days ago at home and I asked her
what the word meant. Does "bitch" really mean my Aunt?

Mama got to the front door and my Uncle, the one
with the white suit, grabbed her arm.

"What did you do to my nephew?"

I was frightened. I hid behind Mama.

She had an air of superiority and power that deafened
me. "Let me go, this is my child! Not yours!"

He snatched Mama by the hair and her wig came off.
She shook her hair loose, opened her purse and pulled out
a gun, aiming at him.

He ran for dear life. She started shooting, making
people duck for cover. My Daddy ran out the back door,
holding my Aunt's hand.

"Wait here, Sweetie," Mama said. She uttered
something in Creole. I didn't know what it meant.

She ran over to the altar, and picked up the bouquet.
She held it in front of her, looking up at the life-sized Jesus
painting.

"Now I pronounce them husband and wife. Psyche.
Lord, forgive me. I know not what I do. I lost my scruples
eons ago. I was always the weak twin. My sister was the
strong one, Lord. Doesn't she understand? It wasn't me
who Grandma liked the best. It was her. That's why she
was easiest on me because I was the slow one and she was
hardest on her because she could put together a cake, a
dresser and change oil in an automobile without breaking a
nail. Why was my sister jealous of the weak one?"

Like a demented beast, she walked, heel-to-toe, up to
the hanging picture of my Aunt and Daddy. I was sitting
on the floor, my knees pulled up to my chest, still upset
that Dad had cut my hair.

Mama turned her back to the photo and said, "Ready to catch the bouquet, sister girl?"

She tossed it over her head and it hit the picture, falling to the floor.

"Oh," joked Mama, shooting the picture off the wall. It shattered all around us.

I jumped up to my feet, shaken from the blast and opened the front door.

"How do you like *that,* Grandma?" Mama yelled, torn from love, hurt by betrayal. "As long as I live, wherever this bitch tries to marry him I will show up and turn her wedding into a funeral."

Mama took my hand and we took our time walking to the backyard, to her car.

She was silent the entire time. But I wanted answers – answers I knew in my soul I would never receive.

But more importantly…why did I have my Aunt's eyes?

I wanted to know the answer.

TOMB 13:

Daughter

The next day a moving company was at our house, packing our things.

"Are we moving, Mama?" I asked, my heart cracking. What about my school and my friends? What about my teachers? They always gave me candy and when they offered to give me a lollipop I would turn it down because Mama said I shouldn't accept lollipops from strangers.

She barely looked at me. She looked a mess. She was still wearing the dress from the wedding.

"Yes."

"Where, Mama? What about my friends?"

She grabbed her purse and keys. "You'll get more."

"But Mama…"

"We have to leave here, Son!"

She told me to open the closet and take out the small

briefcase. I did so without back talking.

She emptied my dresser and neatly put the clothes in the briefcase.

My low-heels and flat shoes with the black bows and my pink sneakers she put in a huge Tupperware bin.

She hadn't slept. Her eyes were narrowed. She looked like the zombies I saw in the horror movies.

"Everything I did for you, Son; I did it out of love."

"I know, Mama."

An hour later, Mama and I packed her car with our clothes and some food.

She checked her wallet. She had about nine hundred dollars.

She called someone on the house phone.

"Do you have the fake I.D.s made up?" She looked at me. "What about the social security cards? Two – one for me and for my daughter."

Daughter? I thought I was her son?

"Good. And they won't be traced back to us? I have my own business so I need all this shit to be legit…I'll pay what it's worth…Good. I'll pick it up when I get into town." She cleared her throat. "I have one thing to say. I just took one of your rooks. You're in check…"

Mama hung up the phone.

I was so distraught I couldn't stop crying. Mama took me into her arms and she apologized for how my Daddy had treated me.

I hated him so much. I didn't think I would ever forgive him for what he did and how he treated me in front of those people. How could he do that?

Did he have a heart? Did he have a caring bone in his body?

Did he hate me?

TOMB 14:
Geometric shapes

Twenty minutes later Mama and I were on I-75, bound for Florida. We were leaving Philadelphia, my Aunt and father behind. Forever.

I would never hear from them again. I was deeply saddened. Why couldn't I spend time with my father? Why was she doing this?

I was in a state of confusion. It was in me to ask Mama about everything she said at the wedding.

What exactly was plastic surgery? And why did she perform it on me? Was it a part of her "internship?" What exactly was that? She was using words I hadn't before heard in my life.

Why didn't she tell me she had an identical twin? My aunt and Mama were the spitting image of perfection. Both drop dead gorgeous. And no matter how much plastic surgery she had she still looked like my Aunt. She still looked more like my Aunt than Grandma.

But I was getting two different accounts.

My Aunt claimed my great-grandma gave Mama preferential treatment – that she had been given the best of everything and my Aunt suffered the shame and rejection.

Yet Mama looked up at the Jesus picture and said it was she who was the weakest, that she was *only* being praised because she was the "slow" one of the two sisters.

With all that going on I came to the conclusion that I really didn't want a sister or a brother.

Best if I stayed the only child and Mama wasn't showing any signs that she wanted to be "fruitful," as she taught me.

When I was riding in Mama's car, I told myself that I didn't want marriage. It seemed to be very hard. Did I want to commit to anyone? Did I want kids one day? I wouldn't cheat on anybody. If one of my friends wanted to marry someone I wouldn't do what my aunt did. I was learning a lot just by observing. I picked up on things and had a knack for putting two and two together. I get that from Mama.

I knew I was good at putting things together because when Mama and I used to put together jigsaw puzzles I would always finish before her and in record time.

She'd still be struggling with her puzzle and I'd go over and help her, kissing her lips. She always told me I was smart.

Was this how life was supposed to be? Was this how I was supposed to learn? My life had become a jigsaw puzzle, only I couldn't put the picture together in record time. I was having problems. Pieces were missing. The seal on the puzzle box was broken before I even opened it.

Was this good for a child to see – grown people acting more childish than me when I play with my dolls?

Why did Daddy call me a "faggot?"

I wanna ask you, Mama. But you seem so out of it, so sad.

Why are you sad, Mama? Was this all about my Aunt? Why didn't you tell me about her? What was it like for you growing up? Why can't I find the voice to ask her?

I looked at Mama and squeezed her hand. She looked at me, her eyes scarlet red. She held the steering wheel with her knee and dug in her purse, pulling out her cigarettes. She extracted one and put it between her lips.

I reached in her purse and handed her a lighter.

"Thank you, baby."

She lit it, puffed on it 'til smoke snaked in the air and she sighed. She then held the steering wheel and my hand.

"What's wrong, Mama?" I asked.

"I'm ok. It's nothing to concern yourself with."

I studied her. "Do you love me, Mama?"

She choked. "Of course I love you. This is all about you. Giving you a life. Protecting you. Overseeing your dynasty until you become an adult woman."

"Am I girl or a boy, Mama?"

She let go of my hand. "What do you think?"

"I'm a girl, I know that, Mama. But why did Daddy call me a faggot? I never heard that word before."

"You're too grown. Don't give five cents to what that man says."

"But he's my Daddy, Mama. I thought I was supposed to love him."

"He doesn't love you."

I was sad. Her words confirmed what I'd been thinking since the wedding.

"He doesn't?"

"No, baby. I love you. I'll die for you. He doesn't love you."

"Why did he say boys play ball and don't have babies."

"Why does it matter? You're a girl, not a boy."

"Oh, yeah. Right, Mama. Well maybe I'm not pretty."

Mama said, "You're gorgeous!"

I was sad. I took one of her cigarettes and put it between my lips, like I'd watched her do for years. I took

Dapharoah69

her lighter and lit it. She sort of looked at me with a smile.

"You know what those are?"

"You smoke them when you're sad."

"They are called Cancer Sticks."

"Cancer Sticks?" I looked at it, the smoke going in my nose.

"Yes. They give you cancer. And cancer kills you."

"So why do you smoke what kills you?"

"Because we're all going to die from something. It's inevitable. It's the one thing God promised, that we will die. We will be judged. We will go to heaven or hell."

The Bible sucks, Mama. All the stories you told me and nothing is happening. God is in the sky watching people cry and hurt and experience their sisters taking their men.

"OK, Mama. You always talk of God but he makes everyone sad."

"No, baby. People make people sad. God loves us. He gives us what we ask for," Mama said, not believing her own words.

I looked at the cigarette then began puffing on it. But I choked so badly that I dropped it on my dress. Mama was laughing as I fanned at it, the tip burning my bare leg.

"It burns!"

She reached over and picked it up. She put them both between her lips and smoked them like a pro.

"Wow, Mama. Two of them?"

"Yes."

"Do all girls smoke?"

"Yes. It relieves stress. After having a hard day, girl, and you light one of these babies, you will feel the change."

"A change, Mama?"

"Yes."

"Can I ask you something, Mama?"

"Yes."

"What is plastic surgery? And why did you lie about me having blackouts?"

She slapped me so hard across the face I was in shock.

"Never call me a liar! I feed you, clothe you. I'm going through training for you, to keep a roof over your head. You kiss my ass, you little dweeb! You do as you're told or I will kick your ass like I whipped your Daddy's. Don't you ever ask me shit like that again?"

I was so scared that I clammed up.

She calmed down. "Plastic surgery is when you bake a cake and I give you a slice. You surgically cut a piece in geometric shapes and your tongue smoothes over the chocolate frosting. That's what I did to your face. So stop with the questions. And I'm going by the store so I can buy you something. My grandma used to slap me when I called her a liar. I only did to you what she did to me. There's nothing wrong with that."

I was really thrown. Sobbing, I looked at her and said, "So I have a chocolate cake face?"

She patted my upper leg.

"Yes you do. Now shut up and let me drive."

I never asked her again. *So you put sleeping pills in my food just to give me a chocolate cake face?*

Life wasn't as simple as I thought.

I continued to ponder the long drive. We were travelling so far away from home I didn't know what was happening. Mama played those medical tapes again. She was bobbing her head, reciting different things. I learned about the joints in the human body before the sun set.

She occasionally glanced at me but I didn't say anything. In fact, I looked away from her. I didn't know if I wanted her to be my mama or not.

I wondered if she remembered she was supposed to take me to the store. I had to pee, badly, but I kept it to myself and after awhile, when the clock changed from 7:30 p.m. to 7:31, I didn't have to pee anymore because I had pissed my pants.

It didn't feel good. In fact it was hot against my skin.

The burn mark had started to heal but the piss had left a terrible odor. Mama didn't mind. Or perhaps she just didn't notice.

Another hour went by and while the piss had dried up now my skin was beginning to itch.

The entire wedding replayed in my mind – I remembered everything. I was Daddy's best man. I was so proud to stand behind him, even though I didn't know what it meant. I just did what Mama had said, being obedient like the Bible states.

And then all hell broke loose. People gawked at me like I was an alien. Daddy called me a "faggot." My Aunt looked into my eyes and shook her head in disgust. People pointed and stared at me. The man who said he was my uncle turned his head and refused to look at me.

Mama jumped on my Aunt, trying to stomp her in the breasts. Frantically, Vanessa was being put on the spot, not believing her eyes.

Daddy was protectively hugging me. I felt connected to him, but after he started cutting my hair I knew I'd hate him forever. Mama had a gun! I never knew she had a gun let alone knew how to use one better than Clint Eastwood in the movies I used to watch.

Why did she shoot Daddy's and Auntie's picture off the wall?

Had they hurt her that much? Was the answer to pain a gun? Did you shoot at people when you didn't get your way?

Yes. Yes. And yes. At least that's what Mama taught me. My eyes were getting heavy so I lay back in my seat and smacked my lips, welcoming sleep.

Mama's medical tapes steadily whirled.

Tomb 15: Barbeques and picnics

When we got to Miami, Florida my life changed. My name was now Hatshepsut Sharp James. My Mama's name was Claire Sharp James and I was to call her "Avarice." I never understood the change in everything, but it happened and she got away with it. I didn't even know how to pronounce my name, but Mama told me it meant Queen of Egypt. I didn't know what Egypt was so she pulled out books and encyclopedias and she taught me about a woman that we had never heard about in school. And I gained a new respect for my black skin.

As I grew up I accepted the fact that I was her daughter. I believed everything she said. She didn't really bother me and I was well taken care of. The wedding had become a distant memory, yet when I would lie down to sleep at night visions of my father danced in my eyes and I would cry. Mama showered me with so much love yet I still could not forget the bad.

We went to church together and we were dressed as magnificent ladies. I was filling out. I had a huge butt and the boys loved it but my breasts didn't grow. I wanted breasts so badly I began to pray about it.

We went on trips, like to Disney World twice a year and we did mother/daughter things. This brought us closer. She taught me about boys and their bullshit. She told me don't give it up to the first cute face that comes across my radar.

She told me to respect myself and wait until I was married to have sex.

She told me she was my mother and father.

I believed her.

ξ

I hated my nose. I figured it was too big. I also told Mama I was going through puberty late. She only laughed and said she'd gone through it late as well.

"Don't be in such a rush to grow up," she told me. "Because when you do grow up you're gonna wanna be a kid again. Trust me."

We smoked cigarettes together and went to the movies together. She told me that anything we did in our home stayed between us, that you never put outsiders in your business because the streets were like crack heads. They'd smoke you, talk about you, sell you and bring you back to yourself a hundred different ways before the rooster crowed. I loved the way Mama used her words. She was quite the storyteller.

We weren't like the average mother/daughter. Mama talked to me about things, told me what was going on in other countries. She taught me about Rwanda and genocide. She taught me about great men like Nelson

Mandela and Martin Luther King.

"Those are real men," she said. "Your Daddy is a piece of shit."

"I got you."

She threw me birthday parties. My favorite one was when I turned thirteen. She dressed me in a huge ruffled dress, my hair up and swept from my face. She hired a photographer and all my friends from school came over. We danced and ate shrimp, lobster and crawfish.

For some reason I wanted to talk to Dad. Why hadn't he come by for my birthdays? Why didn't he send me a gift or a card? All my friends bought me gifts but I didn't have any from him or Auntie.

While Mama talked to the other parents I dismissed myself and went to her room, closing the door. I took her phone from her purse and I scrolled through the list of numbers. Hmm. I didn't know Daddy's name so I gave up.

But before I could put the phone down I saw a phone number with "Dead Beat" next to it.

"Could be Dad. Mom calls him that."

I called him and a familiar voice answered.

"So after all these years you decided to call me, bitch. Where is my son?"

I smiled so big I was about to die. Maybe he wasn't so bad! He missed me and I could hear it in his voice.

"Hi, Daddy! It's me! I'm 13-years-old today?"

He laughed so hard I laughed. We were happy to hear from each other.

There would be barbeques and picnics. My Aunt would come over and we'd be a happy family.

"It's you, Son?"

I blushed, holding my cheek. I felt gorgeous! "Yes, Daddy."

"You sound like a faggot!"

I stopped smiling.

"Oh my God! You sound just like a female. Nowhere in your voice is my son! What did she do to you? You are a boy! You are not…"

"Die, ok. I'm not a faggot. I am a woman and Mama said so. I am prettier than any girl in my school. You are miserable and I'm glad Mama crashed your wedding."

"Shut up, Punk!"

My blood boiled. "What did I ever do to you?"

"Look. I love you. I love you as a boy, as my son. You're my child so I have to love you. If you would have made the choice on your own then I would disown you. But your Mama is sick in the mind."

"Don't talk about her. She's more of a man that you are."

"And she's more of a woman than you are. I love you. I am taking her to court. I want custody of you so I can turn you back into a man. Go sell some drugs or fuck some Hoes."

"What's a Hoe?"

"That's what I'm talking about; you don't even know what men think. We always think about sex."

"What's sex?" He was confusing me. What was sex? I didn't know what that was, Mama never taught me that!

I didn't want to know.

Well, you can't take me to court to raise me. Mama said I'm her pride and joy, and wherever she is I will always be.

I hung up, and lay on her bed, sobbing into my pillow.

When I got home one day from school, a little after I had turned 15, Mama also told me I had a trace of sickle cell. She was clad in spandex grooving to Sam Cooke. Dinner was cooking, smelled like shrimp pasta. I was beginning to wonder was Sam Cooke the only type of music she had.

I was confused. "What is *that*, Mama?"

She smiled. "It's when you have deformed red blood cells." She wasn't too sure herself.

I was saddened. I sat my book bag on the table and looked at the back of her head. She was dancing, snapping her fingers and trying to clean the counter. "And you spring this on me now?"

"Yes. You're old enough to know." She handed me a bottle of pills. "Take these twice a day. I filled the prescription for you so I didn't have to drop it off at the pharmacy. That's one of the perks about having your own business. I know people who know people."

I looked over the small beige bottle. I didn't question it. I took the small pink tablets three times a day after eating breakfast, lunch and dinner.

That night I got on my knees and prayed to God.

"Lord, all the pretty girls have big breasts in school. And those pretty noses. Why am I so different? Why does my vagina get hard when boys come by? Why can't I be like other girls? Please, help. Amen."

I got in the bed and went to sleep.

TOMB 16:

Breasts

I awakened, tired as hell. Again, it felt like I had slept for days. Why did it always feel like that when I awaked? I could barely move. I tried to open and close my hands but it hurt all over my body.

I slowly blinked and turned on the light on my dresser. I looked around. I was unnaturally exhausted, like I'd been run over by a truck.

I looked to my right when I heard strange beeping noises. But what was it? I noticed thick hospital tape on my upper arm, and a needle in it. An IV drip, I knew what those were and what they looked like. I saw the bag with a design on it and different levels.

Then I looked down and noticed I had breasts. They felt sore. There was a huge bandage around them.

I smiled. "God looked out for me."

Mama came in the room. She was holding a chart, clad in a white lab coat.

"My daughter has awakened. Do you like your breasts?"

"Yes, Mama! How is that possible?"

She smiled again, picking up a mirror. She held it to my face and I noticed the huge nose was gone. I had a thin, feminine-looking nose. I rubbed it gently. I loved it.

"You asked God for it, baby. And he sent the answer through your Mama."

"I love you, Mama."

My voice sounded lighter, more feminine.

She kissed me. "I love you, too." She gave me a shot and I felt drowsy.

"Sleep, baby. And heal."

I blacked out.

Engulf me; Lord…I was provisional, uncertain…and hesitant. Watch over me; help me to understand all I didn't understand. Disputatious, I awakened. I felt refreshed, despite the soreness of my chest. Gone from my arm was the needle. I was free to move and roam.

My breasts sore, I walked over to the mirror, clad in a nightgown. Mama must have given it to me.

I lifted it up and saw my perky tits. Wow! They looked full and plump. My nipples were erect.

My hair was in a ponytail. I rubbed my nose. I smiled.

"Look out! Rosa is here and I am here to take your men."

Everything was perfect.

"I am finally like the other girls. I can officially be in their clique and gain the recognition from boys I always wanted."

A few days later I had just gotten home from cheerleading practice, and I felt faint after I ate the cake Mama gave me. My breasts were so sore I couldn't really practice.

I was on cloud nine because, ever since I had gotten breasts and a new nose, all the high school boys were after me. One of them asked me on a date and I declined. For some reason what Daddy said got to me, and I wasn't even thinking about it.

Boys don't date boys.

Well, boys date girls and I'm all woman.

My vagina always got hard. I just never expressed it to the boys or told them I found them to be cute. Mama always taught me that when you let a man know you were interested, they got besides themselves, thinking it was all about them and it was all about the next cute face. You flirted and you got to know more about them; you dated and you felt them out. Life was a big grocery store. Buy fruit as needed, buy meat when desired. You didn't necessarily have to spend your money. You could just go and find out if a sale was going on.

I liked my high school, located in Perrine, Florida. It was very laid back but could get live when it needed to be. I had a thing for the high school quarterback – a tall, gracious boy who seemed to have it all.

Holding a book on Queen Hatshepsut, Mama walked up to me. She said, "I'm going to work. Call me if you need anything."

"OK, Ma. I'm tired. So I'm just going to sleep."

"Make sure you do your homework."

I wanna read that book. I wonder if she would give it to me if I ask for it. After all, she named me after the Pharaoh.

"I will."

Mama studied me, softly squeezing my breasts "Are you feeling ok? You look a little woozy. Are your breasts settling in?"

"I'm fine," I lied, my head throbbing with pain. I couldn't even think straight.

I stood up and didn't know how I got to my room, but somehow I did and once I laid down, that was it.

I was out.

The next few weeks were pretty eventful. I was voted cheerleading captain, and I made a lot of female friends. We sometimes went out for pizza after football games and we talked about what boy was cute and who were players.

We got our hair done together and we always hit the Cutler Ridge Mall. A boy name Ridge was after me, told everybody he was gonna get me but I wasn't interested because everyone had had him already and I didn't do trash. I took it out every Monday and Thursday.

I hardly saw Mama. She'd come home, shower, eat, say a few things to me and sleep. She was slipping into a deep depression. She was letting herself go. She gained forty pounds. Her hair was falling out because she hardly showered.

She always stared at Grandma's picture before she went to bed.

I looked at it myself.

When Mama went to bed the next day I crept into her room and looked around. I started closing her medical books, putting up the journals and I pulled the cover up to her neck.

When I stood up I looked at Grandma's picture.

What's your story? I wondered. *Mama doesn't talk about you, Daddy or my aunt. In fact, ever since we left town with new identities Mama told me, as long as I lived, I was not to talk to or contact the man who left her for her whorish sister.*

I picked up the photo and looked at it.

I walked over to Mama's dresser and I held it up next to my face.

I looked somewhat like her. No big deal.

I replaced the photo and pulled out Mama's photo book. In it were pictures of my family during their younger years. I realized with a jolt it was the same picture book she once pulled Daddy's photo out of.

I had never cared to look in it. But today I had the

urge and I couldn't resist it.

I smiled when I saw Mama when she was eight-years-old. The photos were labeled with names and descriptions of what was going on.

My aunt was in another picture with Mama. They were in their teens.

The photo was labeled, "Rosa and Avarice."

I was named after my aunt Rosa.

Well, that was until Mama changed my name. I had an idea. When I went back to school I would tell my friends to refer to me as Rosa.

But I couldn't tell Mama.

I saw a picture of my aunt Rosa when she was about sixteen. It was a 5x7 close up and she looked arrestingly gorgeous! I hated to say it but she looked better than my mother.

I took out the photo, wondering where I had seen it before. I racked my brain, couldn't put my finger on it.

I walked over to the mirror, Mama turning over, snoring. Startling me, I put the photo behind me, and sort of paced the room, just in case she awakened.

When her lips trembled with sleep all over her face, I was back before the mirror. I held the picture up next to my face.

It was a perfect match.

I looked the spitting image of my Aunt Rosa.

ξ

Nothing seemed real to me anymore. Mama said for years I looked like Grandma, yet I didn't. I only believed her because I felt Mama would never lie to me about anything and she would never hurt me.

Why do I look like Aunt Rosa? I didn't look like

Mama. When I was younger I looked just like Mama and Daddy. From the picture I saw of Daddy I once had his cheekbones, nose and his eyes and forehead. I thought the older you got you looked more and more distinctly like your parents.

Yet I looked full out like Aunt Rosa. I wanted to ask Mama, but she was so busy performing plastic surgery on her clients at the office I didn't want to bother her.

But I knew one thing—

We were growing apart.

And I felt it.

In school I had to take sex education. I didn't really want to take it because my friends made jokes about the class.

"We already know women get wet and men's dicks get hard."

I was smiling at my friend Jane, a pleasantly plump sister from Portland, Oregon.

"Women get hard, girl. Men get wet."

She was laughing at me, patting my shoulder. "No, Girl. Women get wet, Honey. Down there in the flatlands. Men get hard, down there in the South Pole."

I didn't get it, but I had a feeling I was about to find out.

TOMB 17:
Mama's Room

Grudgingly, I watched Mama sleep that night.

I didn't even know she was home. I came in her room to borrow a bra because she hadn't done laundry and I didn't feel like doing it myself, since I was swamped with homework.

If I could be honest with myself I'd admit that something in my soul led me to her room. I knew in my heart that mother's room held some secrets…and I wanted to know them.

One of my friends in school once told me that if you wanted to know about your mother's secretive past then go in her room and snoop around. Take off your mental blockers and probe through letters, old notes from boyfriends, unfamiliar pictures, and the like.

So I used the bra as an excuse.

I was startled to see her. I covered my eyes when I saw a dildo laying on the floor, sheets barely covering the lower half of body. Her hair was like drunken angels in flight all over her plump pillow. The room was a mess. Her skin looked that of a fresh shower – I smelled the faint scent of soap.

She looked peaceful.

On the nightstand Grandma's picture was there to greet me, as always. There was also an empty cup. I had given her lemonade earlier. Thought I'd show my appreciation for her love and devotion and do something out of the ordinary.

I added my special touch, of course. Couldn't make lemonade quite like everyone else, mind you. I already felt myself growing into my own. To have my own individual thoughts and find my own voice in the world was the ultimate goal.

Mama didn't teach me that. I was tired of feeling like a eunuch. Everyone around me wanted to be my teachers, showing me this and that but rarely did anyone listen to me. I had a lot of hurt inside of me, like trying to understand my life story. Trying to understand why my Daddy hated me so much, even though he told me that how I turned out wasn't my fault. Then how was I supposed to turn out? What was I supposed to do and say? Mama taught me to respect my elders yet she couldn't respect Daddy and Auntie at their own wedding.

Being the age I was now, I knew why men and women married, at least according to another adult. But this one claimed God told him. These days everyone keeps saying God is going to tell them something…well, when is he going to tell me?

Attending Bible study in church every Wednesday night opened my eyes about marriage. It's a union between man and woman. Two people in love who want to devote themselves to each other. Yet, even with the vows that were read from the Bible, it didn't say man couldn't marry man. At least from what I understood. This country and their conservative views were just beyond understanding. They beat blacks during slavery, separated them from their families, raped and impregnated their women and hung them from nooses just to turn around and tell people who they could and could not marry. What a contradiction.

I was more aware of things now. Going to school and interacting with people your mother may or may not approve of proved to be the best experience a girl could have.

If I said the wrong thing to a boy my girlfriends corrected me. Never spend your money on him. Let him carry your books, your book bag and open your doors. If he had a car he better drive you home and keep his hand on his own lap. Don't give it up to him just because he has some money, a car or status on a sports team. Just because he's the star quarterback or the fastest runner or best basketball player didn't mean that translated to bed space.

Walking to Mama's closet I remembered when I went to my friend Susan's house a couple weeks ago and she put on a movie. When she pushed the VHS in the recorder I was all ready to watch it. I loved movies and didn't have the opportunity to always see them, even though Mom and I went to the movies when she had free time, which was next to never these days.

Susan was a short, pretty white girl with diamonds in her blue eyes and the softest blonde hair cascading down her back. Her jaw line was more defined than mine and she had big breasts. She made me look at my own. When she moved, her tits shook with fierce abandon.

Mine sort of just sat there. Like hey, Bitch. We're here. Sitting on top of two mountains, stagnated as hell.

Her parents were working and she said she was bored sitting at home, alone, with only her dog. I didn't like her dog. He always tried to snap at my ankles when I visited. I think it was a Boston terrier. Maybe it was, maybe it wasn't. Mama told me I wasn't allowed to go over other people's houses but I was getting defiant and learning to be rebellious. Just because she was Mama didn't mean I had to tell her everything.

So this was my eighth time coming over. I had on tight blue jeans, my "vagina" tucked between my legs and my hair long and curly.

"You'll love this movie," she said, giving me strange looks. I smelled her womanly scent in the air. It made my vagina hard.

When she pressed play two women popped on the screen, moaning and screaming obscenities. Both of them had flat, bushy "penises," like Mama. One of the black girls spread the other woman's "penis" apart and I saw pink, a hole and she was kissing around it, sliding a dildo inside her.

I felt uneasy, a stirring in my loins burning me into silence. I couldn't breathe.

"Susan. Susan, what is this?"

She was leaning over to me, my lips inches from hers.

"I like you," she said, giving me some tongue, like the girls from the video.

I had never kissed another girl before and I liked it.

She wrapped her arms around me and my "vagina" was so hard it came from between my legs and sat on my lap.

Susan pulled away and brushed my hair from my face.

"I like you, Hatshepsut. I'm going to call you 'Rosa.' I don't like your name because it's weird. I'm still confused. Never have I had a friend with so many names. But I like you."

"Hatshepsut was an Egyptian Queen," I said, the chemistry mounting like runaway horses.

"Really?" said Susan, taking off her blouse. She didn't wear a bra. Sliding out of her pants she said, "Can you do to me what the girl is doing on the video. I just know you'll be good."

She sounded so persuasive. Her body was a

magnificent work of art. I envied the tiny muscles forming on her abs every time she inhaled. Her long, slender neck reminded me of swans. Reluctantly, I got on my knees, slowly leaning towards her penis. I was breathing in short gasps…too afraid to touch her. But I wanted to do what the two women did in the video.

I spread her penis open, looking back and forth to the screen. But my "vagina" wasn't a "penis." I was confused. Why did the ladies have a penis and I had a vagina? Why did it look so different? I was a lady, even though Daddy claimed I was a boy, which was ridiculously preposterous

I kissed her penis and ran my tongue over the closed hole. She spread her legs, cooing into her pillow.

"I never received head before. I knew you'd be good. Make me shudder like the girls on the screen. Yes, baby. We can't tell anyone, this is between us. Yes. Push it back and suck my clitoris."

What's a clitoris?

She reached down with both hands, pulled her penis back and a small little thing was visible.

I guess that's the clitoris, whatever that is.

I watched the video. The lady was sucking on the clitoris. The woman on the TV said, "Yes, baby. Suck my clit…ah, yes, baby. Mmm, yea. Make Mama come."

Make Mama come? I'm confused. I don't wanna make Mama Avarice come. That's just nasty! I don't like these incestuous games.

I was out of control, loving the way Susan tasted. She tasted sweet and a little salty. I was using my fingers like the bimbo in the video and Susan could barely contain herself.

"I'm close. Oh my God! I'm finally going to get to come. Keep going, Rosa. Yes." Susan licked her lips and her body went into spasms.

"I'm letting go…it's here, oh God I'm Niagara Falls!"

Something shot on my face and her muscles were contracting in her penis. I was disgusted, as she rubbed feverishly at her penis, growing into a lustful monster.

Dapharoah69   169

When it was over she said, "Your turn, Rosa."

OK, but would I skeet like that?

I lay on her comfy pillows and braced myself. She added that special touch as an addendum to this sexual episode I loved. I was falling deeper and deeper. I had never kissed another girl before. Especially one with the same thing between her legs Mama and the girls on the video had.

Why was I so different? She crawled over me and we kissed. Our heat rose and spiraled towards our bodies. The way she touched me was well thought out. It didn't take a fool to realize she must have planned this because no one woke up and wanted to kiss another girl.

How long had she fantasized about me? While I kissed each of her fingers, how long had she wondered what I tasted like?

She unbuckled my pants and kissed my navel.

I lift my shirt and she reached up and touched my tits.

She pulled off my pants and I spread my legs. I couldn't stop them from trembling.

She closed her eyes and left a trail of warm, moist kisses from my left tit to my navel.

I was smiling. My vagina was so hard I couldn't think straight.

She ran her tongue over my panties and the party stopped.

She sat up, leaning back on her feet. "What the fuck is that? Am I seeing things? This can't be."

"What?" I asked, clearly lost.

She was shaking her head, steamed. Her hands on her hips, she glared at me. I felt her slipping away. What happened? What did I do wrong?

Deliberately, she stopped the video.

"Are you gonna suck my clit?" I asked and she laughed at me so hard I felt foolish.

"Clit? Clit? Bitch, what you got rhymes with clit."

"What do I have?" I wanted to die. I felt the walls

closing in on me.

She looked to her left, sighing. She was shaking her head.

"You got a penis," she said and I knew she was lying because Mama had a penis and it was bushy and looked the way the penises looked on the lesbians in the video.

"Penis and clit doesn't rhyme, OK. And secondly," I said, sitting up, "I don't have a penis, you have a penis. Mama has one. The girls on the porno had one. I have a vagina. Thank you very much."

"Talk like a girl but…Oh, well."

She crawled on top of me and I lay back down. I didn't know what she was gonna do but I felt her grip my vagina and lower herself on it. I felt warmth; the way I slid inside her body gripped my throat and opened my eyes wide.

It felt so good, I couldn't explain it. I was speechless, laying here while she grabbed my tits and rode me like life depended on it.

"Oh my God, Susan. I never knew another girl could feel this good."

"Might as well," she cooed, as I felt the jitters throughout her taut body. "I can't let a good penis go to waste."

I held her hips, my torso coming alive. Tears falling from my eyes from the pleasure, I cocked my legs open, something bouncing between them. I didn't know what they were but Susan gripped them, winking at me.

"Wow, Rosa! You got some good stick," she said. "I'm about to come again. Real soon."

I closed my eyes because something was happening with me. I couldn't explain it but I felt it, getting hotter and hotter. It was building from what she gripped between my legs. It traveled my vagina and it felt so good I moaned out loud.

"Susan…Susan!"

"Are you about to come?" she asked, holding my tits.

"I think so."

She rode me faster, making me grab my hair.

She abruptly crawled off me and it spurted from my vagina, straight in the air, across my abs and tits.

Some got on my face.

Susan licked up every drop of my confusion.

And now I was deep in Mama's closet, turning on the lamp. I was going through all her papers. I was careful to put them back the way I found them.

I didn't find anything worth reading.

A bunch of dresses color coordinated by style. Shoes and pumps neatly placed in little niches.

Filing cabinets with medical bullshit were behind me. I wasn't interested in that, bad enough she drove me crazy with medical tapes.

I replaced everything and turned off the light. I was discouraged.

I then opened Mama's drawer to get a bra. I noticed a small black book. Picking it up, I figured it to be the Bible. So, attempting to put it back it fell on the floor and it turned out to be a diary of sorts.

For some strange reason (call it curiosity) I stuffed it in my back pocket, and got a red bra.

I could wear my red Prada outfit and matching heels, my red bangles and probably put a rose in my hair. I noticed that many girls in school didn't accentuate the hair with flowers.

So I would set the tone, since I was considered the Best Dressed so far.

Closing the drawer, I walked past the nightstand and accidentally hit my toe on it.

"Ouch!" I whispered, the picture falling on the floor. The wooden back came off it.

Damn. I didn't need to hear Mama's mouth. So I got on my knees, my hair in my face and picked it up.

A folded note was behind the picture.

I put it in my pocket along with the diary. I would read it. I replaced the picture, put it back where it belonged and kissed Mama's cheek.

I closed the door on my way out. She would be sleeping for a while.

I had crushed sleeping pills in the lemonade.

A few weeks later, after one of the best pep rallies I'd ever been to in the school's gymnasium, my friends became involved in a heated argument. We were sitting out under the huge oak tree in back of the school for our lunch break. We always hung out here.

I was still thinking about Susan because no one had heard from her. She hadn't been to school. We tried calling her but got no answer. I told myself I would stop by and check on her.

"I don't like gay men," said Henry, a fat, chubby boy from the Circle Plaza Projects.

"I don't, either," said Javier, star of the basketball team. He had a huge crush on me and had told me so several times but I remembered what my friends had told me. Just because he was the star didn't translate to bed space. So fuck him.

I was laughing, "I can't stand them, either."

"You feeling me, girl?" said Veronica, slapping palms with me. She pushed ponytails from her hair. "Any man kissing a man is wrong in the eyes of God."

A jolt shooting through my body, I grew pensive and quiet.

But I'm Mama's daughter. I'm a girl.

Right, Lord?

Ryan, a friend passing by, got in our business. "I feel you. That's why I can't stand faggots."

Faggots!

Faggots!

Daddy called me a faggot. Lord, am I about to find out what that is?

"Faggots?" I asked, shaking my head. Veronica was sipping her soda, laughing.

Ryan bit the hook. "Faggots are men who fuck men. Boys who kiss boys are a sin against the human race. That's what a faggot is."

I closed my eyes so tight I heard cracking in my ears. *Then why does it sound so vulgar?*

Daddy called me that. Was I a man kissing a man? No, because I played around with Susan and it felt good.

She's a girl like me.

So that means we're lesbians.

Yeah, I was sure of it.

When school was over, Mom was out front waiting on me.

She hugged me and took my book bag.

"Hey, baby. You look so good."

"Thanks, Mama."

"Are you ready to go home?"

"Yea, but first do you mind taking a detour. I need to find out something."

Mama opened the car door for me. I waved at my friends and they waved back.

I got inside; put on the seat belt and she closed the door.

When she got inside she turned the key in the ignition.

"So where are we going?"

"Just a few blocks away, Mom."

The medical tapes started to play. "That's not telling me where I'm going," said Mama, a little bothered. She didn't like surprises—she never had. Hell, it took her a moment to drink the lemonade I'd given her. I didn't think she was going to drink it, but she did and minutes later she was out on her ass.

I thought about the diary then. And the letter. I had yet to read it.

"We're going to Susan's house."

Mama's brows rose with curiosity and suspicion. "The

white girl?"

"Yes."

"Cool. I know them well."

I kept quiet. She knew them?

"How do you know them, Ma?"

"I performed plastic surgery on her mother a month or so ago."

"So she has a chocolate cake face, too?"

Mama shook her head at me, putting the car in drive. "Yes."

"Oh."

Weird.

"I have a new nickname for you. It has more meaning than Rosa. Why did you want me to call you Rosa? That's my sister's name. I don't like that name. You don't like Hatshepsut?"

Hell no! "Yes, I do," I lied. "But my friends can hardly pronounce it and don't know who she was."

"Then you school them."

"OK."

She turned onto U.S.1, traveling south. There was a lot of traffic, and it was hot as hell.

"But your new name is Maatkare."

I looked at her. "*Maatkare?*"

"Yes. Maat means Truth. Ka means soul. And Re means Sun god."

"Huh?"

She was laughing, running her hand through my hair. She loved my hair and I loved her attention, but in the back of my mind I still wondered about the lies.

I was glad my hair had grown back. But I still had questions. Why did she give me plastic surgery?

I knew it wasn't to turn my face into chocolate cake.

That worked when I was a child but my awareness of the world changed.

"Together your new name means Truth is the Soul of the Sun God."

"Mama, I don't know about this."

She snapped on me. "You don't have a choice. I just moved my rook two up and one over and took your Queen. You will do what I say. I know what you want and what you need. I'm sure you think that just because you've developed and you're going through puberty doesn't mean that suddenly you know more than me. I had you. You didn't have me, girl."

"Ok, Mama…"

She calmed down. Hatshepsut had changed her name to this, according to the history books. *Maat* is the Egyptian expression for order and justice as established by the gods. When she changed her name to this, she solidified her status as King of the Throne, as a pharaoh who could talk to the gods."

I don't care Avarice. "Interesting."

Mama turned onto Susan's street.

I wanted to see her again. After we were together I thought about her, but I didn't really dwell on it. I was used to people entering my life only to leave without warning.

My heart pounded when Mama stopped in her drive way. I smiled when I noticed the door opened.

My vagina hardened imagining me deep inside her. Feeling her move, watching her come had become an addition.

I got out of Mama's car and walked up the house. I shook my head when I realized the house was empty.

Susan and her family had packed up and moved. And she didn't tell me good bye.

I told you. People always walk out of my life. Why does life play such tricks on me?

Am I not to share my life with friends and family? I can't talk to my father and I can't talk to my aunt.

Why, Avarice?

Why all the secrets.

I swear…I will find out one day.

Good bye, Susan…I love you.

Yes, I do.

You were the first woman I ever slept with. And it was magical and incredible!

You have fire I have never seen before and I hope you think of me and know that I love and appreciate you for making me a woman.

I love you…

TOMB 18:

Sex. Ed.

Sex Ed.

Honestly, I don't know why I came to this class. I knew all there was to know about Sex Education.

Susan taught me that I was a lesbian. That it was perfectly fine to kiss another female and "come" together.

I wondered why her family moved. Didn't Susan love her friends, especially me? Hadn't what we shared bonded us?

My teacher, Mr. Drake, a gregarious S.O.B. walked to the front of the class. "Open your text books to Tomb One: the Male and Female Body."

This was the official first day of Sex Ed. I looked around and noticed all the boys ready and willing to learn.

"Hey, girl," one of the boys called out to one of my female friends. "When we finish with all this wanna fuck?"

he asked naively.

Disgusted, she said, "Grow a pair and we'll see."

"What's a pair, girl?" I asked her.

She leaned to my ear. "Nuts. Testicles. Men have them between their legs."

I was shaking my head. "Sex Ed. Is gonna be so confusing," I whispered, thinking about Susan. She had reached between my legs and grabbed that weird pouch-looking thing when she was riding my vagina.

One of the cute boys, Kenny, looked at me, kissing at me.

My vagina got hard.

See there, girl. I told you women get hard and men get wet. He's wetting his lips now, staring at me like he wants something.

I was sure of it.

Javier walked past my desk and dropped a folded note on it. Mr. Drake was running his flap. I opened the note and it said:

I like you.
Do you like me?

I shook my head, taking my pencil and writing "HELL NO" as big as I could.

I looked back at him, his homeboys snickering and handed him the note.

I faced the teacher with a smile. I opened my text book to the requested page and I looked over the male body.

The minute I did my mouth fell open. I could hardly breathe, the air catching in my throat.

Silently, I put my head on the table.

"Hatshepsut!" said Mr. Drake, with an attitude. "Pay attention. Don't sleep in my class…"

I couldn't. The room was spinning. I didn't want to be

Call Her Queen Hatshepsut   180

in school anymore. Suddenly I feared education. Mama always taught me that knowledge was in books. I believed her because I couldn't recount a time her nose and face weren't in a medical book or a good romance novel, despite books on Egypt and Africa being hidden in the dark, hidden corners of public libraries. I always saw her reading something and that instilled in me an interest in reading. But I was so caught up in school, boys, cleaning up the house and doing homework that I didn't have much time for reading.

I was reverted back to when I first took a shower with Mama.

"Mama, what are those?"

"Breasts," she said. "You have them, too."

"Why don't they stick out?" I asked, careful not to get the plastic cap covering my perm wet.

"Because you're a child."

"And what is that?" I asked, pointing to the bushy area of her hips.

"A penis."

"A penis, Mama?"

She smiled. "Yes."

"And what do I have?"

She pinched the little thing hanging from my groin.

"A vagina…"

"The male has a penis. Also, if you pay close attention to the picture, the urinary track runs through it. Hanging from the male body is the scrotum sack. In it are the testicles, which store sperm. Sperm aides in the conception inside the female."

I could hardly pay attention.

And what do I have?

A vagina.

"Now turn to the female body…" said Mr. Drake.

I was afraid to turn the page, as the truth washed over me, knocking everything Mama taught me to hell.

I wasn't the same. She'd lied to me. But, why? Why

would she?

"Females have breasts, as exhibited in diagram A. Women also have a vagina, and you can read for yourselves the different parts."

"And what is that?" I asked, pointing to the bushy area of her hips.

"A penis."

"A penis, Mama?"

She smiled. "Yes."

She didn't have a penis! She had a vagina! And I had the penis! I feel like such a goddamn idiot. But, why, Mama? Why did you mislead me, and teach me these life-altering things?

I closed my eyes, my heart pounding.

I thought back to Susan and me. Having sex.

She sat up, leaning back on her feet. "What the fuck is that? Am I seeing things? This can't be."

"What?" I asked, clearly lost.

She was shaking her head, steamed. Her hands on her hips she stopped the video.

"Are you gonna suck my clit?" I asked and she laughed at me so hard I felt foolish.

"Clit? Clit? Bitch, what you got rhymes with clit."

"What do I have?" I wanted to die. I felt the walls closing in on me.

She looked to her left, sighing. She was shaking her head.

"You got a penis."

I thought about the wedding, when Daddy cut my hair.

He was pulling pins from my hair. "Son, listen to me…You have a dick. Not a vagina. You are supposed to like girls, not men. Your Mama's a psycho!"

He stood up, reached behind the podium and grabbed scissors.

Like a monster he started chopping off my hair.

"You are supposed to enjoy sports, play ball if you choose to. Date women, have a family with a girl. Men don't have periods and they don't bear children."

I BELIEVE WHAT MAMA SAYS!

Call Her Queen Hatshepsut

I BELIEVE WHAT MAMA SAYS

I exploded so thunderously, I startled everyone. "I BELIEVE WHAT MAMA SAYS!"

My classmates were very quiet. Javier slowly stood up, observing me. Now he would think I was weird. I felt weird, like I didn't belong.

"Mama would never lie to me! I mean, sure, she had her reasons for lying. She had to have her reasons."

My teacher was shaking his head and my friends were looking at me with weird expressions. There was a mirror behind me. I was looking in it, lost within myself. Just like that my life had become a maze and I couldn't find the start or run towards the end because when I thought I saw the end it was the start and behind the start was blackness. Nothing made sense. How could I get out? How would I break free?

Clearly embarrassed, I jumped to my feet and looked at myself in the mirror which stood beside the classroom door. A few people jumped up and ran away from me like I was a monster. But it didn't bother me. Run, people, run! I was a monster. Halloween had come early and I was about to scare the daylights out of them. My hands trembled with fear. My heart beat with trepidation.

I had to scream it again. "I BELIEVE WHAT MAMA SAYS!"

I took my hair from the ponytail and popped the rubber band. I took off my high heels and threw them at Mr. Drake, torn to pieces.

Daddy was right!

DADDY WAS RIGHT!

"Oh my God! My Mama created a monster! She lied to me!" I rushed up to my confused teacher and snatched him by the tie.

"Don't you understand?" I was sobbing so hard he couldn't make out my words. "I wasn't supposed to look like this!"

"Young Lady…" For some reason he hugged me and

held me and I was weak in his arms.

"Mama lied to me! Why would she? You know the one thing about Karma?"

He asked, "What?"

"It comes back…to fuck you…"

"Young lady!"

"No, it's young man!"

Javier was behind me. He looked concerned.

"Hatshepsut. My Rosa. What is wrong? Tell Papi, I am here for you. Who hurt you? What did your Mama do to you?"

I pushed Mr. Drake into Javier. They both stumbled and fell to the floor. I picked up the chalk and wrote, in big letters:

She changed her name to solidify her status.

<u>Maatkare</u>

Truth is the Soul of the Sun God!
Call her Queen Hatshepsut
Not Rosa, you bitches!

Tomb 19:

Your Majesty, Herself!

Distraught, I fled the class. I was running down the hall, tripping over my clumsy feet. They were failing me. The floor felt uneven and I needed the earth to be flat so I could analyze things and be aware and learn and ascertain the truth. If the sunlight was sunlight then damn it, don't try to teach me it's the moon like Mama had done to me. She ruined me.

She destroyed me but why? Now I knew why! She used me to get back at Daddy and my aunt. This was all about her sick need for revenge.

She lost her mind when my aunt stole my father from her. She couldn't live without him and she didn't want my aunt living with him. I sometimes heard my friends telling me about this—that when their parents divorced their mothers used them to hurt their fathers.

Now I felt stupid. My mother had done this to my daddy. Only she hurt him psychologically. I couldn't imagine how he felt realizing his son has long, curly hair, tits and wore dresses and low-heel pumps. That must have burned him alive.

Now I couldn't blame him for reacting the way he had. Mama made a fool out of me and him in front of the family.

But why would she name me Queen Hatshepsut? I thought about it as I ran to the school library. I rushed past a few horny boys and started up the aisle, looking for the "History" section.

When I found it I thumbed through all the books, my breathing coming in spurts. I didn't see a book on her so I snatched an encyclopedia and sat on the floor, opening it. I thumbed through the H's. When I finally saw her picture I started reading, baffled at the information pouring into my eyes and registering in my brain. She dressed as a male pharaoh. She was really a woman.

I read about her reign being erased from history by Thutmose III.

Was it out of jealousy or was it out of spite? He uttered things about Queen Hatshepsut he wouldn't say to her face if she'd been alive.

Why did he wait until she perished to destroy her statues, memorabilia and paintings? Queen Hatshepsut was his step mother and aunt.

Back in those days it was a common practice to marry and screw your sister, half sister, mother and wife and have secondary wives.

Queen Hatshepsut failed at one thing in life, despite her appointing herself king of Egypt the way Napoleon crowned himself king of France. She needed a son to one day ascend to the throne but she was destined to have a daughter.

The building projects in Egypt during her reign were some of the most elaborate in Egyptian history. Two 100-

foot tall obelisks at the great temple complex in Karnak
were created. Each of them weighed 450 tons. Eight
hundred and fifty oarsmen manned 27 ships to tow them
along the Nile River.

*So what about the obelisks of my heart? The fact that Mama
didn't need 850 oarsmen to tow my ignorance to hell crushed me.
What about that building project? Mama reconstructing my face to
look like someone who wasn't me had me completely confused.*

Closing the book, I remembered Mama at the
wedding:

*Tell your son good-bye. He looks nothing like you, does he? He's
gorgeous! He loves wearing dresses and his hair in curls.*

*No, Mama! You lied! You brainwashed me! I didn't know how
a boy was supposed to be. You reversed it all! You tried to play God!*

I had to get out of here. I ran out of the library like it
was on fire. Security appeared out of nowhere and we ran
into each other. I fell to the floor and the stocky man
slammed into the locker. I jumped to my feet and I ran
down the marble hall.

I rushed out the front door, and down the steps. A
few people noticed and said, "Are you OK?"

"No, I'm Frankenstein, bitch! Get away from me!"

I rushed past the trees, and onto the football field, the
scorching sun beaming on me.

I hated the skin I was in. I wished I could burst into
flames and die. I didn't want to be on this vile earth. All
the signs were there. I used to pride myself on being able
to put two and two together, yet I couldn't solve this
puzzle before sex education class?

*A little girl! He is a girl! For years I raised him as a girl! I
taught him that he has a vagina, that one day he would meet a man
and they would marry and have children. That he have his first period
when he was about 13. I taught him about pads, because I didn't
want him sticking tampons in his pussy until he was 18!*

*That period never came, Mama. It was to NEVER COME!
Why did you destroy me? I wasn't born your daughter! I was your
science project! Your experiment!*

Dapharoah69   187

I fell to my knees, sobbing into my hands, remembering Daddy's wedding.

My child will be a pretty ballerina! He starts classes next week. So much for football, huh, you poor thing? You and my sister can have each other! Fuck your wedding; I turned it into a funeral!

I never got those ballerina classes, you were too busy studying your medical books and worrying about the success of your business. And when we did have time we went to Disney World. I remembered Snow White got mad because I was prettier than her and wanted to wear her costume.

I started digging my acrylic nails into the earth, pulling up clumps of grass and dirt, soil falling into my hair. I was a demon possessed.

You pit Grandma against me! She died thinking I actually cheated on my boyfriend. Her last words to me were, 'May your life be filled with whoredom!'

Was this about getting back at Grandma, who was clearly lied to by Aunt Rosa? Why did my Aunt lie? Did she want my Daddy that badly?

Daddy looked at Mama. "Where is my son? You know I wanted him to be my best man?"

Vanessa pointed the camcorder at me, frowning.

"Your son is here," said Mama, pointing at me. She walked out into the front row and up to Daddy.

My aunt dropped the bouquet and snatched the veil from her face, glaring at me.

"That's not my son! This is a little beautiful princess-of-a-girl clad in a light lavender dress, low-heels and curly hair pinned atop her head."

Mama went in for the kill. "That is not a girl. That is your son. Isn't he gorgeous?"

My Aunt Rosa had heart failure, gripping her chest.

Daddy sank to his knees, taking me into his arms in a state of shock.

I held him, not quite knowing what was going on.

Mama looked at Aunt Rosa. "Doesn't he look like

Grandma?"

"You sick bitch!"

I lay on my back, screaming into the sky. I was losing my mind. I didn't want anything or anyone anymore! The sun might really be the moon. The color red might really be the color green. Cars might really be called Greek gods. A horse might really be a leopard. Hatshepsut was Rosa, and Rosa was, shit, what was my name before?

I couldn't remember.

Mama erased me existed from my family's history.

My life was a mockery.

Mama used me to get back at Daddy and Aunt Rosa. But what do she got to do with this? Sure, she took Daddy from Mama but there was something here I didn't see.

What was it?

Someone snatched me off the ground. I noticed it was the police.

"What is wrong?" a tall cop asked me, trying to restrain me.

I was out of control. I didn't want anything touching me. Why didn't people just leave me alone?

"GET OFF ME! LEAVE ME ALONE! LET ME GO!"

I was kicking and spitting and screaming.

Another white male teacher grabbed my legs.

"PLEASE STOP!"

A huge crowd had formed outside the school.

Towards the end of Queen Hatshepsut's reign, she had a second pair of obelisks erected.

One of them read:

> *Now my heart turns this way and that, as I think*
> *What the people will say.*
> *Those who shall see my monuments*
> *in years to come,*

Well the world was watching, Mama. How do I confront you? What should I do now? Should I continue living my life as a girl or do I live my life as a boy? I was so confused I didn't know what to do but I had to do something. Oh yes, mother dear! YES, BITCH! I had to do something. The people were marveling at your creation. They see the bizarre monument you made of my life – even at the wedding they spoke of what you had done. You were my Thutmose III. After I died as a boy and became a woman you destroyed my existence. You erased me from human history. You had fake birth certificates drawn up, fake social security cards and all.

My school papers were fabricated. It was like I was never born. You bought me dolls to solidify my coronation.

You changed my name to seal the deal. You bought me purses and wigs to concrete my insolence. What kind of woman does that?

Now my friends and enemies will speak of what you have done, for years to come.

No respectable man will ever want me. I am the generic brand of a woman. I am a caricature of my mother's design.

All those medical books and tapes she listened to were my enemies.

They schooled her, told her how to recreate me, told her how to destroy me…Mama had me thinking I was having blackouts when in actuality she was putting me to sleep and doing her "internship" on my body. She gave me breast implants. The horror of it all made the earth spin and I was suddenly nauseated.

Like Hatshepsut, *I am Your Majesty, Herself.*

Tomb 20:
Birth Certificate

A few of my friends rushed up to me and said, "Leave her alone!" in my defense.

"She didn't do anything wrong!" shouted Thelma Louise, a chubby girl with two chins.

"Let her go! Rosa, we're right here!"

I was reaching out for Veronica. "HELP ME, PLEASE!"

Hector, Veronica and Javier protectively grabbed my arms and were pulling me away but the police officer wouldn't let me go. He was yelling and barking orders and no one paid him any attention.

"Leave her alone!" Javier shouted. He was getting angrier by the second.

The cop put me down and I hugged Veronica.

"What happened, girl? Who hurt you?"

I was digging into her shoulder, crying so hard it felt like my body was in flames.

My Aunt Rosa, lying on the floor of her wedding, told Mama, "You're crazy. Why..."

Mama said, "Don't worry yourself. You have a wedding to attend, even though I messed it up. He looks like Grandma, doesn't he?" You could see the hurt on Mama's face, the betrayal of my aunt and father she fed from.

Mama sat next to my aunt, and leaned over. Her lips were a few inches from my aunt's right ear.

"I used Grandma's photo on my nightstand when I performed the procedures from my bedroom," she whispered. "...My son actually thought he had blackouts. No..." She was laughing again, people looking at her like she was Satan and I didn't appreciate that because anything my mother did for me was out of love and I understood that. "I always gave him sleeping pills when I fed him. Then I used gas to put him to sleep. I have an EKG machine in my closet I use to monitor his heart. He doesn't remember a thing. I have the manuals all around my bed and floor. After all, I did my internship in there..."

Mama changed my face. I didn't have blackouts. She drugged me then used a gas mask. She did the same thing the night I prayed to God and asked for tits and a new nose. She played God! She must have overheard me; that's the only other answer. She did her internship in her house using my body. Why would she do this to her own child? Why, Mama? Why would you do this? Why did you raise me to think, act and talk as a girl? Did I really have sickle cell? What were those pills I've been taking? The world suddenly changed when I realized that my own mother didn't love me.

I do know that every time I took the pills my voice sounded more and more feminine. I knew in my heart I didn't have sickle cell.

I just got my answer.

She had been making me pop estrogen pills.

GOD!

When I got home, the cop said, "Are you OK?"

I didn't want to respond. Too much was happening too fast and I didn't know how to deal with it. What did I do now?

"Yeah, Man. I'm fine," I answered sarcastically, barely looking at him. I looked a mess. My clothes, ruined. I was the talk of the school. Some people said I was raped. Others didn't know what to think.

Kissing my cheek, Veronica sat next to me and Javier said, "Want me to pour you something to drink?"

"I'm fine," I said, looking across the room in the ceiling-to-floor mirror. I was disgusted with myself.

Avarice did all this to get back at Daddy. To erase his lineage from my face was her mission and she succeeded.

The cop said, "Where's your Mom?"

I hated hearing her mentioned. "Working. She'll be home soon."

"We need to talk to her."

"Well, just come back. I don't want you here right now. I just wanna be with my friends."

"I can respect that. I'll be back."

He tilted his hat and was out the door.

Javier said, resting his hand on my knee. "What happened?"

I stood up and said, "I'll be right back."

Resolute, I closed Mama's creaking bedroom door and slowly looked around her paradise. Where did she keep her important papers? An eerie sense of curiosity washing over me as I cautiously opened the closet and searched for a filing cabinet. There were legions of pants, dresses and shoes all over the place. I didn't find what I was looking for.

Mama would kill me if she found me snooping through her room. She told me umpteen times to stay out when she wasn't home, that she had all sorts of medical stuff I couldn't tamper with. Up until now I listened. Now I needed answers and I had to find them.

Something told me to look under the bed so I did. I saw a huge cardboard storage container. Pulling it out, I opened it and saw papers neatly stacked all over it.

Bingo!

I looked through the papers, looking for one thing in particular.

When I found my birth certificate I looked it over.

Mama had her name signed.

Daddy never signed his.

Why didn't Daddy sign the birth certificate? What was going on? God, please help me. I am so confused. Am I weird for how I turned out? Was this all my fault? All the Bible stories Mama taught me neither one involved a man dressed as a woman. She taught me about Adam and Eve, Peter and the whale and Jesus feeding the thousands. But what about a mother raising her son to be a girl, brainwashing him into thinking he is supposed to grow and live life as a woman. Was it right for Mama to use me to get back at my Aunt and my father?

I slid the container back under her bed.

I opened Mama's nightstand drawer and saw a few credit cards and one of her I.D.'s.

I took the VISA and the I.D. and I stuffed it in my pocket.

TOMB 21:

Javier

I put on some regular low-heeled shoes and cleaned my
face.

"Rosa, are you ok?" Javier asked from the other side
of the door.

"Yes," I said, brushing my teeth.

I heard the door open and he came inside, closing it.

I was a little uncomfortable. I just wanted to be left
alone. Maybe I was being selfish. These people clearly
loved me and cared for me and just wanted to make sure I
was fine.

"What do you want, Javier?"

He walked up to me, clearly concerned. "I like you,
Rosa. I'm checking on you."

He had soft blue eyes and a very sexy body for his age.
He had short-length hair, and looked like a Spanish Fly-

type of guy, mixed with black.

I turned off the water. "Just leave. You and Veronica have done enough. Thank you."

He hugged me and I felt good in his arms. He leaned back and kissed me and it was the first kiss I had ever shared with another man.

My body responded, my "penis" getting hard, pressing against my panties.

He was rubbing my ass, squeezing it.

We both could barely breathe.

"I've always wanted you," he said, admiring me. "You're so beautiful, like a rose. I always play with myself thinking of you. I want to know how you feel and how you taste…"

"Javier…no…It's not right! I'm not ready…"

I was scared of his touch. He kissed me again, holding me, fumbling in my panties, sticking a finger inside my rectum. It was very uncomfortable and I wanted him to stop!

"I want the ass, baby. I hear you're a virgin! You're mine. I'm going save the pussy for when we get married and you make me a man."

I started breaking out in Goosebumps.

God please help me! Why are you giving up on me? Haven't you let enough people hurt me?

"No, Javier…I'm not ready."

I didn't convince myself.

He turned me around, pulled my panties down and ran his tongue all over my butt cheeks. I cooed with delight, trying not to laugh because it tickled.

He spread my cheeks and buried his tongue, slapping my ass and I held the sink, gyrating on his lips.

"This feels so good."

"You like that, Ma?"

Ma. I'm not your Ma. I don't even love my own mother right now. She lied to me and gave me breasts. Men aren't supposed to have breasts. Why did she do this to me? Didn't she love me?

"Yes, Papi…"

He was able and willing and he wasn't about to let me go. I didn't think I was ready for this, I always dreamed about it. In my mind, with the false security Mama planted there, I was supposed to grow up, marry the man of my dreams, have his babies and live my life. But men couldn't have children. Men aren't supposed to marry men, or are they?

"Ready for this dick?"

I want you, Javier! But not like this! I gotta figure myself out! I have things to think about!

"No, Papi. No. I'm not ready!"

He picked up the lotion bottle, squirted some between my butt crack and massaged his finger into my tight hole. I gyrated on it, never feeling pleasure like this in my life. It felt so incredible, my body aching for his passion and his desire, despite the conflict in my heart.

He slid up in me and I yelped. He pulled me to his lips and gave me some tongue, pushing himself deep inside me. I was stunned. It hurt so bad I couldn't do anything. He was pounding it inside me, possessing me, looking into my eyes.

"I love you, Mami."

Then out of the blue the pleasure kicked in and I started to respond. My dick was so hard it fell from the panties and pressed against the sink.

"You are so tight, Mami! You gonna make Papi come?"

"Yes, Baby…" I was lost, knowing I would love this forever. Javier was my first. He was a gentle man who came in my mother's bathroom and took it from me.

"You want me to come inside you?"

I was gone. "Yes, Papi!"

His tongue slithered all over my face. "You gonna have my kids? You gonna be my wife?" He put a foot on the toilet, getting up deeper in me and he leaned back, spreading my cheeks and I felt him throbbing, I felt the hot spurt on my walls. I loved it and I yearned for him. The way he moaned my name and breathed on my neck drove me bananas. I had my head lowered, afraid to look in his eyes. He pulled himself out of me, falling to his knees, panting with a Cheshire cat smile on his face. I wasn't smiling. What just happened here?

Sadly, I pulled up my clothes and knew I had to get out of here. Everyone I loved was violating me and it would keep on happening if I didn't put a stop to it. I had to run; I had to leave before Javier fell deeper in love with me. Before I fell deeper in love. Before I did something like slit my wrists. I loved Mama and she hurt me a million times over. Why didn't I show more self-control? I lost my virginity with Susan and now with Javier. I loved them both. I loved Susan's warmth all over my penis. I loved Javier's throbbing member inside the Senate of my Cabinet. I should be on cloud nine, but that was before sex ed ripped Mama's lies apart.

"I love you," he said, taking me into his arms and kissing me. I cringed inside, wanting him to let me go. "I want you. Marry me, will you be mine. I will die if you let another man touch you…"

"I'm already dead!" I told him. "Do me a favor, Papi." I kissed him, misleading him. "Can you and Veronica go home? I just need to be alone. Call me later. Maybe we can make love again soon."

He gave me some tongue. "I would love that, my future wife."

He caressed my ass.

"I love you," he said, and closed the door behind him.

TOMB 22:
Two things

I opened Mama's bedroom window and crawled out, leaving my friends in the house.

I ran down the street wearing Mama's coat. I hopped on the county bus, paid the fare and I wrapped the jacket around me.

It was cold. I had two things in the coat pocket:

Avarice's Diary.

And my great-grandma's letter.

Part 4
Labyrinth

*For all have sinned; all fall short of God's glorious
standard*

Romans 3:23

*No one is good—
Not even one*

Romans 3:10

TOMB 23:
The Dusty Diary:
AVARICE JAMES:

Dear Diary,

In Port-au-Prince, Haiti, I was born Avarice James back in the 1950's. My life has been a series of gaps and loop holes. Perhaps that is why I have always fancied jigsaw puzzles. Because I got to piece together a touch of heaven, I had the opportunity to piece together something I'm not. I was never a family-oriented woman. In fact, I hadn't ever had a whole family ever in my life. To be brutally honest I don't even know why I'm writing in this diary. Because I am so far gone within myself that it's crazy. I've always felt crazy. I realized that when I fabricated my childhood. I was never attacked by dogs. My mom was never married to a man named Miles. I hated my earlier life in Haiti, I hated when Mom relocated to Jacksonville…so I conditioned myself to believe the fake story I'd made up. Believing my story made me feel like I had actually survived something. In my mind it made me a hero. Young girl survives brutal attack. Girl, almost mauled by vicious dogs, LIVES! This filled me up beyond comprehension. Saying it to myself made me feel better about life. The more I said it the more I believed it. It actually played out in my head like a movie. In fact, I never even met a man named Miles. The thought of my late mother getting married to a man with that name was sheer lunacy. I have yet to rectify the lies I've told in life. For some reason I have always been attracted to Egyptian literature. Out of all the Pharaohs and Queens I was fixated on Queen Hatshepsut. I stumbled across her by accident. I had gone to the market place in Haiti, when I was four-years-old and I remembered helping Grandma carry some tomatoes, which were on the border of spoiling.

In the scorching sun, I was walking down the street, Haitians dancing and doing what they do. Some scantily-clad women were propositioning other males. A few vehicles zoomed by. Grandma held my hand tightly.

I saw a ripped page by a cracked concrete slab. "Grandma, that looks like a picture. Can I get it?"

"Hurry, Child."

I handed her the tomatoes and I walked over to it. The top portion of the magazine page was there. On top was Queen Hatshepsut. I looked it over, going back to Grandma. She took it and looked it over.

"Who the hell is that?"

"I don't even know how to pronounce it," I said. I would show my sister when we got home. She was with one of the church members back at Grandma's bungalow.

I would grow fascinated with Queen Hatshepsut. And the more I learned about her the more obsessed I became. I redefined my life and based it on hers and walked around pretending I had the blood of queens.

This brings me to my son. I am taking out my fears, my anger and my bitterness on my child and he doesn't even know what's going on. Was it my place to tell him? A child should think as a child and do what he was told. But why was I dressing him as a girl? I will get to that later, diary. Just be patient. By the time I am done he will be the prettiest girl in the world! I wonder what his father will think.

My own mother had raised me that way…to do as I was told. As long as I danced to her puppet strings life was good. But if I or my identical twin sister did anything outside of that she viciously attacked us with extension cords and thick leather belts with spikes on the buckle.

The little time she spent in my life wasn't good. Those moments were peppered with salt that stung my wounds whenever I think about her. I try to tell myself that I love my son when in fact I don't. I didn't feel any attachment to him. I knew the reason why but chose to ignore it because it was painful and sinister and so evil not even Satan wanted a part of it.

Earlier in my life, when I first heard him cry and I first changed his diaper, I had a maternal attachment to him because I thought his father was coming back to me. I know I had ulterior motives. I had done something unspeakable in an act of revenge but it was becoming impossible to hide the truth.

Surely having his child would seal the deal. Certainly knowing that a woman carried his child to term would mean so much so I built all these expectations around the man. I would do anything he said. I was his slave. If he wanted it cooked I cooked it in heels. If he wanted it washed I washed it with my tits bare. If he wanted his pussy morning, noon and night I gave it to him willingly. I remember when I found out I was pregnant. I was ecstatic. I kept it a secret, I didn't tell anyone but my sister Rosa. Even though my sister and I weren't close, I even told her around the time I was going to try to get pregnant. I told her my time of the month for my period and she told me it was around the same time of the month for hers, which wasn't surprising.

I had decorated a baby room in my house. Being that I bought the house from a previous owner for little to nothing (because he had a divorce with his wife and he didn't want her having it so he sold it to me for a whopping $45,000, which I gave to him through the scholarships and loans I was applying for since I was in college) meant I had room to spare. I bought blue shirts and little blue pants; I bought a baby bed, playpen and little mirrors. While the baby furniture was being delivered, I had the delivery men set it out in the living room while I painted the room light blue. Helping me was my jealous sister, who tricked me into thinking she actually cared. I knew in my heart it would be a boy because, while I was going successfully through trimesters, I felt his strong kicks and my night sweats. I was losing my hair and my ass stuck out and I just knew.

I wore bigger clothes so no one would suspect. I gained about thirty pounds, so I was at 145, which wasn't that bad. I didn't go around people very much anyway. All I had were my studies, my sister and the man I loved.

I would go to my check ups with the doctors and my boyfriend was right by my side, holding my hand and offering his precious smile. I remembered when my sister came in the room to offer her love and support and it was like Kayak was hit in the stomach with a boulder. My sister and I had on a tight plaid shirt and loose-fitting coveralls. Her hair was swept away from her face like mine and we wore the same earrings. I was smiling, reaching for her hand. Reluctantly, she took it, kissing my lips. We have never dressed alike before and I wondered why she decided to do that now?

"You have an identical twin sister? He asked in disbelief, shaking his head.

"Yes," I said and Rosa smiled, shaking his hand.

"Nice to meet you," Rosa said, staring deeply into his gorgeous brown eyes.

He barely touched her skin.

Grandma knew I was pregnant, I could hear it in her voice whenever she called me but being that I was out of her loony bin of a house and on my own, I felt I didn't have to explain myself to her and I hadn't.

For some strange reason my sweet love Kayak would tell me he was going to the bathroom, or he had something to go and do and I always let him because I never believed in tying a man down, especially when God made them without anchors or harbors to keep them there. I never thought anything about it, as I sat in the hospital lonely, going through mood swings and anticipating the arrival of my baby boy.

When I got home I was tired. As my belly swelled my ankles started to hurt or burn and my thighs would ache and I would call Kayak and he told me he'd come over but I wound up eating fruit, cooking more food than I should and eating myself to sleep. As long as my son was healthy then I was ok. I would clean things that didn't need to be cleaned, dusting shelves that didn't need dusting. I busied myself. I closed myself off from friends. I cut back on working so I could sit at home and care for my man. After all…that's what a woman was supposed to do I thought.

I would want to smoke to relieve stress because when Kayak did come over he would be tipsy or his clothes would be worn out, like he had a hard day at work and sometimes he did. He worked for a landscaping service.

One night, when I was in my sixth month of pregnancy, he drunkenly stumbled into my home, since he had a set of keys and he crawled next to me. He smelled like cologne and beer, which was intoxicating, and I was in pain. In the darkness I was laying on my side, silently whispering to my boy that his Daddy was handsome, strong and dependable, even though he hadn't really done anything dependable since I've been pregnant. He had been mostly missing in action. When the toilet broke he didn't fix it. When there were weird sounds in the house at night he sent me out into the living room and when I came back in the room, upset, he'd hang up the telephone and tell me his cousin needed some advice.

His tender hands caressed my ample buttocks and I responded with a fluid, "Hello, Baby…"

His beautiful lips inches from my right ear lobe, he pressed the product of his nature against my buttocks and he was grinding on me like two pistons and I reached back, cupped his head and we shared a kiss, staring into each other's eyes. Even in the darkness his eyes glowed like glow bugs and I loved the dreams I had when I found myself lost in those pupils. But something was different about him. Something died in his eyes.

His hands found the front of my night gown and he slowly undid each button, his breathing increasing. He was pressed so hard against my ass I could feel his dick throbbing, even the satin of my gown responded from his touch and his urgency to have me and to hold me and to show me how we made this baby in the first place.

He trailed his fingertips down to my thigh and he raised the nightgown, while, with his other hand, pulling down his pants. He gripped the right ass cheek, spread it and he used his rod to slowly and softly tease the back of my dripping anatomy with his bulging head.

"I just wanna slide it in you and sleep holding you close."

"I want that, too," I said. "Your son needs to feel your love."

He was showering the side of my face with tender

kisses, messing up my make-up. I didn't know why I didn't clean my face before bed time, but when you're barefoot and pregnant and trying to go to school for a medical degree, you shunned the norm and got with the new.

He slowly slid his ten inches into my softness and stopped halfway, my body squirming from the pleasure. I always loved how he drove his stick shift.

"You are so hot!" he gushed with zeal, pulling out and using his index fingers to wipe my pussy off his dick and he sucked it off his fingers then he yanked me by the hair in that thuggish way I loved, the type of gestures used to control your woman, and he stuck his fingers in my mouth, watching me as he slid back inside me, this time giving me all his mama and daddy had given him and he tagged it, making my cheeks jump with joy. I held his head, still sucking his fingers, his dick filling me up like water in a tub.

I loved moments like this, when I was reassured that he loved me. That he wanted the best for me and his son on the way.

He was loyal when he wanted to be.

He held my tit and leaned back, lifting my nightgown higher, and he sort of climbed on top of me, lowered pants, unlaced boots, dusty brown hat, opened work shirt and he crawled all through my pussy, giving me orgasm after orgasm. I felt him shudder. He moaned into me ear, the little growls that set a bitch on fire. "This is my pussy, baby. I wanna shower our son with my come."

He started to pound me a little more quickly and harder, arching his back and gyrating his hips like a male belly dancer, hitting the folds of my pussy in ways I never existed.

I had another orgasm.

"It's pulsating on my dick, baby, I feel it contracting, the wetness. I love it."

He started giving me passion marks all over my neck.

"I'm about to come. My son will feel our love."

"Come inside me baby."

He gripped my neck, pressed down and grinded his dick inside me as I felt the hot spurts of a man eager to love me, scared to truly commit to me, eager to possess me.

When it was over he lay next to me, stroking my hair. I refused to meet his eyes. I rest my head on his chest and I fell asleep a very happy, confident woman.

When I awakened the next morning I felt revitalized, like I wasn't pregnant at all. I was rubbing my tummy. I spoke to my son, barely opening my eyes. It took a while for the room to come into focus.

My sister stood in the door way.

She was clad in her fancy dress, bangles and her hair with a lot of weave down to her calves, like a superstar.

"How long have you been here, watching me sleep?" I asked, sitting up. She handed me a cup of coffee. Never had she done this. I sipped it appreciatively.

Rosa put her manicured hands on her hips. "Long enough to know that you must have had an awesome night." She smiled slyly. It was contagious. I smiled.

"Yeah, something like that."

"So how are you? I haven't seen you since you got pregnant. And when I call you're always doing something for Mr. Kayak Burke."

I smiled then, remembering him. I could smell him on my sheets. I kissed my arm and tasted him. It was very soothing.

"I love him." I looked at the clock. "I need to get up and get the house tidy. I'm sure he wants dinner tonight."

My sister stood there smiling. Her eyes lit up.

I stared at her, wondering what I was missing. "What, Rosa?"

She said, "You really don't notice?"

I looked at her. The high heels were extraordinary. The gorgeous legs, that seemed to grow from earth, were breathtaking. The jewels dangerously glittered. I didn't wear all that jewelry. In contrast with my sister, she was elaborate, I was simple.

I looked at her belly. My mouth fell open.

"Oh my God! I'm in shock." I was sitting up and she rushed over and helped me.

"Thanks, Rosa. You're pregnant?"

Fresh tears fell down her eyes. "Yes. I am."

"How many months are you?" I asked. "And I called you and told you I was pregnant. Why didn't you tell me about you? That's not fair," I went on, kissing her lips.

"I'm six months pregnant, sis."

I was looking at her even more fixedly. "So am I."

The news of my sister being pregnant didn't sit well with Grandma. I came home a week or so later and I rushed through the front door because I heard the smoke alarm. Smoke was pouring out of the living room, and my eyes were burning. Oh, no!

I ran into the bathroom, wet a towel and covered my face. I picked up the phone in the living room and before I could dial 9-1-1 I saw Grandma putting a pot in the sink, coughing.

I hung up the phone, relieved to see her.

"Grandma, what's wrong?"

I kept my face covered, trying to figure out how she had gotten into my house. Since she was my grandma, good or bad, and despite how she had treated my sister over the years, she was always welcome.

"I was trying to cook chicken. And I sat on the couch watching TV and I fell asleep and next thing I know," she went on, her clammy skin full of sweat, "the smoke detector started buzzing and all that carrying on and I was startled, thinking the house was on fire."

I hugged her, the cold tap water cooling off the burned pot and chicken.

Dapharoah69

I opened every window from the dining room to the kitchen, and I opened the back sliding glass door.

"There, Grandma. It's all right. We'll order something to eat."

She was stern, as she always had been. "I like to cook meals, they're healthier."

She took the green rag from her head and huge dreads fell to her ass.

"I know, Grandma. And how long have you been in Philly? I thought you were back in Haiti, with your life and your new husband." She looked at me and for some reason I felt like I was being sized up.

"My new husband is not a regular occurrence. I use him to fix things around the house and that is about it. And my plane landed a few short hours ago, when I learned your sister was pregnant."

"I'm just finding out myself."

"So she kept it a secret, like you did from me?"

"Yes, Grandma."

"The last time I was here, a few months ago, I knew *you* were pregnant. The younglings can't fool the elders. We've been there and done that. I birthed your Mama, remember? But why keep it a secret?"

"I don't know, Grandma. I just didn't want to make a huge announcement because I'm not married to Kayak and we haven't even talked about it yet so I'm having a bastard child."

She sat at the table and looked at me. "You were always my favorite. I always treated you differently from how I treated your sister."

The smoke was clearing out so we could breathe easier, even though remnants of burned chicken hovered like an unwanted house guest.

I sat next to her. I cupped her hands. "I know I was your favorite."

Grandma wasn't looking her healthy self. Her face was sagging and her eyes looked sad. I watched how she moved about and she seemed to be in a lot of pain. She always held her left hip and her lips had a twitch I hadn't noticed before.

"Your Mama has been dead for years."

I felt uneasy, knowing what I knew about Grandma and my mother's sour relationship. But since I was so young at the time I never questioned it and as I got older it was hard to care for a woman who put others before her own daughters, so there was some bitterness and resentment there I couldn't control or deny. It was hard to believe in a woman who was the town harlot. Seemingly every man either tasted her or bedded her and that never sat well with me because as I grew older I wanted an understanding of why she felt the need to give her body to men at will. Hadn't her body become her temple?

Grandma inhaled, wide-eyed, and walked past me. Her brown and purple dress smelled old, and her sandals were worn from time. She must have had those sandals for twenty years. She refused to buy a new pair and even when I did a few years ago she set them on fire in her backyard.

"Why do you bring up Mama?" I asked, my brows rising. I toyed around with the salt shaker.

Grandma pushed her dreads atop her head without much effort. "I am hearing rumors." She tied them into place.

"About?" I was shaking my head. I didn't feed into rumors.

"I heard rumors about you having the tastiest piece of pussy in Philadelphia."

My mouth falling open, I stood up, holding my belly. My doctor had advised me to avoid stress or I might my baby and my stress level had just soared to new heights.

My heart pounding, I said, "The tastiest pussy? Are you insane, Grandma?"

She reached over and picked up her frail-looking cane. I hadn't noticed it before.

"No. I'm not making this up. Even when I came here

to your home men in the neighborhood stared at me like I was crazy. One of them mumbled, 'That's the slut's Grandma.'"

"Who could have said that? What is his name? Where does he live? I am dedicated to Kayak; he is the only man for me."

"Does he love you?"

I looked at her. "Yes he does. This is the father of my baby and he wants to be with us."

"Does he spend time with you?"

Not really. "Yes, when he's not working."

She was scrubbing the cane on the floor, looking at the tile. "What man works that many hours, Girl? You are reminding me of your mother. She used to make excuses for being a whore and from what I can see…" She looked up into my watery eyes. "You are the second coming of Jezebel."

I threw the salt shaker at her and it smashed into her chest. "How dare you come in my home and curse me." I couldn't believe my outburst, but it had happened and I wasn't backing down.

She seemed unfazed. She brushed salt from her garments and said, "I am a strong woman of noble character. I can't be touched. And I have never been a harlot."

"No," I went on. "Just a murderer who has been roaming God's earth for years and never jailed."

She laughed so hard I got nervous. She intimidated me.

"Kayak doesn't love you. Hell your sister doesn't even love you. Better yet, ever since the rumors surfaced your sister has sort of changed for the better. Gone are her whorish ways. Gone is the defiance. She is in school."

"So am I."

I didn't know my sister was in school. This was news to me.

"You used to call me once a day. You hardly call me

now, running behind Kayak. Rosa calls me daily; she makes sure I take my medicine on time. She has even flown to Haiti to check in on me. When was the last time you been to Haiti?”

I wasn't trying to get into it with her. There was still a level of respect I tried to maintain with her, since she was my elder and I wanted her in my son's life. “I have school and a life. And how did you get in my house?”

“We all have individual lives, but you don't forget the hand that feeds you and you don't bite it because Karma will knock your teeth out. Guess what karma does, girl?”

“What, Grandma?” I was feeling small and inconsequently inside my own home. I was supposed to be the Queen Bitch in here.

“It comes back to fuck you. That's what it does. Karma knows all and does all. It does what your dreams and nightmares can't do.”

“Who cares? Karma and I don't care about each other and I am growing weary of this entire conversation. Now how did you get in my goddamn house?”

Her grip tightened on the cane. “Easy. When I was over Rosa's house Kayak gave me the keys.”

I couldn't believe this. He gave her my keys? And what was he doing at Rosa's house? “I have to talk to him about giving out my keys to anyone.”

“So is it true?” Grandma asked, looking at me. Gone was the warm way she used to talk to me. Gone was the face lighting up the room when I appeared.

“What?”

“That half the men in this town have had you?”

“No!”

She was outraged. “Why do you lie? I have looked at your body, even *before* the pregnancy. Your tits are plump and your ass is full. You know a woman doesn't get a body like that unless men are putting in overtime redirecting pipes through your sewage of bullshit!”

Dapharoah69   213

I'd had enough. *This bitch has got to go! And now!* "GO TO HELL!"

She put the hook of the cane on my neck and snatched me to her face. I fell on my knees, pain shooting through them and I felt it in my womb. I felt my son kicking ferociously.

I couldn't move. She leaned into my face, her teeth greenish brown and her breath foul.

"May your life be filled with whoredom!"

Grandma spat in my face and stood up, slapping me with the cane. I fell on my back, pain shooting through me.

I thought about my baby.

She leaned over me, pressing the cane on my left tit. She put her dirty sandal-clad foot on my belly, without pressing too hard.

"Harlots shouldn't deliver babies. Don't you know God punishes the evil seeds through their children?"

I feared for my child's life.

"Please, Grandma. My child didn't do anything to you."

She softened because she had a soft spot for babies.

"I know he didn't. And you need to think about this. I spent money raising you and your sister. I fled Haiti after my late husband was killed and I provided for you in ways your mother couldn't. I cared for you, put you through school, stayed up endless nights chastising you and teaching you womanly things. Never have I been a whore! Never have I brought men around you. You were the poster child. Even your sister hated you. She always wanted what you had. She always competed with you. Being identical twins didn't help matters."

"Grandma…" My lips quivered. I hadn't slept with anyone but Kayak. So who was making up these lies against me?

"Before you ask me I'll tell you who told me you were a whore."

I couldn't wait. "Who?"

"Do you really have to ask? Isn't it obvious?"

"Who?"

"Your flesh and blood. Your sister."

I closed my eyes.

Her games would never stop.

ξ

I was surprised she helped me off the floor. She handed me two pills and some warm water. I was hesitant to take them. I shunned the pain, convinced that I was ok. I was a tough cookie, I couldn't be broken down.

I had hate for my sister She was just here a week or so ago giving me coffee. I had thought that was a friendly, sisterly gesture. I should have known there was more to it.

She was baiting me. She knew Grandma was coming and she knew what she'd told her. Why was she doing this to me? Why had she always hurt me in unnatural ways?

And why was Kayak at her house when he gave Grandma my keys?

I splashed cold water across my face, more confused than ever. I didn't know what to think about anything.

Grandma forced a kiss on my lips. I cringed when she touched me.

The love was back, or so I thought. Her eyes glittered. I fell inside them, the little girl I used to be when she was my world.

"I'm leaving. Your keys are on the table. I'm going over to Rosa's. Remember what I said because I mean it. You are nothing but a whore! Just like your mother!"

She slammed the door behind her. I leaned against it, sliding down to the floor and sobbed.

My sister had finally succeeded in coming between my Grandma and me.

The bitch had won!

Dapharoah69   215

Guess what karma does? It comes back to fuck you.
I looked up, wiping my face.
"And it's going to fuck you good, Rosa!"

Several hours went by and I sought to destroy myself –
drinking alcohol. This wasn't good for my baby but I
needed it, anything to make me forget what had just
happened.

I smoked a few cigarettes, stressed out. The sound of
the TV stressed me. Hearing my own breathing stressed
me.

My phone rang and I didn't answer. I had a bone to
pick with my sister but I decided to let sleeping dogs lie for
now until I was ready for the fight.

A few days later, after getting home from intensive
study at school, I saw one of my neighbors looking at me. I
waved and he said something to his wife and they waved
back.

I walked up the sidewalk, holding my back. I was
drained, having studied the different human joints and
being quizzed on it.

When I got to his house he kissed my cheek.

"Was that your Grandma that visited you a couple
days ago?"

"Yes."

"Nice lady."

"You talked to her?"

"Yeah. She liked the suit my little boy was wearing.
She walked over with her cane and introduced herself."

"I didn't know that."

So she's making friends in my neighborhood. For
what?

"There's a rumor going around that I'm letting men
have sex with me," I told him. He seemed uneasy. Clad in
his county uniform, he took off his hat. "Did you hear
anything like that?"

He gave a half-assed smile. "Yeah I did. My wife, too."

"And you didn't tell me? I thought we were friends?"

"We are. Plus you're always in school. I hardly get to see you. And when I do I'm doing something with my family. Plus I'm going through financial hardship. I had to take on a second job because I may lose my house."

"I'm sorry about all that. But why are people making up rumors?" My feet hurt and I really needed to be getting home.

"I have a confession to make."

"What would that be, John?"

"…I told your Grandma you were a slut."

My mouth fell open. He took a few steps back, like he wanted to run to the opposite end of his car.

My hands were fists. I wanted to kill him.

"You *what*? So you stabbed me in the back by making up lies?"

He was shaking his head. "Well, I was paid to lie."

This was unraveling too fast. I rubbed my belly. "Paid to lie?"

"Yeah. I and every guy on this street were paid to lie and say we've been having sex with you."

"This has *got* to be a joke. Who would pay you to do something like that?"

He lowered his head, taking off his hat.

"Your sister, Rosa."

I went home, and slammed the door.

"This bitch has gone too far."

I had ample opportunity to confront my sister but I didn't. I concentrated on having my baby. I already felt guilty for allowing myself to start drinking and smoking. So I stopped doing it and started eating healthier.

I didn't sweat the rumors anymore. They were what they were and I was a grown woman. I didn't have to justify anything I did. Jesus was sent to earth to die for the sins of man. My name was Avarice.

Kayak stopped by from time to time and I never talked to him about giving Grandma my keys. I just didn't want to be bothered and I didn't feel like talking. Plus he had a nasty temper and I didn't want to upset him. We sometimes had sex, giving him pregnant pussy, and called it a night. He was the same tender-turned-ferocious lover in the bed.

He then told me he wanted to marry me when I had the baby, buttering me up with flowers and candy and gifts. I fell for the charm and I believed him. I told him Grandma thought I had been cheating on him and sleeping with the neighborhood. He told me he knew better. He knew I would never give of myself like that.

At least somebody believed in me.

He started working more and more every day. When I called him he didn't answer the phone. When I went by his job his boss said he was there but he couldn't talk because he was on the clock and personal shit needed to stay home. I would smile and thank the Lord I had a hard working man who wanted to care for me and his son.

So I would cook for him, getting dolled up. I'd do my hair and paint my nails and look real skimpy for him. I know his son wanted to feel him inside me to cement our love but he never showed.

I started calling Kayak even more. Days would go by without our having spoken. One particular Sunday I called him to see if he wanted to go to church and he answered. I heard heavy breathing and the phone hung up in my face.

A few minutes later I called again and he didn't answer. I was getting angry. What kind of relationship did we have? I was about to have his child and I had to sweat him for attention. I had the nagging feeling that he didn't want me and part of me couldn't forget the fact that he once gave Grandma the keys to my home while he was at Rosa's house.

When he did call me, which was rare, he would say he

was busy working around town…I told him that it was fine, that when he found the time come by the house and see about me and his son and he told me he would. Sometimes he did come. My son was named after him, even though I would *never* tell him his real name when he got to an age he could remember it.

By the time I looked up I was deep into my ninth month of pregnancy and I went into labor when I was in the shower. I was so stressed something popped in my loins and the baby was coming fast. Controlling my breathing and holding my belly, my water broke and I smiled. I was about to have my child.

I staggered to the phone but before I could call him Kayak waltzed through the door, smiling. He was holding roses, looking as gorgeous as ever.

"Baby!" Alarmed, he dropped the flowers and I told him I was in labor. He picked up the phone and called someone and told them I was in labor. He was giddy; I fed from it, despite the pain.

He was telling someone our baby was being born.

I felt special. Speaking into the receiver, he said, "Baby, I meant Rosa, she's in labor! I'm, going to be a father!"

And he hung up the phone.

Quietly, he sped in his truck to the hospital. I was trying to control my breathing…huffing and puffing, holding my tummy. I felt like I was on fire and it wasn't a good feeling at all.

Parking in the emergency lane, he put the truck in park and carried me inside. One of the nurses ran up to me and a doctor ordered that I be taken to the delivery room.

I was so happy. Kayak was right by my side.

When I got to the delivery room, he was clad in scrubs. He was holding my hand, telling me to control my breathing. I didn't want drugs or anything. I wanted to naturally have his baby.

As I started to push, the doctor moved between my legs. I squeezed my eyes shut, trying to force it out. Caked in sweat and blood, it felt like my body was being torn apart by Godzilla. This shit hurt and I screamed and breathed uncontrollably after each push.

My hair plastered to my face I pushed again, my pussy feeling like the bombing of Pearl Harbor.

I knew then I would never have any more kids. No, sir!

When my child was born I was laughing and crying, shaking my head. My eyes were still closed as the rest of the pain slowly subsided.

I had carried my baby to term. My man was right by my side.

I opened my eyes to see my baby. And I realized with a jolt I wasn't holding Kayak's hand.

I was holding one of the nurse's hands.

Now as I write in my diary, in tears, remembering giving birth to my son, I know that deep down I am angry. I resent Kayak for leaving my side. I didn't know where he'd gone and he wasn't there when I needed him the most. If I could dig deeper into myself, I think my son Kayak, Jr. was born gay. Because even when he was a little boy, when we shopped in the toy stores, he gravitated towards the dolls. So I bought his gay ass one.

What I absolutely despised was when my friends, simple-minded black bitches who didn't want to elevate themselves, would tell me what black women couldn't do—at least not without man. We eat fried chicken and we cut a bitch when pissed. I hated when I was generalized, and I'd been generalized my entire life by my despicable grandmother. She was always sweet to me as a child, read to me and bought me things. She treated my sister like the slut she was. Even at a young age my sister was always caught letting boys do things between her legs or jacking them off. She then fancied the older men, luring them with her curvaceous body and sometimes using my name when they had sex with her, giving me a bad reputation before I hit the tenth grade.

Of course during that time I truly believed in my sister. I cooked and cleaned for her. When it was cold in Philly I gave her my jacket. I slept with her and read her nursery rhymes. I treated her how Grandma treated me. I wanted to show her that her own flesh and blood sister could give her some heaven during her hellish days with Grandma.

And of course that was all fine and dandy, because I really believed in Grandma back then. She could never do any wrong. If she asked me to do something I did it quick, fast and in a hurry. And I made sure it was done right.

I used to ask her why she treated my sister differently than she treated me, and she told me, "Because she's evil. I can feel it."

Gone from her eyes was the love she had for me whenever I brought up my sister. She turned into a different person. Her words were rushed and forced and she snapped on me. It had gotten to the point where I stopped asking her.

Grandma never allowed us to go in her room. She said she had things in there a kid shouldn't see so she replaced the locks and put three others on her door with three different keys. I remember my sister and I tried to pick it. I used Bobby pins, bending them out of shape.

"We need to find out what's in there," she said exasperatedly.

I agreed. I could smell the oldness coming from inside. I was standing there, my heart pounding.

We couldn't get the door opened so I gave up. We had to come up with another way.

I didn't like or accept the fact that church was forced on my sister and me, just like life. Neither one of us had asked to breathe the air we breathed or eat the food Grandma cooked for us. My own mother, Pauline James, never did anything for us. Grandma didn't take too kindly to her whorish ways. But being in church turned my stomach. Looking at images of a white Jesus Christ didn't sit well with me.

"Who is that man?"

I said, "They say he died for our sins."

"What sins? I'm just a kid."

"I don't know."

Black folks jumping up and down, spitting, clapping and sweating wasn't cute. Praise Jesus! Hallelujah! Amen! It all sounded like a marching band and not morning worship. Women speaking in strange tongues and men catching them when they plummeted towards the mildewing carpet weren't setting the right kind of examples.

The pastor was a fat man who licked his lips every time he looked at me and my sister. One day we were clad in matching dresses with the same type of ponytails. Her dress was green and mine was red.

"He must have had some good gumbo, sis," said Rosa when we were about four-years-old. "Maybe Grandma made it for him."

"I know. He tastes it from his lips." I shook my head. He was sashaying back and forth across the worn stage like women lived in his hips, screaming into the microphone. Grandma was sitting behind him. She was one of the elders in the church.

Rosa was covering her mouth snickering. "But we didn't have any of that gumbo so why is he looking at me?"

"Maybe he's rubbing it in our faces that he had some and we didn't."

Rosa picked up one of the fans. "That's why he's fat. He needs to do something other than study Kitchen 101."

"And we're not fat..." We slapped palms, ignoring service, period.

Hadn't the church understood that they had lost me

and my sister with that picture of a white Jesus picture that contradicted the Bible's interpretation of who he really was, having hair of wool and feet of bronze? So why were we praising a blue-eyed demon with silk hair and clean garments?

After Grandpa Sylmar died Mama grew into herself, even though my sister and I were too young to understand why death made people sad and crazy. Mama loved Grandpa Sylmar. From what I could remember Mama used to always cook and clean for him while Grandma did her thing around the house. Grandma and Mama were close then, doing everything together. Mama was about 17 when she gave birth to us, and from what I could remember, Grandpa loved us from day one. Grandma wanted to hire a midwife, even though they didn't have the funds, to rid Mama of the baby.

But Grandpa, a very homely man, full of humility, wasn't having it. He wanted Mama to have the baby, to carry the bloodline, since he had never fathered any other children.

Mama was a very sweet lady who would do for others before she did for self. I guess she must have overlooked us because we hardly witnessed her affection. Yet when Grandpa died she put herself and her own feelings first.

Rumor had it that Mama had the best piece of pussy in town. She never talked about what she did and she never represented it through her image. She dressed in flowing skirts that hid her ankles and blouses that emphasized her gorgeous eyes. She had bangles and sometimes rubbed mud on the bottoms of her feet when wearing her shoes. Mama felt one with the earth. Women detested her and shunned her away from their men. She often received death threats but remained unfazed by them. She was more concerned with self than her children, and that grew in me. It taught me something, that when I got older I would do my child or children the same way.

I remember when I was a teenager, shortly after the

government had Grandpa slaughtered, and my sister and I were at the dining table eating oatmeal. It had been a very long day and our bodies ached because Grandma had us out in the scorching sun picking green beans and throwing them into woven baskets. Grandma always disciplined us like that, having us do housework. We were like child laborers.

Mama came in the living room and she smiled, with a towel tied around her massive breasts.

Her lipstick was smeared and steam erupted from the bathroom. Grandma was sitting at the sewing machine making our clothes for the day. It only took her minutes to make our little pants and shirts. She was very skilled at what she did. Sewing was one of her life's passions.

"Hello, my daughters," Mama said, kissing my cheek first. My sister Rosa glared at Mama and refused to take another bite of food.

"Mama," she said sassily. Mama tried to kiss her cheek and she wiped oatmeal on Mama's lips. "Why do you always kiss her first? Don't I look exactly the same?"

"Yes," she said, licking at the oatmeal. She yawned, stretching her arms in the sky while holding the towel and shaking her head.

"Then why does she always get the product of your lips?"

I looked at her because my sister spoke with a language far advanced then anything I would ever say.

Grandma looked over her shoulder with distaste.

"A young girl, barely out of the hawk's nest, is speaking with such auras of the tongue."

The needle stopped. Grandma's sandal-clad foot rose from the pedal. She stood up, pink and green material all around her. A huge green rag was tied around her luxuriously-long hair.

Rosa looked at Mama, defiantly. "I don't care what she says, Mama. Why do you always touch my sister first?"

I said, trying to keep the peace, "Rosa. I love you. You

can have the product of my lips. I'm your sister."

She pushed the bowl of oatmeal on the rugged brown carpeting. "I said you're lying! Why does Grandma always worry about the auras of my tongue? I learned how to speak with such fluidity from sitting and watching the elders in town at the local shops gossip about the goings-on in Haiti."

Mama sat next to my sister, handing her a doll. Grandma paused behind her, looking down with anger.

"Listen to her! She hasn't one iota of respect for her elders. She needs to be hanged from the tallest tree trunk in Haiti."

I looked at Grandma. "Surely she doesn't mean it? We're kids."

"Both of you have been watching your mother for too long," she exploded, snatching Mama by the hair and slapping her repeatedly across the face. "Your pussy drives you to destruction." Mama, screaming, was pushed into the sewing machine. "Maybe I should stitch it back together, since it never graduated from the class you so dutifully teach these sadistic men."

She grabbed Rosa by the hair and I grabbed her arms.

Grandma took a switch from her garb and begins whipping her.

"Trust the Lord oh God will deliver thee from whoredom. You will be the whore of Babylon recreated in thy house!"

"GRANDMA!" I was afraid for Rosa. Rosa didn't whimper. She didn't shed a tear.

Mama ran at Grandma and grabbed her, trying to protect her child.

Grandma was too powerful. She slammed the back of her body into Mama and she fell to her knees.

Grandma dropped my sister next to me. Rosa's tears flowed, but she didn't dare whimper.

"You are so quick to run at me, your mother, the woman who helped your father give you life, yet you can't

Dapharoah69

stop running as quickly to these men! You don't think I hear the whispers when I go to the market place, Gurl?"

Mama stood up, letting the towel fall.

"Get on the table, Gurl!"

Mama was defiant, shuddering where she stood.

"No, Mama."

Grandma grabbed the doll, wickedness dancing in her eyes. "You don't do what I say, Gurl?"

"Mama…"

Grandma said a series of chants to the doll, shaking it here and there. I hugged Rosa and Rosa stood in place, ready to attack her. She glared at Grandma without blinking.

"On the table, Gurl! You aren't setting the right example for your children. Both are identical twins. One will grow to be a whore; she studies the lip of the elders. The other will be fascinated with books! She will grow to become a force to be reckoned with."

Mama got on the table, using the cloth to cover herself. The bowls of oatmeal fell on the floor.

Mama was shaking.

Grandma paused in front of her and leaned down, picking up the oatmeal. She smeared it all over Mama's face and laid the doll on her womb.

"Any child you have will be damned to Hell. You have tasted the male flesh and swallowed what it produced. The seeds burn inside the belly of the whore and the protein rejuvenates your womb."

"Mama."

"You are to get out of my house, leave my grandchildren with me. I will raise them; I will see to it that both have a decent education."

"Mama, you can't take my girls!"

"LEAVE THE ROOM, CHILDREN!"

I took my sister's hand and pulled her, kicking and screaming to our room. I closed the door, holding her.

I heard a series of screams and chants. Outside our

home gusts of wind shook the house and rain began to fall. Thunder boomed and lightning lit up the entire room. I was afraid.

I heard Mama scream and then after a few minutes all was quiet. I sit there on the floor holding my sister who was scared out of her mind. Her body shook like earthquakes.

I cracked open the door with Rosa behind me, peeping. Grandma was at the table, eating some greens. Mama sat across from Grandma, looking into her eyes. Her body looked frail and her hands were flat on the table.

I looked closely at Mama when Grandma said, "I won't allow the whore to defile the family."

She looked into Mama's eyes.

I fell to my knees; screaming so loud Grandma was startled. Rosa held me, realizing with a jolt that Mama's eyes had been gauged out.

Mama was dead.

Over the next few years life was a constant blur. My sister and I were too young to understand the power of voodoo and I didn't care to know about it. Grandma became our entire life and we weren't ready for it but we didn't have a choice. I couldn't say that I missed Mama because she was never there, even when she was alive. I remember I used to wait up for her when I was two or three-years-old but she never showed. I sometimes had pretty flowers that I had picked from the neighbor's garden and I used my hair yarn to tie them together and I'd draw colorful pictures of Mama, Rosa and me and I'd fold it and put it in an envelope.

I then fixed Mama some cookies and milk. I'd sit in the living room, staring out of the window. But Mama never showed and after several months of this I grew tired of trying.

She was gone months on end. Rosa didn't care, she never lost any sleep. She was too busy trying to read a book, and hadn't a clue as to what she read. Rosa used to bring the books to me, reading and saying things that didn't match the words. She would have beautiful stories to tell but the book didn't match a single word she uttered.

The funeral was short and sweet. Grandma had it at her church. Many people came. The men who had slept with Mama showed up. My sister and I were clad in black dresses. Rosa sobbed and she refused to stop. I didn't shed a tear, I didn't feel anything.

Grandma said a few words of praise about my mother when she had been a child. She was the quiet, sneaky one. She didn't have brothers or sisters.

Grandma volunteered at the church. She was a devout Christian woman. In fifty years she had never missed a Bible study class, a sermon or a service. We had to go with her, but church really grew on me in a negative way.

As for Rosa, she would have rather stayed home and watched the tube. And I agreed.

My Grandma couldn't tell us apart. We had long, thick, unruly hair.

We'd grown a few inches, weighing about a hundred and twenty pounds. Grandma always stuffed our faces and what we ate always came out.

We then found out that with every meal Grandma laced it with laxatives, to help regulate our digestive systems.

Even during our studies, the boys were crazy about us. Rosa didn't like normal boys, yet when they spoke to me suddenly she wanted to talk to them, to take the attention away from me and at first I didn't care about it. But after awhile it really bothered me how she was in constant competition with me.

I really missed Grandpa Sylmar, even though we barely got to know him.

We were very young when he died. I briefly remember the pineapples he used to cut for me. He cut kiwis for my sister, never giving us the same fruit so we could have

Call Her Queen Hatshepsut

something that was just ours.

Grandma said the Haitian government charged him with treason, giving neighboring countries information about Haiti and its policies, since he was rumored to have worked for the government, and they had him butchered. Haiti was the first country to abolish slavery, from what Grandma said. After Haiti established its independence and a few countries tried unsuccessfully to conquer Haiti, Grandpa made a bold move in an attempt to make his family some money and it cost him his life.

He didn't receive a funeral or a burial. Grandma didn't have the funds. So his body rotted where he was killed.

When that happened, Grandma said she couldn't live without him and she tried to survive alone.

She hoped her daughter, who looked just like him would have grown closer to her and helped her get through it. But she took a liking to sex and that ended the dream.

So after Mama's funeral, Grandma packed up and we came to Philadelphia where I would one day meet Kayak Burke.

And he would become my life.

I would mourn a mother who had hardly done anything for me; the images of her funeral would become my nightmares and be the reason why I went to medical school.

I could have saved her if I was a doctor. So medicines, learning them and anything dealing with medicine, from TV shows and movies became my life and my drive.

But it was also in Philadelphia where I would join a Haitian gang of females—robbing, stealing and shooting to get what I wanted and needed.

Those females were like family, yet my sister Rosa was also one of the members. No one could tell us apart.

No one ever would.

At least that's what Karma said before it fucked you.

<u>Tomb 24:</u>

lakes, dams and oceans

I slowly closed the diary, overwhelmed and yet somehow relieved. The diary felt like flames in my lap but I welcomed the heat. I welcomed the misery. I welcomed my own discombobulating fears. My world was a topsy-turvy affair and there were no guard rails on this carnival ride for me to keep balance. I didn't want balance. I needed its cousin. Her name was "stability." Who was I fooling? I could never recuperate from the confusion. I would never look at Avarice or myself in the same manner I once had. What kind of woman performed plastic surgery on her child? What kind of mother would cause her child harm? What kind of woman would lie to doctors and tell them she didn't know why her child was suffering from blackouts? I knew why! The answer was simple. She had been DRUGGING ME! She turned my room into her

training ground, cutting and pasting my face like a
computer document. She recreated my face into that of a
woman I didn't love. A woman I despised. A woman I had
never met – my grandmother. Well, my great-grandmother.
I looked like her. I had her cheeks and her forehead and
her chin. I had her smile. I DIDN'T WANT HER SMILE!
I wanted my life. My real life – the life with which I had
been born. The life Avarice erased like Thutmose tried to
do to Queen Hatshepsut.

My world wasn't real at all. It didn't have thriving
continents and trees feeding oxygen into the atmosphere.
It didn't have lakes and damns and oceans and rivers
teeming with fish and other species. It didn't have cars and
trucks and houses and roofs and thatches. It didn't have
parades and carnivals and states and boulevards and
streets. It didn't have compassion and passion and
sympathy and empathy and apathy. No. My world was
blank. It was a dark blob and God hadn't said "…Let there
be light!" or "Bring land from my waters". He didn't rest
on the Sabbath day. He didn't touch my world at all. It was
a lump of clay without a shape. It was a blank canvas
sitting on Van Gogh's mantel waiting for colors and
strokes and mental stimulation. Genesis was anything but
friendly in my world. It was Omega without the Alpha. It
was the land of Job after he had lost everything. It was hell
without the flames. It was grimy without the dirt. My
world was a 500-page book without a cover, author or
editor. The pages were white as snow and blank as a
newborn baby's mind. The newborn doesn't know if it has
a vagina or a penis but somehow the child knew how to
piss with organ that he or she did not understand. That
was my world. CONFUSION.

In the blink of an eye my life had become public
fodder. My friends were speculating. My sex ed teacher was
dumb-founded. I could still feel his protective arms around
me. I really needed to be held when I found out the truth
in class. I didn't think he knew why he hugged me but I

was glad he did. I felt safe and secure. The police got involved. Everybody would now have an opinion of me. Did I care to hear what they had to say? Really, no. But part of me needed to hear what they had to say. I was hurting so deeply I felt like an oak tree had taken root in my soul. Did I even have a conscious? I had been deceived by a deceitful woman. And no one warned me.

No one protected me.

Why, Lord?

Sighing, I didn't know what to make of my life or my existence. I didn't trust anybody right now and I didn't know if it would ever change. I mean how could I be the same after this? Was I even old enough to deal with it? I wasn't even old enough to buy a pack of cigarettes or a beer. I really needed Mom to clarify things for me. I just wanted to crawl next to her, tuck my head in her arms and cry, cry, cry. She would stroke my hair and tell me to shut up the noise. She would kiss my cheek and tell me I was a gorgeous angel. She would turn on some music and dance with me, with her medical tapes playing in the background. She would tell me that everything would be ok. She would make sure of it. She would protect me. She wouldn't let anybody hurt me. But how could anybody hurt me as much as she had?

I was now on a Greyhound bus, heading for an unknown place. And it was this unknown destination that I needed to explore that had become my primary focus. I hoped this place would have the answers because I had very few. I was in serious denial about it all. I knew Mama wouldn't approve of me just upping and leaving town when I wanted to but she had deceived me so badly I had to take this trip. I didn't care what she had to say. I didn't care if she called the police and reported me missing. She could do what she wanted. She could die for all I cared. I had absolutely no feelings towards her. Something inside of my heart died when my teacher revealed to me that only boys had penises. A text book shattered all of Mama's lies.

How could she do that to me? My Grandma was a horrible woman. Reading Avarice's diary really opened my eyes. The horror of everything was too much for me to deal with. I didn't want to go back to school. I didn't want the questioning eyes bearing down on me. I didn't feel like being bothered. I knew I was going to drop out. I didn't want to continue living a lie. I was too embarrassed. I didn't even want to look at myself. Going to school as a girl when I was a boy with a penis would prove to be too much. My friends would laugh at me. I really believed this. And to know Grandma's blood pumped through my veins. Having that grotesque woman in my genetic make-up made me feel like slime. I didn't understand human emotion. I didn't understand psychology and why certain people did certain things out of spite and vindictiveness. Why did some people seek revenge instead of turning the other cheek? I had been so naïve when it came to Avarice and she had destroyed me. Turning me into a woman was her great experiment. She became a plastic surgeon…not to give us a better life…but to get revenge on my aunt and my father. This was all a chess game. Giving me breasts implants made her proud. She got off on drugging me, making me think I was having blackouts. She was selfishly performing plastic surgery on my face so I would look like my great-grandmother. That was her game. Realizing this killed me inside. It felt like my life was being sucked out of me.

Hot tears fell down my face. Avarice had betrayed me. I couldn't even call her "Mama" anymore. She was the one person I had been able to trust in the world and know it had been destroyed. God, what had I done? Why didn't you protect me? Why did you let Satan attack me like your servant Job?

The bus traveled throughout the night, half of the patrons snuggly situated under their blankets. A few men were snoring. I on the other hand couldn't sleep. I turned on the little night light and it shined down on Grandma's letter. For some reason I didn't want to read it. I had read enough about her in Avarice's dusty diary.

Inhaling, I closed my eyes, savoring the quietness. I would be in Philadelphia in a few days. This would be the longest bus ride of my life. Buying the ticket was easy. Stealing a few of Mama's credit cards paid off. Plus I had one of her I.D's so if I needed to show identification I could pass as an adult woman. I knew I had to get me something to eat but I couldn't hold anything down. I had to figure out my life, I had to find my purpose. I wanted to find my father but he probably wouldn't want to see me. Avarice made sure she used me as a pawn at his wedding years ago when I was a kid, fixing me up in panty hose, low-heels and with curls in my hair. I can just imagine what my father thought when he realized that the little girl that was talking to him was actually his son.

I stuffed grandma's letter in my jacket and thought about Javier. I couldn't stop thinking of him, my champion. And even though he had violated me, I think it was because he had become obsessed with me. He wanted to be the only boy in my life but it was wrong. I was a man, a man tricked into thinking he was a woman. Avarice told me I had a vagina and that she had a penis. She had carefully and gradually brainwashed me. I wasn't born a woman.

Then my mind wandered to Susan, my friend. I had real feelings for her. I lost my virginity with a white girl and it was the most intimate thing I had ever experienced. Even when she realized I was a boy with breasts she still touched me all the same. I knew in my heart she was a lesbian, and that was her thing. But she was also sucked into Avarice's game. The games of making people think I was a girl. I wasn't a young high school girl. I was a boy – a boy with breasts – a boy who thought like a girl and wanted girl things. The years Avarice dressed me in pretty pinks and grew my hair out, styling it like that of a girl's, she had fake documents drawn up erasing who I was born to be from my memory and making people think she had a daughter. After she destroyed my father's wedding she moved to Miami, Florida to start over. I remember it all as if it was yesterday. I loved Avarice and she was my universe. I would have done anything for her.

Not anymore. I couldn't stand the thought of her. I didn't want ever want to return to that house. That house was a shell. It was the grave. It was the house where the boy in me died and the girl was born.

But now I was really confused. Did I want to be a boy or a girl? How did I control the feelings? How did I make the right choice and could I *choose* at all? I wasn't born gay but Avarice had turned me into a beast and I needed to find out why. I knew the answers were in her diary and the letter – my intuition told me that. So why didn't I continue reading? Was I afraid of the truth?

So far I had already discovered that I was born a Haitian boy – I never knew I had Haitian heritage. Avarice never told me that. But there was more to the puzzle. I had a bigger mission in mind. That was the purpose of this trip.

I have to know the truth. I have to hear it from the horse's mouth.

There was someone I had to see. And I had to see her in a few days.

She had to give me some answers – one way or another.

I was standing by the bathroom of a Georgia Greyhound terminal. I had never been there and I wasn't interested in walking around or talking to anyone. I didn't even care to know what part of the state it was.

Just as long as I got to my destination everything else paled in comparison. I was clutching my backpack, the diary and the letter safely tucked away. I was terrified about being out on my own. I had never traveled without Avarice and I missed her. But part of me didn't care. I tried to get her out of my mind.

You should call her! No, I couldn't. I couldn't call her. Why, boy? Because I'm a girl and big girls don't cry. But you are not a girl. Conscious, what do you know? Avarice brainwashed me. Why should I check in on her? I want her to suffer. I want her to stay up all night crying. I want her to lose sleep. I want her to lose her appetite just like I did when I uncovered the truth.

The terminal was very crowded. A chubby woman with three chins kept staring at me, licking her lips. When no one was looking she started to fondle herself.

Her eyes fluttered, then closed from the pleasure as she gyrated on the plastic seat. I was disgusted and ducked behind a tall, imposing man who was hugging what seemed to be his wife.

A dirty-looking white man was playing the guitar outside the door for change. I really liked the song he was playing. He did it with such determination, but the chubby whore kept trying to look around the tall man to get a glimpse of me.

So I walked towards the electronic doors so I could hear the music.

The chubby lady watched me.

When I passed her she reached out and touched my hand.

"I think I know you," she said. I rolled my eyes and sped out the door.

It was a little cooler than normal but I didn't mind.

When the guitar man saw me he smiled, nodding his head which was filled with huge, long dread locks.

He started to sing a song.

Life is long. Li-feeee is a song
When someone hurts you let it go
Give it da Lawdddddd!
Let him make you whole
A whole flapping dove
Fly, fly away to heaven
Leave behind the hurtttt

I smiled, forgetting the incident inside. He had a stellar voice. I really was impressed. His voice relaxed me. His eyes were sad yet friendly. His music suggested that he had experienced pain in his life as well. The lyrics gripped me in a strange way.

I look in your eyes and see heaven
But all over your body is hell
You are not what you seem to be
Be what you need to be
Whatever it is let it go
Let it go and give it to de lawddd
Only de lawddd can cure your ailing heart
Do it before you fly to heavennn…

A small crowd formed around him and he started to play more aggressively on the cracked guitar. His voice rose with pain and descended like a bird in flight in my ears. He didn't look at anyone but me and I shuddered. At that moment I felt special. I found myself snapping my fingers and tapping my feet to the rhythm. I gave him two shiny quarters and decided to move on. I didn't want to get attached to the man, the guitar and the song. Everything happened in life for a reason. Maybe this moment had been ordained by God – an inspiring chapter for my now bland world. Did He know that one day I would be seeking answers?

I had taken two sleeping pills earlier and the effects were starting to take over my body. We would be boarding the next bus in about ten minutes, according to the monitor. I couldn't wait. I would grab a bite to eat and then board the bus.

I had to suddenly urinate but I kept holding it. I didn't want to go to the bathroom because there was a mirror in there, a big mirror and I would have to look in it. I was afraid of the mirror. The mirror was a truthful object. No matter how one played dress up it would always reveal YOU!

I was about to switch buses and I had to rinse off my face. My eyes were so red I couldn't see the pupils. I decided to go to the bathroom and tidy myself up.

Today had been too eventful and there was absolutely too much going on in my life.

TOMB 25:
Small Heart

When I got in the bathroom I looked around, locking the door. The smell of dried urine was overwhelming. The bathroom was dirty. The floors needed mopping and over in one of the stalls a bum was wrapped in a thick, brown blanket, sleeping. I closed my eyes and raised my shirt. My tits were there, pretty and perky. I started jumping up and down. They didn't move. They just sat there, inanimate chess pieces, waiting for the master to make his move. I lowered my shirt and unzipped my pants. My penis hung. It was short and shriveled. I grabbed it and looked in the mirror…at the monster. A girl with a penis. No…no. I was a boy with long hair, arched eye brows and tits.

"AVARICE WHAT HAVE YOU TURNED ME INTO?" I screamed so loud my voice echoed.

I opened my bag and pulled out the scissors. Grabbing

a hand full of hair, I began to chop it all off but I paused, my heart dropping. This hair had become a part of me. I loved my hair. Women in school adored my hair. They loved brushing it and giving me tips on how to take care of it. The fellahs loved chasing me. Telling me I was beautiful and that they would marry me one day. They tried to take me on dates but I was never interested. Plus Javier was so jealous he either whipped their asses or ran them off, vowing to take my hand in marriage.

Javier…I can never be with you. It would be wrong. It wouldn't be safe to do. A man with a man, in the eyes of God, is wrong. But Avarice has turned me into a girl. Does that count? How did I switch? Did I get rid of the hair and the breasts and be a man or do I keep it all and be who I was?

It was so hard!

I put up the scissors. *Cut it CUT IT CUT IT OFF! Erase who you are! CUT IT OFF!*

"Cut it off!" I was saying, shaking my head. The tears would not stop falling. Why was it so hard? I put some strands of hair between the sharp sheers and I started to cut it but something jerked inside of me and I couldn't go on…I couldn't cut my hair. I started pounding on the counter, throwing the scissors into the mirror. The glass cracked down the center.

"WHO AM I? WHAT AM I, AVARICE? WHAT HAVE YOU DONE TO ME, BITCH?"

Angrily, I, with trembling hands, zipped up my pants and hastily grabbed my bag. I couldn't alter or modify who I was. *I don't even know who I am. I'm a monster. God doesn't love me. He has forsaken me.* Avarice made me this demon. It was my cross to bear. I had to live with it.

I had to take what came with it.

I thought of Avarice. My heart was growing weary from worrying about her. Despite her madness I still felt empathy. She had lost a lot at the hands of her evil sister. Aunt Rosa paid people to lie and tarnish Avarice's image. Before Grandma died she thought Avarice was a whore.

Grandma believed what she heard about Avarice. Why didn't Grandma have faith in Avarice? At the wedding Avarice clearly stated that Grandma loved Aunt Rosa more than she loved her. But I didn't understand the magnitude of it. I was too young then – I could barely grasp it now.

Call Avarice, Hatshepsut. Call her. No. My name is Rosa, no, no it's Hatshepsut. I don't have a name. Call me Exhibit A. I am a Jane Doe. I am an anonymously built bitch!

I started for the door and I unlocked it. I rested my hand on the handle and lowered my head. There was nothing else that could go wrong. Nothing else could bother me. All that I had endured, my Mama's agony, my aunt stealing Mama's man – this all had to be for some reason. But what?

Aunt Rosa and Avarice were identical twin sisters. They were the spitting image of each other. Aunt Rosa tricked Kayak into thinking she was Avarice. She wore Avarice's clothing and played games on her. Kayak was a fool. He didn't know what hit him until it was too late. He was in too deep. Aunt Rosa was having sex with my father the same time he was screwing Avarice. No wonder she went crazy. She loved the man more than she loved herself and that was the problem. I don't think Avarice loved herself. How could she love herself when she did such traumatic things to my body, my psychological state and my face?

I opened the door and the triple-chinned woman was standing there, staring me in my face and smiling.

She was rubbing her vagina, stimulating herself.

She smelled of mildew and moth balls. The black, crummy pants she wore hugged every inconceivable curve on her out-of-shape body. Her breasts were bigger than my face. Her red sweater had a huge picture of J.J. from Good Times in the center. Wickedly, she stared into my eyes and didn't move. I wanted to leave. I had to board the bus in a few minutes and I didn't have time for the drama. Behind her, a few feet away, people moved out and about. No one looked in this direction. I felt a cold chill raise in my throat.

"Are you going to move out of the way so I can enter?"

I cracked a smile, relieved. "Sure. I was just leaving…"

When I walked past her she grabbed me by the hair and snatched me in the bathroom, closing the door. I was clawing at her arms, trying to scream but nothing would come out. When she locked the door she slapped me so hard in the face I fell to my knees.

"I love you. I waited for you all my life, you little bitch," she was saying. "We were supposed to be lovers. We were supposed to get married."

I was trying to kick at her huge ankles but my legs wouldn't move. There was blood on my lips. She towered over me, laughing. Her chin shook. I wanted to die. I wanted to fall into a hole and disappear.

"I love you."

"I don't love you…who are you?"

There were sparkles in her eyes. "You don't know me? You don't remember me? That saddens me. How could you not remember, girl…"

"I'm sorry. You're one sick, twisted woman and I have never seen you a day in my life."

She was rubbing the huge scar on the side of her face. The scar had a story, one I didn't want to know about.

"You said you were going to love me. This is what you promised."

"I don't even love myself, woman."

She closed her eyes, wringing her hands like a school girl. "You know what this means, don't you?" Impulsively, she got on top of me and was trying to take off my clothes.

"Get off me!" I was screaming…

She started laughing. "Scream, child. No one will help you."

I was a mad man. "Please…"

She spat in my mouth the minute I tried to scream again. I was so disgusted I trembled on the floor, about to lose my mind. This type of thing had never happened to me…except when Javier trapped me in Avarice's bathroom and he had sex with me in the anus. It had hurt me really bad but a sudden pleasure had taken over and I actually loved it.

This woman, this beast, didn't touch my tits the way Susan had. Susan loved me with so much passion in her touch…I was trying like hell to get her off me.

She spat in my face and slapped me again, ripping my shirt. She bent over and took one of my nipples into her mouth.

"Yummy! YUMMY! You taste the same! I knew you would come back home to me!" She was pulling down my pants. I was punching at her, but she held both my hands to the floor. She was gyrating on me, making me smell like her.

"Please! Leave me alone!"

She took off her wig and stuffed it in my mouth. I gagged, trying to take it out and she punched me in the gut and the pain was unbearable. I was consumed with fear and tried to protect myself by crawling into a fetal position but she was on top of me before I knew it. She took control quickly, ready to have her way.

"You left me once, you little bitch! You left me like my parents left me. How could you do that to me? You said you were my best friend, that you wouldn't call me obese, that you would always be a good, dear friend…"

Darkness overcame her haggard face.

I took the wig from my mouth, about to puke on myself. *"But I don't know who you are,"* I said, begging her to let me go. "I've never seen you before."

"LIAR! You denounce me? You turn away from our love? I am going to kill you, bitch! DIE!"

"Please, don't hurt me!"

"Come on, pretty lady," she said, repeatedly slapping me. I tried to cover my face but she kept slapping my hands away. "You destroyed me. I remember we made love. You were tender, loving and kind. You gave me such a special gift. At the time I didn't know it would be hell. You made me come over and over with your tongue deeply inside of me. I was a pretty girl." She held my hands again and something in my heart told me to listen…if I wanted to live.

She was crying much harder now. And it occurred to me that this woman thought I was someone she knew – someone from her past. I noticed a tattoo on her hand of a small heart. I closed my eyes then, gasping for air, and waited as she continued.

"I fell asleep after we made love. When I awakened you were gone and I was crushed. You packed up and left. I then looked in the mirror and began to scream. You had destroyed me inside and out. This scar on my face is a direct result of your lies and deceit. You must die! AND YOU WILL DIE!"

"NOOO, PLEASE! GOD HELP ME!"

"SCREAM, GIRL! GOD DIDN'T HELP ME WHEN A SICK WOMAN DESTROYED MY FACE!"

She took a small white card from her bra and put it in my pocket. Then she raised both her hands over her head and as they fell down towards my face sparks exploded from her heart. The bum who had been asleep on the floor suddenly jumped up, snatched her off of me and pushed her huge body into one of the stalls. I jumped to my feet, bag in my hand and ran faster than I ever had. I pushed past anyone who was in my way. I didn't care about respect. No one deserved respect. Some folks were cursing at me, calling me outlandish names and this added to the feeling of abandonment I already felt.

You have no one in the world! No one loves you. You are a boy tricked into being a lady. Your mannerisms are on the feminine side. You sit with your legs crossed. You wear ruffled panties under your skirts and dresses.

NO ONE LOVES YOU!

People were boarding the bus bound to my destination

and I ran up to the front, pushing aside an old woman that
was about to get on.

"Whoa, whoa, little lady," said the driver. I thrust my
ticket at him. He looked over it and said, "Go to the back
of…"

I ignored his comments and ran to the back of the
bus. I sat down, covering my face, my hair hanging. I
shook with fear, the tears soaking my hands and began to
sob. I had almost been beaten to death in a filthy
bathroom.

My life had almost been reduced to a memory.

But who would be the guardian of those memories
when my own mother didn't even love me?

Tomb 26:

Her name was...

When the bus pulled silently into Philly I opened my eyes
and marveled at the sunshine radiating on my skin. I was
so tired. I had taken two more sleeping pills to sleep off
what I had gone through in Georgia. I didn't understand
why I had been attacked, but I had a pretty good idea. The
more I thought about it the more I knew I was right. I
even knew the fat woman's name. When I first
encountered the woman she had been gorgeous. She had
on a lovely dress and had been seated next to Mama at the
wedding.

Her name was Vanessa.

I was looking down at the card Vanessa had slid into my
pocket. She had planned to murder me and leave her
calling card. I knew why she was going to do that. I guess

she figured that if I was found dead investigators would discover the card and Avarice would be alerted. She would find out that Vanessa had killed me out of an act of revenge. Avarice would be devastated. But thanks to the bum who had saved my life that would never happen.

I looked at the close-up picture of Mama. And read over her credentials. The color in the picture had faded with the passing of time. The smile wasn't so inviting. Avarice had had an affair with Vanessa. She performed plastic surgery on her face and turned her into a monster. Gone were her pretty looks. In place of her inviting smile was a huge scar – a nasty, vicious one. I knew who Vanessa was when I saw the small tattoo of the heart on her hand. Only one person I ever met had that tattoo.

I was shaking my head. After all these years of wondering what happened to her after the wedding I had to find out in a grueling way. Avarice destroyed her. Avarice used her to get back at my father. All of Avarice's antics were fueled by her sick need to get back at Aunt Rosa and Kayak, my father. Her deadly obsession had ruined a lot of people on this earth. Why does God allow sick people to live? What sort of pleasure did Avarice get out of destroying people? Did this make her happy?

Why, Avarice? I never knew you were a lesbian. I never knew you secretly were seeing Vanessa behind my back. Where did you find the time?

Did you lock yourself in your room with your medical tapes playing to trick me? Did you crawl out of the window to go be with her?

No. That can't be! Because after the wedding we packed up and moved from Philly to Florida. Did you send for Vanessa?

Vanessa said you two made love and that the two of you were in love. That you promised you would never leave her like her parents did. What kind of monster are you, Avarice?

And did I want to find out?

<u>TOMB 27:</u>
The Document

A few hours later I was gripping the strap of my back pack, staring at a beautiful home. There was a rose garden situated under the living room window and two people were serenely sitting on a huge hammock under one of the huge trees on the side of the house. I wondered what kind of tree it was but didn't waste much time trying to find out. After all, I wasn't there for pleasantries.

A warm breeze blew my hair gently—it felt nice. But I had no time to enjoy the beautiful scene and the tempting winds. It was time to handle business —time to face my future. But was I ready? Everyone has a purpose in life, even if someone like Avarice had tried to use different colored markers and crayons in efforts to create a horrid caricature because of her desire for vengeance. Digging around in my bag, I looked at the two strangers. I didn't know if I wanted to go up to them and talk or not. Hadn't I been taught to never talk to strangers? I didn't even know them. And even though I knew their names, I didn't think they would recognize me. How could they? I didn't know them from Adam. I didn't know what music they fancied. Were they lovers of animals? Did they enjoy apple pie and a warm glass of milk? Did they detest the rise of hip-hop or did they dance to an old Donna Summers cut? Who knew? Frankly, who cared!

There was an abandoned car sitting on cracked cinderblocks by one of the smaller windows. Weeds were growing from the tires. I squinted, trying to make out the make and model but I wasn't an expert on cars. I could barely remember who I was. I was being erased. Hell, I was erased. Avarice and her evil games had forever tarnished the very fabric of my life.

The sun vibrated with love, golden rays sent down from the One of peace and longevity…the huge puffy white clouds weren't the same as the dark ones in my flat, blank world.

I made my way up the mosaic-tiled walk-way, my low-heels dancing to the beat of their own symphony. Each time my feet touched the pavement it matched the thump-thump of my bleeding heart. I didn't have much energy. My gas meter was running on empty, the red indicator light reflecting the bleakness of my soul. As the effects of the sleeping pills began to wear off, I moved along the walkway knowing that my presence would destroy the two people before me.

I made a sharp left and walked over to the hammock. As I approached them they were smiling, hugging each other. They didn't see me.

"I love you…"

"And I love you," he answered, kissing her lips. She was blind in one eye. It was white and scary. But overall she was a beautiful woman. Her husband was the same as I remembered.

Call Her Queen Hatshepsut

When I paused in front of them they were taking off each other's clothes. I didn't want to see them naked so I cleared my throat, startling them.

He looked at me while she discreetly smiled, fixing her blouse. I looked down and noticed his penis was so hard I could see the shape of it. I looked away.

The woman spoke, her voice controlled.

"Hello, Miss. And who are you?"

Before I could answer her husband said, "I think she's the neighbor's daughter – the ones who just moved into the huge house up the block."

"What neighbors?"

He was chuckling. "The ones who brought us the apple pie…"

She smiled then. "Oh, Kelli. That's right. She did say she had a daughter…Hello, child. And welcome…"

"Can I speak to your wife alone, please," I said, looking sad. I lowered my eyes.

They don't even know who I am. Avarice has destroyed my existence. She is Thutmose and she has erased Hatshepsut from Egyptian history…

"Oh, you poor thing. Yes, we can talk. What is it?" She looked at her husband and nodded. He remained quiet, standing up, brushing lint from his slacks. He tried not to look at me.

"If you will excuse me," he said, leaving us alone.

"Ok, pretty girl. We're alone now." She motioned for me to sit down on the hammock. But I was afraid to look into her eyes.

"It's hard to say."

"Baby, what's hard to say? I'm pretty sure that whatever it is it is very small…is it a boy?"

No, I am a boy. Not a girl. "No…it's not."

"Then what is it?"

"I don't know how to say it…"

She was looking at my face. "Why is the side of your

face a little swollen?"

"What are you talking about?" I asked, alarmed.

I can't tell you Vanessa tried to rape me. She thought I was in love with her. She thought I was Avarice…

She tried to touch me and I jumped off the hammock, trembling like I was cold.

"Oh my God! Who hurt you?" she asked.

Her name is Vanessa. And she slapped me and spat in my mouth. She tried to rape me on a bus terminal's bathroom floor. A bum saved my life.

"No one. And that's not why I'm here."

She was quiet, observing me. "There's dried blood on your shirt…"

"I had a bloody nose. It's nothing, really lady. Stop probing…"

"I'm calling the authorities."

"I'll leave before they get here," I warned.

"Please let me help you."

"I will…after you help me."

"Tell me what it is," said the lady. She seemed concerned and wanted to watch after me and protect me. Her hands were trembling.

"Let me help you," she said. "You can tell me anything. You can stay here with me where you'll be safe…"

I handed her the folded document.

She looked at it before she took it. She slowly took it from my hand. I looked up at her.

She opened it up. I held my breath. She read it. I died inside.

She looked at me with her mouth open. I took a few steps back, gripping my back pack, about to run. What would she do with the information?

Her eyes filled up like a well with water. She began to shake while a muffled scream came from deep inside her chest. It came out as gurgling sounds.

Call Her Queen Hatshepsut

"This can't be," she said, standing up and taking both my arms. She fell to her knees and looked into my eyes. She was searching for confirmation—searching for answers.

I couldn't stop crying. "*Yes*, Mama. It is me! It's your *son*! The one you thought died in the hospital."

"Oh sweet Jesus!"

The veil had been lifted. I now knew why I had Aunt Rosa's gorgeous eyes. It was because she was my biological mother. Avarice has been playing chess with my life, secretly hurting my real mother and father by hurting me, their child.

Avarice would pay!

Tomb 28:

From me to her

While Mama kept hugging me, I kept looking at the birth certificate on the ground. It had my name on it. The one Aunt Rosa signed. But she wasn't my aunt. She was my biological mother. Avarice was my biological aunt.

Avarice had played a sick game. Mama Rosa looked me over. "I never *knew*. I thought Avarice was lying at the wedding when I married your father. But to actually find out that it's true! That Avarice's child died in the hospital and she switched her dead child with mine! I cried for months over your death. I blamed myself. I thought God was punishing me for being the evil twin. For taking Avarice's man and making him think I was her. I never planned on falling in love with him. I never knew Avarice would take your young life and destroy it, just to get back at me."

"I…I don't know what to say, Mama. I'm numb inside. I don't know how to handle this, truly I don't. I'm 16-years-old. I'm a junior in high school. I make good grades and I don't make trouble for anyone. I thought I was a girl. Avarice has been brainwashing me ever since I was young, telling me I was a girl. She let my hair grow long and styled it with pretty, colorful barrettes and bows and yarn. My dresses were of satin, lace and the most expensive cotton…"

"I am glad you came to me…"

I opened my bag and handed her the other birth certificate. The one signed by Avarice. She had named her son Baxter Burke. My name was Kayak Burke II. Avarice had erased it all. She gave Rosa years of grief by making her think her child had died…just a few hours after I was born. What kind of woman would switch babies at birth?

Mama Rosa looked over the document. It had Rosa's signature on it.

"Why didn't my father sign the birth certificate?" I asked her.

Withdrawn inside her own private thoughts (or private hell, which ever suited her like those God-awful clogs on her ashy feet), she looked into my eyes, trying to stand up. I took her hand and helped her. The muscles in her hand flinched, which told me that she really didn't want me touching her. Did she see me as a monster also? For God's sake she was my mother. She was the woman who had gone through hours of labor to give me life. She nodded, wiping tears from her eyes. She was silent for a brief moment and the silence fell hard on my ears. I heard ringing noises in my ears and wanted to run but I couldn't. I needed her to speak – I needed to know the truth. I couldn't move on unless I knew it all. No more lies. No more tricks.

"He didn't sign it because we thought you had died after your birth …there was no need for his signature."

Later, Mama handed me a cup of warm tea. The fresh smell of herbs filled my stuffy nose with aplomb. Daddy was looking down at me with a smile.

"So did you two enjoy your talk?" he asked, sitting next to me. He had a lovely smile and he had aged well. He was even more sexy and handsome than he was when I saw him on his wedding day. The day he married a woman I thought was Aunt Rosa but who was actually *Mama* Rosa. I had witnessed Avarice beat my mother and destroy her that day. At this point I didn't know if I loved Avarice or hated her. I have to be honest and admit that part of me still adores Avarice. She is a magnificent woman, a very intelligent specimen who acts on emotion before logic. She is a private woman, a sexy vixen who has used sex for advancement, not for pleasure. But when I think of the lives she has destroyed it makes me sick to my stomach.

Everything now made sense about my upbringing—*everything*. It's like the final piece had fallen in place. I now knew why she brainwashed me. I now knew *why* she gave me breast implants. I knew *why* she changed my face. She didn't want me resembling Rosa or my father. She wanted revenge, and what better way to hurt the man you used to love, a man who married another woman, than to hurt his child. His seed. A man was weakest when he wasn't powerful. Men liked to save the world so the quickest way to castrate him was through hurting his child.

Avarice crushed his manhood with the stroke of her evil genius.

Mama Rosa was so nervous she spilled tea in her lap. But as hot as it was, she barely felt the pain. She raised her napkin to wipe the golden liquid from her stained attire.

"Are you ok?" Kayak asked, genuinely concerned.

"Yes, I'm…I'm fine."

"Liar."

"I have no reason to lie." She busied herself pouring more tea.

Dapharoah69

"L-I-A-R! How long have we been married?"

"Quite a while, honey."

"Then why do you continue to be dishonest? Didn't we enjoy a quiet evening today?"

Her eyes watered. "Yes!"

"So what happened? Is it the girl?" Before she could answer, he glared at me.

"What did you tell my wife?"

"Nothing, I swear…" I said, standing up. I was backing away from him. Mama Rosa reached up and took my hand. She stood firm, her shoulders straight. He looked from me to her from me to her from me to her FROM ME TO HER FROM ME TO HER and he stood up, his hands shaking and a moan escaped his lips and I could tell by the thick lines on his forehead that he had figured it out…that he knew. Then, without warning, he was in my face, falling on his knees and he was kissing my face, hot tears wetting my cheek and my hard walls came tumbling down and my heart opened and light burst through and I was hugging him, sobbing and I fell to my knees and we embraced and Mama was so pain-stricken she grabbed her purse and ran for the door.

Then my father said, "The act is over, you little bitch!"

My gates closed once more. For the last time he had crushed my spirit.

I promised myself that I would never love him ever again.

If my life was a story it would read something like a fairy tale. I once had a good home, or at least I thought I had. My mother, well Aunt Avarice, had been good to me. I was given the finest clothes and my bed was draped with silk and I always had a hot meal and despite the absence of a strong man in the house I was still well-grounded. She supported me reading books; she used to give me little quizzes about all the great books. Alice Walker. Toni Morrison. Shakespeare. James Baldwin. Tales about Harriet Tubman. All of those books helped to shape me. But what stood out the most was the literature she gave me about the Egyptian Queen Hatshepsut. She even named me after her. I would study her life and learn about the challenges she faced. I didn't realize then that in a way I was reading about what my own sick "mother" planned to do to me— dressing me as a girl to hide my true biological status. If my life was the alphabet it would read like this.

<u>TOMB 29:</u>

I'm your creation

A: Apathy
B: Bitch
C: Curt
D: Daze
E: Empathy
F: Fluctuate
G: Gregarious
H: Humble
I: Isolated
J: Juxtapose
K: Kowtow
L: Love

M: Madrigal
N: Naught
O: Oppressed
P: Pretty
Q: Quiet
R: Rendered
S: Stupid
T: Trapped
U: Uniformity
V: Virtuous
W: Willing
X: X-ray
Y: Yore
Z: Zealous
Combined, I had been manufactured into a monster.

ξ

Daddy looked at me, pouring a tonic. I was so nervous I
was about to shake out of my skin. I was beginning to itch
and sweat, moisture gathering under my arms. I sat down
on the chair and he faced me, swallowing the drink and
then slamming the glass on the table.

There was a loud bang sound and I jumped.

"Get out of my house, faggot!" His voice overpowered
my heart beat. It put the fear of God in my heart.

I was crushed and it showed on my face.

"Faggot?" I said, knowing what the word meant.

"Yes."

"But you're my father. I'm your creation."

"Let's get it straight…your Aunt Avarice was a quiet
little whore. When I met her back in high school I wanted
her and couldn't get her the regular, whorish way so I had
to pull up my slacks, tighten my shoe laces, carry a Bible
and voila, instant pussy access. I made a baby with a
project. Not a woman."

"And what are you? Aren't you a whore?"

"I am a man. I am not a boy in drag like you, bitch. You watch how you're talking to me."

"Yet you're not watching how you're talking to me."

"I'm the adult."

"You are a poor excuse for an adult. You are a weak man."

"And you aren't a man at all. Get on your knees and suck it, punk!"

"Dad, please stop talking down to me. I've been through so much already."

"Honor me, like the Bible says…You believe in God?"

"I don't know."

"Do as you're told. Just get out. I don't want to see your face."

"I'm not leaving until I get answers. Why did you stay away from Avarice? Why didn't you demand to see your child?"

"Honestly, I didn't want kids. When I found out Avarice and Rosa were both pregnant by me I was upset. I never knew your Mom had an identical twin sister. I was fucking them both, enjoying the pussy, worry-free. True, I shouldn't have led Avarice on. I left her sitting at home and waiting on me hand and foot. I never knew that her own twin sister would do something like wear Avarice's clothes and style her hair the same just to lure me into her arms."

"But that's why I'm confused, Dad…"

"Stop calling me 'Dad.'"

"I can't stop…"

"Tell me, homosexual…how many men have you slept with?"

"Why are you being so cruel?" I asked, fighting back the tears.

I would not allow him to see me cry. I refused to let him get to me. I knew that he had been hurt just like me. This all had to be doing a number on him as well. The pretty little girl standing behind him when he was to marry

Rosa was his son. That had to crush him. That had to be a devastating blow to his soul.

He was silent for a moment. It seemed that he was somewhere else. "I'm being cruel because I don't understand you."

"You don't understand me?"

"No, I don't, son…daughter, what the hell ever. I just want you to leave." His hands were trembling. "Go back to your sick Aunt Avarice and never bother me and my wife again. I want my life back when it was just Rosa and me and we were happy."

"But I need to understand who I am," I said. "I need an understanding of life. I was thrust into all of this, Dad. This is not my fault. How can you blame me?"

"Call me Mr. Burke. I am not your father."

His words were daggers cutting me to the core. "I know it's all confusing."

"You're what, 16-years-old? And you're telling me about being discombobulated?"

"Is that even a word?"

"Sure it is. I just made it up," he snickered. He poured another drink and gulped it down quickly.

"I never heard…"

"Listen man—get out. I don't have any desire to be with you or be your father or take you around my family and friends. I could never introduce you to the people I love. Are you crazy? To take a creature like you around my people would be an embarrassment. I would be laughed out of town!"

This hurt me beyond measure. Why was he being so cold-hearted? Was he protecting himself? Did he look at me and see his own failure? He had failed to be a father! He had failed to protect me! He was OWNED! OWNED by the games Avarice played with human lives. He was OVAH, as I would say, meaning he was OVER, done with, kaput, wave the white flag, surrender, retreat, go home, get out the way…yes he was all of those things every time we looked in each other's eyes.

I stood up and grabbed my bag. There was no sense in trying to make someone love me. Why should I beg and plead someone that I hadn't spent twenty minutes with in my 16 years of life? I felt myself hardening—I felt myself letting go…I was slowly moving to the wild side and I welcomed it. Did that make me selfish?

"Where are you going?" he asked.

"I'm leaving. Didn't you tell me to go? That you didn't want me here?"

"Yes…But…"

"But what?"

"Do you enjoy being a girl? Are you fascinated with having breasts or looking at them?"

"I am a girl and I am a boy. I am something and then again I am nothing, father. I don't know who and what I am. A sick woman did this to me. I simply *am*. That's all. Nothing more. But through all of this I will keep my head high. I refuse to be defeated."

"Do you think you were born gay?"

"No, father," I said, my eyes becoming a river of tears. "I am not gay. I am Hatshepsut. I am a junior in high school who has made every honor roll since the fourth grade."

"So you have made the choice to be a girl?"

"Avarice made that choice for me. I wasn't born like this."

"How do you know? How do you know that you still wouldn't have turned out to be a butt sniffer if Avarice hadn't played trick or treat on April Fool's Day?"

"Look at me! Look at the facts. I didn't even know I was a boy. I thought I was a girl."

"You make decisions in your life, faggot?"

God I hated that demeaning word. "Please stop calling me that."

"YOU WILL BE A BOY IF YOU WANT TO BE IN MY LIFE!" he exploded, throwing the glass at me. It slammed into my face, the glass shattering. I fell to my knees, fighting the pain. Waves of uneasiness swarmed through my body. Go ahead, Dad. Lash out at the monster I am. You don't love me. Rose hates me. Avarice erased me. What a broken alliance, a disheartened one. Your attack is no better than Avarice killing Miss Seymour and planting my dead cousin in her arms. You're no better. Your hate and your ignorance make you a simple old fool!

Placing my clammy palms on the floor, tiny pieces of glass got in my hand and it stung but I ignored the pain. I would never let this man hurt me again. There was nothing left to feel for him. I didn't even feel for myself. I no longer wanted to live. I didn't want to be a monster, a faggot or any of his other hateful names. There was no escape. How would I survive this? They say God don't allow more than you can bear. But Avarice had come pretty close—encouraging me to put on wigs, earrings and a dress and making me the reflection of my grandmother —even with fake breasts. I was the product of her evil. She was once the good twin. But now Rosa had the upper hand.

My father looked at me strangely. I looked up and realized he was in his boxers. His penis was erect—I could see the imprint. I quickly turned away.

"Are you going to stay a faggot or are you going to change into a boy."

"I can't make that choice, Dad!"

"CALL ME MR. BURKE!"

"I CAN'T…"

He dumped the rest of the liquor from the bottle all over me, soaking my hair and my clothes. It burned the gash on my forehead but I refused to scream. I swallowed the pain.

God please help me. Why must I endure this? Was I somehow being punished because others wanted you to be crucified? I didn't kill you Lord. I didn't put nails into his hands and ankles and hang you on a cross. I had no part of that Lord. I never asked you to die for my sins. So why am I being tortured?

I felt like a cheap whore. I didn't notice when he took off his pants but there he was on his knees, taking my face into his hands. Something in his eyes was wicked.

"You know what I do to pansy boys?"

"Dad, please…"

He took the necklace from his neck and put it around mine. I didn't know why he would do this…maybe it was a sacrificial offering. I cringed when he kissed my lips.

"I fuck pansy boys!"

"Dad. Avarice did to me. You helped give me life. Why would you help destroy me? Please, Dad! Don't hurt me!"

"I'm drunk. I am not thinking straight. I put cocaine in my liquor and it makes me feel invincible! I can do what I want to you and sleep well at night." He started showering my face with kisses…licking my blood and the liquor with his moistened lips. But there was something in his eyes that was both relaxing and inviting. He was a very gorgeous man.

"That's what I call a Bloody Mary," he said, taking my right hand and planting kisses on it. My heart fluttered…I tried to resist but I couldn't.

I tightened my left hand on my bag.

"I hate you!" I said to his face. He planted his lips on mine…His tongue grazed my top lip. I refused to move mine. No matter how men turned me on I would not sink so low as to kiss or roll around the floor with my own father.

"As long as you are a pansy…" He ripped my breasts from the blouse. "I will not be your father. Do you hear me?" he asked, slapping me fiercely. My free hand tightened on the liquor bottle and I slammed it across his head and I used the broken piece of the bottle and I cut him across the abs, running for the front door. I saw one of his jackets. It was a Marine jacket with his last name on the name tag. I took it and put it on to cover my

Dapharoah69

breasts…I ran for dear life, I didn't stop…I didn't know where I was going. I didn't know what I was doing! Avarice's credit card was still in my pocket…I had some cash as well. I didn't want to be in Philly anymore and knew I would never return. I wanted to go back home, back to Avarice's haunted house. I wanted protection. I knew she would protect me. If I went to the cops they would probably only laugh at me. A pansy boy they would call me. They would probably try to fondle my tits to see if they were real.

I was a child with many names. Hatshepsut. Rosa. But never Kayak. I loved men. I loved the way they walked and talked. I loved women. Making love to Susan was one of the happiest moments of my life. Did I have to choose which team on which to play? The Cock Leagues or the Pussy Pumpers?

I couldn't decide whether to remain a boy dressed as a girl or be a boy. I didn't *want* to be a boy. I would NEVER be a boy! I just wanted the old days, when Avarice made all the decisions and all I had to do was eat, piss, shit and go to bed hugging my dolls.

I wanted my dolls now.

Tomb 30:

Where are you?

A few days later, around eight p.m., Avarice poured a cup of coffee, feeling like she had been hit by a train. The phone rang but she chose to ignore it. She had no desire to talk to anyone. In fact she snatched the cord from the wall. She didn't understand why she was so tired. One minute she had been enjoying being at home and the next minute she was fast asleep.

Yawning, she walked across the living room floor in red socks. Settling on the couch, she wondered where her gay nephew was. Part of her was pleased that she had gotten away with switching the babies at the hospital. Rosa never knew. She and Kayak thought they would fuck her over and get away with it but oh no, sister! You may have taken everything from me but I have paid you back. Revenge was everything. Vengeance was sweeter than virgin pussy. There were reactions for every action.

I knew back in the 80's, when I had plastic surgery I would play the game. I wanted my face changed because I had switched babies and I had to change my identity just to be safe. Neither the hospital authorities or the cops knew the babies had been switched…I just didn't want to look like my sister because every time I looked in the mirror I saw her, I saw my sister…laughing at me…screwing the man in my life and making him love her sweet nectar more than my strawberry. And I couldn't take it. So I paid a doctor in Miami, during a freakish storm.

And I have prevailed. I have won. I have been getting my revenge for years.

With that pawn Hatshepsut. A boy I turned into a girl.

Avarice suddenly wanted to see his beautiful face. "Queen Hatshepsut? Where are you…?"

There was no answer.

"Hat…"

She stood up, looking down the dark hallway – an eerie feeling taking over her heart. It wasn't like him not to respond to her call. Avarice was unaware that she had slept for days. She didn't know she had been missing work. She didn't know that four women who needed plastic surgery had been stood up. On her machine were endless phone calls from her superiors.

There was a knock on the door.

"There she goes…" She walked over to the door and opened it.

"Hi Avarice," said Rosa, punching her so hard in the chest she fell backward on the floor.

Avarice closed her eyes.

Rosa entered the home, the lab…the place where her son had been turned into a Frankenstein and slammed the door. The photos on the wall shook. Rosa looked around. The photos weren't family photos at all. They were before and after photographs of her son's face. The processes of becoming a woman were all over the living room. Rosa held her stomach, about to vomit. She was a wreck. Her hair was disheveled. She could hardly breathe. Everything she ever felt for sister, the little respect she did have, was gone. All that was left were her dark, accusing eyes.

Above the mantel were two life-sized posters. One had Hatshepsut's face before the breast augmentations. The other poster, hanging directly beside it, was Hatshepsut after the breast augmentations. A tiny tremor of horror flowed through her veins.

"You destroyed my son," she said, her eyes dark red. Avarice smelled the alcohol on her breath. "For years I thought my child was dead, bitch. I held my son in my hands while you were in the opposite hospital room with your child. I know you didn't know I was there. And you were unaware that Kayak had proposed to me. Yes, I wanted your life, Miss Perfect. I wanted to be you more than I wanted the air itself. But after a couple of hours your child died and my child lived and you switched my child to get back at me and I don't understand why you did that Avarice. I'm sorry. Your child didn't die. You murdered two people. Your son and Miss Seymour, that sweet, innocent lady..." Rosa locked the door.

"Let's talk," said Avarice, standing up. She brushed dust from her pants and laughed wickedly, her voice filling the home and Rosa's ears. Play time was over – it was time to take the King. The Queen was about to get swept off her feet. "How dare you come here accusing me of anything?"

Rosa lowered her head, her eyes staring deeply into her sister's. "You switched my child at birth."

"You stole my man. In fact everything I always had you took it. You once told me you would do this and I didn't believe you. I had fancy dresses and dolls and a room of paradise and your room was next to a cemetery and blackened and wicked and the darkness reshaped you into what you are."

"And what are you? What kind of woman makes up

lies about herself? I didn't have the room by the cemetery. Have you forgotten? You had the room by the cemetery. Your pretty room with all the trappings of life faced a dark, sinister place. You used to tell people that when you were little you were attacked by dogs."

"I was!" Avarice stammered, rubbing her face.

"NO YOU WERE NOT! I was attacked, you little bitch!"

"No, Rosa! I was! I went out into the back yard—"

Rosa slapped her once more. "Snap out of it, Avarice! It was me! I was attacked. It was so traumatic you escaped inside a shell for weeks! You didn't talk to anyone. It was I who went out into the back yard to feed the dogs because I was so jealous of you having dolls and toys and our parents' attention. I was lonely. All I had was the darkness to talk to. I needed an outlet. And the cute dogs were perfect."

"LIAR!"

"What I didn't know was that you wanted me dead! You NEVER accepted me. Grandma adored you. Everyone was at your beck and call. You took everything from me, Avarice! I remember the dogs very well. You crept out the back door before I did and you unfastened the latches, leaving the grill doors closed. You then went back into the house and up to your room. Our parents were making love in their room."

Rosa couldn't hold back the tears. Avarice smiled bitterly, feeding on her sister's misery.

"I just wanted to play with the dogs, Avarice. After all, you had your dolls!"

Avarice was slapping her palms against her forehead, twitching where she stood.

"LIAR! SHUT UP! YOU'RE MAKING THIS UP!"

Rosa grabbed her by the arms, shaking her. "You watched me from your bedroom window, Avarice. Remember, your room faced the cemetery. Your room faced the dogs. I set the pan of bloody meat down on the ground. I let them out and they started tearing through my flesh!"

"IT WAS ME, SILLY FOOL!" Avarice screamed, backing into the corner of the room, appearing almost manic.

It wasn't me, Avarice thought truthfully. *Rosa is right! It was her! I was jealous of her! Didn't she get it? She got more attention than me! I may have had the dolls and bedroom furniture and the wardrobe. But she had my parents' attention. Good or bad it was attention. They left me to talk with my dolls. I became lonely and cold-hearted. They left me to go talk to Rosa. Rosa had to earn her keep, her food and her time spent under our roof. I didn't have to earn it. It was always given to me. I never appreciated it. I never knew the rewards of hard work. But Rosa knew. Rosa appreciated it. My parents were always talking to her and telling her what she did wrong. They always told me what I did right! And therein the problem lies. I was always right. I was holier-than-thou. They told me I never failed at anything, that I was always a success. They always pointed out what Rosa did wrong, telling her she was never right. So how did I know what true success was if I never failed at anything? How did Rosa know what failure was if she never succeeded?*

"Avarice…" Rosa said, snapping her fingers. "Come back to earth." Rosa used the back of her palm, pushing her hair from her face. "The surgery marks are still there. A reconstructive surgeon did his best to give me my face back and he did! He made national headlines, and even then you were distant. You didn't want to talk to me."

Avarice rushed up to her, as if the room was on fire, and she cupped Rosa's face. "I'm sorry! It's just that you were always mean to me and our parents were always in your face giving you the attention I wished I had…the day I went to mother with my doll, wanting help with her hair Mama beat me so badly with the plastic toy, something in me snapped. I found solace in my dolls, telling them I wanted all of you dead! They always listened to me and you didn't…"

"I did listen. I just didn't think you were serious. And

when we grew up we grew apart – you remember that. The only thing we did together was when we formed that gang for protection. We could never forget Grandmother killing Mama, gauging her eyes out. That never left me or you. I just never talked about it. You got all the friends and all the boys wanted you and they looked right past me."

"I'm sorry…"

"But why would you switch my child?"

"You started this! You and Kayak played me for a fool. I remember the times when I sat at home, being a good woman, cooking for him and being his maid and washing his clothes and bending over taking his pipe until he exploded with pleasure. I remember when I told you I wanted to try to have a child. That's when you made your move…"

"Avarice…"

"You once told me you would take everything I ever had. You meant it. You started dressing like me and wearing the fragrances I wore and wearing your hair like I had. I didn't know this then. It became clear that day you visited me during my doctor's appointment and you had on the same plaid shirt and loose-fitting suspenders I wore. I thought you were trying to extend an olive branch. But you were already bedding Kayak. That's why he looked so surprised. He didn't know I had an identical twin sister! He didn't know he was a pawn on your chess board. You were having sex with him during the same time I was and you were tricking him into thinking you were me."

"I am so sorry, Avarice. But I wanted him. I wanted to experience his touch. I wanted the touch of his skin against mine. I couldn't bare you having him as a lover."

"So you got pregnant out of jealousy? Even when I went into labor he called you and said, 'Baby, I mean Rosa,' as if I wasn't there. He had been duped. And when he found out that he had really been banging two women, two sisters, which is every man's fantasy, he chose you. You were filled with fire and I was just ice. He didn't love me or my child."

"Yes he did, Avarice. We had plenty of talks about you and he always praised you. And I was jealous and I couldn't stand it so while he slept I took a male doll and stripped it of its clothing. Tarnishing your name provided a Sèvis Lwa…"

"A Service to the Spirits," said Avarice, her mouth hanging open.

"I placed his photo over the doll and used chicken broth and half-filled the tub and I chanted the powers from the Bankongo of Central Africa…I yelled and prophesized… and performed the ceremonial dance of the Yoruba of Nigeria and I put an egg in his shoe and I said over the doll that he could never leave me. I had never done that before and I didn't know if it would work but it did. He chose me and I was pleased. He stopped talking about you. I chanted over the doll that he could never get along with another woman besides me."

"You cursed him?"

"YES! I had to get you back for unleashing those dogs. I had to make you pay for taking my beauty! I couldn't stand by and cope with my parents praising you more than they praised God!"

"Now you see why I switched your child with my dead son. I had to make you pay, Rosa. All these years of molding him into a female was fun! I knew I would have the last laugh. My internships were performed on his body from his bedroom. I was screwing a very respectable doctor from the hospital. He got me the needles, drugs, gas, EKG machine…everything! I listened to my tapes and read my journals and practiced, over and over, everything I learned in college! My hate for you and Kayak was my driving force!"

"I can't believe I'm hearing this."

"You paid men on my block to spread rumors about me. They told Grandma I was a whore and she believed it. You did that. You put voodoo on Kayak to take him and I

took your fucking child and I hurt you and him.
Remember the wedding? Two families saw your son as a
girl! A lovely girl! Isn't it grand? She will grow to take
another woman's husband, get pregnant, have a baby and
then marry him behind the woman's back…Just like his
whorish mother!"

Rosa brutally punched at Avarice's face with death in
her heart.

TOMB 31

Kayak and Hatshepsut

Kayak sat on the couch, his face in his hands. He was talking to God, wondering if he had made a grave mistake. Right now he needed God. God seemed the only one able to explain the evil events that has taken place on earth concerning his family. One minute he had it all – but that was many years ago. He used to make love to Avarice…her taste still lingered on his skin. He shook thinking about it. And the next minute, after her identical twin sister Rosa walked in the doctor's office, wearing the same plaid shirt Avarice wore, his life was torn apart. He had been making love to both women and hadn't had a clue. And one of his sons died shortly after being born. He would never forget the day he returned from the restroom and found Rosa in Avarice's room, shouting, hollering and screaming at the top of his lungs. His blood curdled in ways it never had before. Huge tears blinded him when he realized that his son, his child had been killed by Miss Seymour. She lay in the hospital bed, her arms around the child…she had injected drugs in her body. Was she some sort of junkie? The earth moved beneath his feet and he took his child into his hands…asking God to spare him. His manhood exploded in his face. How could he be considered a man if he couldn't protect his own child? Rosa was a beast. Several authority figures rushed into the room, guns drawn. When they saw the gory scene one of the Caucasian cops started vomiting all over the floor. Rosa snatched her child from Kayak's arms. "WHY, LORD? WHY MY CHILD? WHY MY CHILD, GOD?"

Now, years later, years after marrying Rosa, Satan had delivered another deafening blow…his son was never dead. He had been switched at birth. And Avarice has transformed him into a woman.

Why had he turned his child away? Why did he blame his son? It wasn't his fault. Hatshepsut just did what he or she or he/she was told by the elder aggressive adult.

It had been days and his wife hadn't returned. It has been days and his son/daughter was still at his home. He wanted his child to leave because he couldn't stand looking at him but the caring part of his nature wouldn't allow him to throw his own child out in the streets. The part of his manhood that had exploded in his face so many years ago when he thought his child had been killed, had suddenly been reborn and he desperately wanted to make up for all those lost years. Maybe if he loved him enough and talked to him enough then he would slowly but surely desire women and want to be a man. But he doubted it. How could he possibly reverse over 15 years of brainwashing? He knew in his soul it was too late. Hatshepsut was a woman. She had breasts, a woman's plump ass and a gorgeous face. Her mannerisms were that of any woman he had ever taken to bed. All the years he dogged women in school, back in his player days, had come back to haunt him through his child. He found it difficult to reconcile himself with the ways he had abused women for his own pleasure.

But can I do it, Lord? I need you, Lord to help me, to get me and my son through this. You know what's best, God…but I can't lie…my faith is being tested.

He tried to be civil, hiding his true feelings and talking to his child. Did they have anything in common? Did he or she like football, basketball and sports? Had he or she had sex? Was it with a man or a woman? He didn't want to know the answers, because he feared the truth. When Kayak did try to have conversations with his seed he couldn't look past the monster Avarice had turned him into. How did he relate with a gay teenager? His name was supposed to be Kayak Burke, Jr. Not Hatshepsut!

Standing up he turned off the TV. Picking up the Bible he opened it, flipping through the pages. His son…his daughter was sitting on the chair, drawn into his/her shell. Damn it! Hatshepsut refused to look at him or talk to him. He refused to eat…he said he thought Kayak may have poisoned the food. He didn't shower nor did he pray. At that point he lost all faith in God. Hatshepsut said he would never believe in God again. Where was God when Avarice kidnapped him and turned him into a girl? Where was God when she brainwashed him, teaching him that his penis was called a "vagina?" Where was God when Rosa had to live all those years mourning the murder of her child? What a sick trick to play on someone.

I should have never come here. I should have never snooped through Avarice's room. I have opened Pandora's Box…and it's eating me alive!

Kayak wondered where his wife was. She bolted and hadn't returned. Was she at the bar having a drink? No. She didn't go to bars. Yet it wasn't every day your son showed up on your door step as a full-figured woman. This had to be a nightmare, something ripped out of a horror book. Kayak didn't fancy homosexuals. Being the son of a preacher, those types of things were frowned upon by his family. It wasn't that he didn't like them, for he loved all people. And he certainly didn't want his friends and family thinking he was one. He was the type of man who took what the public said to heart. He would change his style of dress if a person approached him and said his black shirt was ugly. So he had to play the role society wanted him to play. He wanted people to be his friends so sometimes he would even talk to a few homosexuals in the neighborhood. But it was always in passing, or when the sun set or in the shadows. He didn't want his manhood questioned. So finding out that his son walked down gay alley didn't sit well with him.

His mom and dad already wanted to meet the boy, and they had…at the wedding, as a girl…and when they saw the monster Avarice had turned him into they frowned and told him, bluntly, to keep the sissy away and that had hurt Kayak beyond measure. How could his Christian parents say that about a child? His child?

He wanted to save his son, which was why he had grabbed the shears and begin cutting off Hatshepsut's hair…but the little tart punched him in the gonads and that hurt and he took the brutal assault as something negative and he decided to go through with his marriage to Rosa and move on with his life, without being a father to his child.

And it'd cost him dearly.

I was back on the Greyhound…deeply crushed. I wanted to go back to Avarice. Despite what she had done, she did take care of me. She did provide a roof over my head, she kept warm meals in my belly…I had to go back. I didn't have anywhere else to go. Harriet Tubman had done that once. She had run away from her master and hid in a pig pen. But she went back. She knew what would happen if she did. Slaves were taught that they were inferior to whites. Even if they did escape, they didn't have anywhere to go. Many of their family members, reduced to property, had been beaten, raped – even hung. They had no choice but to stay.

And now I was doing that—going back—returning to a life of slavery at the hands of Avarice. How could I look at her the same?

I thought about school knowing that I did want to finish. But did I finish as a girl or as a boy? Did I go to the administration and tell them the bitter truth. If I did that Avarice might be arrested and if she was then who would take care of me? Dad? Rosa? Nah. I couldn't see that happening.

Whatever name went on my diploma it would still serve as proof that I had at least gotten an education. But what next? College? Did I want to go that route? I could barely figure out my life. I didn't even know what I wanted to be as an adult. Did I want to be a man or a woman? I never had the chance to do boy-like things. I had been robbed of that. I had been robbed of my childhood. I was robbed of being a male. I didn't have a chance to date, even though I had lost my virginity with a girl named Susan. But Susan was a hot and bothered lesbian tart and she thought I was a girl, yet the warmth…the way she felt kissing me, the way I loved moving inside her…that part of me wanted more of that. She was my first, how would I decide…yet Javier raped me…well, I wouldn't say raped. I knew he was in love with me and he wanted to be with me and he wanted to protect me but I didn't want to be protected. I didn't want to be loved. I hated myself. How could I love when I hated myself? I hated what I had become. I hated this program. I hated this virtual video game.

I lay back in the seat and I fell into blackness.

TOMB 32:

The Blood of the Whore

Avarice grabbed Rosa in a bear hug and they tussled all over the living room, matching each other's strength.

"I hate you!" screamed Rosa at the top of her lungs.

Avarice tried to bite her tit. "I hate you, bitch!"

Rosa fell into the coffee table, one of the legs snapping from the rotting wood. Termites scattered, a little white cloud of bugs finding refuge in a crack in the wainscoting. Rosa hopped right back up to her feet, yanking Avarice by the hair. "I never loved you, you wretched whore!"

"I still don't love you!" Avarice was scratching at Rosa's face, drawing blood. Blood was on her nails and on her clothes. The cuts burned Rosa's face but she didn't back down.

"You switched my child at birth!" They knocked over the huge black ceramic lamp by the front door. It fell, breaking into a million pieces. When Rosa tried to head butt Avarice…she tripped over her left foot and slammed into the entertainment shelf. It rocked then fell with a thud to the floor, shattered glass falling on the once beautiful tiles.

"I will kill you for destroying my son!" Rosa promised.

"And I will kill you for taking my life!" Avarice promised.

"Kayak didn't love you, Avarice! Don't you understand? He chose me!"

Avarice ran into Rosa's body and they both plummeted to the floor, pulling each other's hair, spitting and screaming obscenities, small particles of glass cutting into their arms and legs. One of Hatshepsut's "Before" pictures fell from its hook and shattered on the floor next to them.

Blackness colored Avarice's eyes. Rosa was a demon. She wanted Avarice to pay for what she had done.

"When I'm done beating your ass I am calling the police and have you put in prison!"

Avarice quickly jumped to her feet, kicking Rosa in the face. She fell back on the floor, her legs up then falling with a thud. "You fucking snitch! Be a woman and kill me yourself!"

Against the floor Avarice beat Rosa's head. Blood spurted all over the place, including Avarice's face.

Licking her lips she tasted the Blood of the Whore. The Evil Twin.

The Bad One.

Avarice started to yell, losing her mind. At that point she lost all sense of reasoning, every ounce of love and empathy she had ever felt was gone forever. Her heart was now filled with blackness, a pure, dark evil she couldn't control.

Kill the bitch! her mind beckoned. *She took your life! She is the reason your child is dead! She is to blame! SHE TOOK IT ALL AVARICE! FINISH HER! I am the Evil One, I am the*

*One who was thrown from Heaven! I am SATAN! I am the Devil!
You are a woman full of — you are no longer a woman filled with
love. Everyone you have ever loved has BETRAYED YOU
AVARICE! LISTEN TO ME!*

KILL HER!

KILL HER NOW!

"*Yes*, Satan," Avarice said, in a trance. "I will kill her
now!"

Avarice slammed her sister's head against the floor one
last time; a huge chunk of glass pierced the back of Rosa's
bloody neck.

Exhausted, Avarice jumped up, nearly falling to her
knees. Her legs were about to give out. "It's time to meet
your maker, Rosa James. You have robbed me of too
much. Now I'm going to repay you in spades!"

Avarice repeatedly stomped her in the chest, leaning
over and grabbing her by the hair. She dragged Rosa,
weakly kicking and screaming, into the near-by bathroom.
Rosa tried to fight back but she was exhausted.

Avarice put her head in the toilet, piss and feces an
unwelcomed reality, and wrapped her hands around her
sister's neck, wild-eyed, hating her sister, opening the
darkness…letting it overshadow rational thought. She was
so angry she couldn't breathe.

Rosa was flinging her arms wildly, hoping her hands
connected with something…anything to save her…But
Avarice was strong, consistent and eager — eager to end her
sister's life.

"Die, Rosa! You have taken everything from me.
Kayak loved me! He loved his son! But you had to go
behind our backs and play with human lives! Die! DIE
DIE DIE DIE DIE!"

Avarice pressed her face one final time into the toilet
water. Rosa's body gave one final jerk and all life left her
body. Little tiny bubbles noisily floated to the top. Her
arms slumped to the ground and the stamina in her legs
dissipated to nothingness. Avarice was sobbing, huge tears

falling into the toilet water.

"I hate you! I have always hated you! Just because we're sisters doesn't give you the right to take my life! You humiliated me!" Avarice screamed, standing up, holding on the counter for balance. Her body was tired and she was drained. She put her hands to her chest to calm her beating heart. She spat at Rosa. "My parents thought you were the Good Twin. Don't you understand? I was the Bad Seed! I wanted what I didn't have. I never asked for gifts and dolls. It was given to me…to test my loyalty…to see if I would appreciative it but I hadn't …because I didn't pray. I never appreciated the blessings I was given … I was still trying to take things from you, Rosa!"

Avarice leaned over and took her sister by the hands. With all the strength she could muster, she pulled her sister out into the living room, falling on the sofa. She covered her face, balling…she hurt inside. She was on fire. It was over! It was over! She had won! She was the victor! She murdered her own sister for taking her life! She deserved to die! She shouldn't have come between her dreams.

Avarice, looking like a demon, stood up and barely made it to the closet. Opening the door, she searched around the top of the closet for the shoe box with the chalk. Once she found it, she opened the box and took out the chalk. Her shoulders slumped. She fell to her knees, looked over her shoulder then smiled wickedly.

She began drawing a huge circle in the middle of the floor.

Sister you shouldn't have embarrassed me. You shouldn't have paid my friends to lie and say they fucked me. You tarnished my image and I crushed you like the roach you are! Well rot in hell, bitch! Take it up with Satan. My child died without knowing me or laying eyes on his father while you rested comfortably in another hospital room with a healthy child…and Kayak swooning over you and your son!

I had to do it…

Avarice cleared the tables, pushing everything on the

floor. She put her photos on the end table, a picture of Hatshepsut on the other. She went into her bedroom and slowly looked around, suddenly realizing that someone had been snooping in there while she slept. Pushing it to the back of her mind, she opened the bottom drawer of the armoire and took out a photo album. In it were childhood pictures of Rosa. She took out her eighth grade picture and threw the book out the window.

She went back into the living room and set the picture on the other end table. She set up perfume Rosa used to wear, old earrings from her jewelry box and the plaid shirt Rosa once wore on the tables.

She lit some unscented candles and poured salt all around her sister's body. She poured candle wax on Rosa's forehead and she set a huge candle on it, allowing it to dry and stick. She stripped the body of the clothing and put it on the low table for the spirits.

Avarice closed her eyes, leaning on the backs of her feet. "I am a Vodouisant or sèvitè/serviteur. I am a servant of Satan. I will do what he asks. I will do what he requests."

She stood up and walked, as if in a trance, into the kitchen. She turned on the light so she could see and then opened the freezer.

She took frozen fowl from under the boxes of frozen pizza and took a huge pot from under the stove. She put the chicken on the island counter and turned on the water in the sink.

She filled the pot with water. She put in the foul and opened the counter. She emptied all of the garlic powder and other seasonings into the pot.

She put the pot on the open flame and went back out to her sister.

She was on her knees, laughing. "Kayak will pay. He will pay for his betrayal, just like you have."

She spread her sister's legs apart and put her face between them, inhaling her womanly scent. It was a very fresh scent…Avarice pushed the hood of the vagina back and tasted her sister's clit. "Your pussy wasn't that good, Rosa. It smells of yesterday's whores and harlots who sucked and drained you of your true aura." Avarice slowly inserted a finger into the warm vagina and wiped the juices on her lips like lipstick. She smacked them, leaning back away from the deceased whore.

"Now I wait for Hatshepsut to get home."

She started humming French songs.

Then I can start the ceremony…

TOMB 33:

Pennsylvania Hospital.
Avarice's dusty diary
Dear Diary,

It was the late 70's and I had a lot of distorted thoughts, each one ceremoniously pouring into the next like a vortex. I had so much on my mind that thoughts of my child coming into a world sick with racism seemed an utter paradox. But I was there and I was ready to give birth and give Kayak Burke the best gift of his life: a whole family. While I'm surfing this prism, writing in this diary, I smiled because I thought a lot about history. My history. The evolution of my history. From my understanding Pennsylvania Hospital, most nurses are calling "Pennsy," was the first hospital built in the United States, so that in itself made me feel like a part of history. It was founded by Benjamin Franklin and Dr. Thomas Bond in 1751. I was glad Kayak brought me to the hospital, considering that women's medicine wasn't thought to be kosher in those days. From what I hear women's medicine wasn't very important in American society, especially for a black Haitian woman like me.

A lot of my friend girls gave birth to their children at home. A lot of "firsts" happened in this place in the area of maternity. I was about to have my first child here.

In 1803 the hospital established a "lying-in" (maternity) department. It lasted until 1854. Obstetrics and gynecology took a 75-year break at the hospital. The specialties were reinstated in 1929 with the opening of the Woman's Building. It housed two operating rooms, 150 adult beds, 80 bassinets, a series of labor and delivery rooms, and a few outpatient clinics. I smiled now, wiping my forehead, my titties itching.

I was on cloud nine. Part of me was upset that so many months had gone by with me barely seeing Kayak. In fact, most days he was AWOL. He hadn't been there to help me through my pregnancy. He hadn't talked to our child like I had every night, rubbing my tummy. I used to read my favorite poems and books to my child because I know he could hear me. After all, I was his mother. How could he not? I remember during my fifth month of pregnancy, I started eating pineapples and fruits, reading a book on Abigail Adams and what she did for women's rights. I know he loved the fruit because he started kicking my stomach with joy. I laughed, rubbing my tummy, trying to spread love and joy. Pineapple juice spilt over my dry lips when I bit into it, my eyes dancing over the small Times New Roman words of the book.

I was still upset over Rosa spreading rumors about me and angry that she had actually paid people to lie and say they had slept with me. Did she do this out of jealousy?

Did she do this because she wanted my life? Why would she do this? We were identical twins for God's sake! But this taught me the truth about friends. Friends didn't exist in the world. How could they? Friends didn't sell you out over money. This taught me that people would sell their souls to the devil for as little as three dollars and a pat on the back.

But none of that mattered when the nurse, beaming brighter than I, put my quivering son in my hands. His little hands were in fists and he wailed with a healthy pair of lungs. The nurse, Fragile Seymour, had on a dusty-looking black wig that hung to her shoulders. Her glasses were thick and made her eyes looked small.

My son's eyes weren't used to the light…He was used to the dark warmth of my womb.

I was ecstatic, overjoyed, elated as I looked at my son! I held him close to my chest while the doctor and nurses scrambled here and there filling out papers and cleaning their mess and adoring my child and saying kind words and I didn't give a shit about them cleaning and them giving me kind words. When Kayak saw his son he would be happy too.

Even though he wasn't there to hold my hands I knew he would return. Maybe he went to the latrine or something, to drain the weasel. Surely he'd be back. I had just given him a son.

I was extremely tired. I knew at that point I would never have another child. That kind of pain a woman like me could only take once in her life.

Miss Seymour took my baby and was cleaning the blood with some wet rags. She was humming, singing to my baby and he seemed to calm down and I got painfully jealous. That was my child! I should be singing to him.

The after birth came and went and I was too drained to even move. My body was sore, like I'd gotten beaten up in a street brawl.

I just had to close my eyes for a minute.

To rest.

A few hours later I awakened, and immediately looked for my baby. He was in a small crib next to my bed, sleeping soundly. Miss Seymour was cleaning a nearby table. When she turned to face me she smiled.

"Hey, Miss Avarice. You slept soundly."

"I know," I said, yawning. My hair was a mess and my legs felt watery, like they were floating.

"How do you feel?"

"Honestly, it feels like my vagina has exploded."

We shared a laugh. "He is an adorable little boy. I just love babies. They are joyous and bring color to the world."

"Yes they do. I can't wait to take him home."

"I wish I had children…" Her voice drifted off. I felt something there, something sad and my soul opened to accept her. I consider her a friend now. She had helped deliver my child.

"Are you married?"

She looked at me sadly. "I was married. But my husband couldn't stop the women from coming and going. He's a military man and all military men are promiscuous sluts."

The scorn in her voice was undeniable. "I never had a military man. But my child's father is a good man. I love and respect him very much."

She gave me an odd look. "Do you mean the man who was holding your hand when you were pushing out your child?"

"Yes. We are going to be so happy together."

She avoided my eyes. "Humph…"

"What's wrong? You can tell me."

"We're strangers. I don' know you."

"Well come on Sistah. We can get to know each other."

"I really shouldn't. As you know women aren't exactly respected in the work place. Hell my salary is less than the male janitors here. It's like a woman has no rights in this country."

"Double-whammy if you're a black woman."

"Ok! You know what I am saying?"

"Yes, Girl." We shared a laugh. She looked at me, letting down her guard.

"You know I circled 'white' on my application before I got hired."

"Why?"

"If I would have circled 'black' I probably wouldn't have gotten hired."

"But you don't know that."

"But I do." She closed her eyes. "Look, I got to get to work before I get fired."

"Well, I'll be here…"

"OK. I have to go…"

"You never told me why you don't have kids…"

"My womb isn't strong enough to carry them to term."

Sweet Jesus!

She was heading for the door. "Get your rest, Avarice. You and your son will be out of here in no time."

The door closed behind her.

I slept for another thirty minutes. I slept soundly. I wondered why Kayak Burke hadn't returned. Could he be celebrating with the boys? Buying his friends blue cigars and getting drunk because his bachelor days were officially over? I was in pain again and I needed drugs so I called out for a nurse but I was in the room alone with my child. Gathering my strength, I took my time sitting up. Little sharp pains shot through my body but I didn't care. I wanted to feel, breathe and become one with my child.

Everything would be so perfect! Kayak would work two jobs caring for us. I would continue to cook for him and clean and be his bitch in the sheets and his Proverbs wife in the world, in public and in

Dapharoah69295

church and he would love his family and cherish us unconditionally and die for us and defend our honor. My son would grow up to be like his father and even though I hated my sister and her evil ways I would allow her to build a bond with my child. I would never teach my child to hate others. I would teach him how to love his fellow man and treat a woman with respect and he would open doors for women and defend them and he would grow and prosper and get a high school diploma and go to college and be in the State Senate and become a rich man with fancy cars and legions of women and he would fuck each and every one until he found a piece of twat that fit his penis and he would mold her and marry her like his father molded me and he would marry and be faithful and happy and have his own children and I would love him even more for being fruitful and multiplying.

Miss Seymour returned. She looked at me oddly.

"What's…what's wrong?"

She was disillusioned. "You're supposed to be in Room 6," she said, short of breath.

Something's not right! "Um, no I'm…"

She interrupted me. "Who changed your room without informing me?"

What in the hell is she talking about? "No one…"

She waved her hands feverishly in my face. She was pushing me…"You can tell me. Was it one of the white doctors?"

"Race hasn't anything…"

She interrupted me again. "They are trying to get me fired!" she warned. "I need my damn job!" She was rubbing her arms, her teeth clicking together as if she was cold. "…Why wouldn't they fill out the proper forms before they moved you out of your original room?"

What was this bitch on? Hallucinogenics? "This is my original…"

She came closer to my face. "You don't have to lie! Are you in on the games?"

OK, she was really upsetting me. "What games?"

She ran her trembling hands over her disheveled wig. "You are trying to trick me into thinking I'm crazy!"

Call Her Queen Hatshepsut

I need to get out of this hospital. "Have you been drinking?"

"Have you been smoking?" she suggested, insulting me.

I tucked my chin back. "I beg your pardon!"

Her body jolted like she had suddenly realized something. Holding up a finger she vanished. I didn't understand why she left so quickly after accusing me of conspiring with hospital personnel. Why did she think I was in another room?

She returned, waving her hands in retreat. "I am so sorry, Avarice! Now I understand."

I didn't understand at all. "Understand what?"

She picked up my child and handed him to me. He was tightly wrapped in clean blankets. My heart leapt with joy at the sight of him. My Prince. He would grow to be a strong boy! I lay back to receive my bundle of joy. He felt so good next to my heart beat.

Miss Seymour said, "You have a sister name Rosa?"

I fell silent, staring at her. "Yes." *How did she know that?*

She smiled, her eyes sparkling. "An identical twin?"

I said it slowly. "Yes." *Sometimes I wish I wasn't a twin at all.*

"OK, I didn't know that. She also gave birth today."

My mouth fell open in shock. "WHAT?"

"She had a little boy! Seven pounds, three ounces. He's so cute!" She clasped her hands together, ditzy bitch! Now was not the time for games. "They are in the room across from you."

"They? What do you mean by 'they'"

"They, meaning a man is in there with her."

"I never met her man. Who is he? I need to go introduce myself when I heal."

"*Kayak* is his name. And he and Rosa are planning to get married…"

The color left my face. *OH MY GOD!* "Are you making this up?" I asked, barely talking above a whisper.

"No! They are talking about it now, Avarice! They even invited me. They haven't set a date but they are now engaged. I watched him get on one knee, take her hand and place a ring on her finger. And what a rock!"

I sucked in air, hugging my baby close to me. *OK, Avarice. Keep it cool, be a woman about this shit. This dumb nurse didn't know what she was talking about. Kayak would never sleep with Rosa. How could he? He loved me and our baby. There had to be a logical explanation for this.*

"You don't believe me, look…" She opened the door and I leaned forward, looking across the hall.

I SAW THEM!

It was a nightmare!

KAYAK WAS KISSING HER FOREHEAD!

Then he kissed his son's forehead. They looked like a post card.

WHAT ABOUT OUR CHILD! You mean to tell me that…that…Kayak fathered both of our sons? He screwed me and my sister? Was this a sick joke? Was he that heartless? Was he leading me on? How could I have been so stupid? I felt like a fool!

God please let it be a lie!

"Avarice," said Miss Seymour, touching my shoulder.

Don't touch me, please get away from me! I died inside, holding my baby tightly. We had each other; I would never let Kayak see him. He couldn't touch or kiss him. I would raise him on my own. I didn't want my son even knowing his father existed. I have been made a fool by my evil sister for the last time. I could not understand how she could have hated me so much! But I knew that I would forever hate her just as much.

My baby started to cry!

Kayak, I loved you more than I loved myself! "Don't cry…shhh," I said.

"Avarice…"

He had betrayed me. My sister had betrayed me, yet again! Why was this happening to me? What did I do that was so wrong? Why, God?

I needed my baby closer to me…closer to Mama. I squeezed him tightly against my bosom. Feel the love baby because I vow to destroy Kayak and my sister. I would make it my life mission to destroy them. There was no way I was sitting back and letting them get away with this. Did he fuck her like he fucked me? Did they talk about me behind my back, laughing at my naivety and telling each other I was a dismal bitch?

I could not take my eyes off of them. Laughing together, he took her hand and kissed her ring finger.

Miss Seymour's face turned white, like a ghost. "Avarice—oh, God, Avarice!"

My baby was quieting down. I told you, that's all he needed was his mother. He needed to feel my pain and my grief. A child sensed these things. I would always love my child and protect him from Kayak's lying ass.

My sister would never lay eyes on my child. NEVER NEVER NEVER, BITCH YOU STOLE MY LIFE!

I looked down at my child and my heart almost ceased to beat. There was a lot blood on my medical gown. Miss Seymour was in shock, gurgling sounds came from her lips. Wide-eyed she pointed at me. Somehow in my madness I had squeezed the life out of my child! The anger I felt for my sister and Kayak had been taken out on my own child. I shook my baby seeing that part of his head had been crushed. Had I squeezed him that hard? What have I done?

I got up to my feet and Miss Seymour picked up the phone to alert the authorities. I punched her in the face, wrapping the cord around her neck. I walked behind her…pulling, dying, and losing it.

She slumped to the floor.

I gave one final tug and she fell to the floor face first. I turned and closed and locked the door. Think, think Avarice. You killed your child.

But I didn't mean it Lord! I just wanted to love him. Now I have lost EVERYTHING and my sister has it ALL!

Dapharoah69

I took off Miss Seymour's wig, and put it on my head. I hurriedly took off my medical gown and took her garments from her body. I put them on. There were needles in a top drawer and some medicine in small little bottles with silver tops. I put on some rubber gloves, couldn't get any fingerprints on anything…I took a needle and a bottle. I didn't know what drug it was but I pumped her body full of it. She couldn't live. She would rat on me and I didn't want to go to the slammer. *Damn it, Miss Seymour I liked you!*

I dragged her to the bed and laid her under it. The bitch was dead. She could never have kids now.

I put on her glasses. The room was blurry but manageable. I slid into her shoes. I picked up my child, and wrapped him in the blankets.

Good bye baby.

I looked across the hall. Kayak walked out and didn't look at my room. My heart dropped. Rosa was sound asleep.

Her son lay vulnerable.

I slowly opened her door, looking around. I had clumsy footing because with the glasses my vision was blurry. I lifted them above my eyes so I could see clearly. She was out cold. I rushed over to her child and placed the dead child next to hers. I had cleaned the blood beforehand. But now I had a better idea. I took my dead child and rushed back to my original room. I was looking around wildly; making sure no one saw me. I placed my child on the bed, tears falling from my eyes. I pulled Miss Seymour from under the bed and used all my strength to put her in the bed. She wasn't breathing. I checked for a pulse. There wasn't one. *Good!*

I pulled the covers over her and laid my child next to her.

I love you, my little angel! I am so sorry baby! Mama didn't mean it! I swear, baby! I just committed an unspeakable act! I wish I could bury you! But I can't…I can't bare it. I gave you life and death today. I am so upset that your father betrayed me. Please, Lord, pass on a message to my son. Let him know that I love him more than anything. And I vow, Lord, I vow to avenge his death. If Rosa and Kayak hadn't betrayed me then my son would be alive. They would pay.

Miss Seymour had always wanted a child but said she could never carry one to term. Now she could walk to heaven with mine. Well walk with my child in heaven, Miss Seymour. It was nice meeting you.

Thank you. Be his protector.

I would have to live with the fact that I had unknowingly killed him.

I looked across the room, smiling at Rosa's bundle of joy. Oh, yes! She didn't deserve him! She didn't deserve to be happy with Kayak. They didn't deserve a whole family. She would awaken and find what she thought was her son dead with Miss Seymour. I would be long gone, building a life with my nephew.

I would raise him thinking I was his mother. And I would raise him as a girl! I would buy him dolls and pretty dresses. I would let his hair grow long and tell him he's beautiful. Yes, I vowed this.

I would make him into the sister I never had, the sister I had always prayed for. I felt nothing for my nephew. I felt no love. This child had come from a demon's seed. My sister had made this child with the man who once loved me.

This child deserved to die! But I wouldn't kill him. Oh, no!

I would brainwash him like his father had done me. Lying prick! I made a pact with the devil. With Satan's help I would be the victor and have the final laugh. I would destroy Rosa and Kayak.

I would give them sleepless nights, mourning the death of their child.

They would curse Miss Seymour because they will

Dapharoah69301

think she had killed the child herself.

But Kayak and Rosa would see us again.

When the time was right…

You have taken my life, my man and my child I am going to take yours. But you won't know I switched your child.

Maybe I'll tell you when you get married! I will be at the ceremony with bells on, bitch!

Me and your…daughter!

TOMB 34:

The Ceremony

A day had passed since Avarice prepared her home for the Haitian ceremony. She changed the dusty drapes and the worn area rugs. She cleaned the windows with Pine-Sol and bleach, and painted the windows black so no light could shine through. She replaced the light bulbs throughout the house with red ones. Red symbolized blood. She replaced every piece of fabric with black. It took her nine hours to completely paint the living room and kitchen floors black. She burned the dining table to ashes. She then wiped the ashes all over her face, painting her lips black. She shaved off her eyelashes and her eyebrows. She spelled Avarice across her head with her sister's blood. She transformed her living room into the room Rosa once had, the one with black carpets and black curtains. Opened medical books were all over the floor.

The Holy Bible lay open next to Rosa's feet. The Holy Quran was right beside it. She had to light more candles, to keep the spirits entertained. They were getting rather bored looking at the same naked whore lying in the middle of the floor. The room temperature was set at 80 degrees. Clad in a floral dress, her hair was sheered off and stuffed in Rosa's mouth. The fowl had been cooked thoroughly and sat on ceramic plates coated with Rosa's blood. On the walls were the words Whore, Slut and Jezebel.

Avarice stared at the candles, the glow trapped in her eyes, the flames dancing in her pupils.

"Satan, it's time to begin…"

She picked up the huge comforter from the sofa and blew out the candle on Rosa's forehead. Her skin was clammy and sickly. Avarice had scrubbed her body with bleach. She didn't want a dirty pussy going to the spirits.

She covered the body, making sure the top of the head and the bottom of the feet were obscured.

Before she could go into the kitchen for the two flute glasses, the front door opened, a cool Zephyr blowing throughout the room, making the flames on the candles dance.

Devastated and drained, Hatshepsut stood in the doorway, dropping her bag on the floor.

"You're home, my beautiful daughter."

Hatshepsut's eyes were beads of malice. "Yes, *Avarice*…I'm home."

And she closed the door behind her.

Hatshepsut was nailed to the floor. *It's time for the showdown, mother.…Aunt I should say. I see you cut off your hair. That's not all I'm going to do to you for destroying my life.* Hatshepsut refused to move. The sight of a woman she thought was her mother did a number on her. The love and respect had turned into pine tree branches stuffed on Oakwood. She realized the special times they had once shared were just lies. She had to remember that Avarice was the one who killed her own husband…told him something was wrong with her automobile and he sat in the vehicle, breathing in the deadly carbon monoxide…

I loved my step father!

"You've been in my room, child," said Avarice, her eyes glittering. "You were looking for something. Did you find what you were looking for?"

"Yes, Aunt Avarice…I found what I was looking for."

"Why go through my things, daughter?"

"I can't tell you why. It hurts too much. I've been made a fool of for too long."

"Made a fool of? By whom?" Darkness colored Avarice's face. "Did someone do something to you?"

"Yes."

Avarice was a demon. "WHO? I WILL KILL THEM!"

I'm not falling prey to your phony concern! "It was a woman. She tried to erase me."

"What is her name?" Avarice asked, getting defensive. "I will not stand by and watch anyone harm my child…" She fell into a deep silence, her head tilted towards the dining room table. "Oh my God! You called me Aunt Avarice! I'm your mother!"

Hatshepsut reached into her bag and produced a small medical book. She opened it to the bookmarked page and snatched the page out.

"Why are you looking like that?" Avarice asked – her heart shattered.

Hatshepsut moved towards her. "I have my reasons."

"I cooked us a meal, daughter. So we can have some alone time."

"Time alone? With the woman who has abused me all across the board."

"What board? I don't use boards when I share everything I touch."

"Your chess board, Avarice."

"Please, as a sign of respect…call me Queen Hatshepsut."

"Why should I call you Queen Hatshepsut? I have had the name since I was small. It went from Rosa to Hatshepsut…I don't understand you."

"Hatshepsut transformed herself into a man to become King! She ruled as a he and made decisions as a he. That's what I did. I took you from your mother and I had my face changed. I remember handing the doctor a photo of my late grandmother. I told him, well, I asked to make me look like her and I paid him for his time and services, young child."

"I am leaving. I don't wish to stay here. I don't want you in my life. I don't trust you. The one woman I love and trusted in the world has been tricking me for years, brainwashing me…I remember our shower. I asked you what was between my legs you said a 'vagina.' I asked you what was between your legs, the bushy area and you said a 'penis.' I believed you! I was an innocent child. I couldn't hurt you. Why would you hurt me?"

"I hurt you because…anyways, you know this. Rosa took my life and I took her child." Avarice held up her hand. "The ceremony must begin."

Hatshepsut closed his eyes.

And I will battle you until the death.

Haitian Voodoo, Avarice understood, originated in Haiti. It was solely based on the merging of the beliefs and practices of West African peoples (Primarily the *Ewe* and the *Fon*). As African slaves were brought to Haiti in the 16th century, they were forced to take on the religion of their owners: Roman Catholic Christianity.

The principal belief in Haitian Voodoo was that there were various deities, or Loa, who were powerful subordinates to a Greater God, known as *Bondyè*, who does not interfere with human affairs.

Therefore it was to the *loa* that Voodoo worship is

directed

Avarice James was a monster. Every lie she had ever told, every person she had hurt had become like stone to her soul. Quietly observing her living room, she was satisfied how she had transformed her once-lovely home into the bedroom that Rosa had occupied during his childhood. Smiling sinisterly, she covered her mouth, tasting the remnants of her sister's flesh from her chapped fingers. Her nails were cracked and several were bitten to the quick. She had prepared the ceremony with all the hate she could muster. The death of her son was still fresh on her mind and with that hatred she had lost her grip on reality. She could not separate fact from fiction. How much of her life was a lie? Rosa James was the one attacked by vicious dogs in Haiti. Why did she think she was the one who was attacked? Rosa had to have reconstructive surgery to restore her once beautiful face. This was when Avarice had the desire to one day become a plastic surgeon.

Consorting with the evil spirits, Avarice looked at Hatshepsut, who stood by what was left of the entertainment shelf, sulking. He/she wasn't a normal child.

I took my anger and frustration out on him. He/she is the direct result of what hate for people could do. His father cheated on me, led me on. Had me clean our home and I cooked his meals throughout my pregnancy, even when I didn't have strength to move and the whole time he was at my sister Rosa's beck and call. I couldn't have that. And now my son is dead! I didn't mean to kill him. Lord, I swear I didn't. I just wanted to hold him close to me, tell him that he was loved, make him feel the love the closer I pressed him to my bosom and when I looked down and saw his lifeless body and the blood and his head deformed I snapped and I haven't been normal since.

"Hatshepsut, the ceremony is about to begin…"

"What ceremony? I don't have time for your games, Avarice. Aunt Avarice."

"Ah, but you will make the time. You are my slave. I have enslaved you for years…getting you to do what I wanted you to do. I programmed you. I have hated you since your birth. The minute I found out you were born was the day I plotted your death! I applaud you for doing what you were asked to do.”

“I was unknowingly a slave. I thought you were my mother. I thought you loved and respected me.”

Hatshepsut’s heart was becoming steel.

“Feeding me sleeping pills and making me think I had blackouts isn’t my idea of love. Performing plastic surgery on my body and face didn’t tell me you loved me. Giving me breasts and telling me God gave them to me is blasphemy. I look at my face now, through the reflection of the mirror behind you and in my eyes and on my lips and on my cheekbones and can see that they bare no resemblance to my mother, Rosa or Kayak, my disgruntled, self-absorbed father. I am 16-years-old. And I am ruined for life.”

“You were born gay, Hatshepsut…surely you know this.”

“I wasn’t *born* this way, Aunt Avarice. You turned me into this monster. If I was born gay, if I knew I wanted to have sex with men since the age of, say, three, why didn’t I have the natural ability to ride a bike or tie my shoe. Why did I take endless spelling quizzes in school teaching me how to spell my name, where I’m from and words selected from the dictionary? Why was I taught to wash my hands after using the rest room if I was born knowing how to do this? I will tell you why I wasn’t born gay. I was taught the things I believe now—by you. If I had been born gay I would think I was born with knowledge. Maybe some people justify being gay by saying they were born with a chemical imbalance in the brain. There’s no way I was born wanting a damn man Avarice.”

“If you weren’t born gay then why did you run up to a doll when you were a child?”

“Silly woman! Children have blank minds. As they live and experience and watch their parents and TV and interact with disquieting systems of the environment and watch politicians lie on the radio and witness the whoredom of a so-called diverse community they become, they experience and the pages of life fill with filth and utter lies and deceit and trickery!"

"Is that what you think?" Avarice asked, crossing her arms over her chest.

"Yes, Avarice. You brainwashed me…" Hatshepsut tried to walk up to her but couldn't move.

Avarice laughed aloud, her eyes black and deadly. "I control the evil force in this room. Did you ask me to move?"

"I don't believe in voodoo. I don't believe in God anymore. I don't believe in Satan. I believe in believing. You have turned me into a vicious cycle of hate and anger. Without love how does God exist?"

"You are a pathetic little girl."

"I was born a boy!"

Avarice threw up her arms wildly and the flames on the candles shifted and the blackness of the flood seemed to be breathing. Avarice bared greenish teeth. Her face was paling. And it scared Hatshepsut.

"The Ceremony will start with a series of Catholic prayers."

"I will not conform to this…I will fight you with something you can never have."

Avarice shook her head. "When slaves were brought to Haiti from Africa they had to conform to the practices of their owners. I own you. I made you. You are of my design and creation. You will do what I say…or else…"

"Or else what, Auntie? You are wicked and cold. I was a child and you separated me from my birth mother. I can't believe my life has transitioned to this. Javier raped me and I lost my virginity with Susan, my friend from school who packed up and left. They left me a confused fool. Do I want a woman or a man? Susan was tender, sweet and accommodating. She touched the blackness of my skin like moisture to rose petals. I loved the way she looked, felt and yearned from the abyss of love. I fell in love with her when her tight, warm flesh engulfed my penis. I wanted to die in her movement, to become one with her heart. Javier…even though he was vicious, controlling and overpowering…he was a man of love. He taught me empathy…always the first to help a friend in need. In my mind this opened up the empathy that lives in me. I became a better person because of it."

"Ha, ha. Yet Javier brutally took it from you and Susan left town and didn't leave a receipt of purchase. Is that love?"

Hatshepsut was weakening.

"I can't hear you. Is that love? No. That is sex. What do you know about love?"

Avarice clapped her hands and a Zephyr blew throughout the room, and the flames of the candles were no more. Red light beamed down on the two from the light bulbs. It was a soft, warm glow.

"You are distracting me from the ceremony, child. Kiss the boy in you good-bye. You are a woman now. You must talk, look and think the part. The only thing you have reminding you of the boy you were is one thing, and quite frankly it's the thing I fancied from your father and happened to be the dirty little rodent he gave my sister. After we sing French songs, which you must participate in, there will be a gregarious litany in Kreyòl that goes through all the European and African saints and *lwa* honored by the house, and then a series of verses, called the "Priyè Gine" or the African Prayer, for all the main spirits of the house, my house," she went on, extending her frail-looking arms. "This house…" She glared into Hatshepsut's eyes. "This will be the day you die! I will sacrifice your life. I have already taken your soul."

Watching Avarice killed Hatshepsut inside. He loved her and used to adore her. He remembered every memory of their lives together, the things Avarice taught him and

the things she had said out of love. But to realize that it
was all a lie, to find out he was just one of the pawns on
the chess board rendered him speechless. All of his friends
in school now knew he was a boy and had been a boy the
entire time. They were probably blasting him in
conversation and tarnishing his image. The world suddenly
turned into a cold place and he didn't want to live
anymore.

"The saints, Hatshepsut, are missing from this house.
There are only selected spirits and minions present. You
can't see them but they can see you. Satan and your whore
of a mother will do. They are here."

"Mama is here?"

"Rosa is here. She isn't your mother."

"She gave birth to me."

"I gave birth to you, daughter."

"You're still trying to brainwash me."

"No, I don't have to brainwash you. I am not Avarice,
boy. I haven't been Avarice since I murdered Rosa."

"You murdered my mother."

"No, I didn't murder her," she said, her eyes balls of
fire. "Satan murdered her."

"Where is he? Show yourself, if this devil exists…"

"Hatshepsut, I am Satan. I am Satan in the flesh," she
went on, her voice deep, dark and masculine. Hatshepsut
shook where he stood.

Black smoke crawled like ants down his lips.

Part 5
Lucifer

Stop judging others, and you will not be judged.
For others will treat you as you treat them.
Whatever measure you use in judging others
It will be used to measure how YOU are judged.
Why worry about a speck in your friend's eye,
When you have a log in your own?

Matthew 7:1-3

Jesus Spoke

Tomb 35:

Satan

Satan had a delicious body. Abs of steel, gorgeously defined arms. Nothing too showy. He had the most beautiful feet and the creamiest skin. His hair was long and curly, just touching his magnificent buttocks every time he paced the floor.

"Avarice has always been a creature of love and compassion," said Satan, roaming around the living room, his fleshy feet sliding across the black floors that suddenly became flames. "Ever since she was a child I wanted her soul. Ever since Rosa was a child I wanted hers too. I asked God, like I had once done with Job, if I could test their faith in Him. He told me yes, but I could not kill Rosa and Avarice. So I became a seed in their mind, watering it with poison, dripping hate on the sprouting buds and let them kill themselves. What better way to come between two sisters then to place a man in their path that was appealing to their senses…."

"So you started all this?"

"And I ended it." Satan wrapped his arms around Hatshepsut, kissing his lips. "You taste like heaven."

"You…"

Satan brutally punched him in the gut and Hatshepsut fell to his knees.

"I hate tasting heaven," Satan said, rubbing his crotch. On his hips was a twenty-four karat gold kilt.

"You can do what you must to me, Satan. I still have questions."

"Ask."

"Why did you destroy my life?"

"I had to. I am here to test the faiths of the world. I taunt the Buddhists and I taunt the Jehovah's Witnesses. I entice the Muslims and I sit on the pews of the Roman Catholic Church the world over…I once spoke to Avarice…when I took on a bodily form."

"When did you do that?"

"At the Pennsylvania Hospital in the late 70's. In fact Avarice and I had a fantastic conversation."

"What shape did you take on?"

"I think the name would be Miss Seymour."

Hatshepsut's breath caught in his throat. "What?"

"Miss Seymour died a horrible death. She put a bullet in her head when she couldn't carry her child to term. So in reality Avarice didn't kill Miss Seymour. She was already dead. I just wore the skin and bones of her body like a winter coat."

Satan opened his mouth and clicked his fingers and Miss Seymour, bloody, naked, rose from the folds of his tongue, engulfed in sulfuric fire. *"Help me, please! Free me! Free me, Jesus I believe in you now! Give me another chance!"*

Then Satan closed his mouth.

Hatshepsut held his stomach and shook his head.

"The price for suicide is a lifetime with me—Satan."

"Why are you so evil?"

"I have my reasons, child. Do you question…" Satan's eyes cast to the ceiling. "…a Higher Power?"

"No, I don't."

"Then why are you questioning me? I am an adult. I have lived for hundreds of thousands of years. I was once the most beautiful angel in Heaven."

"Until God kicked you out on your flame-broiled ass."

"Ah. Such language. He didn't kick me out. I had a choice. Bow at his feet or do things on my own."

"Let me guess, you chose to do things on your own."

"BINGO! Free will. You see even angels have the power to choose."

"I can feel your evil. It clings to my skin then jumps like a clan of monkeys."

Satan smiled, holding up his hand. His index nail began to grow, spiraling up Hatshepsut's nose, pausing just before the top of the nasal cavity. "I am a powerful creature. The world is my video game. I have niggers killing themselves and wives eating pussy behind their spouses' backs. I have young men worshipping rappers and entertainers, wanting to be like them…trying to become them. I affect millions from their television screens. Just last night I put the seed in Bob's head. He lives in Singapore. He has a wife but every time the naked babes come on television he cheats on her at heart so I set it up for him to meet a woman at a restaurant. Every decision he made was his choice. He slept with her, contracting HIV and he went home and infected his wife. Ah. I love toying with humans. They are meager creatures…just like you."

"I'm not evil."

"Yes, you are. If you're not then call to your God and tell him to show himself."

"I will not call on him."

"Why, Child?"

"I don't believe in him."

Satan retracted his nail. When Hatshepsut blinked, Satan was walking around Hatshepsut, tracing his nails along his arm, then the back of his neck. "I know you want to join me, Hatshepsut."

"No, I will never join you."

"But you have no one. Your own father attacked you."

"All men attack things they don't understand."

"You're a homosexual man living life as a girl. What's not to understand?"

Satan extended his arms and floated to a golden black throne with breasts as his arm rest that emerged from the wall. It was the most beautiful thing Hatshepsut had ever seen. Python snakes slithered in and out of his nose, before settling in the glowing core of his medallion.

"I am not talking to Satan. You will not trick me. Maybe I'm tired. Maybe my mind is so far gone I can't think straight."

"You're right. You can't think straight because you are a confused homosexual. Homosexuality is a very profitable, fulfilling thing. I control millions of souls already chained to the sulfuric lake of fire. Don't you understand this?"

"Avarice, you are trying to trick me. You changed your voice and you perform your play but I am not fooled."

Satan took the dress and snatched it off, revealing Avarice's perky breasts and the bush of her vagina. He raised long, clawed hands and pressed them on Avarice's flesh. She screamed as he pressed his loathsome face against her skull. Hatshepsut vomited onto the floor. Satan snatched her body from his and it became ashes. When the ashes settled by his feet he stepped back, tiny flames still emanating from his toes. He held in the pain, holding his breath.

"Time is running out. I want your soul."

"You can't have it, Satan…"

"Do you love your father?"

"Yes, despite how he feels."

"He attacked you."

"He isn't perfect. He was trapped in this game. My mind is warped. I am not having a conversation with Satan. The devil is a liar!"

Satan ran across the floor so fast thirteen demons leaped from body. Spit flew from Hatshepsut's mouth. He fell to his knees, his lips inches from Satan's flaming penis. The hole in his penis slithered and hissed like a snake.

"That's right. Bow to me like your mother bowed to Kayak. Look up at me."

"No."

"Look up at me!"

"No."

"Who is your master?"

Hatshepsut was quiet, studying…

"So you ignore the King of Darkness?"

Hatshepsut said, "Yes."

Satan clapped his hands and then vanished, lightning lit the room, and a great wind snatched the comforter from Rosa's body. Hatshepsut began to scream. "You killed my mother! How could you?" He stood up, his anger boiling over. In his hands was something of substance.

Satan appeared before him with Avarice dangling from his right hand and Rosa dangling from his left.

"I controlled them. I controlled them through the free will they possess. I didn't destroy them. They destroyed themselves. It was a choice. People choose their destiny. I merely give them what they want….what they desire. If they pray to God," he went on, the word "God" cold on his hot tongue, "and ask for one thing, I am there to offer them even more. They choose it. They sell their souls to me. I don't put a gun to their heads. It's the same with you. *Make* a choice. Live life with me and join me in the sulfuric lake of fire. My days are numbered as well but before my demise I will take as many souls as I can. You can come to my paradise…where men will fuck you to your heart's content and women like Susan will adore you with her haven of lesbians and you can stay a confused little bitch…"

Satan bowed his head. "Join me." From his scalp two curved, porcelain horns extended towards the ceiling. His skin beamed bright red, superimposing with his hatred for mankind. "End your life," he went on, Rosa's soul burning in his left eye and Avarice's soul burning in his right. "It is really of no consequence. I already own your body and your soul."

Hatshepsut grunted. "But you don't have my heart!"

Screaming, he wiped Avarice's ashes all over Satan's face and his face exploded, blood splattering all over the floors and his lips. The room shook like a great earthquake…his mother's body slammed into the wall; Avarice's lifeless body flew into the front door, slumping to the floor.

"This can't be real, Lord!"

TOMB 36:

Call Her Queen Hatshepsut

The noise stopped. The blackness vanished from the floors. His mother's body lay on the floor by the couch. Avarice, with her head shaved, lay on the couch.

Hatshepsut, sweating profusely, looked around. There was no sign of Satan. No sign of life. No sign of entry. No sign of ashes or blood. Hatshepsut looked at his hands. They were the same as he remembered them.

"What is going on? Did I imagine all of that? Am I going crazy?"

He slowly walked over to his mother's dead body, lowering himself to his knees. He took her into his arms and wept. "I never…got the chance to know you or love you. I was robbed of that opportunity … And now you are gone. Why?

He kissed Rosa's head, gently laying it on the floor. He rose to his feet, glaring at Avarice's dead body. He shook with fear. Confusion overwhelmed him. Nothing made sense. The living room was a graveyard – the scent of death and evil in the air. He went into Avarice's room and stared at the poster of Queen Hatshepsut, from Egyptian times. He reached up and took it down. Taking the back from the frame he took out the poster. He looked around for scissors. He searched through the nightstand and found a pair. He cut the face from the poster. He then gauged out the eyes and the mouth and put it over his face. He took the duct tape from his mother's – rather his aunt's night stand – and taped the mask to his face.

He turned and looked in the mirror. "Call her Queen Hatshepsut. It is time to take my seat on the throne."

Nothing would ever make sense.

"Avarice. Sweet Avarice," he began, picking up a wooden bat from behind the couch. "I hate you. I will always hate you. Hate festers in my heart. I will never forgive you. I will never forgive my father for not taking on his responsibility. I am his child, his seed and he has lashed out at me because of your wrong doing. I had nothing to do with this. I didn't ask to be a woman. I didn't know you were performing surgery on my body to erase my male existence. I am a victim of hate, pain and circumstance. But I will not live in fear. I will not live in the shadows of impurity. The way I turned out, in some sick way, was meant to be. If it wasn't meant to be it wouldn't have happened. Now I'm left without an aunt or a mother. Now I have to use the power of free will to live the rest of my life. God watched this and he didn't stop it. I want to hate Him but how can I when I have *never* seen Him or spoken with him?"

Hatshepsut brought the bat to his face, his hair dusty.

He ran his tongue across the tip of the bat, huge tears spilling over his eyes. "I am to be a transvestite. I will be this way until I die. It's the only life I know how to live. I love men and I love girls but I desire men and I don't want girls touching me because Susan abandoned me. She took my virginity and left me hungering for more. Javier changed me, despite his taking me by force. Still I do not know who or what I am."

Hatshepsut turned around and swung the red bulb from the lamp and the ceiling fan. "You programmed me, Avarice. Rosa took my father and your life and you took me and my life and you molded me into something hideous – something that I will never understand."

Hatshepsut shook, feeling abandoned. He felt as if no one loved him. He would never see Javier or speak to Susan again. They were in his life to teach him about himself. Both were now closed chapters in his book of life.

He began to scream, swinging the bat wildly. He swung it for the memory of a mother he never knew he had and then again for being kidnapped and for his own insolence. He tore holes in the walls and shattered pictures from the dresser in Avarice's room. He began to destroy the tape deck, savagely attacking her medical tapes. He wanted to erase her memory like his had been erased.

He went into the living room and put a medical tape in the tape deck and pressed "play." As a Caucasian professor explained the different bones in the body Hatshepsut beat at the kitchen counters, throwing pots and pans, immune to the pain. He was a demon – possessed.

He went into the laundry room, grabbing a can of gasoline. He poured it all over the bedrooms, his bedroom and his mother and Avarice's body. The smell made him nauseous.

"My dolls and my clothes were lies. Avarice turned my bedroom into the bedroom she once had, when she had everything but my grandparent's attention. I lived her life! I look at the pink on my walls and realize that she recreated

her childhood and made me live it to indirectly hurt my
natural mother and father."

His life, Avarice's life, Rosa's life – there were all a lie.
It was all deceit and betrayal and monuments of hate.

I'm a boy.

I'm a girl.

I'm a boy.

I'm a girl.

*I'm a boy! I'm a boy! I'm a goddamn boy! I am a manufactured
mess. Society will talk about me. The public won't understand.
People will call my family freaks. I won't be accepted in church. I
won't be taken seriously. I hate myself. I don't love myself. I never
had the option of deciding what I wanna do with my life. What a
mockery. This is an injustice!*

*I have no one to help me. I have only myself and I will survive. I
will go on. I will graduate school and I will make something of my
life. I stand alone. I don't need anybody. I don't' want anybody. I
don't need to feel anything for anybody. There is no God. God is not
real. God is dead. The clouds have disappeared. The sunshine and the
oceans and lakes and damns are all lies, lies, lies on the planet I
thought was Earth.*

I'm a girl.

I'm a boy.

I'm blank.

Blank pages.

I'm gay.

I'm bisexual.

I'm a transsexual.

I'm just me.

What am I?

I'm just me. I will be.

Be what, Hatshepsut? *My bubble sheet has no valid answers, no
directions and no time limit. Is this simply a test? No, it isn't.*

a).

b).

c).

d). None of the above.

Call Her Queen Hatshepsut

On this True and False sheet were multiple choice answers. Why would God give me essay questions when I don't understand the test?

Avarice once told me that Job, in the Bible, lost it all. Fuck Job! I ain't Job!

"My Dad doesn't love me. Mom will never want me again. My aunt never cared for me. Adults trapped a child in their games and ruined me. I hurt, Lord," Hatshepsut said, holding his heart, turning around in small circles. "I am in pain. I call out to you. I call out to the air and the trees and the shores. Surely those things had a maker -- surely it was you, Lord. Reveal yourself the way Satan revealed himself to me! My father doesn't love me. I was made in God's image…look at me. I am a fucking woman, Lord. Is this your image? I want to go to my father and see if he has changed his mind but I can't. He doesn't love me. Did he ever? He hasn't been given the chance. How could he? He and Rosa thought I was dead. They were caught in a game without their knowledge. I was a clown. No. I was a puppet. As long as I did what Avarice said their life was a crystal stair. But the minute I moved on my own accord, accepting candy from strangers or allowing people to kiss my cheek, she lashed out at me."

Hatshepsut lit a match. "Now it all ends."

He dropped it on the bed, and the flame ignited, exploding with the gas, gradually erasing his life, his memories and his love.

He walked to his closet, engulfed in smoke, and put on a pair of high heels. He took off his clothing and put on a lace blouse and a leather jacket. He turned to look at the fire. He loved fire. Fire didn't lie. It was what it was. It was the truth.

Checking his hair, he slid into a flowing skirt and walked out of the room. On his neck was the necklace his father had given him

He looked at his mother one last time. The flames were advancing, licking at the torn walls…ravaging the ceilings. Then the flames were on tickling his mother's beaten body, jumping to her breasts and eating through the couch...then Avarice was engulfed in flames and black smoke.

Hatshepsut was dead inside, he had to go…he had to leave before the authorities got there and thought he was responsible for the murders.

He walked to the front door, the flames racing towards the heels of his shoes, and he lowered his head, crying. He was scared. Where would he go? What would he do? Who would look out for him?

The branches of his mental oak tree had pine needles and weak roots. He couldn't think – he couldn't breathe.

He opened the door, his hand on his hip. Cold, drizzling rain fell on his skin, but he didn't care. Sashaying up the sidewalk, he closed his eyes, the heels clicking against the sidewalk as behind him his home, his life, Avarice, his mother, the lab, all the lies, the EKG machine, the medical tapes, the medical books, everything, went up in flames.

Rest in peace Aunt Avarice and Rosa.
You destroyed each other.
Free will has given you your destiny…

TOMB 37:
Suicide

As the memories of that fire burned in my mind, I realized I was crying while trying to do the show at the Bumperton. Janet Jackson's "Discipline" had long ago ended and I didn't know if I was coming or going. I didn't know what I should say. Everyone in the room had come to see me perform and I had let them down. The fire I was known for had turned into bullshit.

I was an adult woman now with real raw feelings and I didn't want to go on. My show was ruined. Even from their graves my mother and aunt were affecting my life.

People looked at me with tears in their eyes, silent and unmoving, like a still lake. I wondered why they stared at me as if I were a ghost. As I looked at the lipstick on the microphone, I realized that I had shared my life story with them. They know knew the evil that Avarice had done. But

I am the Grand Diva. I was a superstar. I have performed
all over the world. I have dined with bishops and I have
spoken at local churches, urging the youth to love
themselves and to be themselves. And now I no longer
desired to live the diva life. I walked off the stage, covering
my face. A few people hugged me, telling me they
understood…that everything would be alright. But I didn't
believe it. And because I had been let down so many times
before I didn't need their empathy. I died for the love of
my mother. I died for the love of my aunt. I died because I
was a woman with a dick between my legs, and as long as I
had a penis another man wouldn't want me. They didn't
want a make believe woman. They wanted a real woman.

I ran out of the club to my car. I pulled my keys from
my bra. I unlocked the door and I cried all the way to the
nearest drug store.

I walked around the aisles looking for some pills. I had a
headache and it wouldn't go away. I needed something and
I needed it now. I stared at the beer. No. Alcohol wouldn't
do. I thought about the graves of my mother and aunt
behind the house. I didn't want to go there again. After I
had the house rebuilt, with the money I inherited from
Rosa and Avarice, I never told my father where it was. I
told my lawyers I didn't wish to speak with him. From my
understanding Kayak didn't want anything with Rosa's
name on it but his half of the money. He sold their home
and my lawyer got me the furniture and everything with
my mother's name on it. Her bedroom furniture was in my
room. Her photos and everything hung all over my walls.
There wasn't a single picture of Avarice nor did I want any.

I paused before a row of Tylenol. I grabbed the
economy size bottle and a pack of razors, paid for them
and was back in my car.

I was preparing for my death.

AVARICE

ROSA

I hated cemeteries. After my Mom was killed I refused to go to another funeral. I lost the desire to watch ceremonies of that nature. I never forgot I once had a conversation with Satan, when he talked to me about free will. But this cemetery was a place to which I had become addicted. I was a part of this place. Whether I was happy or sad, I would often come here, sometimes bringing a small, handheld TV and a lawn chair, watching my favorite programs. I paid Lance, a landscaper, fifty dollars a week for its upkeep. Weeds grew around Avarice's tombstone. Rosa's tombstone shined with brilliance. Sometimes I cleaned the dirt and grime from her name myself. After all, good or bad, she was still my mother. And nothing could replace a mother's love.

This was a position I had never imagined; it was a place I never desired. There weren't bodies in the ground. No. The bodies were ashes that once burned to the ground. I had started the fire. Fire was the truth.

I no longer wanted to live. It had been years since my father and I had spoken – years since he threw a drinking glass into my face. Now he was living his life and had forgotten that I ever existed. He was a preacher now, I heard through the grapevine, right here in Miami. I heard he moved here, found a white wife, made a few mixed breed children and was living happily ever after. I heard his congregation was a thriving affair, having made several newspapers for winning several out of state Bible Bowls. I was glad he moved on with his life. I was glad he pretended he didn't have a transvestite daughter. But I wondered how he could sleep at night, knowing he had turned his back on his child because he was different. What kind of father does that?

God, if you are there, listen to me. I don't want this, I don't want this life. I don't want a life, period. I don't want to do any more shows. I don't want people looking at me like I am a freak. I don't want to be loved for something I am not. I don't want to be hated for something I am, something Avarice made, something I had no control over. Give a horse an apple he will munch and chew until he's through with you. I have to go. Lord. I can't bare the thought of my father loving his other children — my brothers and sisters — but never having loved me.

My hands trembling, I opened the bottle of pills and poured them into my mouth. Good-bye, world. Good-bye to the monster that I had become. Good-bye to the bashing and the hate and the finger-pointing.

I picked up the bottled water.

And I ended the life Avarice gave me.

God in heaven, be with me.

TOMB 38:

Pastor Kayak Burke

A year later, Kayak Burke was in his office, arguing with one of his assistants. A week before, he had a falling out with his wife Olive Hills and they weren't talking and hadn't been talking for the next few days. She went out with her friends, a bunch of nosey white bitches and he went out with his boys, getting caught up in what he used to be. Wild. Obnoxious. He fought himself internally, wanting to love his son, but knew he couldn't love a transvestite. Rumor had it that he/she committed suicide. He was too afraid to find out. There was fear there. He already thought he lost his child once. Now he might never see him again.

"I am about to go out and give the sermon and you haven't finished typing the memos, inviting neighboring churches to my organization for service."

Sammy Dawson was frustrated. "You told me to put that on hold and concentrate on developing our youth ministry. Remember your speech. The children are the future."

"And there are bills too, like lights and water but that's beside the point."

"I have to get out here, Pastor Burke. The church is filling to capacity…"

"Why doesn't your girlfriend do that, Sammy?"

"Because she is helping the young adult female ministry and she's only one woman."

"Hogwash. You two were fighting…"

"No, we weren't fighting…and why are you in my business, Pastor."

"When are you two getting married?"

"When doves cry."

"You know…having sex before marriage is frowned upon…"

"Did you ever have sex before you married?"

"Well, yes."

"Good-bye, Pastor. I have to make sure today's events run smoothly."

"I don't understand you sometimes."

"Pastor…I don't understand myself sometimes."

"Join the club."

"I'll talk to you after service. Good luck. And don't forget your portfolio on the table."

"I stayed up all night rehearsing for today's sermon. I don't need those notes."

"Ok." Sammy shook his hand. "Bye."

Kayak Burke had become a changed man. He did things out of love and did things for the soul. He was a wreck the night God called on him to start a ministry and he'd been running from it for several months. No matter what program he watched, no matter what magazine he read, he saw theology advertisements, offering classes at affordable prices.

He swallowed his pride and called the number, enrolling in school. Reluctantly, he began rebuilding his life. He put his heart and soul into it. He tried to correct his wrongs by studying his assignments and excelling. He would repeatedly make the Dean's List.

He still missed his wife and so he tried to forget the past and their life together. The memories hurt too badly. When he found out she had died in a house fire with Avarice he was never the same. He had the two women he loved the most, two women he cared for, two identical twin sisters that gave birth to his children.

His son would never be in his life as he continued to deny his existence. Kayak tried to pretend he didn't exist when he married his lovely wife Olive Hills, a Caucasian Yale graduate with a degree in business. She was the church treasurer, secretary and hostess.

There were many nights over the years, when he strengthened his relationship with his wife, by talking to her about the mistakes of the past. She knew the entire story, the bitter truth and she loved him for being honest.

She always told him he should find his son and build a relationship with him but Kayak was adamant.

"I will never talk to him. He's a woman now. And I don't want a daughter for a son."

She dropped the subject.

Setting a huge off-white colored Bible on the podium, Kayak smiled at the congregation.

"Good morning, Covenant Church of Christ Written in Heaven."

Everyone in the room stood up clapping. They loved and adored Pastor Burke. He was a passionate man who believed in equality, spoke out against homosexuality and was a man for the people. He was available morning, noon and night for his members.

"How are you all doing today?"

"We're fine, Pastor Burke!"

"Amen!"

"It's time for the Word, Pastor!"

"Before I get started," he went on, loosening his tie, "I have a few church announcements…you may all take your seats."

He looked resplendent in a purple robe with golden cuff links. He was meticulously barbered. The ladies in the audience crossed and uncrossed their legs. Several men, looking handsome in black suits, secretly imagined they were in bed with him…enjoying his aura…and feeling his presence.

"If you haven't gotten your money in for the Orlando trip then I urge you to turn it in with the proper forms to Miss Sue Daniels by the end of service today. We have to secure the charter buses and book the hotel rooms and we can't do that if we don't have an accurate count on who is attending, praise God."

He flashed a smile. "You all look wonderful today."

"So do you, Pastor."

"A man of God looks the best!"

"You're so crazy, Pastor!"

His smile widened when he saw several new faces in the crowd.

"How many of you, by a show of hands, have already paid your Orlando trip fees?"

He counted about forty hands.

"Amen! How many of you still have to pay your fees?"

About thirty-four hands went up.

"Make sure you have your money in by the end of service but if you cannot afford it at this time, please see me and we can make special arrangements. I'm telling you…it's very important that we plan and do things as one body, one unit. There's strength in numbers and one individual lacking faith can make the entire church body weak."

"Yes, Lord."

"Amen, pastor! I'll help pay for some people who can't afford to go…"

"I'll pledge a hundred dollars, Pastor, towards helping the less fortunate as well."

His eyes scanned the congregation as he smiled.

But before he could say anything the breath caught in his throat and he started to choke, gasping for breath.

People were on their feet and a few of the ushers rushed to his side.

Sammy was so worried he picked up the phone, dialing for medical assistance.

"Pastor, are you ok?" a concerned usher asked, taking Pastor Burke by the hand, urging him to sit down.

Pastor Burke stormed past him and into the third row of the church.

Angrily, he snatched the visitor by the arm and yanked her to her feet.

"I told you I didn't want you in my life!"

"But…"

"But hell! You are my son!"

Gasps filled the church.

The Pastor has a transvestite son?

Oh my God!

This has to be a grave mistake.

Get him/her, Pastor!

Teach him the Word of God, Pastor!

I can't let my congregation down, thought Pastor Burke. *I have to lead by example if I'm going to be an effective leader. I love my son, Lord I do but I will not accept his lifestyle. Son, forgive me but I will fight Satan to save you.*

"And I don't condone homosexuality in God's house or in my life!"

A shockwave went through the church.

"Hatshepsut. I love you. Yes, you are my child but I can't support you as a woman. I'm sorry. It's bad enough that Rosa is dead and I am still coping after all these years. Get your purse and get out!"

Dapharoah69

"You can go to hell!"

"You're already in hell. Look at you. You are a faggot dressed as a woman! Get it through your head! You are not a woman, Son!"

"You are not my father! You never were!" She snatched her floral hat from her head, slapping him repeatedly in the face with it. "I hate you! You have no right to talk about me in front of these nosey bastards!"

Pastor Burke yanked her through the polished oak wooden doors. She was kicking and screaming, her wallet falling from her huge Chanel purse. He picked her up, one of her heels falling off her foot. He threw her out on her ass.

"Why are you treating me this way?" she asked, frowning. "God said I can come as I am, Pastor! I can come as I am, you fucking crummy son of a bitch!"

The doors closed in her face.

Full of himself, Pastor Burke looked at Sammy. "Make sure she never comes back," he said, disappearing into his main office, slamming the door and leaving people in the congregation to gossip.

The door was yanked open and Sammy stormed inside, his face a twisted mass of anger.

"You turn your own son away?"

He looked up from the Bible. "I'm trying to meditate…"

"Meditate? You are a hypocrite."

"I believe in what I believe in."

"Do you now?"

"Yes, Sammy. Why are you so defensive? You don't know my son."

"You are supposed to be a leader."

"I am. I lead this congregation every Sunday, Wednesday and Friday. I give this church my last. I take care of my kids and my wife."

"Yet you just threw your son out on his behind."

"Let's hope it shakes that wig loose."

Sammy shoved her wallet in his back pocket. "I am leaving this church."

Kayak's eyes bulged out of his head. "What?"

"You heard me! I can't belong to an organization of prejudice and judgment. We all fall short of God's glory. We all owe our lives to God. His son gave his life, and his blood for the continuation of civilization. He died for our sins, and the sins of your son."

"My son wants to be my daughter and I can't have that in my life. That's why I didn't accept him when he showed up on my door step in Philly when he was 16-years-old. I told him then I would never accept him but I guess because the years have passed he thinks he can waltz in my church, sit in my pews and chant, participate in the Holy Communion, despite his impure way of life."

"Your heart and mind aren't pure," said Sammy, taking off his jacket. "You are carrying grudges. You have to forgive your child. He is being himself and I respect him for that."

"Well go fuck him in the ass then," the Pastor said angrily, wishing immediately that he could take back his words. "I am so sorry, Sammy. I didn't mean to curse in God's house."

"This is why I'm leaving. You get angry, you call him names and you defile the Lord's house – and you justify your actions because of your son's appearance." Sammy walked out the door. "You will need someone else to lead your youth ministry – or perhaps the youth can teach themselves!"

He closed the door behind him.

Sammy was looking through the wallet, deeply upset. Rage burned his eyes when his woman called the phone.

"Yes, baby."

"I heard…are you ok?"

"Yea, I'm ok…where are you?"

Dapharoah69

"Still in the church. I have work to do; I can't leave…so Pastor Burke said you're leaving."

"Yes, I am. And you are, too."

"Um…..no I'm not."

"But you're my lady."

"If you like it then you should put a ring on it. Until then, we are building and strengthening our relationship. We haven't even had sex yet, Sammy."

"…We had sex once, baby."

"Ok, and? I'm not leaving. I love working with the youth. They are the future."

"Fine. Stay there, betray me."

"I'm betraying you by keeping my church home?"

"You are either with me or against me."

"I'm sorry you feel that way."

"Why are you being a bitch?"

"Because you're being a spoiled brat. The world turns the opposite way for an hour and suddenly it's only you with feelings. I have a life. I love you, yes, but I will not wrap my entire universe around you."

He hung up in her face.

TOMB 39:

Hold Your Hand Out

Putting the key in the ignition, Sammy turned the key, the car quietly cranking up.

Forget her! She can have this phony church! What man throws his own child out of the House of the Lord?

He put the car in "reverse," and the passenger side door opened.

It was Kayak Burke.

"We need to talk," Pastor Burke said, getting inside. Gone was the purple robe. He looked around for any signs of his gay, wanna-be-a-woman son.

"About what?"

"I have been through hell and back, Sammy, dealing with my son. I was robbed of him at birth. Avarice, my son's mother, murdered her child and had me thinking the son I fathered with her sister was dead. She switched her dead child with my living son and had me living all those years in denial. Yes, I knew Avarice had my son. But the son I thought was dead was the son that actually lived."

"Are you serious?"

"Yes. You see when I met Avarice she was a sweet girl. I was used to making women drop their panties in Philly. But Avarice made me work for it and I fell in love. When we did try to make a child I didn't know she had an identical twin sister. Rosa, her sister, was dressing like Avarice and walking and talking like her and she threw herself at me and I thought I was screwing one woman. I wasn't. I was boning both sisters and they both turned up pregnant around the same time."

"Wow, man…are you busy right now? Let's go grab a bite to eat."

The back driver side door open and Sammy's woman got inside.

Her face was flames. "I'm going too."

Sammy, looking at her through the rear-view mirror, closed his eyes.

Please don't start with me today!

They were at a local restaurant and pub in Kendall, just after S.W. 152nd Street.

"Kayak, I can't stay at your congregation."

"Why?"

"Because I can't believe you threw your son out. I can't look past that. You are supposed to be a father, good or bad."

Kayak struggled with his inner feelings and what the public expected of him. It rendered him speechless.

Sammy looked at his lady. "What do you think?"

"I agree with Sammy, Pastor Burke. And if he wants to leave the congregation that's on him!

Sammy said, "I am not trying to be difficult. I just want to work with intelligent leaders —men who can set an example for me—men who have knowledge to pass on to me so that I can become a better man. I struggle with myself every day. I have weaknesses; my flesh gets weak, yes. But I pray and I give it to God. There was a time I didn't believe in anything, Kayak. I never knew my father and my mother was too busy hurting the ones she loved to care about me."

"My son went through that. But why did he choose to live his life as a woman? I know the answer to that. Avarice wanted to destroy me and Rosa for betraying her. OK, hurt me; hurt Rosa but to harm my child? I will never forgive her."

"But you want God to forgive you for your sins? What if God said 'No, not until you forgive your child?'"

"If God speaks it then it'll be."

"That simple."

Kayak said, "Yes. Can we order something…I just left my congregation behind. I can't give a sermon today. I can't face them. They have questions. They want to know my business. I can't handle it. I can't deal with it."

Sammy said, "I have your son's wallet. It fell out of his purse when you were throwing him out. I went snooping through it."

"You what?" said his lady, infuriated. She brushed her blonde hair from her lightly made-up face. "That's an invasion of privacy!"

"No it's not."

"Yes it is, Sammy. What has gotten into you?"

"Nothing…Kayak, we have to seriously talk."

"Ok. But I hope that means you won't leave the church. I need your help. I can't do it alone. I can't run that church by my lonesome."

"If you do something for me then I will."

"Name it."

"Hold out your hand."

"Why would I do that?"

"Just do it, man. Hold your hand out!"

Dapharoah69

<u>Tomb 40:</u>
Sammy's Free Will

Kayak held out his hand. Sammy put the I.D. from the wallet in his hand.

Kayak looked down at it, grinning. "So the person I threw out the church was a real woman." He looked over the I.D. "Pretty lady."

"Pastor, this is serious. You falsely accused a real woman of being your son dressed as a woman. You embarrassed her. You hatred for Hatshepsut goes beyond anything normal."

"You wouldn't understand."

"Hold out your other hand," Sammy said, his heart falling into his gut.

Kayak held out his other hand. Sammy put a necklace in it and closed his hand, bringing it up to his lips and kissing it.

"Why are you giving…?" Kayak opened his hand and saw the necklace he once gave Hatshepsut.

"Hi, Daddy. My name is Sammy. It used to be Hatshepsut. I am no longer a woman."

Susan, the love of Hatshepsut's life, the woman he lost his virginity with, the woman he loved with everything in him, smiled, wiping tears from her eyes.

Kayak jumped up to his feet, wiping his face. He looked at the necklace, and looked at Sammy. "Stand up! Now!"

Sammy stood up, grinning.

"Or dear God! Oh dear God! You mean to tell me my right hand man, a man I have confided in, a man who teaches my youth ministry is Hatshepsut, my son?"

Sammy smiled. "Yes Dad. It's me. I had the breasts removed. I received hormone injections. And I continue to go to counseling three times a week Dr. Kind who helps me battle my inner demons. I have gotten better by accepting my past so I can have a future. I really battled myself the day I tried to kill myself at my mother and aunt's grave behind my house. Yes, I killed the transvestite, because you were the only parent I had living and I was robbed of being in your life so I transformed back to a man over the years. And it was hard!"

Susan hugged him. She kissed his lips. "The day I met Hatshepsut I knew she was my soul mate. I thought she was a woman. We were 16-years-old and in high school. When I found out she was really a he I still made love to him. He felt so good and so warm and despite his outer appearance, his inner beauty and his soul set me on fire."

Kayak's knees buckled and he lowering himself to his chair. He folded his hands to hide his tear-stained face

"Dad, I'm not promising that I am completely healed. I'm not saying I will never desire a man again. But I am willing to try to change for myself. I'm not doing this for you. I don't do this because I was hurt. I do this because I once had a conversation with Satan, in my mind, about free will. A person can suffer abuse for years…but if they don't learn to forgive and let go…if they don't give it to God, if they carry the grudge and the anger over and over into the next day…then the victim becomes a perpetrator in their own mind, destroying themselves if they don't seek help. Help is always available. People decide to shun it thinking they can do it without God. When a victim is raped, robbed of their innocence or abused it is not the victim's fault. But it becomes the victim's fault if they don't learn to forgive themselves for what happened. It is not their fault."

Sammy took his father's hand. "It was not my fault; it was not your fault. It was not Rosa's fault for Avarice's scorn. Her scandal nearly destroyed me. I have some news for you."

Kayak Burke was about to hyperventilate with joy. *God is so good! Yes he is! Just when I think God had gave up on me and didn't hear my prayers He does the unthinkable. Anything is possible, Lord!*

"Yes Son. Anything…Anything."

Sammy tenderly grabbed Susan's soft, bejeweled hand. "Susan and I are getting married. She's also pregnant with our child."

"Are you serious my boy?" Kayak asked, beaming. He stood up, grabbing his son and Susan in a bear hug. "Please tell me you're serious."

"I am, Dad. I was raised as a girl. I made the choice to change that. I go through the highs and lows of it daily; it is not easy. I may slip back into that mentality. But my beautiful fiancé and my unborn child will guide me through. They are giving me a sense of purpose. I never told anyone this but, even as a girl, I lost my virginity with Susan. She indirectly made me a man during our love making. I'm almost embarrassed to talk about it," Sammy went on, the love of the memory and the memories themselves washing over his face, releasing joy throughout every limb on his semi-muscular body. "When we made love her parents packed and moved away…I thought I would never see her again but we found each other when I joined a gym. She was my trainer after I went through the surgery to reverse the implants so I could become the man I was born to be. When it dawned on us we knew each other and remembered what we shared we became inseparable. I now have my own family and I have to protect my future wife and my child and my household."

"I will help you. I will give you whatever you need."

"Thanks, Dad."

"No, thank you."

"Thank me for what?"

"Thank you for teaching me how to forgive."

"You know she's pregnant with a girl."

Kayak embraced her. "Congrats…all these months of seeing you in church and I didn't suspect you were pregnant."

On the radio Beyonce's "If I Were a Boy" came on. Sammy smiled, kissing Susan.

Susan said, "And we are naming her Rosa Hatshepsut Burke."

"Son, what is your legal name?"

"Sammy Kayak Burke."

"I think it sounds wonderful!"

And they embraced.

Sammy thought, *Oh, God! Help me. I am having feelings for the man at the table behind us. I love the bend of his lips and the elegance of his body…his skin is the color of dark chocolate and the texture of his hair reminds me of Javier.*

He keeps winking at me. I felt the stirring in my loins.

Satan, clad in a black suit, sipped his tea…Watching.

Waiting to test Sammy's free will.

Satan never took his fiery eyes off Susan's unborn son.

And I'll be testing your free will too, little one…

www.ingramcontent.com/pod-product-compliance
Lightning Source LLC
Chambersburg PA
CBHW020737020826
48980CB00018B/655/J